Pendant of God

by

Christopher Gorham Calvin

Table of Contents

Chapter One The Day The Sky Opened   7

Chapter Two Write What You Know   11

Chapter Three Old Friends   15

Chapter Four The Pendant of God   18

Chapter Five Which One Are You   22

Chapter Six Terminal   26

Chapter Seven Paranoia   30

Chapter Eight Pursuit   33

Chapter Nine Artifact Manor   37

Chapter Ten Absolute Power   41

Chapter Eleven Cannes Tower   45

Chapter Twelve Contamination Protocol   49

Chapter Thirteen The Old World   53

Chapter Fourteen Shifa   56

Chapter Fifteen Evidence   59

Chapter Sixteen The Weapon   63

Chapter Seventeen Caught   67

Chapter Eighteen An Insignificant Lie   70

Chapter Nineteen The Decoy   74

Chapter Twenty Takeoff   78

Chapter Twenty-One New Tech   82

Chapter Twenty-Two Small Talk   85

Chapter Twenty-Three The Competition   88

Chapter Twenty-Four Arrival   92

Chapter Twenty-Five Gearing Up   95

Chapter Twenty-Six The Veiled Bird   99

Chapter Twenty-Seven Brainstorming   103

Chapter Twenty-Eight Standoff   107

Chapter Twenty-Nine Gus   112

Chapter Thirty Safi   116

Chapter Thirty-One Tareq Sabir   120

Chapter Thirty-Two Procession   124

Chapter Thirty-Three The Sundown Trek   128

Chapter Thirty-Four Into The Cave   132

Chapter Thirty-Five The Blessed Burial Ground   135

Chapter Thirty-Six Wearing Down   139

Chapter Thirty-Seven Revitalized   143

Chapter Thirty-Eight Casablanca   148

Chapter Thirty-Nine Trust Issues   152

Chapter Forty Stonewalled   156

Chapter Forty-One Patience   159

Chapter Forty-Two Adila Benkirane   163

Chapter Forty-Three Breakthrough   167

Chapter Forty-Four Lingering Questions   171

Chapter Forty-Five Reunion   174

Chapter Forty-Six Two Vans   178

Chapter Forty-Seven Vehicular Warfare   182

Chapter Forty-Eight Tension   187

Chapter Forty-Nine Three Bags   191

Chapter Fifty Isla de Cabrera   194

Chapter Fifty-One Light   198

Chapter Fifty-Two The Disc   202

Chapter Fifty-Three Orientation   206

Chapter Fifty-Four Mind Of The Mechanic   210

Chapter Fifty-Five Worthy   214

Chapter Fifty-Six Red Flags   217

Chapter Fifty-Seven Crosswinds   220

Chapter Fifty-Eight Airborne   224

Chapter Fifty-Nine Descent   228

Chapter Sixty Falling   232

Chapter Sixty-One The Lock   237

Chapter Sixty-Two The Leak   240

Chapter Sixty-Three Submerged   244

Chapter Sixty-Four Heat Shield   249

Chapter Sixty-Five Fireball   253

Chapter Sixty-Six Revelations   257

Chapter Sixty-Seven The Observer   260

Chapter Sixty-Eight Down The Barrel   264

Chapter Sixty-Nine Judgment   267

Chapter Seventy The Truth   271

Chapter Seventy-One Research   274

Chapter Seventy-Two Unveiled   277

Chapter Seventy-Three Hunted   281

Chapter Seventy-Four Caught   284

Chapter Seventy-Five Caged   288

Chapter Seventy-Six Twenty Questions   292

Chapter Seventy-Seven Face To Face   295

Chapter Seventy-Eight Fireworks   299

Chapter Seventy-Nine Partners   303

Chapter Eighty More Time   307

Chapter Eighty-One Into The Veil   311

Chapter Eighty-Two Unseen Resistance   314

Chapter Eighty-Three Speechless   318

Chapter Eighty-Four The Thousand Year Man   322

Chapter Eighty-Five A Question Of Worth   326

Chapter Eighty-Six Village De Alegranza   331

Chapter Eighty-Seven Moving On   334

Chapter Eighty-Eight The New Survivors   338

Chapter Eighty-Nine Arsenal   342

Chapter Ninety Last Supper   345

Chapter Ninety-One Early Warning   349

Chapter Ninety-Two The Coup   354

Chapter Ninety-Three A Changed Man   358

Chapter Ninety-Four Crosswalk   361

Chapter Ninety-Five Wayward Souls   364

Chapter Ninety-Six Awake   368

Chapter Ninety-Seven Scorned   373

Chapter Ninety-Eight Puzzle Pieces   377

Chapter Ninety-Nine The Common Outcome   381

Chapter One Hundred Ocean Bound   385

Chapter One Hundred One Sikes   388

Chapter One Hundred Two Defensive Planning   392

Chapter One Hundred Three The Calm Before   396

Chapter One Hundred Four The Storm Begins   400

Chapter One Hundred Five Race Against Time   405

Chapter One Hundred Six Back To The Beginning   409

Chapter One Hundred Seven Whatever It Takes   413

Chapter One Hundred Eight Man Versus God   416

Chapter One Hundred Nine Nature's Course   421

Chapter One Hundred Ten Closure   427

Chapter One Hundred Eleven Blue Skies   431

Chapter One Hundred Twelve The Day The Sky Closed   433

Author's Note   437

Chapter One
The Day The Sky Opened

New York, New York
The Day The Sky Opened

Gabriel and Lisa pushed through the chaos and raced up the stairwell to the Astoria-Ditmars subway platform. With no time for common decency or lawful behavior, they knocked other pedestrians aside and hopped the turnstile without swiping their MetroCards. The police were busy dealing with panicked New Yorkers on the streets below. They wouldn't interfere, and Gabriel and Lisa needed to catch the N train that would depart at any moment. It might be their last chance to get into Manhattan.

"Talk to me, Nate!" Gabriel shouted into a walkie-talkie as he and Lisa ran the length of the train to locate a car with enough room for the two of them.

"It's a war zone out there," Nate responded, his voice crackling with interference. *"We're tracking two Phoenix choppers. They've left a trail of destruction from the Upper West Side heading southeast across Central Park. Current trajectory looks like Cannes Tower. Where are you?"*

"We just boarded the N train in Queens," Gabriel said as he and Lisa slipped into a car near the southern end of the platform. "We'll be in Manhattan in twenty minutes, give or take."

"You're going to want to get off as soon as possible. There's no telling when they'll shut the system down."

A couple of eavesdropping passengers stared fearfully at Gabriel.

"Don't worry," Lisa told them. "We're the good guys."

The subway doors closed, and the train began moving. As it pulled out of the station, the platform walls gave way to the Manhattan skyline. Passengers gasped at the sight of thin plumes of black smoke rising in the distance. Gabriel and Lisa didn't share their shock, but rather stared determinately at their destination.

"Samantha?" Gabriel said into his walkie-talkie. "Are you with Nate?"

"Of course, boss. We're in the air and heading to intercept now."

"Great. We're unarmed down here, so I'm going to need you to be our firepower from above."

"No problem."

The subway train stopped at its next elevated platform. Spooked passengers scrambled to get off while new passengers, who were either naïve about the situation unfolding in Manhattan or who, in true New Yorker fashion, didn't care about it, replaced them. Gabriel held his breath, expecting the conductor to get on the intercom to announce the closure of the subway system, but no such announcement came and soon the train was moving again.

"We're going to be lucky if we make it," Lisa said as the smoldering skyline came into view again. "They won't hold us under the river, but we've got five more stops until then."

Gabriel knew she was right. Taking public transportation while the city was in a state of upheaval was risky, but it was also the only option they had. There wasn't enough time to get to Manhattan on foot from Queens. Judging from the chaos filling the streets, there was also little chance of getting a car across one of the bridges connecting the two land masses. Five stops. They just needed to make it through five more stops.

The first and second mimicked the stop they had already made. Passengers who hadn't been aware of the extent of danger in Manhattan exited the train while others got on. On the way to the third stop, Thirty-Sixth Avenue, an explosion boomed in the distance, and a fresh fireball rose from the city's skyline. Gabriel thought for sure that would be the end of their journey.

"Ladies and gentlemen," the conductor said over the train's intercom, *"I've been ordered to bypass Thirty-Ninth Avenue and to unload everyone at Queensboro Plaza. We need this train to help with evacuations in the city. Please prepare to disembark."*

Lisa stared at Gabriel as if to say, *what now?*

"They won't delay the train for a couple of stragglers," Gabriel assured her as the Thirty-Ninth Avenue platform passed by in a blur. "Just stay put."

Their N train pulled to a stop at the Queensboro Plaza station, as promised. The conductor repeated his instructions over the intercom, stressing that it wasn't safe for anyone to remain on board. Gabriel and Lisa ignored him, as did a handful of other stubborn New Yorkers, and soon the train continued its journey.

"Nate? Samantha?" Gabriel said into his walkie-talkie. "We're about to head underground. See you soon."

The train tracks dipped as they approached the river. Soon, darkness enveloped Gabriel and Lisa. Focused on getting into the city, they didn't consider the risk they were taking by riding through an underwater tunnel while explosions rang out nearby. It was too late to worry about that now, however.

"So what do we do when we get there?" Lisa asked.

"The only thing we can do. Find Porter before it's too late."

Lisa released a tense breath. "And if it already is?"

Gabriel shrugged. "Pray."

A few minutes later, they pulled into the underground station at Lexington Avenue and Fifty-Ninth Street, where a hoard of panicked New Yorkers and tourists were primed to charge the train. When the doors opened, Gabriel and Lisa pressed against the flow of the crowd, ramming and elbowing their way out of the car, off the platform, and to the city street above. They emerged at an intersection of skyscrapers, people screaming as they raced in every direction. Gabriel heard an unusual whistling noise coming from the north. A second later, a smoking missile blasted through the sky overhead. Gabriel and Lisa couldn't see where it struck, but they felt the rumble of the explosion and saw the tail end of its impacting fireball dissipate into the sky.

"Come on!" Gabriel yelled.

He and Lisa ran toward the direction of impact. In fact, they were the only people running toward the impact, for everyone else had enough sense to get away from the imminent danger. Gabriel and Lisa rounded a corner and saw the blown-out side of a tall building. Not far in the distance, Cannes Tower loomed over the surrounding architecture. Two attack choppers passed overhead and glided straight toward it. Gabriel and Lisa followed down the now empty street, each hoping that there was still time.

"Holy shit, boss!" Nate's voice crackled over Gabriel's walkie-talkie. *"Are you seeing this?"*

Before Gabriel could answer, a bolt of lightning streaked across the sky above Cannes Tower. It left a deep, red gash in its wake, as if the sky was a tangible surface that could be scarred through physical force. Another bolt of lightning shot across the sky, then several more, each of them leaving similar gashes behind.

Lisa shivered. "Oh, no."

The gashes began to widen like wounds being ripped open by some otherworldly force. Beyond them was a sea of clouds and stars, all cast in the same blood-red glow. The ground beneath Gabriel's and Lisa's feet quaked violently and the wind instantly accelerated to tropical storm speeds. Litter and debris flew through the air. Smells of chemical accelerant and smoldering rubble spread through the deserted streets. Stray animals cowered in fear and the sky grew darker. Gabriel had never before wondered what the end of the world might look like, but he had a feeling he was getting a front-row seat to it now. Most people in his situation would start questioning their morals and religious beliefs, preparing for whatever judgement or lack thereof waited beyond mortal life. But all Gabriel wondered was, *how the hell did I let it come to this?*

Chapter Two
Write What You Know

New York, New York
Two Weeks Before The Sky Opened

Gabriel stood before the auditorium of English students and felt the sweat beading on his forehead. He loved giving guest lectures to up-and-coming novelists. It gave him a sense of tangible accomplishment that his millions in book sales could never deliver. But those stage lights... every time he stood under them, he remembered how much he hated them. He hated their glare; he hated their heat; and he hated the fact that, without fail, they would force him to repeatedly pause his lecture to wipe his face dry and take a swig of water.

Ten years earlier, when Professor Wilson Mead first asked Gabriel to provide his students with motivating words of wisdom, Gabriel had been unprepared for the harsh conditions that accompanied such a request. He showed for his first guest lecture in shorts and a button-down, his typical day-to-day attire, with no prepared notes and nothing to drink. Gabriel had assumed the students would have so many questions for him that he would spend the entire ninety minutes fielding their inquiries. He couldn't have been more wrong. Not only did the students not have questions for him, barely a handful even knew who he was. He was Gabrielle Dunne, best-selling author, winner of numerous writing awards, and apparently a complete nobody to anyone under twenty-one. To say that first lecture didn't go well would be an understatement.

But Professor Mead was a fan. He gave Gabriel some postmortem tips and invited him to try again next semester. Gabriel accepted the challenge and committed to being more prepared the next time around. And he was... sort of. He showed for his second guest stint still wearing his usual attire, and still without a drink, but he had rehearsed a speech that time, and even brought a note card to reference if needed. Student reception was better, but Gabriel still fell about fifty minutes short of his planned lecture duration. He tried to elicit questions from his audience, but that only lasted about ten more minutes before Professor Mead dismissed the class early. Gabriel and Professor Mead had another heart-to-heart, and they arranged for Gabriel to make a third- and possibly final- attempt.

The next semester's guest lecture was a hit. Gabriel swapped out his shorts for dress khakis, brought a bottle of water to keep his throat moist, and prepared an even longer presentation, this time accompanied by a handful of visuals to stimulate the students' attention. But none of that mattered. In the months between his second and third guest lectures, one of Gabriel's books had been optioned for a movie. It wouldn't release for another year, but it had two high-profile stars attached and the hype train was full steam ahead. Gabriel's book sales skyrocketed, and he was no longer a nobody among the college community. Students shot questions at him as soon as he took the stage, and he still hadn't answered all of them when time expired.

This interaction continued for the next several years. Gabriel discovered quickly how hot he could get under the auditorium stage lights when he actually had to move around and talk for ninety minutes straight. He began wearing a sports coat to hide the sweat stains under his armpits, carried a handkerchief to wipe his forehead, and doubled up the bottles of water to ensure his throat never went dry. To anyone who hadn't witnessed those first couple of failed lectures, Gabriel carried the facade of a seasoned professional speaker. Over the years, as buzz for his novel-turned-movie died down, Gabriel returned to filling some of the lecture time with rehearsed speeches, and by the time he reached his twentieth appearance, he had found his stride with a mix of prepared lecture, popping visuals, interspersed audience polling, and finally, a window for questions and answers to satiate students' curiosities.

"My number one rule," Gabriel said to this year's newest crop of students, "is to write what you know." He clicked a portable remote, and a slide of rowdy youngsters watching sports at a bar projected onto a screen overhead. "This," Gabriel pointed, "is what you know. Or at least it's what you know if you're anything like I was at your age."

A wave of chuckles rolled down from the crowd.

"But seriously," Gabriel continued, "for some of you, this is what you know. For others, it's your studies. For others, hobbies. For others, family. Whatever it is, write about it. Nothing draws a reader in more than the authenticity that empowers the words on the page." Gabriel clicked his remote, and a map of the world replaced the projection. "This is what I know." He clicked again, and the map was replaced by pictures of archeological digs, ancient sunken ships, artifacts on display in a museum, and other similar photographs, repeating on a loop. "I know geography. I know history. I know the thrill of discovery. These are the things I write about, because they're the things that have impassioned me for the better portion of my life. So," he turned the projector off, "write what you know, and your readers will appreciate you for it."

A hand went up in the audience.

"Yes?"

A tall, curly haired student in a white tee shirt and jeans stood. He had a class clown vibe to him, and Gabriel braced himself for whatever smart-ass comment might be headed his way. "The main protagonist in most of your books is a treasure hunter," the curly-haired student said. "If you write what you know, does that mean you're secretly a treasure hunter, too?"

Gabriel smiled. "I wish I had time for that. Unfortunately, between researching, writing, editing, marketing, and speaking with fine students such as yourselves, the only time for treasure hunting in my life is the hunting I do in my head." Gabriel paused while the student reclaimed his seat. "And that brings me to my second rule: don't adhere too strictly to the first rule. You're the writer. You're the creator. Take some liberties and introduce some unreal into the real. Mingle them so fluidly that the reader doesn't know the difference."

Gabriel's eye caught a familiar face watching him from the back of the auditorium. He couldn't be certain through the glare of the stage lights, but he was pretty sure it was someone he hadn't seen in a very long time. If so, it was someone who knew the true Gabriel, the one behind the novelist, whose identity had been fictionalized and put to the page for the rest of the world to enjoy. Gabriel broke contact with the unexpected visitor and finished his thought.

"You never know what kind of magic your imagination might produce."

Chapter Three
Old Friends

New York, New York
Two Weeks Before The Sky Opened

Gabriel finished his lecture to a round of fierce applause. He touched base with Professor Mead while the students filed out of the auditorium, then grabbed his water bottles and presentation materials before strolling out into the bright midday sun. Seated on a landscaping ledge just beyond the auditorium doors was the familiar man Gabriel had spotted during his lecture. He was dressed in a pressed suit and tie that Gabriel suspected cost more than his annual book royalties, and he wore dark shades beneath slicked back hair.

"Porter Cannes," Gabriel said as he approached the man.

"Gabriel." Porter hopped off the ledge and greeted Gabriel with open arms. "How long has it been?"

"At least twenty years. How the hell have you been?"

"Eh," Porter said with a dismissive shrug. "How about you? How's Lisa?"

"Lisa and I are both doing great," Gabriel replied. "I've got a new novel releasing in a few months-"

"Yeah, I read an article about that."

"-and Lisa... well, she's just being Lisa."

"Still obsessed with ancient history?" Porter asked.

"Of course. And you? Still obsessed with making the world a better place using futuristic technology?"

"I wouldn't have it any other way."

The last time Gabriel had seen Porter was at a high school reunion. Gabriel's writing career was just kicking off and Porter's company, Cannes International, had just held its initial public offering. Porter had designed some new method for microchips to transfer data between one another without making physical contact. The technology was beyond Gabriel's understanding, but it must have been a big deal, because Porter's net worth shot from ramen level to caviar level overnight. Porter didn't have time for high school reunions after that.

"So, what are you doing here?" Gabriel asked.

Porter played coy. "I came to hear your lecture."

"Bullshit. The only fiction you care about is the science fiction you can make a reality."

Porter laughed. "Okay, you've got me there." His laughter gave way to a more serious expression. "The truth is, I'm here for a business transaction. I need your services."

Gabriel shot him a puzzled glance. "Working on your memoirs already? There are more qualified writers than me for something like that."

"No," Porter said flatly. "I need your *other* services."

Gabriel deflected. "I don't do that anymore."

"Now who's bullshitting?" Porter asked bluntly. "I remember you and Lisa every weekend in college, hunkered down in your dorm room, marathoning Indiana Jones movies. Remember what I used to tell you?"

"That it wasn't real archaeology?"

"That's right," Porter said, smiling at the memory. "Do you remember what you used to tell me?"

"That we didn't care because it looked like so much damn fun."

They shared a chuckle.

Porter continued a moment later. "A passion like that doesn't just go away. A passion like that is for life. Besides, you don't think I got where I am today without knowing how to dig up information on people, do you? I know about your little mansion in the hills. I bet you even gave it a kitschy little nickname, too."

"Artifact Manor," Gabriel admitted.

"Ha! Not exactly subtle, huh?" Porter draped a friendly arm around Gabriel's neck and whispered as if he were divulging state secrets. "My people tell me our old pals Samantha Collins and Nathan Bellows spend a lot of time there- maybe even live there. I also know they get regular deposits in their checking accounts despite being unemployed, suggesting *someone* has them on an unofficial payroll. There's no way your book royalties can cover that amount of money, which means you're on an unofficial payroll, too."

Porter had Gabriel nailed, but Gabriel shouldn't have been surprised. Information was like gold in the business world, and Porter's legacy was so shiny and yellow it would've made King Solomon jealous. Gabriel wanted to know what Porter's angle was before confirming too much, though, so he kept quiet and listened.

"I need services like yours," Porter told him. "I know there are other treasure hunters out there who would champ at the bit to get a taste of my wallet. I've got dossiers on every one of them stacked on my desk back at work. But I need someone I can trust. I need a friend."

Porter quickly pulled away as a coughing fit overtook him. He stifled his outburst with a handkerchief, looking uncharacteristically embarrassed for what was a common human reflex, then apologized as he straightened his jacket and tie.

"Here," Gabriel said, passing Porter one of his unopened bottles of water.

Porter took several gulps, then place his hand back on Gabriel's shoulder. "See? You haven't changed in twenty years. I can't tell you the number of people who'd rather watch me choke to death than offer me a drink." He took another sip, then capped the bottle. "You're the person I need for this job. You, Lisa, Nate, Samantha... we all go back a long way, well before I made enemies in this world. You're the only qualified people I can trust with this job. And don't worry, I'll pay you five- no, ten times your normal rate. Just because we're friends doesn't mean I expect a discount."

Gabriel smiled. "Given your net worth, I wouldn't dream of it." He and Porter shared another laugh. Then it was time to have an honest conversation. "So, assuming you're right, and that my team and I are still involved in the activities you think we are, what exactly do you want us to find?"

Porter released Gabriel's shoulder, the businessman within him rising to the surface. He stared at Gabriel with deadly serious eyes and asked a single question. "Have you ever heard of the Pendant of God?"

Chapter Four
The Pendant of God

New York, New York
Two Weeks Before The Sky Opened

Gabriel blinked skeptically at Porter. "I think I'm going to want to sit down for this conversation."

"Sure," Porter said. "Let's grab some food. It's on me."

They walked in silence to a campus deli and each ordered a sandwich. Gabriel was having a BLT on white bread. Porter was having a club sandwich on wheat. Some things never changed, Gabriel thought as he grabbed two bottles of root beer and Porter paid. They sat across from each other at a corner table, away from the prying ears of students who had been on the tail end of the lunch rush.

After savoring a few bites of his sandwich, Gabriel was ready to continue their conversation. "You asked if I've heard of the Pendant of God. I have. It's a fabled piece of jewelry described in the Book of Damien. Religious scholars dismiss its existence since the Book of Damien was never officially deemed a canonical entry into the bible."

"Correct," Porter said. "And do you know the story of the pendant?"

"My memory's a little hazy," Gabriel admitted, "but I believe it was a weapon entrusted to Damien by God himself to prevent a mass genocide."

"Very good," Porter said. "Only it was so much more than a weapon. May I?"

Gabriel was happy to give his voice a rest. Besides, now he was getting a free lunch and entertainment to go with it. "Sure," he said.

"The Book of Damien actually begins with the story of Lyrus, a servant boy loyal to God at a time when the Hebrews were losing faith due to harsh living conditions. A sect of unfaithful Hebrews banned together to denounce God's love for his people. They established a creed that man should take what man wants and preached against the tyrannical hand of morality. Eventually they grew violent, and the remaining faithful Hebrews prayed for God to intervene on their behalf."

"In stepped Lyrus, I assume?" Gabriel asked.

"Correct," Porter confirmed. "God was angry with the violence befalling his followers, so he called upon Lyrus to rise from his servant status and become a leader of other faithful men. Lyrus obeyed, and with God's blessing, created an army to fight back and eventually subdue the insolent Hebrew sect."

"Okay," Gabriel said as he swallowed a bite of sandwich. "I'll admit I wasn't familiar with the Lyrus tale. How do Damien and the pendant fit in?"

"I'm getting there," Porter assured him. "Once the fighting subsided, the surviving Hebrews expected their lives to return to the status quo, which also meant they expected Lyrus to return to being a mere servant boy."

"I take it he didn't agree with that?"

"No, he sure he didn't," Porter said. "I can't blame him. He had spent most of his life near the bottom of the class hierarchy, but rose to power and risked that lowly life to defend those of a higher status than he, only to have them look down upon him once more when he was no longer needed." Porter shrugged as if he could relate to the feeling. "That sort of thing can piss a person off. The army of men who had fought and bled by Lyrus's side were still loyal to him. If the rest of the Hebrews wouldn't recognize Lyrus for the leader he'd become, then they didn't deserve his, or their, mercy."

"This is how the genocide began," Gabriel deduced.

Porter nodded. "It sure is. Following in the footsteps of Lucifer himself, Lyrus misused God's blessing to establish his own rule on Earth. He plunged the world into a dark age marked by mass death and destruction. God called on Lyrus to stop the terror, but Lyrus saw God's calling as another form of servitude, and he was done being anyone's servant. So God called on another of his faithful to step in."

"Damien."

"Damien," Porter repeated. "Instead of providing Damien with an army of men, God presented him with a single chained pendant. He told Damien that he had imbued the pendant with a mere fraction of his own power, but that it would be enough to stop Lyrus and return the Earth to the light. Damien challenged Lyrus and his army to a battle. Of course, Lyrus thought it was a joke. One jewelry-wearing man versus an army that numbered in the hundreds of thousands... Damien didn't stand a chance."

"Damien, the man, didn't stand a chance," Gabriel chimed in.

"Right. But Damien, the wielder of God's strength, was unstoppable. He single-handedly crushed Lyrus's army, then publicly executed Lyrus as an example of the fate that lay in store for anyone else who defied God's will. No one really knows how Damien accomplished such a feat, but accounts from Lyrus's execution suggest that whatever the tyrannical leader witnessed on the battlefield drove him mad."

"So it is a weapon?" Gabriel asked, revisiting his earlier claim.

"It was that day," Porter explained. "But once Lyrus's reign had ended, Damien offered to return the pendant to God. Recognizing the unending good in Damien, God instructed him to keep it, explaining that the power within was not just derived from God's might, but also from his love. He told Damien the world needed his love more than ever, and so Damien kept the pendant and swore to put it to proper use."

Porter grew silent as Gabriel flicked the last piece of sandwich into his mouth. "And then?"

Porter shrugged. "No one knows for sure. That's where the Book of Damien ends. But I have my theories."

Gabriel eyed Porter as if to say *spill it.*

"Records from the region around the implied time of Lyrus's defeat suggest a prolonged period of peace, health, and prosperity followed. The average lifespan of men during that time was fifty percent greater than the periods immediately before or after. Ailments such as disease are all but absent from historical accounts. There was no war, no famine, barely even a mention of crime. I think Damien did that. I think that's how he used the pendant. It was his way of sharing God's love with the world."

Gabriel eyed Porter suspiciously. "Ever since we were kids, your beliefs have been rooted in science. You built your entire career, hell, your entire life, around science. You don't believe in this stuff. I can't count the number of times I've heard you speak about religion as if it's a plague on mankind, both privately and publicly. Religious scholars don't even believe the pendant is real. Are you trying to convince me you believe it is? Why?"

Porter nodded, acknowledging that everything Gabriel had said was true. He then leaned forward, his eyes narrow. "Because I have evidence," he said confidently. "The pendant is real, Gabriel. It's real... and you're going to find it for me."

Chapter Five
Which One Are You

New York, New York
Two Weeks Before The Sky Opened

Porter leaned back and smiled, as if he knew he had Gabriel on the hook now. Gabriel had been raised in a religious household and schooled in traditional Christian beliefs. His parents forced him to attend church despite it being an utter bore, and though he dropped that tradition as soon as he was a grown man, Gabriel remained a believer at heart. Maturity and years of knowledge had transformed his view of the bible from a divine record of man's relationship with God to one of many historical accounts of ancient civilization. It was written by man and thus could be flawed like man. This also meant it could be incomplete, leaving room for the omission of any number of valid books, including the Book of Damien.

Gabriel tended to only accept jobs with a high probability of success. Those jobs were usually rooted in accepted historical facts. They involved artifacts that had been lost in time, but for which multiple corroborating pieces of information evidencing their existence could be obtained. The Pendant of God was not one of those artifacts. It was a legend that may or may not be true- with most scholars leaning toward the latter. Any time or effort spent in pursuit of it would more than likely wind up wasted. Unless...

"What sort of evidence?" Gabriel asked.

"A collection of scrolls written over thousands of years and preserved by monks stationed in temples throughout the world," Porter told him. "I've been painstakingly collecting them for the past eighteen months."

"That doesn't make sense," Gabriel argued. "If scrolls

documenting the Pendant of God were out there, surely someone would have discovered them long ago."

"True. These-" Porter's voice caught in his throat as he broke into another coughing fit. This time, he had his bottle of root beer to help stymie the attack. "These scrolls don't mention the Pendant of God," he said once he regained composure.

"But you said-"

"I said I had evidence that the Pendant of God exists," Porter cut in. "The scrolls themselves are actually quite benign. They contain population data, demographics, accounts of significant events, technological breakthroughs... basically a greatest hits collection of census data and newspaper headlines. It's not until you compare the data in the scrolls to similar data from the rest of the world that a pattern emerges."

"Peace, health, and prosperity," Gabriel said, channeling Porter's earlier words.

"Exactly!" Porter leaned forward with excitement. "Believers in the Book of Damien estimate his last known location was somewhere around modern day Israel. Approximately three hundred years after Damien's battle with Lyrus, the abnormal prosperity in that region dissipated. Why do you think that is?"

"Because the power of the pendant ran dry?" Gabriel was only half serious.

"The power of God himself dried up? Your mother would be so disappointed."

Gabriel shrugged.

"The way I see it," Porter then explained, "if we take the power of the pendant as absolute, then only one of two things could have happened three hundred years later. Damien, or whomever succeeded Damien in possessing the pendant, either left Israel, taking the pendant's blessing with him, or changed his mind about sharing God's love with man."

"It if was the latter, we probably wouldn't be having this conversation," Gabriel concluded. "So where did Damien- or whomever- go?"

"Egypt," Porter replied. "For about one hundred years. Then Libya, Algeria, Morocco, Spain, France, Austria... round and round the

Mediterranean Sea, changing locations every fifty to one hundred years."

"Sharing God's love beyond the boundaries of Israel?"

"Or trying to keep it a secret," Porter countered. "Too much prosperity in one place for too many years could draw unwanted attention. Imagine if Hitler had gotten a trajectory on the pendant's location during his artifact obsession... the world could be a much different place."

"So, where is it now?"

"Well, that's the tricky thing," Porter said. "The evidence always lags the pendant's current location. By the time a pattern of prosperity can be identified in one country, the pendant has moved to the next."

"Where was the last pattern?"

Porter smiled. "That's the good news. Morocco. The pendant has consistently moved clockwise around the Mediterranean Sea for several thousand years. Morocco is at the Northwest corner of Africa and at the Southwest corner of the Mediterranean. To continue clockwise around the sea requires crossing the Straight of Gibraltar-"

"Which would put the pendant in Spain." Gabriel recalled from his studies of European geography. "Or possibly Portugal."

"Yes," Porter agreed. "Though based on previous cycles, Spain is the more likely of the two."

Gabriel took a moment to consider the implications. "So where in Spain do we start? It's not like we can trek door-to-door across the country asking people if they've seen a pendant that gives the wearer god-like capabilities."

"That, my dear friend," Porter said with a mischievous grin, "is what I'm going to pay you big bucks to figure out." He began to cough again, but stifled it.

Gabriel ran some rough calculations in his head. He didn't know the exact count, but he guessed Spain had to be home to at least forty million people. He also guessed, based on mental recollections of world maps, that it was approximately the size of Texas, maybe a little smaller. Finding a mythical artifact in an area of that size and population density was going to be like finding a needle in a haystack. Still, it was one hell of a needle. Mythical religious artifacts were the first place trophies of the treasure hunting game. It didn't matter whether they lived up to the often exaggerated legends from which they sprung. Their existence, and attainment by those lucky and skilled enough, made them the ultimate prize.

A thought popped into Gabriel's head. What if the Pendant of God *did* live up to its legend? What if, tucked safely away in a hidden corner of Spain, was a piece of jewelry that didn't simply symbolize the power of The Almighty, but actually contained a piece of it? God entrusted Damien with the pendant because Damien's heart was pure and devoted to God's word. But what if Damien had been like Lyrus? What if the temptation of mortal supremacy could have corrupted his devotion to God's ways? As Porter himself had put it, the world could be a much different place.

Gabriel sized up his old friend, a friend that appeared out of the blue after twenty years to implore his unique services. A friend who already had about as much power as any one man could expect in life. A friend who appeared quite healthy, but had a suspiciously nagging cough…

"There's one thing I'd like to know before I take this job," he told Porter.

"Shoot."

"Damien and Lyrus each used the gifts God gave them to achieve extraordinarily different goals. Not that it's likely, but let's assume for a moment that the pendant truly contains the power of God, both his love and his destructive capability. Let's also assume I'm able to find it for you." Gabriel stared hard into Porter's eyes so he could get an accurate read on his friend's next reaction. "Once you have that kind of power in your hands, which one are you going to be? Damien… or Lyrus?"

Chapter Six
Terminal

New York, New York
Two Weeks Before The Sky Opened

Porter glared at Gabriel as if offended by the question. "Now what do you think? I'm Lyrus. I'm going to use that pendant to infuse my tech empire with the power of The Almighty. Then I'm going to use my empowered empire to rule the world with a steel fist and army of God-infused robots at my back."

Gabriel sat in stunned silence as Porter let his plan sink in.

A moment later, the businessman busted out with laughter. "I'm just bullshitting you, Gabriel! Oh God, you're just as gullible as I remember. You should see your face. You're whiter than the mayonnaise on my sandwich!"

Gabriel released a tense chuckle. He was glad Porter still had a sense of humor after all these years, twisted as it might be. But he still wanted an answer to his question, so he waited.

"The truth is," Porter told him after settling down, "I don't want to be Damien or Lyrus. I'm Porter Cannes. I'm the man who has more wealth than most men dream of. But you know what I don't have? Treasure. Sure, I can buy just about any historical object I want. Famous paintings, priceless jewelry, ancient inventions, revered artifacts... I've bought them all at one time or another in life. Hell, I think I even own a museum somewhere in Europe. But none of it feels like treasure to me. So I asked myself why."

"Because you're so disgustingly rich you can't remember what you've bought?" Gabriel snickered.

Porter flipped him his middle finger. "It's because I'm so disgustingly rich that purchasing objects has lost all meaning for me."

"I could help take some of that wealth off your hands," Gabriel offered. "In the interest of restoring meaning to your life."

"Hardy har," Porter replied. "Unfortunately, even if I returned to our penniless college years, I suspect buying objects would never be enough. I want to discover, Gabriel. Like you. I want to obtain something grand through hard work and perseverance."

"Isn't that how you got your company?"

"Yes," Porter admitted, "but even it has a price. I want to obtain something so unique and so valuable that a price tag could never be placed on it. I want a treasure of my own, and the Pendant of God might very well be the greatest treasure in existence today."

Gabriel pondered over his intentions for a minute. "Not to potentially ruin the financial windfall headed my way," he then said, "but if you hire me, won't I technically be the one making the discovery?"

Porter grinned as though he had anticipated the technicality. "That's why I need someone I can trust. It's also why I'm going with you. We'll follow the clues and make the discovery together. What better way to reignite an old friendship?"

While Gabriel had no problem with Porter's suggestion, he wasn't sure his team would feel the same. Oh well, that was a problem for later. Gabriel was intrigued enough to formally accept Porter's task, but before he could, the businessman broke out into another coughing fit. This time, he didn't cover his mouth quickly enough, and a light spattering of blood landed on the remnants of Porter's sandwich.

"Shit," Porter muttered when the fit subsided. "I guess that cat's out of the bag."

Gabriel's eyes swung from Porter's face to the blood on the bread, then back to Porter's face again. "This isn't just about finding your treasure in life, is it?"

Porter wiped his lips with his handkerchief and examined the red streak they left behind. "What I told you was true. But yes, I have a secondary motive for pursuing the Pendant of God instead of any other of a thousand artifacts hiding out there. Eighteen months ago, an x-ray revealed a mass in my lungs. The prognosis was... well, let's just say we probably won't be having lunch again this time next year."

"Treatment?" Gabriel asked, deep down already knowing the

answer.

"It was too late for most, and the others are too ineffective." Porter frowned. "It's funny, really. I've got all the money and connections in the world, and it's all worthless when it comes to saving my life." He looked at Gabriel with solemn eyes. "But you're not. You can help me extend my time on this mortal coil. You can help me live again."

"Porter," Gabriel said. "There's no guarantee we'll actually find the pendant. Even if we do, we don't know for certain it has the power you think it does. It could be an inert relic, nothing more."

"You're the best there is at this sort of thing," Porter said with a confident smile. "We're going to find the pendant. If it has the power to save me, mission accomplished. If it doesn't, then at least I can die having lived my last days to their fullest." He sighed with heavy acceptance. "That alone is pretty priceless."

Gabriel frowned. "Why didn't you just come clean from the start? You know I would have-" He paused, having answered his own question. "You didn't want me to pity you. You wanted me to take the job because I wanted to take it, not because I felt obligated."

"I've never been a pity kind of guy. I don't show it to others, and I don't expect anyone to show it to me." Porter wrapped his sandwich remnants and pushed them aside. "So, ignoring the last five minutes of our conversation... I'll pay ten times your normal rate and keep the cash flowing until we find the pendant or until I drop dead. I'll give you a twenty-thousand dollar deposit up front to cover any return expenses should the latter happen mid-journey. You will, of course, keep everything we discussed today and everything that happens related to our business agreement going forward strictly confidential. If word got out about my condition..."

"I get it," Gabriel told him. "You're trying to protect your company. My team and I will sign whatever non-disclosure agreements you need us to."

"Your word is plenty," Porter said. "Let's keep the lawyers out of this. I've already taken my fair share of scoldings from them and my financial advisors over the laws I've bent and money I've burned to get those scrolls."

"I've never cared for lawyers, anyway."

"Well, then?" Porter asked. "If the terms are acceptable, shall we do business?"

Gabriel probably should have discussed the proposition with his team, but he didn't want Porter to sense hesitation in him. Porter may have been an old friend, but he was in businessman mode. He would just as soon offer the same deal to the next most trustworthy treasure hunter should he get the idea Gabriel would flake out. Besides, Gabriel could only think of one or two reasons his team might oppose the arrangement. Given the stakes, he was willing to risk their unhappiness. "Yeah," Gabriel nodded. "Let's go find that pendant."

Chapter Seven
Paranoia

New York, New York
Two Weeks Before The Sky Opened

Porter and Gabriel conversed for another twenty minutes before heading their separate ways. Porter invited Gabriel and his team to stop by his office the next day to review the scrolls he had amassed and to discuss any further business arrangements that needed to be made. Gabriel accepted the invitation, expressed his remorse for the circumstances that had reunited him and Porter, and ensured Porter he had entrusted the right person with such an important task. He then began his trek across campus to the visitor parking garage.

Gabriel noted that Porter headed in a different direction, and assumed he had more privileged parking somewhere nearby. *It must be nice to have that type of money*, Gabriel thought as he walked the landscaped paths of campus and took in the sights of students going about their days. It wasn't that Gabriel was poor; far from it, in fact. But most of his income, both from his legitimate job and his more secretive, but highly lucrative one, went into one of two ventures. The first was funding future excursions, for which he rarely received advance payment. The second was collecting historical relics for safekeeping in his museum-like mansion, itself the source of a hefty property tax bill. Gabriel spent very little of the money on life's luxuries and conveniences. Maybe he would if he had ridiculous amounts of wealth like Porter did. Then again, maybe he would just spend it on more of the same. It was hard to know without having the opportunity to test those rich waters.

"Watch it!" A student exclaimed as he barely avoided crashing into Gabriel at a blind corner.

"Sorry about that," Gabriel replied, his cheeks turning red with embarrassment.

It was funny how the universe had subtle ways of slapping people on the wrists when they needed it. *That's what I get for having money envy,* Gabriel told himself. He continued down the sidewalk, more alert to his surroundings. Gabriel watched as some students passed him by on their way to class, while others tossed footballs or frisbees on the lawn, and as the rest drowned out the natural world to focus on the screens in their hands. Gabriel had nothing against technology, but he would never understand how today's youth got the same satisfaction out of their devices as he did out the tangible feel of a piece of history.

He passed the library, where an attractive male and female student leaned against a stairwell railing, their eyes glued to their phones instead of to each other. *I hope those things start coming with reproductive organs*, Gabriel thought. *If not, humanity is screwed.* As if hearing Gabriel's thoughts, the male student glanced up at him briefly. They made eye contact, causing Gabriel to question whether he had accidentally vocalized his comment. But then the student returned to his device, confirming that the glance was little more than happenstance.

Gabriel reached an intersection and took a slight left onto the path that would take him directly to his parking garage. He didn't know why- call it intuition- but he had a sudden urge to check the status of the library couple before he lost his line of sight. When he looked back, he caught the male staring at him again. The student tried to play it off by turning away and running a hand through his hair, but Gabriel was certain about what he had seen. Did he have a 'kick me' sign on his back or something? Gabriel's name was famous among up and coming English majors, but his face was another story. Maybe the student had recognized him from one of his novel covers or a talk show interview. *Unlikely,* Gabriel decided.

A moment later, the library and its tech-obsessed students were gone from view. Gabriel reached the parking garage, took the stairs up two levels, and found his car. As Gabriel tossed his presentation materials on the front passenger seat, he thought he heard a cough echo off the garage walls. Gabriel had seen no one else in the garage, despite there being only a few parking spots left, so he glanced around for the source of the sound. All was quiet.

Gabriel knew he should shrug the noise off. Why did it matter if there was someone else in the garage? It was a public place, after all, and clearly Gabriel wasn't the only visitor to campus that day. But his clandestine profession had taught Gabriel to be observant when his surroundings didn't feel right, and this parking garage was feeling about as right as a left-handed guitar player. If he had noticed another person on his way to his car, Gabriel probably wouldn't have given the cough a second thought. But an unseen person trying to mask a cough... well, that was a different story altogether.

Gabriel closed the front passenger door and walked around to the other side of the vehicle, trying to act natural as his eyes scanned his closest surroundings. Nothing triggered his warning lights. Gabriel then opened his driver-side door and was pretty sure he heard a quick patter of footsteps timed with his own noise. He froze and pretended to check his smartwatch as if he had received a notification. Unfortunately for Gabriel, the footsteps had been to his backside. Turning toward them would be too obvious, but proceeding into his car would be noisy enough to entice his potential assailant forward.

A wave of girly laughter echoed from the stairwell Gabriel had taken to this level of the parking garage. A moment later, two chatty teenagers emerged from the stairwell and started down Gabriel's aisle. Seizing the unexpected opportunity, Gabriel flung his car door open, jumped inside, and slammed and the locked the door behind him. He caught a brief glimpse of a suited figure dashing out of sight as the teenage girls neared. Gabriel started his engine and peeled out of his space as soon as the girls were clear, then raced for the exit ramp. The headlights of a black sedan illuminated his car as he passed, its engine springing to life. Gabriel summoned his phone's virtual assistant and instructed it to call his wife.

"Hey, how'd it go?" Lisa answered after two rings.

"Hey," Gabriel responded as he watched the black sedan pull into range of his rearview mirror. "I'll tell you about it later. Right now, I've got a problem."

Chapter Eight
Pursuit

New York, New York
Two Weeks Before The Sky Opened

Gabriel's tires squealed as he took a hard right out of the campus parking garage and sped toward city streets. He pounded his horn at students crossing the road, swerving around them so tightly that he may have even clipped a backpack or two. The black sedan pursued, less cautious with its actions, sending students diving for the sidewalk to avoid being run down. At the edge of campus, Gabriel made a left onto Broadway.

"You need to cut over to Third Avenue as soon as possible," Lisa guided through his speakerphone. *"Otherwise, you'll hit too much pedestrian traffic."*

Gabriel glanced in his rearview mirror. The black sedan was still on his tail, but it had lost some ground exiting campus. Gabriel shifted his vision ahead, where red lights dangled across the approaching intersection. He muscled his way into the right lane, spotted a gap in the mob of pedestrians crossing the adjacent street, and blasted through the gap without slowing. Gabriel was heading east now, with nothing but green lights on his path. He gunned the gas through a nearby intersection, then two more, before he saw his next set of red lights approaching.

"North or south on Third?" Gabriel asked.

"North," Lisa instructed.

Gabriel maneuvered his way to the leftmost lane. This time he couldn't speed through the red light without risking a major accident, so he took his place in line in the turn lane. A pedestrian vehicle immediately sandwiched him in. Then another pulled to a stop behind it. The black sedan followed. Gabriel leaned from side to side to get a better look at his pursuer, but the man was too obscured by the cars that stood between them. How long had the man been following him? He had returned home from his most recent treasure hunt nearly six days ago. The mission had experienced some *complications,* as Gabriel liked to call them, but to the best of his knowledge, everything had been settled by the end. Was it possible some lingering threat from that mission had been tracking him for six days without his knowledge? If so, why wait until now to strike?

There was another possibility, though Gabriel didn't want to acknowledge it. The suited man, whoever he was, might have been following Porter. He might only be after Gabriel because of Gabriel's new business arrangement. But would a tech billionaire's fascination with a mythical religious artifact really garner this type of attention? Porter mentioned something about making enemies... but Gabriel had assumed he was speaking hypothetically. *Well,* Gabriel thought, *you know what they say about people who assume...*

The turn lane light turned green. As soon as he was able, Gabriel pulled forward and passed through the intersection. The larger width of Third Avenue at his disposal, he then gunned the gas once more, hoping to recoup some of the distance he had lost between him and the black sedan.

"Where to now?" Gabriel asked Lisa.

"There's only so long you can evade by car," she replied. *"My map shows a public parking garage to your right when you reach Thirteenth Street. Park there and ditch. You're going to lose me until you get back outside. I'll figure out your next move by then."*

Gabriel continued using the full width of Third Avenue to swerve around slower vehicles and put critical space between him and his pursuers. When he crossed Twelfth Street, he pushed his way to the right lane, careened around the corner of Third and Thirteenth, and checked his rearview mirror. He didn't have sight of the black sedan, which meant it didn't have sight of him, either. Gabriel turned into the first parking garage he saw, grabbed a ticket to raise the gate, and sped deep into the structure.

He took the first available parking space he spotted and killed his engine. Then Gabriel hopped out of his vehicle and ducked down just before the black sedan pulled in after him. The sedan crept slowly down the entry lane, and Gabriel knew it wouldn't be long before the driver identified his car. Staying low, he tiptoed to the next row of vehicles, then double-backed toward the garage entrance. The sedan stopped near Gabriel's parking spot. As his assailant investigated his abandoned car, Gabriel reached the end of the row and assessed his situation. The entrance to the parking garage was only about twenty yards away, but all twenty of them were out in the open, with nothing for Gabriel to hide behind. The black sedan was about eighty to one hundred yards away, having not moved since locating Gabriel's vehicle. But the sedan had wheels and a gas engine, two things that, the last Gabriel checked, didn't come standard on the human body. Even in reverse, it could close that gap about as fast as Gabriel could close the one to the entrance.

He would have to chance it. His pursuer knew he was in the garage. It wasn't like Gabriel could simply wait him out. Gabriel took a deep breath and set his eyes on the bright sunlight streaming in from the garage entrance. Twenty yards... it didn't sound like much, but it might be the difference between life and death. *Oh well,* Gabriel thought. *Let's get this over with.* He pushed off with his dominant foot and ran into the twenty-yard clearing. His pursuer was on him quicker than expected. The sedan's reverse lights lit up immediately, and its tires screeched as it launched backwards.

Gabriel slammed on his own internal gas pedal. The sunlight grew brighter as he closed the gap to the entrance. The roar of the sedan's engine grew louder as it closed its gap to him. Gabriel gritted his teeth as he charged ahead, praying that he felt the heat of the sunshine before he felt the heat of the sedan's exhaust pipe as it passed over his pancaked body. He had less than five yards to go, but the sedan's engine sounded as if it was less than five feet from his ears. Gabriel channeled his inner football player and dove forward. The draft of the sedan twisted his body in midair, sending Gabriel tumbling awkwardly onto the concrete sidewalk that lined Thirteenth Street.

The sedan took out the guardrail that blocked the garage entrance, nearly crashed into a passing taxi, then spun one hundred eighty degrees before coming to a stop in the middle of Thirteenth Street. Gabriel pushed himself up and eyed the vehicle. The glare of the sun prevented him from seeing its driver, but Gabriel knew the driver was eyeing him right back. Seeing as how they were in different weight classes, Gabriel in the lightweight and the sedan in the ungodly overweight, Gabriel thought it best to hightail it out of there. He bolted toward Third Avenue, not looking back as the sedan's tires squealed once more.

A familiar face rounded the corner ahead. It was Samantha, walking toward Gabriel as cool and collected as ever, a small steel container in one of her hands. Samantha removed the lid from the container and tossed its contents into the street. As Gabriel ran, he heard the familiar clinks of a dozen spiked steel balls spreading across the concrete. The sedan contacted the first of them and skidded out of control as its front tires popped. This brought it into contact with the rest of the balls, which blew out its rear tires and sent the sedan flipping end over end into the intersection of Third and Thirteenth. Gabriel paused at the corner and watched as oncoming traffic narrowly missed hitting the smoking overturned vehicle.

"Come on," Samantha said once she reached him. "There's a subway station at Fourteenth Street. We can lose him underground."

Gabriel saw his unidentified assailant squirm behind cracked glass. The man then freed himself of his seatbelt and kicked at the passenger side window. Gabriel didn't wait around to see what happened next, and instead followed Samantha to the safety of the subway system.

Chapter Nine
Artifact Manor

New York, New York
Two Weeks Before The Sky Opened

Gabriel and Samantha hopped subway lines for nearly an hour to ensure they had lost any potential tails. Then they caught a cab to Grand Central Terminal and took the Metro-North to Bedford Hills. Lisa parked near the Bedford Hills station over an hour earlier and had been keeping her eyes peeled for any suspicious activity. Comfortable that all was normal, she picked up Gabriel and Samantha and took them home to Artifact Manor.

At first glance, the mansion looked like any other celebrity home in the area. It was a luxurious multi-winged structure surrounded by thirty acres of lush greenery. It had a garage the size of most people's houses, a tennis court, basketball court, and a swimming pool that would make proprietors of five-star hotels jealous. Though Gabriel and his team used the amenities from time to time, they primarily existed for show, to detract the attention of anyone eyeing the property from its true value, which resided on the inside.

Gabriel had been in the treasure hunting game for so long, he had amassed a small village's worth of ancient artifacts. Many were his own, collected during quests that held personal significance to Gabriel or members of his team. Others belonged to various museums and preservation societies Gabriel had networked with over the years. He had earned a reputation for meticulously protecting relics of the old world, so whenever these organizations needed safekeeping for their excess or particularly valuable exhibits, they turned to Gabriel. He offered his protection services at minimal cost, and often reciprocated with a pledge to donate one of his own artifacts upon his death.

Gabriel saw it as his duty in what had become mutually beneficial arrangements to preserve objects of historical relevance. He got to enjoy and protect treasures that would otherwise be inaccessible to him, and the museums and societies received protection and grew their collections in return.

Artifacts were showcased throughout the mansion. Some were encased on top of standalone pedestals. Others were displayed on bookshelves, walls, and mantles. A select few- the most valuable of those in Gabriel's possession- were kept in the vault, an underground showroom with an extra layer of security between it and the rest of the mansion. Not that the artifacts in the common areas of the mansion were unprotected. Gabriel had installed advanced sonic fencing along each property line of his estate. It was one of the many technologies Cannes International had made available for commercial purchase and it allowed strong physical protection of any area without the ugly sight of a physical barrier. Technically, the fencing wasn't approved for residential protection, but Gabriel's residence and business headquarters were one and the same. Whether it was commercial systems or taxes, Gabriel often leaned on whichever classification was necessary to get preferential treatment.

Gabriel had also installed a vast network of security cameras throughout the estate's acreage. They fed into a security console in the underground vault that also actively monitored motion, moisture, temperature, ultraviolet radiation, air purity, and a handful of other statistics from every portion of the mansion in which an artifact was stored. Should any portion of the sonic fence be disturbed by something larger than a stray animal, or any camera detect a remotely human figure, or any sensor within the mansion record a reading outside of its established standard parameters, each member of Gabriel's team would receive an alert directly to their phones. Should the need arise, any of them could remotely, or from the security console, trigger a mansion lockdown that would immediately drop containment doors between each room, over every window, and at every exit.

Of course, such an elaborate security setup was only as strong as its weakest link, and in this case, electricity and a stable network were the portions of the safety chain most easily broken. To counter this possibility, Gabriel installed solar paneling on the mansion's roof and an enormous array of battery storage in the underground vault. He wired the entire security system and its communication network into this storage to provide a failsafe should anyone attempt to break those weak links. In the event that still wasn't enough to stop intruders, Gabriel had made good friends with the Bedford Hills PD, who would drop everything to come to his aid at a moment's notice.

Upon arriving at the mansion, Gabriel headed up to his and Lisa's bedroom and took a hot shower. Sweat induced by the stage lights at his guest lecture would have likely forced him to take one when he got home anyway, but the additional perspiration and sidewalk gunk accumulated during his chase around Manhattan had sealed the deal. As elaborate as the rest of the mansion was, its bathrooms were surprisingly plain. Gabriel had long ago given up on trying to battle humidity and air purity in confined spaces to which both problems were inherent. So he minimized the space consumed by bathrooms in the mansion and reduced them to their most basic requirements: shower, toilet, sink. At the urging of his team, he at least kept the number of bathrooms sufficient to serve everyone at once, with a few to spare in the event they hosted company.

While Gabriel showered, Lisa sat on their bed scanning news networks for any stories about her husband's pursuit through Manhattan. One of their team's cardinal rules was to avoid trouble on home soil, because once you brought trouble into your own backyard, there was no way of avoiding it other than to move. Luckily, when Lisa finally found coverage, reporters were treating the overturned car at the intersection of Third and Thirteenth as a freak accident. The driver had fled the scene, possibly out of embarrassment or fear, though the police had produced a sketch of his appearance and asked that anyone who saw him contact them. There was no mention of Gabriel or of the high-speed pursuit that preceded the accident.

"We're in the clear," Lisa told Gabriel when he stepped out of the shower. "Three different stations are all reporting the same thing. Random accident."

Gabriel toweled his hair as he considered the story. "That doesn't make sense."

"Why not?"

"Samantha blew out the car's tires," Gabriel explained as he crossed into their bedroom. "The police would have found her spike balls. They would have traced the balls to Thirteenth Street, seen the broken guardrail to the parking garage, pulled traffic cam footage, and likely back-traced it all the way to the university." He wrapped the towel around his waist and sat next to Lisa. "There's no way they don't have me, or at least my license plate, pegged."

"You think they're keeping it under wraps?" Lisa asked. "Why? You did nothing wrong. Well, except for speeding, but it was to save your life."

Gabriel rubbed his chin as he tried to connect the dots of the day's events. "If they were simply keeping it quiet, they would've already sent units here to question me. It's more like..."

He trailed off, but Lisa had already figured out where his mind was headed. "Like it's being suppressed," she said. "Who would have the power to do that? And why?"

Gabriel had the answer before she even finished her questions. He smiled. "I still haven't told you who I met with today, have I?"

Chapter Ten
Absolute Power

New York, New York
Two Weeks Before The Sky Opened

"Cannes?" Nate asked from his perched seat atop a couch armrest. "*The* Porter Cannes? As in, the asshole who always competed with me for best-in-class?"

"That's the one," Gabriel confirmed.

After his shower, Gabriel had asked Lisa to corral the team in the downstairs great room. He knew there would be questions about Porter's request, and likely some hesitation regarding Gabriel's decision to accept it. As was his typical style, Gabriel wanted everyone together to air whatever concerns or grievances they might have and to ensure team unity going forward.

"Porter..." Lisa said. "After all this time. What did he want?"

"Probably to buy the manor," Nate grumbled.

"Yeah, right," Samantha said. She was seated at the other end of the couch from Nate. "Porter never cared about history. He was always Mr. Future-Focused. Doesn't he have, like, a gazillion dollars or something by now?"

"Something like that," Gabriel replied. "And no, Nate, he doesn't want to buy our home or your affection. He wants to hire us for a job."

Gabriel relayed the day's events to his team, from Porter's unexpected appearance at his lecture, to their conversation over lunch, to Porter's terminal condition- which Gabriel emphasized must be kept in strict confidentiality- and finally, through the car chase that ended Gabriel's outing. When he finished, Gabriel was met with three sets of quiet stares.

"Huh," Nate eventually said to break the silence. "So money and fame really can't get you everything in life. Poor Porter." He didn't even attempt to sound sincere.

"For what it's worth," Gabriel said, "Porter is entrusting his life to the four of us. That includes you, Nate, regardless of your feelings toward him."

"Did you negotiate the return of my Seventh Annual Engineering Build-Off trophy when agreeing to this ridiculous mission?"

Samantha groaned. "Dude, you've got to let that go. It's been like thirty years."

"I don't care," Nate replied. "He cheated, and I got stuck with second place. If we save his life, I want my first place trophy back." Nate thought for a moment, then added, "And a public apology."

"Do you even have proof that he cheated?" Lisa asked.

"I did," Nate told her. "But my backpack got stolen the day of the competition and the proof was inside."

"Yeah," Samantha chimed in, "I bet the dog ate your homework the night before, too."

Everyone but Nate shared a laugh.

"I'm serious," Nate said to Gabriel. "You tell Porter I want an apology, even if it's a private one. Then, maybe..." He backed down from his rigidness, as if suddenly aware of how childish he sounded given the gravity of the situation. "I'll help save his life."

Lisa looked at Gabriel. "Did you warn Porter that we may not find anything? Or that even if we do, it may not be the mystical artifact he thinks it is?"

"I did, and he wants to try anyway."

Lisa pursed her lips in thought. Though they were usually in tune with one another, Gabriel wasn't sure what had her reluctant to get on board. Had Gabriel gotten swept up in the possibility that a religious relic largely believed to be a myth might actually turn out to be real? If he was being honest with himself, probably so. But that was no different from any other mission he and the team undertook. Maybe Gabriel had been biased by Porter's deteriorating health condition. It wasn't the typical reason for taking a job, but it wasn't a bad one, either. In fact, it was more altruistic than most reasons Gabriel and his team agreed to hunt down ancient artifacts. Maybe Lisa was just worried he had gotten in over his head.

"If this is about the car…"

"It is about the car," Lisa said with a heavy sigh. "And Porter, and the myth. I'm concerned, Gabriel. We've never faced this kind of heat within minutes of taking a job. And the end goal has never been so unclear."

Gabriel cocked his head curiously. "We've been on plenty of assignments where we weren't sure if the artifact we were chasing existed, or what condition it was in, or what it could do-"

"Yeah, but we're talking about the power of God here," Lisa cut him off. "Setting aside anyone's personal beliefs, that kind of power is terrifying. In the right hands, it could be used for great good, but in the wrong hands, or even misguided hands…"

"Absolute power corrupts absolutely," Gabriel quoted. "Like the story of Lyrus."

"Exactly."

A heavy silence hung over the room. Once again, Nate was the one to break it.

"If you're worried about the pendant being in the right hands," he said with a mischievous grin, "I know of a middle-aged tech engineer with a ton of ideas that could better the world if he had the right resources."

"Oh, you mean like Porter Cannes?" Samantha asked, feigning ignorance.

Nate flipped her a middle finger.

"Now, now, children," Gabriel said. "Look, if none of you feel comfortable with this, I can call Porter in the morning and back out."

"Who said anything about being uncomfortable?" Samantha asked playfully. "I think I'd look pretty damn hot with a god-like pendant hanging around my neck. The world could use a little more female power of the supreme-being type. I say let's go for it."

"Look at her," Nate said. "She doesn't even have the pendant yet, and it's already corrupted her."

"Yeah," Gabriel said with a smile. "Note to self: Samantha doesn't get to touch the pendant."

Samantha threw a decorative pillow at Gabriel, then another at Nate, which instigated a wrestling matching between the two of them. Gabriel ignored the more childish members of his team and sought

Lisa's advice.

"You make the call," he said sincerely. "Either we're all on board or we pull out. Just keep in mind, if we do pull out, Porter's going to find someone else. His life depends on it."

Lisa knew what Gabriel was hinting at. "There's no guarantee the next treasure hunter in line shares our morals," she said. "Now that Porter set his sights on the pendant, the only way to ensure it doesn't get abused is to be on the front line with him."

Gabriel nodded.

Lisa chewed her lip as she processed the information, then watched as Samantha pinned both of Nate's arms to the ground. Lisa cleared her throat loudly, bringing the wrestling match to an abrupt halt. "My official vote is that we retain our agreement with Porter and retrieve the pendant."

Samantha grinned. "Female power, here we come. I'm in."

Nate rolled his eyes, then looked at Gabriel and Lisa. "I still want my apology, but I'm in, too."

Gabriel took an accomplished breath. "Well, you already know my position." He took Lisa's hand and gave it a loving squeeze. "Let's get some good food and a good night's rest. We'll kick off planning tomorrow."

Chapter Eleven
Cannes Tower

New York, New York
Thirteen Days Before The Sky Opened

The next morning, Gabriel and his team took the Metro North train back into Manhattan. They had debated driving, but between traffic, parking, and the risk of losing another vehicle should anyone show unwanted interest in their excursion, they opted instead for public transportation. When they arrived at Grand Central Terminal, Nate insisted on a detour through the line at Magnolia Bakery for banana pudding, exposing the real reason he didn't have breakfast with the rest of the team before they left Artifact Manor. It was a pleasant day outside, so instead of hopping subway lines, Gabriel and his team strolled up Lexington Avenue until they reached Fifty-Seventh Street. There, they hung a right and laid eyes upon Cannes Tower in the distance.

The tower was located off of Second Avenue between Fifty-Seventh and Fifty-Eighth. It was the global headquarters of Cannes International and the personal residence of Porter Cannes. Rumor had it the tech billionaire had called in a number of political favors to place a hundred-story building at that intersection. Rumor also had it he had greased some palms to get the permit for a single private residence to be housed inside the building. In public, Porter insisted that he had done nothing wrong. He expressed how his business was an extension of himself, an organic entity necessitating his nourishment and constant attention. He saw no reason why he should be forced to place artificial commuting distance between it and him.

In the end, whether through nefarious means or not, Porter got his way, as most men of his stature did. Now he lived on the top two floors of the building, supposedly the penthouse to end all penthouses, while beneath him were ninety-eight floors of technological achievement in action. Cannes International had its hand in everything from consumer electronics to corporate software and hardware solutions to custom military grade technology. Their established revenue streams were as consistent as a company could hope for, and their ever-growing product line only grew the number of those streams over time.

Porter had had the foresight to anticipate consumers' desires for privacy protections before a series of data leaks and foreign government spying revelations made those desires commonplace. Everything designed by Cannes International was done so in Cannes Tower, on the local soil of its primary customer base. Software products were produced solely in-house, and hardware products that required foreign outsourcing flowed back through Cannes Tower for quality control before being mass distributed. The handful of times products returned to the U.S. with *undesirable modifications*- the PR-friendly way of saying they'd been tampered with- Porter had made public spectacles of the attempts and banned those third-parties from future business. The combination of lost profit and political embarrassment successfully dissuaded additional tampering efforts.

Cannes International's dedication to privacy won it devoted customer bases at both the consumer and corporate levels and also made it a prime candidate for lucrative government contracts. Porter had earned his riches honestly, even if he had broken a few inconsequential rules and stepped on a few toes on his way to immeasurable wealth.

"So that's what first place in a kids' engineering competition gets you these days, huh?" Nate asked upon seeing Cannes Tower for the first time.

Samantha rolled her eyes.

On the outside, Cannes Tower didn't actually appear to be anything special. Its height was impressive for this area of the city, but skyscrapers of similar height were scattered about other sections of Manhattan. Cannes Tower also stood out as more modern than the buildings around it, but again, modern design had been popping up around Manhattan for decades. What made Cannes Tower special was on the interior: the multitude of floors allocated to design studios, research and development labs, and testing facilities, as well as rumored entertainment and relaxation stations to help keep Cannes International's employees' minds healthy and fresh.

Unlike the other famous skyscrapers in the city, Cannes Tower was not open to public visitation. In fact, a network of digital access rights secured nearly every door in the building, from the front doors to the elevators to even the restrooms. Porter ensured that anyone entering the building was supposed to be there, and that anyone with the right to be there only had access to the areas of the building needed for their jobs. Porter never publicly admitted what other security precautions were in place should someone breach an off-limits part of the building, but he hinted they would sufficiently stop any such perpetrator within seconds.

On the roof of the tower, three high-tech cranes were currently removing long metal beams from stacks positioned along the perimeter. The cranes were unlike standard machinery used for construction. They were less bulky and appeared to move with more care and precision. They also appeared to be unmanned, and Gabriel suspected they were themselves a product of Cannes International, one of Porter's many ventures into automation, artificial intelligence, and robotics.

"What do you suppose that's for?" Lisa asked.

"Porter's ego," Nate quipped. "He finally got the memo that his tower wasn't the tallest in the city. Notice how from here it looks like a giant d-"

"Nate?" Gabriel cut him off.

"Yes, boss?"

"You're going to play nice in there, right?"

Nate grinned. "I'll do my best."

"Please do," Gabriel requested.

He looked at Cannes Tower, only a few blocks away. Gabriel then glanced over his shoulder, as he had already done numerous times during their stroll, before also discretely examining the crowd passing by. Lisa grabbed his hand and gave it a squeeze.

"We're clear," she said.

Gabriel smiled. He should have known Lisa would also be on the lookout for any unusual behavior. She probably had Samantha doing it, too. And while Gabriel knew the risk of being attacked two days in a row was slim- after all, today's trip into Manhattan wasn't a publicized event- he couldn't shake the feeling that he hadn't seen the last of his anonymous pursuer. Gabriel looked at Cannes Tower again.

"Okay," he said. "Let's go."

Chapter Twelve
Contamination Protocol

New York, New York
Thirteen Days Before The Sky Opened

Porter's personal assistant, who introduced herself as Nadine Walsh, met Gabriel and his team at the front door of Cannes Tower upon arrival. She guided them to the ground floor security office, where an armed guard scrutinized each of their IDs before giving them temporary Cannes International badges. The guard emphasized that the badges granted minimal access and should not be used for any purpose other than entry to the building, passage to the eighty-third floor, and use of the eighty-third floor's facilities. While receiving their lecture, Gabriel caught Nate scoping out the security office, likely noting any exploitable weaknesses in Porter's supposedly rock-solid system. The tech engineer just couldn't help himself.

Once they were clear of security, Nadine escorted Gabriel and his team to the central elevator shaft. She had Gabriel test his new badge to ensure it worked properly, then rode with the team to the eighty-third floor. Gabriel noted that the elevators rose so quickly he could feel gravitational pressure pushing down on his shoulders. Surprisingly, the sudden change in altitude didn't trigger any discomfort in his ears.

"Each elevator car has a dynamic environmental system," Nadine explained upon noticing Gabriel's curious look. "They counter the fast changes in altitude using predictive A.I. that triggers a rapid injection or expulsion of temperature controlled air as needed to maintain comfortable pressure levels."

"Fancy," Gabriel acknowledged. "If a bit over the top..."

Nadine raised her brow. "Take enough trips on these things each day and you'll have a greater appreciation for them."

She had a point. Gabriel shrugged, acceptingly.

The elevator made a soft, ear-pleasing *bong* as it stopped and opened its doors to the eighty-third floor. Nadine motioned for Gabriel and his team to exit into the awaiting corridor, which was barely long enough to hold all of them and abruptly ended in what appeared to be an airlock door. Nadine had Lisa try her badge on the door, which slid into the ceiling with a loud hiss. The team then proceeded into a changing room. Benches ran down the middle of the room and electronically locked steel lockers lined the two parallel walls that stretched from the first airlock door to a second at the other end. Most of the lockers had nameplates over them, and a group down the far-right side displayed G. Dunne, L. Dunne, N. Bellows, and S. Collins.

"Mr. Cannes is very protective of the materials you'll be working with," Nadine said. "You should leave any loose items in your locker and slip the containment suits inside over your current clothing." She motioned to a valve and hose system installed in the far wall. "Once you have your suits on, use the buddy system to check for any tears or loose seams, then hook up to one of these hoses like so." She demonstrated with an example containment suit. "Press this green button and approximately two hours' worth of oxygen with fill the air sacs in your suit's lining. When the air stops flowing, disconnect the hose, and you're ready for entry."

Nate glanced at Samantha. *Seriously?*

"The disinfecting chamber on the other side of the next door will fill with poisonous gases," Nadine continued, "so never enter without first confirming that your suit is sealed and primed with air."

Without further instruction, Nadine removed a containment suit from a locker with the nameplate N. Walsh and began the described procedure. Gabriel saw his team was hesitating, so he led by example and motioned for them to get moving. A few minutes later, all team members were suited, inspected, and inhaling the first breaths of their two-hour air supplies.

Nadine showed the group that temporary badges were embedded in the right sleeves of each of their suits, which would allow them to move freely throughout the eighty-third floor without needing to carry loose, and potentially contamination-riddled, badges. She had Samantha try her badge on the next airlock door, which also slid into the ceiling with a hiss. The group stepped into the disinfecting chamber Nadine had referenced, which was just another sterile-looking corridor with steel tubing jutting from the ceiling. The airlock door shut, and a series of gasses began spewing from the tubes.

"Well, this is fun," Nate said as the gasses expanded to fill the chamber.

"Maybe I'm a bit late asking this," Samantha then said, "but what happens if one of us needs to use the bathroom? Did Porter invent some sort of super absorbent liner for these suits?"

"We encourage everyone to empty their bladders before entering the eighty-third floor," Nadine said, explicitly answering Samantha's first question and implicitly answering the second. "But in the event of an emergency, there's a restroom in the middle of the floor. It requires passage through a disinfecting chamber like this one, and of course bringing a buddy to help with your suit on the other side, so I don't recommend making a habit of using it."

Gabriel couldn't see Nadine through the thick clouds of gas, but he could feel her displeasure at their presence. Maybe she wasn't used to outsiders having such precious access to Cannes Tower? A ventilation system kicked on loudly and cleared the chamber of gasses within a matter of seconds. An affirmative buzz let the chamber's occupants know it was clear to proceed, so Nadine approached the next airlock door and motioned for Nate to test his badge on it. Nate waved his right arm in front of the digital reader beside the door, but a red LED light flashed at him and the door didn't open.

"Hmmm," Nadine said. "Please try again."

Nate did as she asked, but the door still wouldn't open.

"It's okay," he told her. "I'm the one member of this group Porter probably doesn't want running around unsupervised." Nate glanced at the steel tubing on the ceiling. "That, or he wants to kill me."

"I'm sure that's not the case," Nadine said, failing to clarify which of Nate's claims she was referring to. "I'll have your access repaired by end of day."

Nadine swiped her own arm badge over the digital reader, and the next airlock shot into the ceiling. Beyond the open door was a long, white hallway, similar to those found in the surgical wards of hospitals. The hallway was staggered with observation windows and glass doors to what Gabriel could only assume were various laboratories and examination rooms housing the collection of evidence Porter had amassed. Waiting in the hallway was Porter himself, almost unrecognizable with his expensive suit hidden behind the same style contamination outfit Gabriel and his team now wore.

Porter grinned upon seeing his guests. "Welcome to the Old World!"

Chapter Thirteen
The Old World

New York, New York
Thirteen Days Before The Sky Opened

As Porter showed Gabriel and his team around, Gabriel thought the eighty-third floor looked much more like a world out of a futuristic science fiction movie rather than the Old World of ancient technology and artifacts. Every piece of equipment within every lab or exam room had the sparkle of newness and innovative design. Some equipment Gabriel recognized: microscopes, x-ray machines, ultraviolet lights, pH testing kits, magnification and photography devices, an assortment of preservation and restoration tools, and other like items. Granted, all of this equipment was fancier than the counterparts Gabriel had used or observed being used during his career. However, he supposed if he was rich like Porter and his life was on the line, he would spare no expense either.

The floor also held a noticeable amount of equipment Gabriel didn't recognize. In one lab was a large white cylinder, about the size of a standard kitchen trash can, that glowed blue at one end and red at the other. It had no visible ports and its state never changed to indicate it was actually doing something, leaving Gabriel to wonder if it wasn't actually equipment, but some overly expensive piece of contemporary art. Given the seriousness with which Porter appeared to treat the eighty-third floor, Gabriel doubted that this was the case. Then again, people with the type of money Porter had were usually a bit eccentric.

In one exam room, set inside a thick glass casing in the middle of a wall, was a parallel series of seven thin glass tubes with filaments running down their centers. At first, Gabriel assumed these were light bulbs for some kind of fancy display, similar to the back-lit boards doctors might hang x-ray pictures on. But upon passing them, Gabriel saw waves of purple electricity spiral down each of the filaments in succession. Then something in the wall clicked, and a deep hum sounded for about twenty seconds. This led Gabriel to think the tubes were part of some larger mechanism, the bulk of which was not visible from the eighty-third floor hallway, and that the glass case was simply an access point to swap out its tubes if needed. The scope of the unseen mechanism, and more importantly its purpose, had Gabriel stumped.

In fact, a number of other mystery objects left Gabriel stumped as well. In one room, there was a white box with ventilation holes on top, similar to what one would see in a standard desktop computer tower. The box had a single analogue dial on its side, and a digital display on the front that contained a series of gibberish letters, numbers, and symbols. If Gabriel didn't know better, he would have pegged the box for an over-the-top password generator, but he assumed Porter had more elegant ways of doing that.

In almost every room, there was a white orb affixed to a ceiling corner. The orbs occasionally glowed with a pale orange hue, beeped, and then returned to their dormant states. Before Gabriel could even contemplate what they were, Nate tapped him on the shoulder, pointed, and mouthed *what the hell?*, the tech engineer clearly as baffled as Gabriel. Also in every room were white rectangular prisms about the size of a standard power strip. In some rooms, they were magnetically attached to the edges of tables. In others, they had been adhered to the walls. And in one room the prism was hanging from the ceiling by something equivalent to straightened fishing wire, though Gabriel assumed it was probably much stronger and much more expensive. The prisms had no ports, no displays, and no discerning characteristics to suggest they were anything more than artsy paperweights. Again, Gabriel could only scratch his head as to what purpose they served.

In a less formal situation, he would have picked Porter's brain about the mysterious technology implemented throughout the floor. But this was work, and to maintain professionalism, Gabriel thought it better to focus on the task at hand. To that end, he noted that within almost every room that lined the central hallway of the eighty-third floor was an ancient scroll on display within a glass box. No two looked alike- their parchments differed, the languages written upon them differed, their ages varied significantly- yet each appeared to have been treated with the same amount of care and reverence as the rest.

"We've tried to assign rooms by chronological order," Porter explained as he led Gabriel and his team past the series of observation windows on each side of the central hallway. "The first room we passed contains a scroll confirmed to have been written sometime around 1400 BCE. The room at the far end," Porter pointed ahead of them, "contains a Moroccan scroll that was written only seventy years ago. We've periodically left rooms empty to accommodate any additional scrolls we might still discover."

"I take it that's the Moroccan scroll that led you to believe it was the pendant's last location?" Gabriel asked.

"That's correct," Porter confirmed, already a step ahead of Gabriel's thoughts. "You're concerned about its dating."

"Well, yeah," Gabriel said. "Seventy years for the scroll; tag on another five to twenty for the time span it documents... You told me the pendant changes location every fifty to one hundred years. Even if Spain was its next destination after Morocco, there's less chance of it still being there than there is of it having moved on. To maximize our chances of finding it, shouldn't we wait for more recent evidence out of Spain and track the pendant to its subsequent destination? With modern censusing and easy access to historical data, surely we'd be able to see some evidence within just a few years of the pendant's departure."

"Ideally, we'd do exactly that," Porter admitted with a sad smile. "Unfortunately, we don't have that kind of time."

Right, Gabriel thought, ashamed he had let himself slip so quickly into treasure hunting mode that he lost sight of the reason they were going on this journey. Porter nudged his head as if to say *don't worry about it*, then continued leading the team down the hallway.

"Let's start at the Moroccan room," he told them. "I want to show you something."

Chapter Fourteen
Shifa

New York, New York
Thirteen Days Before The Sky Opened

"The Moroccan scroll documents some of the more prominent events of the early 1900s," Porter said as he guided Gabriel and his team to the far end of the eighty-third floor hallway. "The Algeciras Conference, the Treaty of Fez, the end of slavery... they're all listed as milestones in Morocco's socioeconomic evolution. But these larger scale developments had nothing to do with Morocco's secret period of prosperity, at least not directly anyway. In a rather minor side note, the scroll also documents rumors of a small village in the Atlas Mountains. As best we can determine, it was located somewhere near the modern day village of Imlil. Normally, a small village like this wouldn't be worth the ink required to note its existence in historical records. But this village, which the scroll refers to as Shifa, was said to contain magical properties. Starving farmers, laborers down on their luck, and men, women, and children afflicted with medical ailments made pilgrimages to Shifa to receive the blessing of its village leader. They believed he could cure whatever troubles haunted their lives." Porter stopped outside the viewing window of the final examination room in the hallway. "Some didn't survive their pilgrimages, but those who did supposedly experienced unexplained crop resurgences, well-compensated job opportunities, and prosperous health that extended their lives at least fifty percent longer than the average Moroccan lifespan at that time."

Lisa looked puzzled. "There's no way that scroll could document lifespans like that. According to your math, some of those children could still be alive today."

"Some of those children are," Porter acknowledged. "And you're correct, the scroll itself doesn't document their extended lifespans. It included a short list of names of Shifa travelers who shared their experiences with the scroll's authors. We've cross-referenced the names against other historical records to calculate our numbers."

"How old are the ones still alive?" Gabriel asked.

"There are three we know of. The oldest is eighty-four, the second oldest is seventy-nine, and the youngest is seventy-five." Porter must have spotted the confusion on Gabriel's face, for he explained further. "It doesn't sound too old by today's standards, but remember, the average lifespan of a Moroccan in the early 1900s was less than fifty years. The odds that multiple children with serious health issues lived into their seventies and beyond are astronomical... unless something not only cured those children of their ailments, but granted them increased longevity as well."

Gabriel caught a tone of hope in Porter's voice. No wonder the billionaire saw the pendant as a divine detour that could divert him from his approaching rendezvous with death. Of course, there was one missing, but nonetheless critical, element to this story.

"So the scroll supports *something* in Shifa granting the type of healing you're seeking," Gabriel said. He then motioned to the previous labs and exam rooms they had passed. "And I assume those other scrolls tell similar stories. But what makes you think it's the pendant? Just the circulation of prosperity around the Mediterranean tracing back to Israel?"

Porter signaled a technician in the room with the Moroccan scroll. "Each scroll you see contains a description of its respective village leader. The descriptions vary slightly from one another, but they all tell of a kind-hearted man with a gentle face and eyes that have seen a lifetime of hardship. The man wears layered robes and jewelry, and he heals his visitors with a single touch of his hand."

Gabriel could see the assumption Porter was making, but it was far from hard evidence. "Do any of the scrolls describe the jewelry as a pendant?"

"No," Porter admitted. "The descriptions were all quite vague. Until Morocco..."

The technician Porter had signaled earlier turned down the lights in the Moroccan room and flipped the switch on a high-tech projector. A small, crudely drawn image of a man in robes with his right hand on the forehead of a second, kneeling man appeared on the wall. Porter extended his hand for Gabriel and his team to get closer.

"The authors of the Moroccan scroll asked one returning traveler from Shifa to describe what he saw there," Porter explained. "But instead of recording the man's description in words, they drew this image in the scroll's margin."

Porter signaled to the technician again, who repeatedly pressed a button atop the projector. The drawing of the healer zoomed in with two times magnification, then a digital processor refined the edges of the image to remove artifacts from the zooming process. This repeated five more times, until the projection was so large it filled the wall of the examination room. Porter smiled as Gabriel leaned even closer to the observation window, his eyes fixating on the projection.

"This was one of the first scrolls my contractors located," Porter said. "And yet it wasn't until last week that we stumbled upon this detail." Porter joined Gabriel at the observation window. "It was right in front of us the whole time."

Gabriel could only stare. Until now, he had silently believed his mission to find the Pendant of God was much more likely to end in failure rather than success. But that changed the moment Porter's technician magnified the scroll's drawing, revealing what appeared to be a necklace with a round decoration at the end hanging from the neck of the robed man. It was the pendant, as described by the first-hand account of someone who had not only seen it, but received its blessing. Gabriel felt a sudden sense of determination, an urge to defy the odds and find the artifact that had eluded historians, archaeologists, and fellow treasure hunters for thousands of years. The treasure hunting blood within him pumped with excitement, coursing through his veins like adrenaline feeding a marathon runner. Gabriel made an internal oath to himself that failure was no longer an option. He was going to find the Pendant of God, and in doing so, he was going to make sure his friend lived a long and healthy life.

Chapter Fifteen
Evidence

New York, New York
Thirteen Days Before The Sky Opened

Shortly after revealing the Moroccan drawing to Gabriel, Porter excused himself to handle company business. Before leaving, Porter assured Gabriel that he and his team were authorized for free rein of the eighty-third floor. Porter encouraged them to approach their examination of the scrolls with a high degree of scrutiny. He told Gabriel that he trusted their opinion more than his own and wanted to ensure he hadn't overlooked any significant details, regardless of their implications for the mission. Porter then instructed Nadine to remain nearby to provide Gabriel's team with any assistance they might need. Gabriel noted that she didn't seem too thrilled with her orders.

Nonetheless, Nadine provided the team with sterilized tablets and styluses they could use to take digital notes. She promised Gabriel she would forward the notes to him via secure email by the time they got back to Artifact Manor. Nate, ever paranoid about Porter's intentions, pushed for a physical pen and paper so Porter couldn't retain his own copy of anything they jotted down. But Nadine claimed physical paper and flowing ink would compromise their sterile environment. Nate pushed back, but Lisa convinced him to back down, supporting the merit of Nadine's claim.

"Fine," Nate eventually acquiesced, "but I'm logging anything of real importance up here." He pointed at his head.

Gabriel and his team spent the next seven hours examining Porter's scrolls. The process was tedious, for every ninety to one-hundred twenty minutes, they would have to drop what they were doing, return to the locker room to refill the air sacs in their suit linings, and then get disinfected again upon return. Nate made the procedure even more troublesome than needed, for he demanded they do it in pairs rather than as a group. That way, two of them would always be within the Old World to make sure no one tampered with their work. The one benefit of the periodic air refill was that it also provided a chance for the team to rehydrate. Working in contamination suits and breathing processed air while constantly talking was a surefire way to dry one's throat. Luckily, Nadine had foreseen this and ordered refreshments to be staged in the locker room.

"I don't like the way she stares at us," Nate said to Gabriel as they returned from their most recent refueling trip. "I bet she knows how to read lips. The tablets were just a way to deflect our attention."

Gabriel glanced at Nadine, who was toiling away on her own tablet in one of the empty examination rooms. "She's not even looking at us."

"Right now," Nate said. "But she does. I've been keeping an eye on her."

"Maybe you're being a little *too* paranoid?"

"We'll see."

The pair continued down the main corridor until they found Lisa and Samantha in a preservation lab, hovering over a scroll from Macedonia. They had already examined this scroll once before, but Lisa wanted to view it again after recalling a possible connection to the Moroccan scroll. Gabriel let Nate enter the lab first, then glanced once more at Nadine, who he thought he saw hastily divert her gaze back to her tablet. Had she been watching them, or was Nate's paranoia rubbing off? Gabriel supposed it didn't matter either way.

"So," he said upon entering the lab, "what's the conclusion?"

"Well," Lisa responded without looking up from a digital touchscreen embedded in one of the lab's tables, "Porter's claims check out. There's a clockwise progression of small pockets of prosperity around the Mediterranean from the time of Lyrus all the way to seventy years ago in Morocco. Every scroll mentions either a small or traveling village established in a remote region of the land. They also note that people journeyed to the village to meet with its leader, who was claimed to have mystical healing powers. Some describe the man as wearing jewelry, though, as Porter already admitted, none specifically mention a pendant. With that said, the prosperity observed during the leader's presence in any given area is too great to chalk up to coincidence." Lisa grabbed her tablet and referenced notes she had taken earlier. "Now, playing Devil's advocate for a moment, nothing confirms the Pendant of God is actually the source of the prosperity. Sure, we have the drawing from the Moroccan scroll, but it's crude at best. We also have the progression around the Mediterranean tracing back to the Israeli region around Lyrus and Damien's time. But even then, we don't actually know whether that was the origin point, or just another stop in a Mediterranean rotation that had already been in motion for hundreds of years."

Gabriel pursed his lips. "I guess the question then is: do we actually care whether the pendant is the source of healing and prosperity, or whether something else is driving these events?"

"From Porter's perspective, it shouldn't make a difference," Lisa said. "He wants to be healed. Something out there is healing people, and he's hired us to find it."

"So we assume it's the pendant unless we find evidence to the contrary." Gabriel drifted off. He had had another thought, but it slipped his mind. "Anything else?"

"Just the standard disclaimer that none of this is based on our own work," Lisa told him. "Porter's technicians appear to have done a thorough job, and as best we can confirm, everything they've done is on the up and up, but there's always a risk we're being played."

"Let's hope an old friend wouldn't do that to us." Gabriel looked around the lab and at its high-tech equipment. "You trust that these devices..."

"They're clean," Lisa assured him. "All cutting-edge and, as far as I can tell, calibrated to much higher standards than any equipment I've ever used. Unless the reports themselves have been manipulated, there's no reason to doubt their results. These scrolls are what Porter claims they are."

Gabriel's eyes shifted to the hardware he didn't recognize: the blank rectangular prisms, the orbs attached to the ceiling, the glowing cylinder... "Nate, putting your paranoia aside, what about the rest of this stuff? Any cause for concern?"

"What? You mean the weird alien technology all over this floor? Nah, no cause for concern at all."

Gabriel shot him a look that said *cut the shit*.

Nate sighed. "Okay, those white orbs in each room? I've been stewing on them and my best guess is they have something to do with periodic static electricity sanitation. I notice they do their glowing thing more often when someone is in the room with them, and even more often when multiple people are in the room. That suggests they're measuring something generated by us- or more specifically, by the movement of our contamination suits- and neutralizing it when the buildup reaches a certain threshold."

"That's pretty nice," Lisa said admirably. "What about the rest?"

Nate shook his head. "Not a clue."

"That's because you're the wrong person to ask," Samantha chimed in. She pointed at the rectangular prism in their current lab, then motioned toward the exam room where Gabriel had seen a series of glass tubes embedded in the wall. "Most of this is outside of my wheelhouse, too. But that right there?" She pointed to the lab where the trash can sized cylinder that had first caught Gabriel's eye upon entering the Old World stood. From their current position, they could see the top of the cylinder and the glowing blue ring around its circumference. "That's a weapon," Samantha continued. "And a pretty damn scary one at that."

Chapter Sixteen
The Weapon

New York, New York
Thirteen Days Before The Sky Opened

Gabriel stared at Samantha with his mouth hanging open. "What sort of weapon?"

Samantha smiled nervously. "The kind that makes sure you can't identify the bodies- or anything else that was once on this floor- should someone ever detonate it."

Gabriel shared a worried look with Lisa.

"I've never seen one in practice before," Samantha told them. "But I have seen the preliminary designs, and it's pretty unmistakable. Two blue rings? That means it's disarmed. One red and one blue like it is right now? That means it's armed. Two red rings-"

"And we're all seconds away from finding out if God really exists," Nate said.

"That's one way to put it," Samantha confirmed.

"Why the hell would Porter have something like that here?" Lisa asked. "Is he that desperate, or paranoid, or-"

"Psychotic?" Nate asked.

Gabriel took a deep breath as he processed this new information. He asked himself why he might want such a weapon in this situation. "It's a failsafe," Gabriel concluded a moment later. "It's a way to guarantee if Porter doesn't find the pendant, no one will."

"What a conceded jackass!" Nate yelled. "He'd blow up all this history, destroy any evidence about the pendant's existence, just because he didn't get his way?"

Gabriel noticed that Nate's volume had caught Nadine's attention, so he signaled for his teammate to calm down. "You're just assuming his intentions are self-centered," Gabriel whispered. "Remember, the pendant has as much power to destroy as it does to heal. Maybe Porter just wants to ensure it doesn't fall into the wrong hands."

"Optimism at its finest," Nate whispered back. "But you must have your own doubts. It's why you're quizzing us so much about the authenticity of this place. Even if Porter's intentions are noble- and I'm not saying they are- clearly he's not being completely forthcoming with us."

"Or he didn't want to scare the shit out of us," Gabriel countered. "You wanted him to tell you there was an armed thermonuclear bomb sitting fifty feet from us?"

"It's a next-gen thermobaric explosive, actually," Samantha corrected.

"Thermonuclear, thermobaric... either way, it's death in an unassuming can and we're well within the blast radius." Gabriel forced himself to pause for a relaxing breath. "I'm guessing Porter knew we wouldn't be able to concentrate under those conditions."

Nate glanced over Gabriel's shoulder. "Well, it looks like you have a chance to ask him."

Porter had just come through the disinfecting chamber. Nadine joined him as he marched down the eighty-third floor hallway with a small but thick silver briefcase in his hand. Porter caught Gabriel's eye and pointed to an empty exam room.

"Let's keep the bomb talk to a minimum," Gabriel told Nate as they relocated to the indicated exam room. "For now, anyway."

Porter set the briefcase on an examination table and grinned as the team joined him. "How are things going?"

"I think we're just about done here," Gabriel replied, glancing at Lisa for her agreement. "We'll need to regroup back at the manor, go over our notes, get supplies moving, make travel arrangements-"

"That last one's already done," Porter interrupted. "I've got the six of us booked on a flight tomorrow morning from LaGuardia to Marrakech. Unfortunately, it was the only flight I could get for all of us on such short notice. We'll have a layover at Dulles and then again in Lisbon, so bring entertainment."

"Marrakech?" Gabriel asked. "Morocco? How'd you know I'd want to start there?"

64

"I saw the way your eyes lit up when you heard there were survivors from Shifa," Porter said. "You were worried about finding a needle in a haystack in Spain. Those survivors could be our metal detectors. One is in Marrakech, another is in Safi, and the third is in Casablanca. I figured we'd start south and move north toward Spain."

Gabriel was impressed. Porter had approached the search with brains and efficiency, just as he would have given the time to plan it himself. "Sounds good."

"Um, what's with the public transportation?" Nate chimed in. "Don't you have a bazillion dollars and access to private jets and stuff?"

Porter smiled, but it was more of a *how naïve* smile than a friendly smile. "I'm trying to attract as little attention as possible." He turned his focus to Gabriel. "I heard about your incident after our meeting yesterday. To be honest, that was probably my fault."

Gabriel caught Samantha shooting a *see?* look to Lisa.

"The government's been all over me since they caught wind of me sneaking ancient relics into the country," Porter continued. "I still don't know who tipped them off, but they know what I'm after, and they want it first."

"Why does the government care about some dusty old pendant?" Nate asked.

"Because that pendant gave a single man the power to destroy an army," Porter replied. "What government wouldn't care about something so threatening?"

"Or useful," Lisa added.

"Exactly," Porter agreed. "In any case, after yesterday, I can't be certain how closely they're watching me... or you, for that matter. I'm scheduled to speak at a tech conference in San Diego in two days. We've submitted flight plans, booked a hotel suite, and made restaurant reservations for the duration of the conference to give the impression that Nadine and I are going. As for the four of you, your bank accounts each just received a ten thousand dollar advance from a potential client in Canada. That same client booked you on a flight to Toronto for tomorrow evening. Tonight, you'll call me on a line I'm certain is tapped and you'll turn down my job offer, citing the Canadian opportunity as one you can't pass up."

"Won't this whole ruse get blown out of the water as soon as we go through LaGuardia security tomorrow?" Samantha asked.

"That's what these are for," Porter said as he clicked open the silver briefcase. Inside, neatly displayed in molded foam, were passports and state driver's licenses containing each of their pictures. "Go on," Porter encouraged.

Gabriel grabbed the documents allocated to him, then stepped aside to analyze them as the rest of his team did the same. The forgery work was impeccable. Both the passport and license looked authentic, containing specialized inks and watermarks that were used to distinguish legitimate government documents. The forgeries had some wear and tear to disguise the fact they had been freshly printed, and the passport contained backdated stamps from a handful of countries Gabriel was familiar with, should he be asked anything about them.

"Gilbert?" Nate asked, staring at his driver's license. "You thought I looked like a *Gilbert*?"

Porter shrugged. Some things never change, Gabriel thought.

"These are nicer than the ones I'm usually able to get," Samantha said, a hint of glee in her eyes. "How'd you get the watermark so perfect?"

"You'd be amazed what my technology is capable of," Porter told her with pride. "Now, as far as supplies are concerned-"

The entire eighty-third floor went dark for a half-second before red floodlights washed over Gabriel and his team. The door to the disinfecting chamber opened, revealing two hard-nosed security guards, who headed straight for the examination room. One guard ushered Porter aside and spoke as softly as a person could while still being heard through a contamination suit. Gabriel couldn't make out the guard's words, but he saw the guard's eyes, and then Porter's eyes, swivel to Nate. Gabriel looked questionably at his tech engineer.

"Whoops," Nate said with a guilty smile.

Chapter Seventeen
Caught

New York, New York
Thirteen Days Before The Sky Opened

"Mr. Bellows, please come with us," one of the security guards told Nate. The words may have been a request, but the tone was an order.

Gabriel kicked into damage control mode. "Porter, whatever he's done, the rest of us weren't aware of it. I can assure you-"

Porter held up a hand to silence him. "Don't worry, Gabriel. Nate is clearly up to his old tricks. We'll contain the situation, and then I'm expecting you to keep him in line going forward. This doesn't change our arrangement."

"Thanks, Porter."

Lisa tapped Gabriel on the shoulder. "Why don't you go with him and find out what he did? Samantha and I can finish here."

Gabriel nodded, then expressed his appreciation for Porter's leniency again, before joining Nate and the security guards. As they walked toward the decontamination chamber, Gabriel could hear Porter running down a list of supplies, then Samantha questioning those supply choices with a bit more criticism than she probably should, given the strained dynamics Nate had fostered. Gabriel considered saying something before exiting the Old World, but stopped himself. He knew whatever criticisms Samantha was leveling at Porter would be in the best interest of the mission. Letting the politics of a childhood rivalry influence that would do more harm than good.

"Gabriel," Nate whispered as they trailed behind the security guards. "I just wanted-"

"Shut up," Gabriel instructed. "The less you say, the better."

They went through the decontamination procedure with the two security guards, then exited into the locker room. The guards unsuited and ordered Nate to do the same. Gabriel kept his suit on in case he was needed back in the Old World.

"Confirm whether this is your locker," one guard told Nate as he pointed to the nameplate that read N. Bellows.

"Obviously," Nate said antagonistically. After getting a glare from Gabriel, he changed his tune. "Yes, sir, it is."

"Open it, please."

Nate reluctantly joined the security guard at the locker and did as he was told. He stepped aside as the guard performed a visual examination of the locker's contents, which on the surface didn't trigger any red flags. Gabriel noticed the second guard had stepped away to rummage through an unlabeled locker on the other side of the room.

"You sure this is the one?" The guard examining Nate's locker asked.

"That's where we triangulated the signal," the other guard confirmed.

The examining guard stepped back to make room for Nate. "Please remove the prohibited item."

Nate looked at Gabriel for instruction. Gabriel knew what the tech engineer was thinking. If the guard couldn't find the item on his own, why should Nate voluntarily reveal it? Why not play dumb and cast doubt on whether the accusation of a prohibited item was valid? In certain situations, Gabriel would have approved of the tactic. But not here and not now. Porter would only have so much patience for Nate's antics, and Gabriel was certain the tech billionaire had the equipment to sniff out whatever Nate was hiding, even if this guard couldn't. Gabriel motioned for Nate to give it up.

Nate sighed and reached toward the metal lip that hung down from the roof of the locker. He fiddled with an unseen object for a moment, then Gabriel heard a magnetic release as Nate removed a small black box with a flexible wire antenna from behind the lip. He passed the box to the nearby security guard, who held it up to his partner.

"Is this what we're looking for?"

The guard at the unlabeled locker glanced back. "Yep, that's it."

He carried what appeared to be a shoebox, only made of dense steel, across the room. He opened the lid of the box and held it out for the other guard to place Nate's equipment inside. The guard then closed the box and pressed a recessed button on top that originally glowed green, but then switched to red as a hum emanated from its steel walls. Twenty seconds later, the button turned green again, and the guard removed Nate's equipment from the box. The equipment was smoking and partially melted, and there was an odd smell in the air that Gabriel couldn't quite place. The guard handed the ruined equipment to Nate before returning the steel box to its locker.

"Thanks," Nate said sarcastically as he dangled the equipment from two fingers like a soiled diaper.

"You know, you guys are lucky," the examining guard said. "Mr. Cannes doesn't normally stand for shit like this. I'm surprised he didn't have us throw you out on your asses."

Nate smiled wryly. "We're old friends."

"Hmph," was the guard's reply.

Gabriel thanked both guards for bringing resolution to the situation. He asked about returning to the Old World, and the guards told him he could, but they *strongly encouraged* Nate to call it a day. Trusting that Lisa and Samantha had things under control, Gabriel offered to escort Nate out so the guards could get back to their normal duties. He unsuited and gathered his belongings, silencing Nate multiple times as the tech engineer tried to repeatedly explain his actions. Gabriel then led Nate downstairs as promised, and soon the two were back on the street like tenants that had been booted from their expensive new condo.

"So," Nate said so casually that he appeared blissfully unaware of the trouble he had just caused, "you want to grab a snack while we wait on the ladies?"

Gabriel stared at him with deadpan eyes. "How about instead, you tell me what the hell that was all about?"

Chapter Eighteen
An Insignificant Lie

New York, New York
Thirteen Days Before The Sky Opened

"A transmitter?!" Gabriel's volume attracted stares from a handful of curious bystanders. He bit his lip and took several deep breaths before continuing in a more inconspicuous voice. "You really thought you could sneak a wireless transmitter into the headquarters of the world's brightest tech entrepreneur?"

"Technically, I did sneak a transmitter in," Nate retorted. "I just got caught after-the-fact. Also, I have serious reservations about referring to Porter as the world's *brightest* tech entrepreneur."

"Are you trying to get us kicked off this job?"

Nate huffed. "No, but one of us has to play the objective observer in this charade. You're still too buddy-buddy with Porter. You don't see him for the underhanded opportunist he is."

"And you can't see past him beating you in your little science fair thirty years ago."

"It was an engineering competition," Nate corrected.

"Whatever!" Gabriel shouted, once again drawing glances from nearby pedestrians. "The point is, you're just as biased as me regarding Porter Cannes."

"Good," Nate said with a firm nod. "That means our views offset one another."

"Yeah," Gabriel agreed, "but my views won't get us booted from an opportunity to find one of history's most controversial relics." He took one more meditative breath as his brain crafted a compromise. "Look, we're all entitled to our own opinion. Can you just keep yours on the down-low, at least when Porter's around?"

Nate chewed on the request for a moment. "Can we pick up another pint of banana pudding on the way home?"

Not in the mood to humor Nate, Gabriel blinked with purposeful silence. As he did so, his eyes glimpsed a small security camera perched on a mechanical arm above the front door of Cannes Tower. The security camera was pointed directly at him and Nate. Gabriel scanned the front wall of the tower for additional security cameras. He spotted one near the building's corner at Second Avenue and Fifty-Seventh Street. It was pointed at the intersection, an early warning system for any threats that might approach from that direction. Gabriel spotted a second camera on the opposite side of the front door, this one pointed down the Second Avenue sidewalk that ran along Cannes Tower toward Fifty-Eighth Street. *So*, Gabriel thought, *the front entrance is protected from the north too.*

The only direction left to protect was west, from which an attacker could jaywalk toward the front door of Cannes Tower while threading between the other cameras' fields of view. There was no way Porter would leave such a direct approach unmonitored, and Gabriel quickly surmised that to be the job of the camera perched directly above the front door. Only that camera wasn't pointed west, for Gabriel and Nate weren't standing west of the entrance. How long had it been rotated out of position? And who was watching- and likely listening-on the other end?

"Let's grab that banana pudding now," Gabriel suggested.

Nate must have sensed Gabriel's hidden motive, for he followed his boss away from Cannes Tower without protest or commentary. Gabriel desperately wanted to look back to see if the front door camera was tracking them, but he knew better than to tip his hand that he had noticed the surveillance. He led Nate north to Fifty-Eighth Street, then west toward Third Avenue, where he recalled a Magnolia Bakery location being nested inside a Bloomingdale's department store.

"Okay," Gabriel said once they were halfway between Second and Third Avenue, "I'm putting my objectivity hat on. Tell me why you tried to plant the transmitter."

Nate shrugged. "I was hoping we could get into Porter's system. The transmitter would have scanned his corporation's wireless network, hacked through whatever so-called security it uses, and then opened up an access tunnel through a series of public relays and VPNs all the way back to the manor."

"Yeah, but for what purpose?" Gabriel clarified.

"That's the thing," Nate said. "I'm not really sure. It was more of a fishing expedition to explain anything unusual we saw while in there."

"Like an armed thermobaric bomb on display like a piece of contemporary art..."

"That," Nate said, "and those weird electrical tubes embedded in the wall, and the locked door Porter and Nadine conveniently didn't address."

Gabriel shot Nate a confused look. "What locked door?"

"It was at the end of one of the Old World hallways," Nate explained. "Heavy steel, no handle, looked like it was controlled via a nearby touchscreen monitor with interactive keyboard overlay. No four digit pin codes for that sucker. Whatever's behind it, Porter wants to make sure only those who are authorized have access."

Gabriel tried giving his friend the benefit of the doubt. "Maybe it's some other pet project unrelated to the pendant."

"Maybe," Nate admitted. "Or maybe it's just one more lie Porter's trying to sweep past us."

They reached Bloomingdale's. Gabriel pulled Nate away from pedestrian traffic. "What do you think he's lied about?"

"Not think," Nate told Gabriel. "I know he's lied. Did you get a good look at that Moroccan scroll image? The one of the pendant?"

"Of course."

"Did you notice the date Porter's technicians scribbled in the margin next to their notes?"

Gabriel had noticed the date. It was the thing that had slipped his mind when he and the team were discussing the collection of evidence Porter had collected. Now he knew exactly where Nate was headed with this line of questioning. "It was dated almost three weeks ago."

Nate smiled. "And do you remember when Porter claimed they found the drawing?"

"One week ago."

Nate cocked an eyebrow as if to say *explain that, detective*. Gabriel wrestled internally. On the one hand, Nate was correct. They had caught Porter in a blatant lie. On the other hand, what reason was there to lie about something so insignificant? Whether three weeks ago or one week ago, Porter's crew had found the drawing, and the drawing supported the existence of the pendant- or at least, *a pendant* associated with magical healing abilities. Could the slip-up have resulted from Porter's deteriorating condition? Or was there something more nefarious Gabriel wasn't seeing?

"I wanted inside of Porter's system to find out what else he's lying to us about," Nate said. "I don't trust him, even if you do. And you should be glad you've got me around to maintain skepticism."

Gabriel nodded. "I am glad to have you around, as nuts as you might drive me sometimes." He then admitted, "I'm also not mad that you tried to plant the transmitter in Cannes Tower. I just wish you hadn't gotten caught."

Gabriel strolled to the door to Bloomingdale's and held it open, but Nate didn't follow.

"You really mean that?" The tech engineer asked.

"Of course."

Nate took a heavy breath and grinned. "Good. Because that's going to make what I'm about to tell you so much easier."

Chapter Nineteen
The Decoy

New York, New York
Thirteen Days Before The Sky Opened

Gabriel stared silently again, waiting for Nate to extend his confession to whatever other bad deed he had done while inside Cannes Tower.

"The transmitter those guards fried," Nate said. "It was a decoy. I stashed the real one in your locker when you weren't paying attention."

Gabriel hadn't been sure what to expect from Nate's extended confession, but it wasn't that. He stood speechless as his tech engineer walked past him into Bloomingdale's, then led the way to the counter of the Magnolia Bakery within.

"I don't understand," Gabriel said as Nate ordered banana pudding for both of them. "If it was a decoy, why did the guards triangulate your signal to it? And how the hell did you get the real transmitter into my locker without me noticing?"

Nate avoided eye contact with Gabriel as he paid for the pudding. "Lisa."

"Lisa?"

"Yeah. I told her what I wanted to do, and she offered to distract you when the opportunity arose. Good thing those containment suits aren't easy to put on without help."

Gabriel's brain churned through the implications of what Nate had told him. He should have been pissed that his wife conspired with Nate to carry out a clandestine operation Gabriel would have never approved of beforehand. Then again, if Lisa was willing to go that far, maybe Gabriel needed to rethink his own objectivity- or lack thereof- regarding Porter's virtue. After all, evidence was mounting against him...

"The decoy was real," Nate continued explaining as he found open bar seating against a window that overlooked Third Avenue. "It was just meant to be found. I couldn't risk putting a fake transmitter in my locker. If they discovered it was fake, they would have searched until they found the real one."

"So you expected to get caught," Gabriel surmised.

"For sure," Nate replied as he dug into his banana pudding. "I may not like Porter, but I'm not about to underestimate his capability." He took out his phone and launched a custom-built app that sacrificed an attractive user interface for textual information display. After scrolling through a few screens, Nate continued. "According to my logs, it took Porter's system less than five minutes to flag the intrusion. The good news is that my transmitter established a workable connection in only two minutes. The bad news is that the connection only stays open for as long as the transmitter keeps operating."

"So factoring in time for the guards to physically locate and destroy the device-"

"We'd have maybe six to ten minutes of unrestricted access to Porter's internal network." Nate shrugged. "It's not enough for me to root around aimlessly, but it may come in handy in a pinch. Consider it our miniature Trojan horse, should the need to use it ever arise."

Gabriel had to hand it to Nate. Despite his emotional misgivings toward Porter, the tech engineer had taken a methodical, long-game approach to protecting the team against the possibility that Porter had more nefarious motives for hunting down the Pendant of God than he was letting on.

"Good job," Gabriel said. "Let's hope we never have that need."

As Gabriel started on his own pint of pudding, he saw Lisa and Samantha cross Third Avenue. Samantha had her serious face on and was engaged in a heated discussion on her cell phone. Lisa was looking from left to right, presumably searching for Gabriel and Nate. A moment later, she was standing on the sidewalk side of the bakery window, giving them eyes that screamed, *really?* Samantha broke away from her phone call to mouth what appeared to be *I told you so* before Lisa headed inside.

"It looks like I'm on dish duty tonight," Lisa said as she joined

Gabriel and Nate at the window seating. "I told Samantha there was no way you'd reward Nate's behavior with more banana pudding."

She reached for Gabriel's spoon, but he slid it out of reach. "Apparently, I shouldn't be rewarding you either."

Lisa feigned confusion for a moment, but realizing she'd been outed, quickly dropped the act and looked over Gabriel's shoulder at Nate. "You told him?"

Nate shrugged innocently as he finished off his second pint of the day.

"It's fine," Gabriel said, passing his pudding to Lisa. "We always watch our backs on other jobs. I don't know why I'm treating this one so differently. I think it's just... seeing an old friend, the same age as us, with so much promise, about to lose his life well before his time..."

Lisa placed a comforting hand on Gabriel's back. "We're going to do our best to save him. But we've also got our own lives to look out for."

"Yeah, I know," Gabriel said solemnly.

Lisa offered him a smile and the next bite of his commandeered pudding. "So, do you want a rundown of what you missed?"

Gabriel gave her a muffled acknowledgment.

"Porter's arranged travel accommodations throughout our three destinations in Morocco, including hotel rooms and a car to get between cities. He's waiting until we gather our Moroccan intel before making arrangements in Spain. I warned him that our Spanish might be a bit rusty, and that none of us were fluent in Arabic, but he said he's got that covered- whatever that means. We can expect supply shipments in each city, including fresh clothes, toiletries, bottled water, snacks in case we don't care for the local cuisine, and tools that we might need for excursions into undeveloped areas."

"Self-defense?" Gabriel asked. It was his subtle way of inquiring about weapons, which were sometimes a necessity in their business.

"That's what Samantha's working on out there," Lisa said with a point to their fourth team member. "Porter's not a fan. He said he doesn't approve of violence."

"Oh please," Nate grumbled.

Lisa ignored him. "But Porter also said he wouldn't stop us if we felt the need to bring basic protection. Samantha's working with some of her overseas contacts to procure our usual assortment of gear."

"I hope she ensures our names don't appear on any documentation that gets processed through official channels," Gabriel said. "We're supposed to be going to Canada."

"Samantha knows what she's doing," Lisa assured him. "We *all* know what we're doing," she added, hinting at her and Nate's clandestine operation. "Porter is just another client, and this is just another job. Let's treat them that way and do what we do best."

Gabriel nodded in agreement. The problem was, Porter wasn't just another client. He was a friend- a *dying* friend- and that made their business arrangement inherently more messy than it otherwise needed to be. And sure, this was just another job, but the target of the job, if real, would be the highest profile relic Gabriel and his team had ever hunted. The stakes of this mission were far grander than any before it, but maybe that's why Lisa's suggestion made so much sense. Gabriel needed to push the emotions and high-stakes aside. He needed to focus on the task at hand. He needed to do what he did best, and he needed to trust his team to do the same, if they were going to succeed in finding the Pendant of God and saving Porter's life.

Gabriel gave Lisa a grateful kiss and leaned his forehead against hers. "Thank you."

Chapter Twenty
Takeoff

Flight 4832: LGA to IAD
Twelve Days Before The Sky Opened

After leaving Magnolia Bakery the prior evening, Gabriel and his team returned to Artifact Manor to pack their bags and perform a final information debrief. Gabriel asked his team to disclose any other secrets or misgivings about the situation, but thankfully no one dropped additional bombshells on him. Before heading to bed early, Gabriel placed the phone call Porter had instructed him to. He pretended to decline Porter's request to seek the Pendant of God, apologizing profusely and claiming that his team had too many reservations about working with Porter. Given that part was actually true, it wasn't difficult for Gabriel to sound as genuine as a professional actor. He then informed Porter about the manufactured Canadian opportunity, to which Porter feigned extreme disappointment, leading to accusations of not caring about Porter's health and an angry disconnection that left Gabriel shaken. Gabriel might have channeled his inner Pacino for his phone performance, but Porter had topped him with a taste of Brando.

Reminding himself the phone conversation had been an act, Gabriel then went to bed. He had a strange dream of combing through jungle terrain and stumbling upon a hidden temple. Inside the temple was a cult of robed worshipers. Who or what they worshiped, Gabriel didn't know, but they kneeled to him and presented him with a shiny golden pendant. As Gabriel took the pendant, it dissolved into ash. The worshipers disappeared, as did the temple itself, into a cloud of darkness that cracked with lightning and swirled around Gabriel as if ready to swallow him whole, his punishment for disturbing God's will.

Gabriel's alarm woke him from the dream just after four in the morning. He snoozed it a few times before Lisa tired of listening to its annoying ring and forced Gabriel out of bed. Technically, the entire team should have been getting up around then, but the others had long learned if they slept a little longer, Gabriel would do the heavy lifting to get them out of the manor on time. Today was no different, for Gabriel had most of their luggage ready at the front door by the time anyone else came out of their room. Each member of the team grabbed a quick snack of his or her choosing, then carried their own luggage to the taxi van that arrived outside the premises shortly thereafter, and they were off to LaGuardia Airport.

Shaken by both the heated phone call with Porter and his disturbing dream, Gabriel wondered whether Porter would actually be at the airport to meet them. He wondered whether there was some authenticity behind Porter's striking accusations that would drive him to pull out of the arrangement at the last minute. Gabriel also wondered whether his dream was actually a premonition that something would prevent the mission from succeeding, be it manmade interference or something of a more celestial nature. But his worries were unnecessary, for Porter and Nadine were at the airport right on time, arriving in a taxi and wearing far too casual clothing and goofy headgear that screamed *don't look at me; I'm someone in disguise!*

The team made it through airport security without issue, though a thick metal briefcase Porter sent through the x-ray machine received a fair amount of scrutiny before being cleared. They made it to their gate, boarded the awaiting plane, and were in their seats, ready for takeoff just as the sun peeked over the horizon. The first leg of their journey was a brief ninety minute puddle jump to Washington D.C. It took a little over twenty minutes for the plane to reach cruising altitude, and it would only be another thirty or so before passengers were requested to take their seats to begin the descent, which left little time for conducting business once the stewards and stewardesses had cleared the aisles from passing out drinks.

"The first Shifa survivor is Faras El Mehdi," Porter said as he crouched near Gabriel and handed him a manilla folder. "You'll find some background information in there. He visited Shifa when he was seventeen. At the time, he had a debilitating muscular condition that had nearly paralyzed him from the waist down. Rumor has it his family carried him most of the way up the Atlas Mountains, but that he climbed back down on his own. He traveled around the Middle East for nearly twenty years after that, enjoying his mobility and founding a trade business that dealt in rare fabrics, before one day returning home to Marrakech to marry and have kids."

Gabriel flipped through the manilla folder. "Where is he now?"

"Our intel suggests he never leaves his house. Apparently, old age is finally catching up with him. His wife died over ten years ago, and he insisted his children move out to live their own lives instead of taking care of him. He employs a paid servant to clean his home, make him food, help him bathe... that sort of thing."

"Does he know we're coming?"

"We've been in contact with the servant. He tells us Faras has agreed to meet with us to share his tale. The servant claims no one believes Faras' story about being healed anymore. Most people think he's senile. So the prospect of us coming to listen excited him greatly."

"Could he be senile?" Gabriel asked.

"I suppose anything's possible," Porter admitted. "But that doesn't make what happened to him any less true." He guided Gabriel to one of the rear pages in the folder. "It's not much, but we located hand written medical records mentioning a young boy from Marrakech who was stricken with a paralyzing malady doctors of the time didn't understand. The records refer to the boy simply as Patient F, and his age matches with that of Faras. We couldn't find any follow-up records on Patient F from a later date, suggesting maybe his ailment was cured."

"Or that his condition killed him," Gabriel offered as a devil's advocate suggestion.

Porter frowned. "Unfortunately, that's a possibility as well. That's why I need you-"

He broke off as a coughing fit overtook him. Porter covered his mouth with a handkerchief to catch the spatters of blood before anyone else could see them. As he did so, Gabriel thought he caught a look of embarrassment from his old friend. It wasn't as if Gabriel hadn't seen Porter's condition manifest firsthand before, so Gabriel surmised Porter's embarrassment must be related to the other passengers whose attention his coughs had attracted. Gabriel supposed Porter wasn't used to displaying weakness in a public setting. His appearances were likely well planned and controlled, so that he always portrayed the brilliant and infallible tech entrepreneur people took him for.

Gabriel's default was to be himself regardless of his setting and regardless of what other people thought of him, and he couldn't imagine trying to paint a continuous facade of perfection over that. Then again, even Gabriel had learned of the need to adapt to the expectations of his audience when delivering guest lectures, so he had a vague understanding of Porter's inner conflict. He smiled compassionately as Porter folded his handkerchief and returned to Gabriel's side.

"That's why I need you to siphon out fact from fiction when we get to Marrakech," Porter completed his thought. "We can't proceed on false intel, so I want you to take the lead when we interview Faras. Let's find out how much of his story is true, and whether any of it helps us find the current location of the pendant."

"I'd be happy to run the show," Gabriel said, "but my Arabic-"

A loud bing sounded through the cabin as the fasten seatbelt light came on. A stewardess toward the front of the plane informed everyone that they should return to their seats to begin the descent into Washington D.C. as two stewards started down the aisles collecting garbage.

"That was fast," Gabriel said, losing his train of thought.

"Yep," Porter added as he stood. "You keep the folder. We'll discuss your Arabic on the ground."

Chapter Twenty-One
New Tech

Washington, D.C.
Twelve Days Before The Sky Opened

Porter's steel briefcase hit the small waiting area table with a solid thud. Gabriel recognized it as the same briefcase that had drawn scrutiny from the security screeners at LaGuardia. Porter clicked open its latches and displayed the contents of the briefcase to Gabriel and his team. Similar to the briefcase that had held their fake IDs, the inside of this briefcase was padded with molded foam. Nestled inside the foam was a five by ten grid of electronic devices no wider than a penny and no thicker than a pencil eraser. They were a light shade of gray, and their surfaces contained subtle contortions.

"Lisa mentioned your team might be *linguistically challenged* where we're headed. These," Porter said proudly, "will be our translators on this little adventure." He removed one device from the case and pointed out pin-sized holes on each side. "They're programmed with every language still in use by mankind today. Foreign words go in, a self-contained operating system identifies the language and translates those words- to English in our case- then plays them back in your ear like so."

He inserted the translator into his own left ear. It was so tiny Gabriel couldn't see it without standing and getting a direct angle on Porter's ear canal.

"*Quelle est la rapidité de la traduction?*" Gabriel asked.

"Nearly instantaneous," Porter responded without skipping a beat. "The speaker even mimics the voice of the translated individual. It's not perfect, but it's more than enough to tell people apart when they're speaking in close succession. We're planning a voice upgrade in the next model."

"I didn't realize these were on the market already," Gabriel said.

"They're not. In fact, most of my products don't launch until version two or three." Porter winked. "I'm kind of a perfectionist."

Nate fetched a translator and held it up to examine under the bright airport lights. "Battery life must be a bitch on these things."

"Why do you think I brought so many?" Porter asked rhetorically. "The good news is there's a backup battery embedded in the case. Whenever your translator dies, swap it for another, and the used one will recharge by the time you need to swap again." Porter stepped aside to give the rest of the team access. "Go on. Our next stop is foreign territory. May as well get used to wearing them now."

Gabriel let Lisa and Samantha go first, then grabbed his own translator. For some unexplainable reason, he felt hesitant about putting such a sophisticated piece of technology in his ear. He supposed it was no different than a pair of high-end wireless headphones, which he didn't have a problem using. And yet, whether it was his dream, or the seed of doubt Nate had planted in him regarding Porter, or his own questioning of his objectivity, Gabriel was uncomfortable with this particular aspect of their mission. His team didn't seem to share his discomfort, for they seemed excited to give the translators a try. Even Nate had put his in without hesitation, and he must have sensed Gabriel's trepidation, for he gave Gabriel a subtle gesture that it was okay.

Well, Gabriel thought, *if Nate doesn't have a problem with Porter's tech...*

He planted the translator in his right ear canal. It was so lightweight that Gabriel could barely tell it was in there. The only giveaway was a slight difference in the way ambient sounds flowed through to that eardrum versus the one without the translator. They came with something of a white noise undertone, as if they were also being processed by the translator, but not actually translated.

"*Da quando hai i piedi freddi riguardo alla nuova tecnologia?*" Lisa asked in smooth Italian.

Gabriel didn't actually need the translator to understand her, but he was impressed when a robotic version of Lisa's voice began in his ear only milliseconds after she started talking: "*Since when do you get cold feet about new tech?"*

Gabriel knew she was just pushing his buttons, so he ignored her comment. He turned his eyes back to Nate, who was hounding Samantha with his pitiful attempts at Spanish.

"*¿Qué hora es?*" Nate asked in overly loud, stilted words. He sounded like a football player that had received one-too-many concussions.

"Time for you to actually learn some foreign languages," Samantha snapped. "Hey Porter, can we take Nate's translator away? This is *literally* the worst thing you could have ever given him."

Porter laughed. "I'll do an audit of my stash when the job's done."

"Actually," Nate said, "I think you should make a contact lens version of these things. I'm so tired of pointing my phone at foreign signs to read them."

"Then learn the damn languages!" Samantha scolded him.

Lisa tapped Gabriel on the shoulder to draw his attention away from their less mature team members. She flashed him a flirty smile. "*Ehi roba bollente, vuoi prendere un caffè prima del nostro prossimo volo?*" Gabriel's translator repeated it, "*Hey hot stuff, do you want to grab a coffee before our next flight?*"

Gabriel chuckled. "Sure."

Chapter Twenty-Two
Small Talk

Washington, D.C.
Twelve Days Before The Sky Opened

Gabriel and Lisa snuck away from the group to grab that coffee. Samantha had strolled off moments before them to take a phone call, probably having to do with her gear requests from the day before. That left Porter and Nadine to babysit Nate, which Nadine seemed so thrilled about that she quickly found her own excuse to walk away.

"Oh boy," Gabriel said under his breath as he and Lisa headed for the nearest cafe.

"What is it?" Lisa asked.

"Nate and Porter, *sans* supervision."

Lisa giggled.

"What?"

"The translator," she said, pointing at her ear. "It actually translated your Middle English." She grabbed Gabriel's hand. "Come on. Leave them be."

Gabriel huffed, but obeyed. He considered whether leaving Nate and Porter unsupervised was a mistake, and whether he should go back to play mediator between the two tech rivals. Then again, maybe it was better that they hash out their issues now rather than at a more critical stage of the mission. Surprisingly, as Gabriel looked back after reaching the cafe line, it appeared as though Porter and Nate were getting along just fine. Nate was fascinated with the briefcase of translators, and Porter seemed to bask in the opportunity to tell Nate about the technological intricacies that went into developing them. Gabriel would never understand the relationship between those two.

"So you're headed to Morocco? I hear it's nice this time of year."

85

Gabriel heard the words not from a person's mouth, but from the translator nestled in his ear. The voice that had spoken those words was in a language Gabriel didn't understand and guessed to be Arabic. It came from a short and skinny man, around his age, speaking to Lisa as they weaved through the cafe line.

"I'm sorry?" Lisa asked the man.

"Oh, my apologies," the man said. "I just assumed you were fluent- I said Morocco has nice weather during this time of year."

Gabriel knew Lisa had understood the man with the help of Porter's translator, just as he had done. Her confusion wasn't the words; it was how this man knew anything about their destination.

"That's nice," Lisa said, a subtle suspicion in her tone. "Are you going to Morocco?"

"Oh, no, I'm on my way to Seattle for a business trip. I thought you and your friends were headed to Morocco. I heard you talking about it on the plane."

Lisa looked at Gabriel. He knew she was hoping for a confirmation that he recalled the man from their flight, but unfortunately, Gabriel had no confirmation to give.

"I see I've startled you," the man said, as his cheeks turned red. "I didn't mean to come across as creepy. It was such a short flight, and you were deep in conversation. You probably didn't notice me. Forgive me, I was just making small talk while we waited."

They reached the front of the line, and a barista took the man's order. Lisa looked at Gabriel with wide eyes as if to communicate *I have no idea who this guy is*. Gabriel mimicked her gesture: *Ditto*.

The barista took Lisa's order next, then she and Gabriel checked out before joining the mystery man at the pickup counter. He seemed friendly enough, and his embarrassment at failing to strike up a more meaningful conversation appeared genuine, but no matter how much Gabriel tried, he couldn't recall the man's face from the first leg of their flight. Luckily, the coffee orders took no time to arrive.

"I really am sorry to have unnerved you," the man said as he grabbed his cup. "Please enjoy the rest of your trip."

And with that, he was gone, presumably to catch a flight to Seattle. A middle-aged, Arabic-speaking, New York businessman flying out of LaGuardia to get to Seattle and supposedly sitting close enough to

Gabriel and his team to casually overhear their plane conversation. Something didn't feel right.

Lisa passed a cup of coffee to Gabriel as he discretely scanned their surroundings. Though Gabriel had his concerns about everything falling apart at LaGuardia, he had convinced himself it would be smooth sailing once they boarded that first plane. The biggest concern he had about this one hour layover was whether they would have enough time to run to their next gate before the second leg of their flight took off. But while time turned out not to be an issue, Gabriel now wondered if something else would. Porter had said the government was monitoring him, and here they were, on the ground in the heart of government territory. Maybe Porter's fake IDs, staged phone call, alternate travel plans, and silly disguises hadn't been enough. Maybe they were being tracked, right here, right now. Maybe they were walking into a trap.

The problem was that this was an airport, a place where everyone was being monitored and tracked by all sorts of people and devices as part of the day-to-day norm. It was also a place where anyone suspicious or acting unnatural could just be an ordinary citizen, thinking everyone around them is equally suspicious and unnatural. There was no way Gabriel was going to spot someone or something out of the ordinary in this environment. He checked his watch, then confirmed Samantha and Nadine had successfully returned to the waiting area outside their next gate, and that Porter and Nate were still there, pretending to be best buds. Gabriel saw the gate attendant move aside the ropes blocking the entrance to the jetway. He then watched her get on the intercom to make a boarding announcement. Gabriel breathed a sigh of relief.

"Come on," he told Lisa. "Let's get on that plane while we still can."

Chapter Twenty-Three
The Competition

Lisbon, Portugal
Twelve Days Before The Sky Opened

The seven and a half hour flight from Washington, D.C., to Lisbon was surprisingly uneventful. Gabriel insisted the team stay awake for the duration of the flight to minimize the impact of changing time zones on their biological clocks. Lisa spent that time reading a book she had pre-loaded on her tablet. Samantha spent it studying satellite imagery of Marrakech, Safi, and Casablanca, then plotting out their travel within and between the cities. Nate attempted to distract himself with the in-flight entertainment system, but that only lasted for two movies and twenty minutes of digital solitaire. Afterwards, he asked Nadine to swap seats with him. She had been perfectly fine scrolling aimlessly through digital magazines on her own tablet, but she was sitting next to Porter, and Porter was engrossed in design blueprints for some new invention he was working on, which was infinitely more interesting to Nate. Once they swapped, he refused to give the seat back, even when it was time to land.

Gabriel had also packed a book for the flight. It was a paperback, for he far preferred physical paper to digital screens for his pleasure reading. But he mostly watched what the others were doing instead of reading. He held an occasional powwow with Samantha to discuss logistics. He tried to strike up a conversation with Nadine a couple of times, but she made it evident she wasn't interested. At one point, Gabriel added a second set of prying eyes to whatever Porter was working on. All Gabriel could tell from his brief glimpses of the blueprints was that it involved some sort of mechanical claw that pointed upright with pinched fingers, as if waiting to grab something, and that it was attached to a ton of circuitry. He was sure Nate- who was giving Porter a grand inquisition about the design- would explain it to him later. The rest of the time, Gabriel mostly stared quietly at Lisa, reminding himself of how beautiful she was and how much he loved having her as his life partner.

When their plane landed in Lisbon, Gabriel was pleasantly surprised at the modern design of Humberto Delgado Airport. It wasn't as though he thought Portugal was a third-world country or anything; he just didn't expect the airport to essentially mirror those he frequented in the U.S., only with all signs, menus, instructions, and labels written in Portuguese instead of English. Gabriel wished the written words would simply read themselves aloud so his earpiece translator could do the heavy lifting as they maneuvered through the airport, and he realized Nate was on to something when he encouraged Porter to make translator contact lenses. Gabriel would never travel internationally without them.

"Local time is about nine-thirty," Porter said as he checked his watch. "We have four hours until our next flight. I'm going to stretch my legs a bit and then find a good restaurant. Dinner's on me for anyone who'd like to join."

Nate jumped at the offer. "I'm in!"

The only thing Nate loved more than technology was food, and it seemed both had the power to overrule his disdain for Porter. Nadine was, of course, staying by Porter's side, and Samantha said she would join as well after placing a few more calls. Gabriel dreaded to see next month's cell phone bill.

"Well?" Lisa asked.

Gabriel was hungry and had no issue going to dinner with Porter. He just wasn't sure whether he wanted to sit for another hour or two, or to simply grab something quick he could eat on his feet. Lisa batted her eyes at him. She loved international travel and cuisine, and Gabriel knew she was going to dinner with or without him, though she would rather have him by her side.

"Sure," he caved. "Let me find a restroom first."

Gabriel had already spotted one restroom near the gate their plane had landed at, but it had a line out the door he didn't feel like standing in. Gabriel took off in the opposite direction from the group and weaved through the crowd of diverse passengers that made international airports so distinguishable from their U.S. counterparts. He located a less busy section of their current terminal and found a nearly empty restroom there. Gabriel emptied his bladder, then took a few moments at the sink to freshen up from their lengthy flight. He was nearly done when an unmistakably cocky American voice startled him from behind.

"No shit!" The voice exclaimed. "Gabriel Dunne. What are the chances?"

Gabriel hoped the chances would be zero, but clearly, he wasn't so lucky. He turned to face Byron Coltrain, a rival treasure hunter he'd had the displeasure of crossing paths with on more occasions than desired. Byron came from the school of thought that if something didn't have legal documentation to prove its present day ownership, then that ownership was up for grabs for whomever claimed it first. He was also the type of treasure hunter that gave treasure hunters poor reputations, disrespectful of other cultures' practices and beliefs, carelessly destructive of ancient places and property, and always on the lookout to make a buck, no matter what making that buck entailed. The only good to come out of Byron's existence was its inspiration for most of the antagonists in Gabriel's novels.

"Hello, Byron," Gabriel said as cordially as he could muster. "What brings you to Lisbon?"

"What else? A job," Byron said truthfully before turning on his bullshit spigot. "This rich pyramid fanatic hired me to retrieve a pharaoh's ring from some off-limits dig site outside of Giza. My team and I are waiting for our connecting flight." He eyed Gabriel suspiciously. "What about you? Business or pleasure?"

"Business," Gabriel admitted. He couldn't risk Byron seeing the rest of the team and calling him out on a lie. But that didn't mean he had to be honest about the nature of his business. "Some rich jackass caught wind of a newly unearthed ancient burial site near Bilbao. He's hired us to go in and see what we can find."

"Spain, huh?" Byron said. "I bet Lisa's looking forward to that."

"She is," Gabriel replied. "Just as I bet your team is looking forward to Egypt."

"They are," Byron said with a fake smile.

If there was one thing both men knew about each other, it was that neither one was headed to Giza or Bilbao. Gabriel had played this game with Byron enough times to know the rules, and the number one rule was to not provide any information that would give your rival an edge over you. The number two rule- sometimes difficult to adhere to- was to never physically harm your rival. You were both in the same line of work, and you never knew when you might be reliant on one another to get out of a sticky situation. That left the third rule: avoid spending more time than necessary with your rival, so that neither of you was tempted to violate rule number two. That was the rule Gabriel decided it was time to invoke.

"Well, Byron," he said, "my rich jackass has offered to treat me to dinner, so I'm going to be on my way."

Byron smiled again. It was the arrogant type of smile Gabriel wished he could smack right off of Byron's face. "Yeah, I'd better get some food, too. I've still got a long flight ahead." He stepped aside to give Gabriel unblocked access to the restroom's exit. As Gabriel walked out, Byron added, "I'll be seeing you around. Maybe back here in Lisbon... *or wherever.*"

Gabriel didn't respond nor look back, but he had an unsettling feeling that reunion would come far too soon.

Chapter Twenty-Four
Arrival

Marrakech, Morocco
Twelve Days Before The Sky Opened

The team's third plane of the day touched down at Marrakech Menara Airport just after three o'clock in the morning local time. Even though the team was still running on New York time, it was just after ten o'clock there, leaving everyone sluggish and ready to call it a day given the early starts they had had. The 'car' Porter had arranged for the team turned out to be a luxurious passenger van large enough to hold all of them and their luggage. It was waiting outside the baggage pickup zone, where a rental company employee requested Porter to sign off on delivery before passing him its keys. Porter signed using his fake identity, then immediately offered the keys to the first taker from the group, his interest level in playing chauffeur somewhere between zilch and none.

Nate started for the keys, but Samantha swiped them away from his grasp. When he protested, she reminded him of the last rental car he drove while overseas, a rental car that was now *under* the sea following a series of blunders in judgement. That was all Porter needed to hear to cast his vote for Samantha taking official driving duties for the rest of this road trip.

It was a thirty-minute drive to The Oberoi Marrakech, a luxury hotel that looked more like a private palace than a holdup for tourists. It was nestled among hundreds of acres of olive groves and citrus orchards, giving it the feel of a secluded resort. Its pillared walls had been carved from marble, and its high ceilings and open spaces made the lobby, hallways, vast courtyards, and guest rooms feel grand in scale. Meticulously crafted gardens and waterways adorned the grounds, intertwining the manmade structure with the nature that surrounded it. The sun hadn't risen yet when Gabriel and his team arrived, but Gabriel suspected once it did, the hotel would provide one hell of a view.

Bellhops and a valet greeted them at the curb. As the bellhops unloaded the team's luggage, Nadine stopped by the front desk to confirm the reservations she had made. She returned with digital keycards- one for Gabriel and Lisa, one for Samantha, another for Nate, and a final one which Nadine pocketed herself. Gabriel wondered why she hadn't given Porter his own keycard, but Nadine's smoothness in diverting attention to the valet before anyone could ask questions provided Gabriel with a hint at the answer.

"We'd like the van ready at eleven o'clock sharp," Gabriel heard his translator say in a robotic version of Nadine's voice. She had spoken in Arabic to the valet, and it was in that moment that Gabriel realized at least one reason Porter had brought her on this adventure. The earpieces would translate Arabic into English, but they wouldn't speak Arabic back for the team. Nadine was going to be their one-way translator. As was becoming common for Porter, he made sure the translator was someone he could trust.

A bellhop informed Samantha that a crate had been delivered for her shortly before the team's arrival. He said it was too heavy to move to her room, but offered to take her to it at the hotel's loading dock. Samantha accepted his offer, told the others goodnight, and followed the bellhop down a pathway around the side of the main building. Nate took Samantha's departure as his cue that it was alright to leave. He hit up Porter for a thousand dirhams to tip his bellhop, then galloped off for what he claimed would be the most luxurious four hours of sleep he'd ever have. It was honestly hard for Gabriel to tell how much of Nate's claim was sarcasm.

Gabriel and Lisa's room and Nadine's- and presumably Porter's- room were in the same direction, so they hung close and discussed next-morning logistics as they followed the bellhops there. Once those logistics had been squared away, Nadine made conversational small talk about how lovely the hotel was. Her mood had lightened considerably since the team's arrival, to where she didn't act as though Gabriel and Lisa were a bother. Maybe they just needed to warm up to her. Or maybe...

They arrived at the rooms, but stayed in the hallway to chat while the bellhops carted their luggage inside. Lisa caught a glimpse of the grandeur of her and Gabriel's room through its open doorway and marveled at how beautiful it was. Gabriel caught a glimpse of the pleased look on Porter's face and realized he had chosen this hotel for a reason. At first, Gabriel assumed it was because Porter didn't know how to live a simple lifestyle anymore. Now he understood Porter had actually chosen the hotel because he knew the impression it would make on them. Porter wanted to earn the team's admiration, and by extension, trust; something he must have discerned was lacking.

The bellhops excused themselves after unloading the luggage and receiving a generous tip from Porter. The remaining team members exchanged goodnights and went their separate ways, though Gabriel lingered back just long enough to confirm Porter and Nadine were indeed sharing a room. He considered for a moment the room could be a suite with multiple beds and that them sharing it was nothing more than a cost effective and efficient manner for Porter and his assistant to continue getting work done. But then Gabriel saw the way Nadine tugged at Porter's shirt, and the boyishly stupid grin that spread across Porter's face, as she pulled her boss into the room and slammed the door behind them.

Lisa popped her head back into the hallway. "Did they just-"

"Uh huh," Gabriel confirmed.

"Huh... didn't see that coming." She spotted the mischievous grin Gabriel was flashing her. "Don't even think about it, Dr. Jones," she said, referencing the fictional character that had inspired their careers. "This damsel needs her beauty sleep... right after a hot shower."

"Can I at least join you?"

Lisa faked contemplation. "Judging by the size of everything else in this place, I'm guessing there's enough room for both of us."

She smiled and pulled him into their room. Lisa may not have had the same intentions for Gabriel as Nadine did for Porter, but Gabriel was going to enjoy his night nonetheless.

Chapter Twenty-Five
Gearing Up

Marrakech, Morocco
Eleven Days Before The Sky Opened

Gabriel's alarm sounded at eight o'clock the next morning. His body wasn't ready to get up, but his mind was already racing with excitement at the thought of their expedition getting underway. He rolled over to find Lisa's half of the king-sized bed empty, her silky sheets stretched tight and pillow fluffed and neatly propped against the headboard. It wasn't unusual for Lisa to wake before Gabriel on international trips. Sometimes she would sneak away for a morning stroll. Other times she would grab a coffee and relax poolside until Gabriel came to find her. Today she was standing on the walk-out patio attached to their room, leaning gracefully against a decorative railing that lined its perimeter.

Gabriel spotted her through the sheer curtains that filtered sunlight through the patio door. They danced playfully as a cool morning breeze flowed into the room. Gabriel rose from bed and pulled the curtains back to join Lisa, and that's when the true beauty of their present location washed over him. Beyond the deep green trees of the hotel's gardens and surrounding orchards, nestled against a skyline of bright baby blue, was a picturesque view of snow-capped mountains that stretched from one end of the horizon to the other. The view was so crisp in the morning sun that Gabriel could make out distinct peaks, ridges, and slopes throughout the entire range, as well as areas of rock, snow, and vegetation. It was as if he had stepped out of real life and into one of the most astonishing paintings he had ever seen.

"Is that-"

"The Atlas Mountains," Lisa replied, anticipating his question. "Where the sick, poor, and in-need once ventured to receive the blessing of a pendant-wearing healer in a little-known village called Shifa."

So Porter hadn't picked this hotel just to impress the team. Though Gabriel couldn't see Porter's patio, he imagined the tech billionaire was standing outside just like he and Lisa, staring at the Atlas Mountains with reverence, feeling an illogical emotional connection to the majestic formation. Porter longed for what travelers to those mountains obtained, and being within visual proximity to their source of healing likely instilled him with hope that he could accomplish the same.

"I guess it's time to get moving?" Lisa asked, disappointment clear in her voice.

Gabriel smiled and put his arm around her shoulders. "We can afford a few more minutes."

They stood there for nearly ten more, just staring, taking in the majesty Mother Nature had to offer, before they finally accepted that their job could wait no longer. Gabriel and Lisa got dressed, joined the rest of the team in the hotel restaurant for a light breakfast of M'semen- a Moroccan flatbread- served with sides of honey and olive oil to suit the desires of both sweet and savory diners, and hot tea. After breakfast, the team migrated out front, where the valet had their van ready for eleven o'clock as promised.

Samantha popped the rear of the van open to reveal she had stocked its cargo compartment with a variety of gear from her previous night's delivery. She passed around cargo vests to the entire team. The vests' pockets had already been stocked with basic supplies they might need throughout their journey: compasses, binoculars, sunglasses, sunscreen, insect repellent, and utility knives. Samantha left a few pockets of each vest empty for stashing backup earpiece translators and personal belongings. She also informed everyone that the cargo vests could serve as temporary flotation devices in the event of a water emergency. Should a more predictable water scenario arise, Samantha had certified life vests and two self-inflating life rafts in the van.

She had sun hats and canteens available for anyone that wanted one, but didn't pass them around as they probably weren't needed right away. Samantha also had hiking boots on-hand and encouraged anyone wearing casual shoes- she particularly eyed Nadine when saying this- to swap them out. Samantha had retrofitted a section of the van's cargo space with a portable water tank that held about seventy gallons and could be easily refilled anywhere fresh water was available. Next to the tank was a box containing enough MREs to feed the team for three days should they become stranded away from other food sources. There was also a duffel bag containing an assortment of rope, straps, hooks, tools, and other miscellaneous items the team could need in specialized situations.

Last, there was the arsenal. Samantha had requisitioned handguns for everyone, Porter and Nadine included, though she wouldn't force them to take the weapons. She provided the choice of waist or ankle holster, as everyone had their own preference regarding weapon access. Lisa and Samantha liked their guns close, but concealed, and tended to wear them positioned at the base of their spines. Gabriel never intended to use his gun, and carried it only as a weapon of last resort, so he kept it hidden beneath the leg of his cargo pants. Nate, on the other hand, liked to pretend he was a gunslinger in the Old West, so he wore his gun traditionally, hanging off his right hip for the world to see. Everyone's holster had a secondary slot for a twelve-inch bowie knife, which Samantha also distributed to the group.

For defense and recovery, Samantha had kevlar vests and first aid kits available for the entire team. The kevlar vests weren't compatible with the cargo vests she had passed around, and would stay in the van unless the team anticipated getting into a firefight. The first aid kits were never intended for use, as the team made their own safety a top priority on any mission. But Samantha always stocked them just in case, and the team had used in them in the past more often than they would have liked.

Porter nudged Gabriel's arm. "What? No whip?"

Gabriel laughed. "Only for Halloween." He pointed to the spare weapons waiting in the back of the van. "You should seriously think about carrying one of those. You don't have to use it. You just never know when you might need it."

"I'm already living on borrowed time, my friend," Porter said with a frown. "What happens will happen."

"Fair enough." Gabriel looked around to ensure everyone had their vests on, and that those with weapons had secured them properly. Satisfied, he slammed the van's rear doors. "Alright! Let's roll!"

Chapter Twenty-Six
The Veiled Bird

Marrakech, Morocco
Eleven Days Before The Sky Opened

The team headed about ten miles south through a mix of farmland and open country until they reached a small neighborhood of perhaps forty or fifty houses, by Gabriel's rough estimate. The houses appeared in stark contrast to the hotel the team had left behind. They were in decent enough shape, but they were packed closely together and painted in pale pastels, with plain stucco sides, flat roofs, and little to speak of in terms of gardens or other decor. Nadine guided Samantha to a corner home set one street back from the main avenue they had traveled on to get there. Before anyone could exit the van, the front door of the home opened, and a man dressed in an off-white djellaba stood waiting.

"Is that Faras El Mehdi?" Nate asked, peering over Samantha's shoulder from the middle row of seats.

"Too young," Gabriel answered. "It must be his servant."

Porter briefly assessed the situation, then opened his door. "Everyone else wait here. Nadine and I will confirm we're still welcome."

The two of them exited the van and approached the man at the house. Gabriel watched as the man spoke a greeting, then shook Porter's right hand before bowing his head to Nadine. Porter spoke- and Nadine translated- what appeared to be an explanation for the presence of Gabriel's team, for he motioned several times toward the van. The man seemed to understand, and a moment later, Porter waved for the rest of the team to join them.

"Gabriel Dunne, this is Jalal Ismaili," Porter said.

"Hello," the earpiece translator said in a robotic imitation of Jalal as he greeted Gabriel in his native Arabic tongue. *"It's a pleasure to meet you. I've read some of your books."*

"It's always nice to meet a fan," Gabriel said, then waited for Nadine to translate.

Jalal greeted the rest of the team the same way he did Porter and Nadine, with a right handshake for the men and a head bow for the women. After all greetings had been exchanged, Porter took charge of the conversation once more.

"I hope this isn't a bad time for Mr. El Mehdi," he said. "We would love to speak with him."

Jalal's face drooped. *"I have some bad news, I'm afraid. Please, follow me."*

Without further explanation, he returned inside the home, leaving the door open for the team to follow. Porter started after Jalal, but Lisa grabbed his arm and instructed him to remove his shoes first. He obeyed, as did the rest of the team, and then one-by-one they filed into the home and proceeded down the main hallway. Jalal was waiting for them near a dining room, where a spread of traditional Moroccan dishes lay waiting for consumption.

"Mr. El Mehdi insisted I feed you well while you are here," Jalal said. *"Please help yourselves."*

"Thank you," Porter told him, "but we'd prefer to speak with Mr. El Mehdi first. You said there was bad news. Has something happened?"

"I'm afraid so."

Jalal continued down the hallway, around a corner, and to an ornate door that was currently shut. He waited until the team caught up with him before opening the door, revealing the home's master bedroom inside. As Gabriel entered the room, he saw cleansing bowls and washcloths lined up on a dresser, then a linen wrapped body lying in the middle of the bed. Gabriel watched Porter's shoulders slump. In an unusual sign of weakness, the tech billionaire staggered backwards, as if the sight of what was presumably Faras' dead body had stabbed him in the chest. Nadine caught Porter by the arm and rested her head on his shoulder.

"When did it happen?" Porter asked.

"During the night," Jalal said. *"He must have sensed it was coming. He insisted that I treat you as his guests even if he didn't make it until your arrival. He also insisted I wait to deliver his body to his final resting place until you saw him for yourselves."*

Porter regained his composure, though Gabriel could still see in his eyes the toll this blow had taken on him. He silently gestured for Samantha and Nate to head back outside to give them a little more space. Lisa gripped Gabriel's hand and gave it a gentle squeeze.

"Was he ill?" Porter asked. "Were there any signs that he-" He couldn't finish the sentence.

"It was just his time," Jalal said. *"He was at peace, though he was hoping to survive long enough to share his tale with you."* Jalal opened a drawer of the dresser containing the washing materials and removed a small piece of stiff paper. *"Mr. Mehdi asked me for this paper and a pen yesterday evening. He didn't have enough strength left to write or even dictate his story, but he managed to draw this. He asked that I give it to you should he not be able to himself."*

Gabriel joined Porter as Jalal passed him the piece of paper. Crudely drawn on its surface, in almost hieroglyphic fashion, was a small bird. Squiggled over the bird were two deliberate wavy lines. Porter studied the image, then shook his head.

"Do you know what this is?" He asked Jalal.

"I was hoping you would," Jalal replied. *"Mr. El Mehdi called it 'The Veiled Bird,' but that's all he would tell me about it."*

Porter looked at Gabriel. "Does this mean anything to you?"

Gabriel frowned. "No." Then, seeing the disappointment on Porter's face, he added, "But we'll figure it out. Faras wouldn't have instructed Jalal to delay his burial to give it to you if it wasn't important."

Porter passed the paper to Gabriel for safekeeping, then looked to Jalal. "I'm very sorry for your loss. Thank you for carrying out your boss's last wishes."

"It was my honor and my duty," Jalal said. *"You seemed very troubled by Mr. El Mehdi's passing. I hope those troubles don't prevent you from achieving whatever it was you sought to achieve by coming here."*

Porter nodded his head solemnly. "So do I."

There was no need for Nadine to translate that last part. Porter's body language spoke universally to everyone present.

Chapter Twenty-Seven
Brainstorming

Marrakech, Morocco
Eleven Days Before The Sky Opened

"What do you want to do now?" Gabriel asked Porter as they headed back to the van.

"Let's grab our stuff from the hotel. We have a two and a half hour drive to Safi. If we get moving, we can reach the second Shifa survivor by nightfall."

Porter stifled a cough, but more quickly followed, doubling him over as bright red blood spattered across the dirt at his feet. Nadine rushed to Porter's side and helped him clean his mouth with a handkerchief. Samantha and Nate started to climb from the van to assist, but Gabriel motioned for them to stay back. He understood the last thing Porter would want right now was to be treated like a wounded animal. The one thing the team could do was let him keep his pride by refraining from acting on his illness.

"We need to take new scans," Nadine said. "I'm concerned your progression is accelerating."

"After Safi," Porter replied.

Nadine didn't press him further. Gabriel wasn't sure if it was because Porter was her boss, and therefore did as she was told, or if it was because of their personal relationship, one in which Porter was the dominant decision maker. Either way, he agreed with Porter's choice to delay what Gabriel assumed were medical scans of Porter's lungs. Knowing whether Porter's condition was progressing wouldn't change their current course of action. They needed to push onward to Safi, find the second Shifa survivor, and hopefully obtain more clues to the pendant's whereabouts.

Once Porter could stand upright again, everyone piled into the van, and Samantha drove them back to The Oberoi Marrakech. Nadine called ahead to let the hotel know about the team's impending checkout so it could have bellhops on-hand to help with luggage. It took less than twenty minutes for everyone to pack their bags. They were all quite experienced at coming and going on short notice, and Porter's incident leaving Faras El Mehdi's house had emphasized the urgency with which they needed to act. Within thirty minutes, the team was back on the road, skirting the edge of downtown Marrakech, passing north through Harbil, and entering the hilly agricultural terrain of western Morocco.

"I assume you have a way to communicate with your Old World team back at Cannes Tower?" Lisa asked Porter, just shy of an hour into their trip.

"Of course," Porter said over the noise of the road. "Why?"

Lisa showed him the drawing of The Veiled Bird. Gabriel had given it to her upon leaving Faras El Mehdi's house, and aside from the ten minutes she put it down to pack her luggage, she had been studying it ever since. "You should send them a copy of this. See if they can find any reference to it in the scrolls you've collected."

Porter nodded to Nadine, who took the paper from Lisa and scanned it with her phone.

"What's on your mind?" Porter asked.

"We've been assuming the pendant moved to Spain after it left Morocco," Lisa explained. "Because, based on the scrolls you've found, it moves clockwise around the Mediterranean." Lisa pointed to the drawing still in Nadine's possession. "That thing looks Egyptian, which is a problem on multiple accounts. For starters, Egypt is counterclockwise from Morocco in the Mediterranean rotation. It's also not the next country in line. There's Algeria, Tunisia, and Libya between here and there. If Faras El Mehdi was pointing us toward Egypt as the pendant's current location, it would mean whomever bears the pendant broke from the rotation it's maintained for thousands of years."

"You don't think that's likely," Porter surmised.

Lisa shook her head.

"What about the name Faras gave it?" Gabriel proposed to everyone in the vehicle. "The Veiled Bird? Can anyone think of a historical reference involving veils, birds, or anything tangentially related in either Spain or Egypt?"

"Ancient Egyptians worshiped the ibis," Nate said. "That's a bird."

"That's right," Samantha called from the driver's seat. "The moon god, Thoth, had an ibis head. He was also the god of wisdom, science, and judgment, if I remember correctly."

"A veil of wisdom?" Nate suggested.

"Possibly," Gabriel responded. "Counterarguments?"

This was the team's normal brainstorming routine. Someone would throw out an idea, others would provide corroborating support, then they would open the floor for anyone to play devil's advocate. For this suggestion, Lisa was the first to wear the horns.

"Why would a Muslim man who believed he was the recipient of a monotheistic God's healing power give us a polytheistic clue?"

No one had a valid response to this, so they moved on.

"Egyptians depicted the goddess Nekhbet as a vulture," Porter offered as a contribution to the brainstorming session. "But I suppose that faces the same polytheism problem as Nate's suggestion."

"Right," Gabriel agreed. "Let's take polytheistic-based explanations off the table. What else?"

"Spain owns the Canary Islands," Lisa said.

"Yeah, but they're not named after the bird," Samantha called back. "The name comes from *Canariae Insulae*." Samantha didn't need to translate, for everyone's earpieces converted the Latin to English: *Island of the Dogs*.

"Also, where's the veil fit in?" Nate asked.

Lisa shrugged.

"The national bird of Spain is the imperial eagle," Nadine said, holding up Faras' drawing. "It's head sort of looks like this." Nadine paused as Gabriel's team stared at her with bewilderment. "What? I know things."

"She likes to watch nature documentaries when I'm not dishing out orders," Porter explained.

"Okay," Gabriel said with an apologetic grin. "Any thoughts on the veil?"

"The imperial eagle is afraid of man," Nadine said. "Maybe the veil is a veil of secrecy, representing the eagle hiding."

Gabriel pondered over the suggestion. In all honesty, it was the best theory they had come up with so far. "Okay, chalk one up for Nadine. What else have we got?" Before anyone could respond, an odd noise overtook the loud hum of the road. Gabriel held up his hand to silence the team as he listened to a pair of overlapping repetitive thumps grow louder. Soon he ascertained a rough direction of origin, first to the rear of the vehicle, then shifting overhead. "Samantha?"

"I'm on it," she said as she leaned forward to peer through the top of the front windshield. "Shit... it's two Phoenix choppers."

Gabriel saw Porter shoot him a concerned stare, but he and the others didn't seem to grasp the implication of Samantha's observation.

Porter clarified. "It's the U.S. military."

Chapter Twenty-Eight
Standoff

Jnadgha, Morocco
Eleven Days Before The Sky Opened

Gabriel squeezed through the gap between the two front seats and looked up through the front windshield. He could see the two helicopters, black and sleek, with tinted windows and mounted machine guns and missiles. Even though the helicopters had advanced from behind the van, then started to pass overhead, they had now slowed to hold their position in tandem with the team.

"Any chance this could be a coincidence?" Gabriel asked Samantha. "Are there war games or joint military exercises you're aware of in the region?"

"No, on both accounts," Samantha replied.

Gabriel returned to his seat and stared at his feet. The van was commercial; it wasn't outfitted for a gunfight. And the weapons Samantha had procured were only good for ground combat; they'd be useless against a superior air-based opponent. Unless...

"Is there any arsenal in the back you haven't shown us?" Gabriel asked.

Samantha glanced over her shoulder with a knowing stare. Gabriel smiled. He knew Samantha liked to over-prepare for missions. It increased their out-of-pocket costs, but Gabriel viewed it like insurance: better to have it and not need it, then get caught without it. He climbed past the rest of the team and into the van's rear cargo area. Lisa followed.

"What are you looking for?" She asked.

"I'll know it when I see it."

The cargo area was crammed tight with Samantha's gear and the team's luggage. Gabriel twisted his body around the stacks of suitcases and travel bags, pushing what he could aside until he found a long, black case similar to those that would hold musical instruments. Gabriel flipped the latches on the case and lifted its lid, revealing a miniature shoulder-mounted rocket launcher. Nested next to the launcher were four color-coded missiles: two blue and two brown, representing surface-to-air and surface-to-surface projectiles.

"God bless you, Samantha," Gabriel muttered.

Lisa peered over Gabriel's shoulder at the artillery. "You can't seriously be thinking of using that. That's the U.S. military out there! Our own government!"

Gabriel removed the launcher from its case and loaded a blue-tipped missile. "We won't use it if we don't have to. But right now, we're sitting ducks in open terrain, and we've got two heavily armed hunters looming overhead." Gabriel leaned his head around Lisa and yelled, "what's going on up there?"

Samantha peered up at the clouds. "Nothing. They're just staying put."

Gabriel made his way back to the front of the van, the rocket launcher in tow.

"What the hell is that?" Porter asked, though the uncomfortable tone in his voice made it clear he already knew the answer.

"Insurance," Gabriel replied. He then leaned next to Samantha. "Any one of us can shoot this thing, but we're more likely to hit the moon than those choppers."

"Speak for yourself," Nate called out behind him.

Gabriel ignored him. "I'd feel a lot more comfortable if you were squeezing the trigger."

Samantha looked at the van's speedometer, hovering at just over fifty miles per hour. Then she looked resolutely at Gabriel. "Stop and swap on three?"

Gabriel nodded.

Samantha confirmed there were no cars trailing close behind them, while Gabriel warned everyone to grab hold of something stable. Samantha then counted to three and slammed on the brakes as she swerved the van off-road. Its tires squealed and kicked up plumes of dust that engulfed every window. Samantha covered her face, threw open the driver's side door, and hopped out. Gabriel listened to the thumping of the helicopter blades continuing forward as he took Samantha's place behind the wheel. Lisa held a rear door open just long enough for Samantha to climb in and take Gabriel's former position by the rocket launcher.

"Should I floor it?" Gabriel asked.

"No, wait," Samantha instructed.

They were still concealed by dust clouds, but that would only last for so long. The thumping of helicopter blades was duller than before, the Phoenix choppers having moved far ahead of the van following its unexpected stop. The problem was that the sound wasn't getting any quieter, which meant the choppers weren't moving farther away, either. Samantha pushed her way to the window near Porter. It was the largest window that would directly face the helicopters once the dust settled. She rolled the window halfway down and stuck the warhead end of the rocket launcher out of the van.

"Ummm..." Porter said hesitantly. "You're not going to fire that thing in here, are you?"

"I might," Samantha said coolly. "You should probably find a different seat."

Without argument, Porter unbuckled himself and squeezed into the van's cargo area. Nadine did the same, which made room for Lisa and Nate to clear themselves of the rear end of the rocket launcher. Gabriel watched his view through the front windshield begin to clear.

"You realize the moment she fires that thing, we've committed treason, right?" Lisa asked.

"She won't fire it unless she has to," Gabriel assured her.

The dust was settling. Gabriel looked out of the front side window facing the sound of the helicopter blades. He could barely make out the black outlines of the two choppers. They were maybe a quarter to a half mile away, and they had turned to face the van. More importantly, their weapons were facing the van.

"Samantha?" Gabriel asked

"I see them."

Samantha peered through the rocket launcher's reticule and adjusted her aim. Lisa looked worriedly at Gabriel, but he signaled for to hold tight. Samantha kept one hand near the rocket launcher's trigger while she reached into a cargo vest pocket with the other. She removed a foldable mirror, opened it, and held it up next to her weapon. She then flicked her wrist back and forth to catch reflections of sunlight.

"What the hell are you doing?" Nate asked. "You want to provoke them?"

"No," Samantha said calmly, without changing her readied position. "But I want them to know the consequences of firing on us." She flicked the mirror a few more times, then set it down and returned her second hand to the rocket launcher. "The ball's in their court now."

Gabriel could feel his muscles tightening as he stared at the black hunks of metal hovering in the distance. He counted at least eight missiles mounted under each side of the choppers. All it would take was one to wipe him and his team off the face of the planet. Even if Samantha got a shot off, it would serve only as revenge, for it wouldn't stop the incoming fatal projectile that triggered her response. Gabriel closed his eyes and breathed rhythmically in an attempt to steady his pulse. He could hear his own heartbeat- *thump, thump, thump, thump*- at first erratic, and then growing more regular as it slowed and softened. Soon Gabriel's heartbeat began to fade, and for a moment he thought maybe the helicopters had opened fire, that maybe he had died before hearing even the first shot, and that maybe his heart wasn't simply slowly, but stopping, as his soul departed a soon-to-be-lifeless body.

Gabriel heard multiple sighs of relief and opened his eyes. The thumping he had heard softening wasn't his own heart; it was from the blades of the Phoenix choppers as they abandoned their intimidation tactics. They had turned away from the van and were continuing down their original path. Samantha waited until they were specs on the horizon before finally lowering the rocket launcher and joining the rest of the team in a subdued victory celebration.

"Good job, Samantha," Gabriel said.

"Yes," Porter agreed. "Excellent job."

Samantha took the praise humbly as she removed the surface-to-air missile from her rocket launcher and climbed out of the van to take a less constrained path to the rear cargo area. The others maneuvered back to their original seats, except for Gabriel, who rested his head against the driver's seat while waiting for Samantha to return. He noticed Lisa fidgeting nervously as she stared out of a window facing the departing helicopters.

"What's wrong?"

"I don't think we've seen the last of the U.S. military," Lisa replied.

"Why not?"

She bit her lip as she shifted her gaze to Gabriel. "Those choppers? They're headed straight for Safi."

Chapter Twenty-Nine
Gus

Jnadgha, Morocco
Eleven Days Before The Sky Opened

Lisa's words fell over the van like an ominous cloud. No one was deceiving themselves about what had just transpired. The team was lucky to be alive. The next time the U.S. military intercepted them, it would be in a less direct manner. They wouldn't give Samantha the opportunity to ready a lethal counteroffensive. Hell, they might even just take the team out in secret and from afar... they'd be easy pickings for a well-trained sniper once on foot.

"Maybe they're just passing by Safi on their way to the next city," Nate suggested hopefully.

Lisa lowered her head with a disappointed shake. Nate had never been good at geography.

"That's unlikely," Porter told him.

"Why is that?"

"Because Safi's a coastal city. Unless the military has a naval vessel anchored just offshore, that's where they're headed."

Nate pursed his lips. "Awesome."

Samantha shut the rear cargo door and reclaimed her position behind the wheel, while Gabriel returned to the back and sat next to Porter. Soon they were back on the road, the only casualty from their military encounter being the twenty minutes of transit time lost. On a typical mission, that twenty minutes would be meaningless. Gabriel and his crew frequently spent more time than that arguing over which fast-food restaurant to grab lunch from. But on this mission, that twenty minutes could be the difference between Porter surviving his illness or succumbing to it. Gabriel had to think of a way to avoid further delays.

"Maybe we should head to Casablanca next," he suggested. "We could swing back down to Safi once the military figures out we veered off course."

Porter shook his head. "Too inefficient. We'll lose a minimum of four hours with the back-and-forth trips."

"We'll lose a lot more than that if the military intercepts us in Safi," Gabriel pointed out, unsure if Porter was considering all the possibilities.

"It's a risk we'll have to take," the tech billionaire replied. "They already got visual confirmation of our van, which means they're probably tracking us by satellite as we speak."

Gabriel noticed Lisa look to Samantha, who nodded in agreement.

"If we divert to Casablanca now, they'll do the same and they'll beat us there." Porter stared out of his window as he rubbed his chin in thought. "We need to knock out their eye in the sky; get them chasing their tales."

Nadine cleared her throat, drawing Porter's attention. "I could send a message to Gus."

"Who's Gus?" Gabriel asked.

Nadine raised her eyebrows as if to silently ask *what do you think?* while Porter looked hesitantly between her and Gabriel.

"Officially, Gus is in military intelligence," Porter explained. "Unofficially, he's on my private payroll. He gives me inside information about the technology needs of the government so I can get a head start on competitors in meeting those needs. It helps secure lucrative contracts that fund the majority of Cannes International's R&D."

"Once a cheater, always a cheater," Nate mumbled loud enough for everyone to hear.

Porter glared at him. "A little hypocritical coming from someone who got caught hacking into my network two days ago, don't you think? Besides, I didn't cheat you out of winning that competition."

"You didn't *get caught* cheating me out of winning."

"Nate..." Lisa said sternly as she observed the exchange from the front seat.

"No, it's fine," Porter told her. "It's about time we hashed this out." He stared hard at Nate. "Believe what you want, but I bested you fair and square when we were kids. I can best you fair and square now. Despite your inexplicable lack of geographical and cultural awareness, you're a genius, Nate. You're the brightest tech engineer I've ever known. But unfortunately for you, your parents and mine were on the same child-rearing schedule. You'll always come in second place to me. You'll always be the one who gets caught. And if you can't get rid of that damn chip on your shoulder, you'll never live up to your full potential!"

Porter sounded angry, but not because Nate had accused him of cheating his way to a first place trophy in a kids' engineering competition. Gabriel suspected Porter was really angry because he couldn't stand to see Nate waste even a fraction of his inherent talent. Gabriel glanced nervously at Nate. He half-expected his tech engineer to fire back with the truth about his clandestine activities to break into Porter's network in Cannes Tower. Gabriel would have if Porter had pushed him into a corner like that. But Nate kept his cool and didn't say a word. Instead, he lifted an outward-facing fist into the air, turned an invisible crank to the side of that fist, and erected his defiant middle finger. Nadine stifled a chuckle.

"Real mature," Porter said.

Nate smirked and removed himself from the conversation.

"So this Gus," Gabriel said, steering them back on track, "can he help us avoid our government companions?"

"I assume so," Porter said, his body language still hesitant.

"What's the problem, then?"

"He'll burn his inside man," Lisa explained. "With the type of interference required to shut down an active satellite tracking operation on short notice, there's no way Gus could avoid detection. He'll probably go to prison for it."

"Gus is talented enough to make it look like an accident," Porter countered. "But yes, he will get caught and likely fired for negligence. He already knows not to worry if that ever happens. I've got a retirement account set aside to ensure he never wants for anything in life."

"It's not Gus you're worried about," Gabriel concluded. "It's your company. How much of your operating budget do those government contracts represent?"

Porter looked at Nadine.

"Ninety-six percent, by our most recent estimates," she said.

"Shit," Nate finally spoke again. "Talk about putting all your eggs in one basket."

"We won't lose them all-" Nadine started.

"We'll lose enough," Porter said. "Even with a shift in focus to our commercial and corporate sectors, we're still looking at significant losses for decades to come." He shook his head. "It's not worth it. It-"

Porter choked on his words, a convulsive coughing fit demanding the attention of his body. He bent in half and spasmed as he did his best to suppress his respiratory outburst. Gabriel saw Nadine shut her eyes, her body tense and emotions visibly rattled by the display. A half-minute later, he saw Porter's body relax, though the tech billionaire remained hunched over, sticky globs of blood dripping from his bottom lip into a small pool in the palm of his hand. Porter stared into the dark pool as if he were staring into the depths of death itself.

"Message Gus," he said softly. "Tell him to get us off the grid... no matter the cost."

Chapter Thirty
Safi

Safi, Morocco
Eleven Days Before The Sky Opened

Nadine received a response from Gus within minutes. He instructed the team to take a decoy path until further notice. Samantha turned the van north at Echemmaia to comply. She would have preferred to turn south to deter any suspicions that the team might have an interest in Casablanca. But given they initially started their journey northwest out of Marrakech, a sudden southern diversion would have raised red flags for anyone monitoring. The good news was that going north, instead of northwest, from Marrakech would have been a straighter shot to Casablanca. Samantha hoped their late turn north would point their military observers to El Jadida or one of its surrounding regions instead.

After about forty minutes of driving- and forty minutes of Porter's frustrated tapping- Gus sent a new message that the team should be in the clear for at least twenty-four hours and that they shouldn't engage in further communication with him. As Samantha rerouted the van toward Safi, Porter instructed Nadine to have their corporate legal counsel assemble a team for Gus' eventual defense. Nadine suggested he also schedule time with Cannes International's board of directors upon his return, but Porter wasn't receptive to the suggestion. Gabriel figured some part of his mind was churning through potential solutions to his company's impending revenue hit, no matter how unlikely those solutions might be.

The team arrived in Safi a little after five o'clock local time. The sun was still glowing vibrantly from over the Atlantic Ocean, casting an orange radiance over the coastal city of mostly white stone buildings and brown castle-like structures. Lisa noted how the occasional splashes of bold color among the otherwise neutral architecture reflected ancient Safi's Portuguese influence while also capturing the aesthetic of the coastal city's well-known pottery trade. In contrast, Nate noted that he wasn't as impressed by Safi as he was by Marrakech.

"You barely saw Marrakech," Samantha reminded him from the van's driver's seat.

"And I've barely seen Safi," Nate replied, "but unless we're headed to another spiffy hotel-"

"We're not going to the hotel," Porter chimed in with more tension in his voice than usual. "We've lost enough time today already. We'll head straight to the second Shifa survivor's home."

"Not even a bathroom break?" Nate asked.

Gabriel glared at him, noticing that Porter was doing the same. Why couldn't Nate just keep his mouth shut sometimes? The mission had already gotten off on the wrong foot with the unexpected death of Faras El Mehdi and the arrival of military heat they hadn't counted on. Given the circumstances, Porter wasn't exactly in a chipper mood, and he and Nate had gone one round with each other already. Gabriel wasn't ready to entertain round two just yet.

"You can ask to use the bathroom at our destination," he told Nate. Gabriel then turned to Porter. "It might help if we know where that is."

"Samantha's already got it programmed in the van's navigation system," Porter said. "It's the home of Tareq Sabir. He lives in an apartment complex just south of *Le Grand Tajine*."

Gabriel heard his earpiece translate: *The Great Tagine*.

"What the hell is a tagine?" Nate asked.

Samantha groaned at his ignorance. Lisa was nicer about it.

"It's a Moroccan cooking pot," she explained. "The one Porter's referencing is about the size of a small house. It's a popular tourist attraction in Safi."

Nate huffed. "Must be some pot."

Once again, it was up to Gabriel to steer the conversation back on course. "We weren't supposed to move to Safi until tomorrow. Has anyone confirmed Mr. Sabir is okay with us showing up this evening?"

Porter was silent.

"I take that as a *no*," Gabriel continued.

"Actually," Nadine clarified, "Mr. Sabir doesn't know we're coming at all. He ignored all of our outreach and unfortunately doesn't have a servant to field meeting requests through."

"Oh."

Lisa looked back nervously. "I don't mean to be the one to ask the hard questions, but do we even know if he's still alive?"

"He was four days ago," Porter said. "He initiated a large fund transfer between his and a family member's bank accounts. The transaction details showed his bank's local branch verified his identity in-person."

Gabriel eyed Porter suspiciously. That wasn't the type of information that was publicly available or easily- and maybe not even legally- obtainable.

"Desperate times call for desperate measures," Porter said in a tone that was more informative than defensive. "I greased a few palms at the bank's corporate headquarters."

Nate chuckled as he dropped his forehead into the palm of his hand, but for a change, he kept his mouth shut.

"So how do you want to handle our arrival?" Gabriel asked, staying on track. "I assume Mr. Sabir won't appreciate you disrespecting his privacy."

"Probably not," Porter agreed. "But everyone has their price. Mr. Sabir transferred almost every dirham in his name to his granddaughter. A person doesn't do that without a reason. We just need to coax out of him what that reason is and offer to cover any shortfall in funding his family still needs."

"Have you considered just saying *please*?" Nate asked. When everyone except Samantha stared at him, he explained. "Some people don't want to be bought. Some people just want respect, or at least a little recognition, for whatever they might be going through."

Gabriel sensed there was more than friendly advice behind Nate's words. Porter must have sensed it too, for his freshly frozen veneer melted ever-so-slightly.

"Okay," he told Nate. "We'll try it your way first. *If* it doesn't work, then we'll try mine."

The two stared at each other as if unsure whether to shake hands or start throwing punches. After a few moments, they each turned their gazes elsewhere, round two postponed to another time. Lisa and Gabriel shared an *it's only a matter of time* glance before resuming their touristy intake of the sights of Safi. A silent nervousness hung in the air as each team member waited for another to speak. It was Samantha who finally broke the silence with her best airplane pilot impersonation.

"Attention, passengers," she said as she held an invisible radio to her lips. "If you look down the street approaching on your right, you'll be able to see the world's largest cooking pot."

Everyone on the left side of the van shifted to the right, hovering over those seated to catch a glimpse of the squat hut in the distance. It was pink with a blue and white cone-shaped roof that ended not in a point, but in what could best be described as a flattened lid handle. The building was situated in the middle of a pedestrian courtyard and protected by chain-link rope hung between decorative posts.

"Huh…" Nate said. "So that's the famous cooking pot."

Porter smiled peacefully at him. "*Le Grand Tajine.*"

Nate returned the gesture with an accepting nod. "Okay."

Gabriel watched the odd exchange between the two tech geniuses, and though he couldn't even begin to comprehend the words that weren't said, it left him with a feeling that everything might turn out okay after all.

Chapter Thirty-One
Tareq Sabir

Safi, Morocco
Eleven Days Before The Sky Opened

Samantha stopped the van outside a white three-story apartment complex with bright blue accents above each of its windows. She offered to remain on watch while the others went inside to find Tareq Sabir. Gabriel knew it wasn't so much an offer as a declaration of intent, for Samantha wasn't taking chances the U.S. military would show and either raid the apartment building while the team had their defenses down, or worse, rig the van to have an 'accident' as soon as the team was back on board.

Porter led the way up a stale-smelling stairwell, past a pair of stray cats, and to the closed door at the far end of the third-floor interior walkway. Nadine checked the apartment identifier against the intel on her phone, then gave Porter a confirming nod. He knocked and waited patiently for a response. When none came, Porter knocked again.

"Not to point out the obvious," Nate said, "but what if he's not home?"

Gabriel strolled back to the stairwell and glanced down at their van parked out front. Samantha was standing near the open driver's side door, one hand near her gun and the other ready to blare the horn should her keen eyes spot anything suspicious coming down the road. Porter knocked again, this time louder and more forcefully than before. Gabriel heard a bolt lock retract and saw one of the neighboring apartment doors crack open before quickly shutting again. Lisa had seen it too, so he motioned for her to take the lead.

"Excuse me," she called out as she gave the neighboring door a light rap. "Could you help us? We're looking for Tareq Sabir. Does he live in this building?"

Silence. Lisa looked at Gabriel for advice, but he knew their options were limited. They were Americans on foreign soil, facing both a language and appearance barrier. In hindsight, Gabriel realized they should have sent Porter up to the apartment alone, or at most, with Nadine to accompany him. The two of them would have been much less intimidating than an entire squad of armed foreigners intruding on someone's home.

"Let me try," Nadine suggested.

She joined Lisa at the neighboring door and repeated the request for help, only in Arabic, in case whoever lived there didn't understand English. When that didn't work, Porter gave Tareq's door one final, but pointless, try. Visibly frustrated, he squeezed his hands together and stepped away in defeat.

"I know everyone's tired," Porter said. "Gabriel and I can stay here to wait for Mr. Sabir to come home. Nadine can get the rest you checked in at our hotel. There should be a decent restaurant on the premises in case anyone's hungry."

Before anyone could respond, a muffled male voice spoke from behind the neighboring door. "He's not coming back."

The door opened, revealing a middle-aged man in traditional Moroccan garb. Behind him stood a middle-aged woman, presumably his wife, and a young girl.

"You speak English," Lisa said.

"Yes," the man admitted. "Forgive my hesitation. I didn't know what you wanted with Tareq. He's a very private man, and clearly he didn't expect you."

"Then why'd you open your door?" Nadine asked.

The man shrugged. "You seem like nice enough people. I didn't want you wasting your time. Tareq left before sunrise with his family. He stopped by on his way out to give me this." The man showed them a decorative fez. "I believe it was his way of thanking me for being a good neighbor for so many years."

"You think it was a goodbye present?" Gabriel asked.

The man nodded.

"Was Mr. Sabir leaving to live with his family?" Porter asked.

"Maybe we could visit him at their home."

"No, no," the man said, shaking his head. "Mr. Sabir and his family left on foot. They had supplies for at least two days' worth of hiking with them."

"Do you know which way they went?" Gabriel asked.

"South, I believe. But to what destination, I am unsure."

Gabriel shared a glance with Lisa, who, as usual, was on the same page as him. If Tareq Sabir truly left on foot, then with the help of technology and a little luck, they'd be able to track and catch up to him. But it would be a lot easier to do so before the black of night set in, which meant they needed to hurry. Porter must have been thinking something similar, for he thanked the man for his information and even offered him a significant amount of dirham. The man declined, but Porter insisted he take it and spend it on his daughter. The team returned to the van, where Samantha was waiting for an update.

"Get in touch with whomever you know that has access to current satellite images for the region south of Safi," Gabriel instructed her. "We're looking for a family traveling on foot."

"No can do, boss," Samantha replied. "My contacts use the military satellite network. When Porter's contact took it down, they took my guys down, too."

"Damn," Gabriel said. He turned to Porter. "Decision time. If we head south, we're driving blind and it'll be getting dark soon. If we head north, we risk driving straight into the military opposition we diverted that way, but we could get to our next target sooner."

"You think we should abandon the search for Mr. Sabir and head straight to Casablanca?" Porter asked.

Gabriel shook his head. "I honestly don't know. We know Mr. Sabir's alive and have a general direction in which to find him. But there's an entire continent's worth of land south of us and no guarantee we'll take a close enough trajectory to intercept him. On the other hand, we've struck out twice so far with Shifa survivors. There's no guarantee Casablanca won't be strike three."

Porter looked at Nadine for her opinion. She said nothing, but based on her expression, Gabriel guessed she would rather them hunker down in Safi for the night so she could get those scans of Porter's lungs she wanted. Porter appeared as though he might cave in to her despite the urgency looming over them, but before he vocalized his thoughts, the young girl from the third-floor apartment came running up to his side.

"*Mister*," Gabriel heard her translated voice say through his earpiece. "*Are you the dying man?*"

The question caught Porter off-guard. "What?"

Nadine translated.

"*Are you the dying man?*" The girl repeated. "*You don't look well.*"

As stoic a facade as Porter usually maintained, the young girl's comment seemed to make him crumble. His mouth hung open as he tried to find the words to respond, and in those awkward moments, Gabriel realized just how much his friend had deteriorated since their first conversation three days earlier. His sickness was rapidly advancing, and apparently it took the observation of an innocent stranger to make them all see it for themselves.

"Yes," Porter replied with an uncharacteristic quiver in his voice. "I am the dying man."

After Nadine translated, the young girl handed Porter a folded piece of writing paper. "*Mr. Sabir was a kind man,*" she said. "*He didn't want to ignore you. He just didn't have much time left to get his own affairs in order. He asked me to give you this should you show up after he was gone.*"

Porter looked at the girl as if in awe of her maturity. Gabriel couldn't help but linger on the way she spoke, as if Tareq Sabir may not be as alive as they initially believed.

"Thank you," Porter said.

The young girl ran back to her parents, who had walked downstairs to keep an eye on her while she fulfilled Tareq Sabir's request. Porter unfolded the paper and read its contents. His face didn't change much, but Gabriel thought he spotted a hint of relief as the muscles in Porter's body relaxed ever so slightly.

"What is it?" He asked.

Porter turned the paper around to display its contents to the group. "Coordinates."

Chapter Thirty-Two
Procession

Safi, Morocco
Eleven Days Before The Sky Opened

"Give us the rundown," Gabriel said to Samantha once the team was back in the van and on a road headed south.

"Mr. Sabir's coordinates point to a mountainous region south of Tnine Rhiate. The good news is that we've only got an hour's drive ahead of us. The bad news is that no roads go to the exact coordinates Tareq Sabir left us, so we'll have an hour to hour and a half hike over uneven terrain after that."

"We're going to be pushing sundown at that rate," Lisa commented.

"What's at the coordinates?" Gabriel asked.

Samantha shrugged. "Best I can tell, the only human constructs are some agricultural plots. Beyond that, it's nothing but Mother Nature."

"There's got to be something there," Porter said confidently. "We may not have met Mr. Sabir, but we did our homework on him. He wasn't the type of person to send a dying man on a wild goose chase."

"Even if that's true," Gabriel said, "you shouldn't get your hopes up that he's leading you to the pendant."

Nadine's sudden frown hinted that she already had. "Why not?"

"The Veiled Bird," Gabriel explained. "Remember, these coordinates weren't the first note we received. Two Shifa survivors, two notes... so far anyway. Unless we can figure out how The Veiled Bird and these coordinates fit together, we shouldn't hold our breath over what we might find."

"Way to be a buzzkill," Nate said, followed by a nod of agreement from Porter. "Let's assess what we do and don't know. First question: why did the Sabir family go on a hike to the middle of nowhere?"

"The pendant," Porter suggested. "That little girl said Mr. Sabir was getting his affairs in order. It's probably what his parents did before taking him to Shifa. The journey was dangerous, so travelers made sure their personal matters were tidy before making it."

"Okay," Nate said. "Why go back to the pendant after all these years?"

"His granddaughter," Lisa said. She didn't sound confident so much as she sounded like she was shifting puzzle pieces around a table in her mind. "Porter said he transferred his savings to her a few days ago. What if she's got a serious ailment? The money might have been to pay for treatment, but sometime during the past few days, Mr. Sabir decided to take more drastic action."

"It's plausible," Nate said. "Anyone want to dissent?"

"I've already mentioned The Veiled Bird," Gabriel said. "But let's set that aside for a moment since we don't know what The Veiled Bird actually tells us. The pendant shouldn't be in Morocco. Given its relocation history- and some common sense- there's little chance it moved from the Atlas Mountains to a smaller mountain area less than two hundred miles away."

"Fair point," Nate admitted. "So back to the original question..."

"Maybe they went camping," Samantha suggested from the front seat. "They could simply be fans of the outdoors."

"You really believe that?" Nate asked.

"No."

Nate rolled his eyes. "Okay. Second question: why'd they leave on foot?"

Lisa shrugged. "Why not?"

"We didn't," Nadine chimed in.

"She's right," Gabriel added. "It never crossed our minds to walk from Safi to wherever those coordinates are taking us. We're driving as far as roads will take us. Why didn't they?"

"I'm guessing no one's thinking they just like exercise?" Porter asked rhetorically.

"Ceremony," Lisa said. "Plenty of cultures engage in walks for ceremonial reasons."

"Walking is a significant part of the Hajj," Samantha added. "I'm guessing Tareq Sabir was Muslim, so he'd be familiar with the tradition."

"But this isn't the Hajj," Gabriel pointed out. "So, what ceremony was it?"

"Maybe it wasn't an official ceremony," Nate suggested. "Maybe it was a walk of personal reflection, or of honor, or respect."

Nadine scrunched her face. "Like...?"

"Like a funeral procession," Nate said bluntly, his words hanging heavily over the team.

There had been far too much discussion of death on this mission so far, so Gabriel tried to pivot to a different suggestion. "I don't think-"

Porter cut him off. "Nate's right." He glanced solemnly at Gabriel, silently communicating that he was okay discussing it. "Think about it. The transfer of his life savings. Moving out of his apartment. A mysterious hike into the wilderness with his loved ones. It's Faras El Mehdi all over again. Mr. Sabir knows the end is near. He's going out there to die."

"Well, as of this morning, he was still alive," Gabriel reminded Porter. "And apparently healthy enough to make the journey south. Even if he went out there to die, we still have a chance of getting to him first. Remember, he wanted you to follow him."

Porter nodded before looking down at his feet. Nadine, clearly in denial, chewed her lip as she turned her eyes to the surrounding countryside. Gabriel gave Nate a *you had to go there?* look, to which Nate raised his brow with an expression of *you know it had to be said.* Gabriel took a deep breath and thought about their current course of action. A matter of hours had been the difference between them meeting Faras El Mehdi and arriving after he had already passed. A matter of hours had been the difference between meeting Tareq Sabir and chasing him to a mysterious destination. Now they were going to spend at least two more hours getting to their destination, and another two and a half getting back to Safi. Would those four and a half hours be the difference between reaching the final Shifa survivor in Casablanca before he or she disappeared into death's embrace?

Would they be the difference between a genuine lead on the pendant's location and just another cryptic clue? Gabriel supposed there was no reason to worry about it now. Their course was set; he had to hope it was the right one.

Chapter Thirty-Three
The Sundown Trek

Tnine Rhiate Region, Morocco
Eleven Days Before The Sky Opened

For the next twenty minutes, no one spoke. The team passed through Tnine Rhiate and continued on a southeast heading until moderately populated areas gave way to open farmland, and then eventually to sparsely populated hills that gradually transitioned to mountains. After another twenty minutes of winding along a paved mountain ridge, Samantha pulled the van to the shoulder of the road and turned off its engine.

"This is as close as we're getting with wheels," she told the team as she hopped out.

The sun was just starting to drop behind the horizon. It filled the sky with shades of hot pink and deep orange that cast a colorful glow over the land. As the team filed out of the van, Samantha opened the cargo area and assessed their most important needs. She filled canteens from their portable water supply and passed them around to each team member. She then confirmed that everyone was wearing appropriate shoes before handing each of them a cellophane package small enough to slip into a cargo vest pocket.

"What are these?" Porter asked.

"Foil blankets," Samantha replied. "Just in case we get stuck out there. It's going to get cold at this altitude after dark." She grabbed an empty backpack and filled it with a dozen MREs. "I'll need someone to carry this as well. Just in case."

It surprised Gabriel when Nadine volunteered. She was slowly warming up to the team, and now it appeared she was even trying to play an active role on it, almost as if she wanted their respect. Unable to ignore his inner gentleman, Nate intercepted the bag and reminded Nadine that he was being paid for his labor. Nadine reminded Nate that she was too, and held tight to one of the backpack straps until he relented. Gabriel could see why Porter liked her. She wasn't just some run-of-the-mill administrative assistant with little investment in her job. She had a strength and confidence to her that would naturally appeal to a man who was used to being the smartest and most confident person in the room.

"What can we do?" Lisa asked on behalf of her and Gabriel.

"Take this," Samantha said, passing her the duffel bag of ropes, hooks, and other miscellaneous items. "I'm not anticipating the terrain ahead to be too difficult, considering the Sabir family has already crossed it. But you never know when a little climbing gear could come in handy."

"Samantha?" Gabriel asked as he eyed the mound of kevlar in the back of the van. "Are we good with just our cargo vests?"

"We should be in and out of wherever we're headed long before the military gets their satellites back online. Given we know nothing about our destination, I'd rather have gear instead of protection." Samantha grabbed another empty backpack and shoved a handful of first aid kits inside. "Here," she said, handing the backpack to Gabriel. "Now we're protected against bullets and any other dangers we might run into."

Samantha made one final assessment of the team and their gear, then shut and locked the van. Gabriel wondered whether it was safe to leave it on the side of the road, especially considering the firepower inside. Then again, it wasn't like anyone was going to be driving down this curvy mountain road once dark had set in. The risk was probably minimal.

Once Samantha was satisfied they were ready, she checked their compass bearing on a handheld GPS system and set off toward a rocky slope. *Here we go*, Gabriel thought to himself as he followed Samantha, the rest of the team filing into place behind him. They hiked for thirty minutes, their shadows elongating against rock and sand in the diminishing light. Then the team stopped for a water break. The aridness of the region was sucking moisture from their lungs with every breath, and each inch closer to their destination brought them into slightly higher altitudes with thinning air.

Porter seemed to be handling the trek the worst so far. While the rest of the team was simply thirsty, he was downright winded, his ailing lungs struggling with even the slightest bit of aerobic activity in this climate. Nadine tried to convince him to return to the van, that they would bring Tareq Sabir to see him there, but Porter refused to listen. He removed a tablet from a shoulder satchel he had brought with him and insisted he'd be fine if he distracted himself. Unable to dissuade Porter from continuing, the team got moving again.

"Reviewing blueprints for another invention?" Gabriel asked Porter during the next leg of the hike.

Porter showed him the tablet's screen, which was filled with tables and charts containing financial figures. "Nope, just trying to figure out how to save my company."

That explained why Nate wasn't breathing down Porter's neck.

"Have you considered getting into the exotic tourism business?" Gabriel said in jest. "You could offer treasure hunting excursions around the Mediterranean. I even know an experienced treasure hunter you could pay handsomely to lead the excursions."

Porter wheezed out a chuckle. "I'll be sure to get in touch with Lisa once we get that launched. Who knows? She might even meet a suave treasure hunting companion during those excursions. I hear those Mediterranean boys can be quite the catch."

"Hey now..."

Porter elbowed him playfully. It was like being back in college again.

"I hear you two talking about me back there!" Lisa called from the front of the party.

"No, you don't!" Gabriel called back with a grin.

Nate dropped back to join them. "Personally, I think you should pivot into movie-making. The money you'd make on this story alone-" Nate jumped into character, mimicking the deep, brooding voices of movie trailer narrators. "Coming this summer, a jackass genius billionaire sacrifices everything to find a piece of jewelry that could save his life..."

The boys on the team shared a laugh while the girls rolled their eyes at the idiocy.

"The only problem with that idea is it isn't a recurring revenue stream," Porter said once he caught his breath. "A one-and-done blockbuster can only stave off bankruptcy so long."

"Are you kidding me?" Nate asked. "That's what sequels are for. In part one, you're just a simple man trying to survive. By part six, you'll be fist-fighting anacondas in space. People flock to theaters for that shit!"

"I do like the idea of punching a snake in space," Porter said, musing on the idea. "Write me a six-movie outline and I'll consider it."

"Done," Nate said.

By then, the sun was almost gone, and the brightest stars had started to peek from the black and blue blanket of the nighttime sky. When it was time to stop for water again, Gabriel saw Lisa motion for Samantha to keep going. He knew what she was thinking. The boys were being boys, just as they had been in the good old days, and it was taking Porter's mind off of his condition. There was more harm in interrupting than not. After another twenty-five minutes, Samantha led the team to the peak of a rocky hill and paused. She checked her GPS, then scanned the dark horizon, the lack of sunlight inhibiting long-range vision.

"What is it?" Gabriel asked.

"We're here," Samantha said.

Nate looked around the star-lit field before them. "I don't see anything. Are you sure-"

"Wait," Lisa cut him off. "Look over there."

She pointed toward a steep mountainside just past the open field. Gabriel squinted, but saw nothing. Then, as his eyes adjusted, a soft orange glow faded into view. A barely visible blue glow soon joined it, both emanating from an opening in the mountainside. It was a cave, and the lighting coming from within wasn't natural, which meant someone was inside. *No,* Gabriel thought. *Not someone. Tareq Sabir, the second Shifa survivor and the team's best hope of locating the pendant.* Gabriel shot Porter a relieved smile.

"Okay, team," he then said aloud. "Let's go."

Chapter Thirty-Four
Into The Cave

Tnine Rhiate Region, Morocco
Eleven Days Before The Sky Opened

As the team neared the mountain cave, the orange and blue lighting grew stronger. Gabriel noted that the orange light flickered against the visible interior cave wall, as if cast by a large flame. He also noted that the blue light rippled ever so slightly over the same rocky surface, as if reflecting off of moving water, though Gabriel knew that could have been an optical illusion from the overlapping orange movement. The team was at the cave entrance within minutes. There, they found a group of camels tied to a post permanently embedded in the mixture of sand and rock that comprised the soil in this area. Beside the camels was a harness attached to a wooden cart with wheels and a pile of luggage bags.

"The Sabirs?" Lisa asked Gabriel.

"Probably."

Samantha crept to the cave entrance, one hand ready to draw her gun should the need arise, and peered inside. The tension in her body eased a moment later, at which point she turned to Gabriel. "It's your show now, boss."

Samantha stepped aside so Gabriel could peer into the cave's mouth. Inside was a hollowed out tunnel large enough for several people to fit through simultaneously. The tunnel curved after what Gabriel estimated to be fifty feet, and the sources of the orange and blue glows were somewhere beyond that curve. Gabriel observed a pair of metal prongs on each side of the cave entrance. They were torch holders, he recognized, though they held no torches right now.

Gabriel also saw that the ripples in the blue light weren't an illusion after all, and that they became more prominent the closer they got to the bend in the tunnel.

Gabriel's eyes scanned the inner circumference of the hollowed cavity for any other signs of unnatural formations, human construction, or abnormalities that might suggest the presence of booby traps or other dangers. Finding none, Gabriel slowly proceeded into the tunnel, signaling for the others to follow. About halfway down the corridor, he heard running water. As the ripples in the blue glow grew stronger, so did that sound grow louder. Soon it was joined by the echo of quiet voices, too distant for Gabriel's earpiece to pick up, but definitely speaking Arabic.

When Gabriel reached the bend, he held up a hand, signaling for the team to stop, then peered to see whatever awaited them next. About ten feet beyond its curve, the tunnel opened into an enormous cavity inside the mountain. From his current vantage point, all Gabriel could see was a portion of a waterfall surrounded by lush green vines. The Arabic voices were clear enough now for his earpiece to partially translate. As best Gabriel could tell, they were praying.

He put a finger to his lips to signal the team to stay quiet, then moved forward toward the cavity. Where the tunnel ended, a downward stone staircase began, and at the foot of that staircase began three rows of marble burial vaults. To the left and right of the primary cavity were stone columns and archways, beyond which Gabriel could see several more rows of burial vaults. Burning torches lined each column, creating the flickering orange glow the team had seen from outside. At the far end of the main chamber flowed a bright blue waterfall. It splashed into a pool at its base that then channeled around the edges of the side chambers, where smaller waterfalls added to the gathering water before it emptied into an unseen location. The water must have been fresh, for the lush greenery Gabriel had glimpsed from the tunnel was actually quite extensive, hanging from the ceiling overhead and draping the stone archways that supported the mountain cavity.

"How does plant life grow in here?" Lisa asked curiously.

"Maybe sunlight gets in through holes in the ceiling we can't see at night," Gabriel suggested. He had no idea if he was correct. It just made more sense than the alternative, that some force of nature beyond human understanding was feeding jungle-like plant growth in this cave.

Gabriel's eyes traveled to the base of the main waterfall, where the three primary rows of burial vaults ended. The vault to the left was sealed and decorated with a wreath of fresh flowers. The vault to the right was open and empty. The vault in the middle, however, was partially open and surrounded by three adults and two children, a boy and a girl. They paid no attention to the new arrivals and instead continued praying.

"Porter," Gabriel whispered. "Are any of them Tareq Sabir?"

Porter took a moment to study the faces of the mourners positioned around the vault. A moment later, his own face dropped. "No, but that little girl is his granddaughter."

It was an innocent observation, and yet Porter's words carried more meaning than what was apparent on the surface. Those people were Tareq Sabir's family, and they were standing around a burial vault, praying for the body within, the one member of the family no longer living among them. Tareq Sabir was dead. Porter knew it, and that knowledge swept his legs from under him as he staggered toward the tunnel wall and dropped to the ground. Gabriel knew it, too. He closed his eyes, kicking himself for not turning the team around sooner, for not putting their chances of success in the hands of a Shifa survivor who might still be alive and well in Casablanca. Instead, Gabriel had let them trail a dying man to his grave, and in doing so, may have sealed Porter to the same fate.

Chapter Thirty-Five
The Blessed Burial Ground

Tnine Rhiate Region, Morocco
Eleven Days Before The Sky Opened

"Mr. Cannes?"

Gabriel heard his earpiece translator repeat the words in a voice he recognized, but couldn't immediately place. He looked around for the source, his eyes soon falling to Jalal Ismaili, who had just rounded a column to the left of the main staircase. Jalal's arms were full of loose flower buds.

"Mr. Dunne, is Mr. Cannes okay?" Jalal asked. *"Shall I bring water?"*

"No," Gabriel called out. "We have water. Mr. Cannes just needs a minute."

Upon seeing Jalal's quizzical expression, Gabriel motioned for Nadine to translate. He then asked her to join him while he climbed down the stone staircase to meet with Jalal. Lisa tagged along while Nate and Samantha hung back to watch over Porter. A few members of the Sabir family glanced back to see why there had been a sudden commotion, but then returned their attention to their prayers.

"Jalal, what are you doing here?" Gabriel asked.

After Nadine translated, Jalal replied, *"I have brought Mr. El Mehdi to his desired resting place. If I had known you were coming here too, I would have offered to travel together."*

"We didn't exactly know where we'd be going after Safi," Gabriel explained.

Lisa motioned to the rows of burial vaults. "What is this place?"

"I don't know," Jalal said. *"Mr. El Mehdi gave me a map many*

years ago. He instructed that when his time came, I should bring him to the spot marked on the map. He said there would be a place waiting for him." Jalal extended his hand in a welcoming gesture. *"Please, follow me."*

He led Gabriel, Lisa, and Nadine down the nearest row of burial vaults, toward the waterfall end where the Sabir family continued their mourning. Gabriel glanced back to find that Porter was back on his feet, the sight of Jalal apparently restoring a glimmer of the hope that had been lost minutes earlier. Nate and Samantha were monitoring him as he took one cautious step after another down the stone staircase. Soon, Jalal stopped near the burial vault with the fresh flower wreath on top. He shifted his bundle of flower buds into one arm and pointed to the side of the vault, where the name *El Mehdi* was engraved on its surface.

"I didn't know what to expect when I got here," Jalal explained, *"but as you see, Mr. El Mehdi was correct. There was a place waiting for him."*

Gabriel rubbed his fingertips over the name. It appeared as though it had been etched long ago, the engraved lettering showing the same wear from the passage of time as the surface it had been etched into. Gabriel caught a member of the Sabir family- he presumed Tareq Sabir's eldest daughter by her age and the way she exuded familial authority- eyeing him uncomfortably.

"May I?" He asked Jalal, motioning to the flower buds.

"Of course," Jalal said.

Gabriel took a handful of buds, as did Lisa, and they helped Jalal place them across the surface of Faras El Mehdi's vault. "So Mr. El Mehdi never told you why he wanted to be buried here?"

"He never offered, and I never asked. Remember, my duty was to carry out his wishes, whatever they happened to be."

"Of course."

Gabriel saw the suspecting woman excuse herself from her family. He had hoped helping Jalal would be enough to take attention away from them, but that appeared not to be the case. Porter, Samantha, and Nate arrived at the burial vault just as the woman approached Jalal. She spoke softly, but with a harsh tone that commanded respect. Gabriel angled his ear just in time to catch the woman's words.

"They are outsiders. They do not belong in here."

Thankfully, Jalal defended them. *"They are guests of Mr. El Mehdi. They have a right to say goodbye."*

Gabriel saw Lisa nudge Nadine, then approach the woman.

"Miss Sabir?" Lisa asked, having come to the same conclusion as Gabriel about the woman's identity. "My name is Lisa Dunne. We're very sorry for interrupting. We didn't know your father had already passed. We'd been looking for him. We had questions-"

"About his time in Shifa," Miss Sabir said, responding before Nadine's translation was complete. *"You and everyone else. You all want to hear my father's fantastical stories of the magical place where people go to be healed."*

"You sound like you don't believe such a place exists," Porter said.

"My father and I didn't share the same beliefs. I am much more grounded in my faith. I believe in Allah just as he did, but I believe the time of prophets and intervention with mortal man ended long ago, well before his time, and certainly not during ours. I don't believe in magical cities or mystical tokens that heal travelers of their woes. I look to Allah to guide my life choices, to make me a better person. I look to science when I need to be healed."

Porter approached Miss Sabir with his arms outstretched, as if to show he meant no harm. "I'm a man of science myself. Unfortunately, my need for healing has surpassed the capabilities of modern medicine and technology. That mystical token you speak of may be the only chance I have left."

"Look around you," Miss Sabir said as she waved an agitated hand over their surroundings. *"Everyone buried in this cave thought they had been blessed by the power of Shifa. They even nicknamed this place The Blessed Burial Ground, a place where those touched by Allah could all be together at the end."* She swallowed hard, as if fighting back deep-rooted emotion, and stared into Porter's eyes. *"Do you know what I see? Death. Rows and rows of death. There's nothing blessed about that. My father is gone, and now it's on me to ensure my family's continued survival. Where is the magical city he claimed to have visited? Where is the mystical token that could have extended his life and kept him here among us? If such a thing existed, why did we come here instead of going to it? Why did my father walk*

into death's embrace so willingly?" Miss Sabir lowered her eyes, and with them, the strength in her voice. *"When you figure out the answer to those questions, you'll realize there is no magical salvation awaiting you. You'll realize that you should use whatever time you have left to make your lasting impact on the world... because soon you will be gone, too."*

Porter didn't respond. Gabriel wasn't sure if it was because he was angry, in shock, saddened by Miss Sabir's words, something else, or all of the above. All he knew was that Porter stood motionless as a statue as Miss Sabir turned away to rejoin her family. She was done with them, regardless of any questions they might still have.

"Don't get discouraged," Gabriel whispered to Porter. "We're not giving up yet."

Porter closed his eyes in defeat. "Maybe she's got a point. I'm wasting what little time I have left chasing a fairy tale supported by circumstantial evidence, at best."

"Yeah, maybe," Gabriel admitted. "But if there's even a slim chance the fairy tale could be true, wouldn't you give it your all to find out? Besides, there's still one more Shifa survivor who may be able to guide us to the pendant's location."

"If she isn't dead yet," Porter replied bluntly.

Gabriel smiled, aware that his treasure hunter brain had already processed a key observation Porter had overlooked in his despondent state. "She's not." He pointed past the Sabir family, toward the final open burial vault, the one still awaiting its passenger to the afterlife. "Miss Sabir said everyone in this place was a Shifa traveler, and by the looks of it, they're still missing one of their own." Gabriel put a reassuring hand on Porter's shoulder. "Which means we still have a fighting chance."

Chapter Thirty-Six
Wearing Down

Tnine Rhiate Region, Morocco
Eleven Days Before The Sky Opened

Gabriel and Lisa could have hung around The Blessed Burial Ground for weeks if given the opportunity. The names etched into each burial vault would have provided a rich source of history that could expand the little knowledge they had about Shifa and its travelers. The compilation of that knowledge would likely fill at least one historical non-fiction book and serve as the inspiration for a handful of fiction novels. That alone would make the time invested worth it, financially speaking, and any personal enlightenment Gabriel and Lisa received from their investigation would be icing on an already delectable cake. They would also likely stir up interest from religious scholars looking to reignite debate over the Book of Damien, as well as biologists who would undoubtedly want to perform tests to understand the thriving biome that had grown inside the burial ground despite its inhospitable conditions.

For now, though, Gabriel could only dream of what might have been. His team was in a time crunch to find the Pendant of God before Porter became the next life lost during this mission. That didn't mean he and Lisa couldn't return once the mission was complete, so Gabriel- and by necessity, Nadine- shared a brief aside with Jalal before they departed.

"I'd love to come back here one day to do some book research," Gabriel told his foreign fan. "Do you mind if we keep in touch? You could be our guide when we return."

"Name a character after me in your next novel and you've got a

deal," Jalal said with a friendly grin.

"Deal."

Lisa tapped Gabriel on the shoulder. "I think we should get going before we disturb the Sabirs any further."

"Agreed," Gabriel said, the sight of Miss Sabir glaring at them clear in his peripheral vision. "I'll round everyone up."

"Okay. I'm going to hang back to ask Jalal a few more questions. Then Nadine and I will be right behind you."

Gabriel nodded in acknowledgement, then signaled for Porter, Nate, and Samantha's attention before circling his fingers in a *wrap it up* motion and leading them back to the stone staircase. Despite his renewed hope, Porter didn't seem to move with his usual power swagger. At first, Gabriel chalked it up to the emotional swings his friend had been through during these first three Moroccan encounters. But then Porter stumbled trying to climb a solid stone step, his foot simply failing to support his weight as he tried to lift himself higher. Porter caught himself as he pivoted forward, and Gabriel could hear him wheezing quietly, as if trying to hide the fact that he couldn't take in enough air.

Gabriel nodded his head toward the tunnel entrance at the top of the stairs, silently ordering Samantha and Nate to proceed without them. He then bent his head under Porter's arm and rose, taking Porter's weight on his shoulders as he placed a supporting hand on his friend's back.

"I shouldn't have come," Porter wheezed. "I'm just slowing you down."

"You just need some rest," Gabriel countered as he helped Porter climb the next step.

"There's no time for rest," Porter said. "We need to get to Casablanca."

"You aren't going to make it to Casablanca if you don't take a break." They climbed another step in unison. "Frankly, we're all exhausted, even those of us without a terminal lung condition. If we don't get rest, we're going to start making mistakes... there's nothing deadlier than that when out in the field."

Porter glanced at him with sunken eyes as if to say, *are you sure about that?* The two reached the top of the steps, paused for a few moments for Porter to catch his breath, then followed the tunnel passage back to the mouth of the cave, where Samantha had a canteen ready for Porter's consumption.

"What's the next move, boss?" Nate asked.

"We check in to our hotel in Safi," Gabriel said. He saw Porter's eyes shift toward him, but the businessman didn't challenge Gabriel's decision. "Samantha, you have contacts in Casablanca, don't you?"

"I'm sure there's at least one or two friendlies I could ask for a favor," she replied. "What do you need?"

"Get the details of our last survivor from Porter. Have them find her, confirm she's alive and in good health, and have them keep watch on her. They're to notify you immediately at any sign of health concerns, military intervention, random walks into the desert... you get the idea."

Samantha nodded. "Yeah, you got it."

Gabriel turned to Porter. "There. Can you take a few hours to get sleep now?"

Porter lowered the canteen, swallowed, and took several deep breaths to replenish his lungs. "Fine," he eventually said. "You win." Porter then made an exaggerated glance to his left, followed by one to his right. "Should I take the cold, rocky ground, or the even colder rocky ground?"

Yeah, Gabriel thought as he bit his lip, *that's going to be a problem.* The team still had an hour and a half walk just to get back to their van. There was no way Porter was going to make it that distance in his current condition. And while Gabriel had already decided the team needed rest, sleeping outdoors on a low-lying mountainside wasn't exactly what he had in mind.

"Miss Sabir said to take their camels and cart," Lisa announced as she and Nadine emerged from the cave opening. "She said that even though we don't see eye-to-eye, she wouldn't be able to face Allah if she let Porter drop dead out here."

Gabriel saw conflicted relief wash over Porter's face.

"Miss Sabir will also need the location of our van so she and her family can retrieve the camels once they leave," Lisa said to Samantha, who gave her a thumbs up. Lisa then looked at Porter. "She didn't ask for compensation, but it may not be a bad idea to make a generous donation to the family for their trouble. I'm guessing you have enough information about their bank accounts to pull that off."

Porter rolled his eyes at the accusatory assumption, but didn't deny it. He then gave a confirmatory nod to Nadine, who typed a note into her phone. Lisa smiled with gratitude before walking to Gabriel and locking her arm in his.

"I need to talk to you privately," she whispered.

Gabriel instructed Nate to help Porter into the wooden cart. He presumed the Sabirs had used the rickety transport to escort Tareq Sabir, a man on the verge of death, to The Blessed Burial Ground. Now he and his team would use it to escort another man on the verge of death away from that same burial ground. The dichotomy was funny, but not in a ha-ha way, Gabriel considered, as he and Lisa casually strolled away from the group. One man was ready to embrace death; the other was fighting vehemently against it. One man was from a life of wealth and privilege; the other lived much more simply. Yet both men were traveling the same path, in the same vehicle, each at the mercy of a rapidly declining lifespan, and, depending on the success of this mission, both headed to the same destination.

"What's going on?" Gabriel asked once he felt comfortable he and Lisa were out of earshot range.

"Do you remember how Miss Sabir alluded to others wanting to speak with her father about Shifa?" Lisa asked rhetorically. "I asked Jalal if that had been Faras El Mehdi's experience as well. He said no, that while Faras liked to tell his tale, no one had actively sought him out like we did."

"Okay..." Gabriel said, unsure where Lisa was going with this.

"Jalal then told me he didn't doubt Miss Sabir's claim, though, for someone had shown up here just a few hours before us and mere minutes after Tareq Sabir had passed. He said the man harassed the Sabir family while they were trying to complete their burial customs. Jalal didn't hear most of what the man's translator said, but he remembers hearing the word *Shifa*."

Now Gabriel could see where Lisa's story was headed. His eyes shut and his shoulders drooped. "Don't tell me..."

"I'm afraid so," Lisa said. "I asked Jalal for a description of the man. It was Byron Coltrain."

Chapter Thirty-Seven
Revitalized

Safi, Morocco
Ten Days Before The Sky Opened

Gabriel woke to the sounds of a bustling market on the street outside his hotel room. He rolled over to find Lisa still asleep, then checked his watch and saw that it was nearly ten o'clock. Gabriel hadn't intended to sleep so late, but in hindsight, he had needed it following the high emotional and physical tolls of their previous lengthy day. After Lisa had informed him about Byron's presence in Morocco, the team carted Porter back to their parked van. Riding camels was a welcome reprieve from hiking over uneven terrain, especially in the dark of night, when even the simplest of land obstructions had a high probability of causing an ankle sprain.

Gabriel and Lisa agreed to keep the news about Byron secret until the next morning to avoid anyone dwelling on its implications when they should be resting. Nadine, also in on the secret because of her role as the team's sole translator, didn't like the idea of keeping secrets from Porter, but agreed to do so in the interest of his health. Not that it would have mattered, for Porter passed out within minutes of settling into the Sabirs' wooden cart. The contraption hadn't looked the least bit comfortable, but apparently it was enough to allow Porter to get some much needed shut-eye.

Once the team arrived at their van, Gabriel offered to drive since Samantha had been awake the longest of all of them. It only took an hour to get back to Safi, but that was one more hour of sleep Samantha wouldn't otherwise be able to get. Gabriel encouraged everyone to do the bare minimum required to get to bed after they arrived at their hotel. Most of their luggage stayed in the van, and no one took time to explore whether their new hotel was as luxurious as the last. Instead, they dispersed to their rooms with little fanfare, and Gabriel hoped the rest of the team was as efficient as he and Lisa at cleaning up before hitting the sack.

Gabriel now climbed out of bed as quietly as possible so he wouldn't wake his wife. He peeked around the nearest window curtain and saw a mob of merchants, local customers, and tourists swarming makeshift retail stands that lined the road that ran along this side of the hotel. Surely their noise had already woken some of the other team members. Why had no one come to wake him and Lisa yet?

Curious, Gabriel threw on his clothes from the day before and crept out of his room. The adjacent hallway was empty, so Gabriel meandered toward what he thought was the lobby based on his hazy late night recollection. A concierge soon spotted him and waved him over. The concierge then escorted Gabriel to a private dining room where Porter, Nadine, Samantha, and an assortment of Moroccan breakfast dishes awaited his arrival. Samantha was picking at the remnants of her plate while she hovered over her phone. Porter was seated stiffly upright, his shirt unbuttoned and open while Nadine passed an eight-inch wand that looked like an elongated light bulb over his chest. The wand was plugged into a port on her tablet, and Nadine was watching its screen intently.

"Good morning," Gabriel said to no one in particular as the concierge shut the dining room doors to ensure their privacy. "How long have you three been up?"

"About two hours," Porter said, his posture and vocal strength both significantly improved from the night before.

Nadine quickly shushed him. "No talking while I'm scanning."

Porter gave Gabriel a quirky smile as he rolled his eyes.

"I'm surprised you haven't beaten down my door to get moving yet," Gabriel commented.

"We've got eyes on our final Shifa survivor," Samantha informed him. "She's alive and well and hanging around her home, which is apparently quite extravagant."

"Nothing suspicious to worry about?"

"Not unless you consider paying someone to walk, feed, groom, and massage your three Siberian Huskies suspicious." Samantha tossed a morsel of olive oil soaked bread into her mouth. "Personally, I'm a bit leery."

Gabriel chuckled as he grabbed an empty plate and loaded it with food. "Nate's still asleep?"

"Of course," Samantha replied. "That, or he snuck out before us to go chasing women around the market."

"Let's hope not," Gabriel said with another laugh.

Nadine's tablet beeped. She unplugged the wand and set it on the table before Porter, then swiped through several screens of what Gabriel assumed were test results.

"Well?" Porter asked as he buttoned his shirt.

Nadine turned the tablet where he- and in turn, Gabriel- could see. On display was a three-dimensional image of Porter's lungs, or the interior of them, anyway. Within each lung was a large black mass, one slightly bigger than the other, both consuming more than half of the available space. A red glow highlighted the outer half inch of each mass.

"Red's usually a bad thing," Gabriel said. "Are they reaching some sort of critical size?"

Nadine tossed the tablet onto the table in frustration. "They reached critical size weeks ago. The portion in red is new growth in the last forty-eight hours. Their expansion is accelerating."

Porter stared at the ominous image on the tablet. "Assuming that pace continues, how long am I looking at?"

"Eight to ten days, assuming an ideal diet, exercise, plenty of rest, and access to oxygen tanks," Nadine said, her eyes welling with tears. "If our current conditions don't improve, cut that estimate in half."

Porter reached for the tablet and turned it off. "That's why they're estimates," he said emotionlessly. Porter then turned his attention to Gabriel, moving on as if he hadn't just received terrible news. "I hear we've got a competitor in the field."

"Yeah. Byron Coltrain. Barbaric, ruthless, and quite the jackass to deal with."

Porter smiled. "I know all about Mr. Coltrain. He was next on my list if you turned me down."

Gabriel's eyes went wide with surprise.

"Don't look at me like that," Porter said. "You're the best. We both know that. But personality aside, Byron Coltrain's the second best. I had to consider him."

"Then let's be glad I didn't turn you down," Gabriel said. "You don't want to do business with that man." He turned to Samantha. "You've given his description to your Casablanca contacts, right?"

"Of course," Samantha replied. "And if they see him, they'll run interference as long as they can. But there's no guarantee they'll be successful."

"All the more reason to get moving once everyone's up," Gabriel said. He thought it was out of character for Porter not to be the one pushing for them to hit the road. Then again, Porter had just recovered from a pretty rough day, and his morning medical update wasn't exactly heartening. Maybe his mind was just in other places. "Any particular departure time you have in mind?"

"Samantha tells me it'll take four hours to get to Casablanca since we need to avoid the El Jadida region," Porter said. "Let's aim for noon. That way, we all have a chance to freshen up while still getting there with a few hours to spare before sundown."

Porter held Nadine's hand and nodded toward the dining room doors. Gabriel wondered if the freshening up time he had referenced was really just time he wanted to grant Nadine to deal with her emotional burden. It was obvious how much the two cared for one another, and though Porter was taking his revised expiration date in stride, Nadine was struggling much more with it. The two excused themselves, leaving Gabriel to eat in silence while Samantha continued focusing on whatever logistics she was arranging on her phone.

"What's up, boss?" Samantha said after a few moments.

"What's up with what?"

"You," Samantha clarified. "You look like something's bothering you."

Gabriel's initial instinct was denial. The mission was in a better spot this morning than it had been the previous day. They had gotten a clue from one Shifa survivor in the form of The Veiled Bird, they had discovered The Blessed Burial Ground, they had surveillance on their next target, and they had gotten a refreshing night's sleep. What could be wrong? And yet, once Samantha had asked the question, Gabriel knew something was indeed wrong. Something was bothering him deep inside, something he didn't understand, nor even realized until Samantha had called him out on it. What that something was, though, Gabriel wasn't sure.

Chapter Thirty-Eight
Casablanca

Bouskoura, Morocco
Ten Days Before The Sky Opened

The first three and a half hours of the drive from Safi to Casablanca were fairly uneventful. Porter continued reviewing his company's internal financial reports, this time scribbling digital notes in the margin of those reports as he fleshed out a game plan to restructure its revenue streams. Nadine read a book on her tablet, at least for the first hour, until her troubled mind forced her to give up and rest her eyes. Nate drove this time around, not because he wanted to, but because Gabriel felt more comfortable with Samantha's eyes- and potentially weapon sights- glued to the sky instead of the road. Meanwhile, Gabriel and Lisa resurrected the team's discussion of The Veiled Bird, though after three and a half hours they were still no closer to solving its meaning.

"I don't suppose your crew at Cannes Tower has cracked this thing?" Gabriel asked Porter.

He looked to Nadine, who opened her eyes and shook her head in the negative.

Gabriel sighed. "Well, for what it's worth, at least it's a clue we have that Byron doesn't."

Nate glanced back from the driver's seat. "I'm sorry, who?"

Lisa smiled sarcastically. "Our dear friend, Byron Coltrain."

"Byron's in Morocco?"

"Where have you been?" Samantha asked flatly.

Nate huffed. "Clearly not in the inner circle!"

"Or maybe just asleep while the rest of us discussed important matters," Samantha retorted. She then added, "you nitwit."

Nate flailed his right hand blindly behind him, playfully slapping at Samantha's arm. Already at DEFCON 1, Samantha instinctively grabbed his hand and twisted it, eliciting a yell from the front seat. The van swerved wildly as Nate tried to rip himself free of Samantha's grasp, sending the remaining passengers careening into the vise grip of their seatbelt retractor locks.

"Whoa, you two!" Gabriel shouted. "The rest of us would actually like to make it to Casablanca in one piece."

Samantha released Nate's hand. "Next time I cut it off."

Instead of cowering, Nate goaded her on by mimicking her in an unattractively high pitched voice. Lisa glared at him: *enough.* Their surrogate mother having stepped between them, Nate returned his eyes to the road and Samantha resumed her surveillance of the sky. Gabriel made a mental note to talk to both of them about their professionalism during missions once this one was over, though it wouldn't be the first time and he was already certain it wouldn't be the last.

After a few minutes of uneasy silence, Nate broke the tension in the air. "If Byron's here, it means he's on a job. So, who's he working for? Porter has us. The U.S. government has the military doing its bidding. Who else would be interested in the pendant?"

"Who wouldn't be?" Lisa asked.

Nate shook his head. "No, you're missing my point. Of course, anybody would be interested in the pendant at any given time. But I'm talking about right now. Porter's the only one with evidence suggesting the pendant was last seen in Morocco, and he's the only one who's collected records of the Shifa survivors. The government's been monitoring him, so we can chalk up their presence to following in our footsteps. But what about Byron? He didn't follow us to The Blessed Burial Ground. He beat us there, which means whoever's employing him has access to the same information we do... possibly more."

Gabriel shot Lisa a worried stare. They both knew Nate had made a good point. Until now, their only race had been against Porter's ticking biological clock. Now another competitor had entered that same race, and there was a good possibility he was already a lap ahead.

"I don't suppose you hired Byron?" Nate asked, eyeing Porter through the rearview mirror.

"That would be counterproductive, don't you think?" Porter replied.

Nate shrugged. "We build redundancies into hardware and software as failsafes all the time. Maybe Byron was your failsafe for this mission."

Porter blinked at Nate's reflection with deadpan eyes. "I didn't hire Byron Coltrain." He then looked out his window and muttered, "though I almost wish I had."

"I'm going to assume that comment was targeted at Nate and not the rest of us," Gabriel chimed in to keep the peace.

"Oh, it was," Nadine answered without bothering to open her eyes.

So much for Porter and Nate getting it out of their systems, Gabriel thought. *Oh well, there were bigger concerns to deal with.* "Porter, how would Byron have enough information to be a step ahead of us? Those scrolls in Cannes Tower were originals. Did you make any copies?"

"No."

"Are the digital analyses locked down on Cannes International servers?" Lisa asked.

"Every one of them," Porter replied. "I didn't even put copies on my personal devices. I access everything remotely through a secure tunnel into the company's intranet."

"And you're sure you've had no breaches?"

Porter glanced toward Nate with disdain. "Just a single *attempt.* But you're already aware of that one." Porter's face then eased as he swung his gaze to Gabriel. "My best guess is that someone paid off one of my technicians. I compensate them well above market to avoid corporate espionage, but there's no way to stop it completely. I bet whoever hired Mr. Coltrain wasn't even looking for information about the Pendant of God. They just stumbled across the right person with the right access at the right time."

"Sounds like some shit luck," Nate said.

"Actually," Gabriel cut in before Nate's commentary started another skirmish, "it's probably the best scenario we could hope for."

He saw Porter eye him curiously. "Think about it. If it was corporate espionage, then at best, Byron has the same information as us, not more. I thought we had an edge since we have The Veiled Bird, but since we sent a picture of it to the Old World, we'll have to assume it's been compromised as well."

"But Byron's got the jump on us to Casablanca," Lisa reminded Gabriel. "He may have already found the last survivor."

"I'm not worried about," Gabriel said. "I suspect he won't get very far with her, even if he has."

"How so?" Porter asked.

"Because he doesn't have you." Gabriel shot him a sad smile. "It's the one benefit of not being long for this world. Faras El Mehdi wanted to tell you his story if we had made it to Marrakech in time. Tareq Sabir, despite not making time to speak with you, left you a breadcrumb trail to aid in your journey. They tried to help you because they related to your plight. They wouldn't have related to the quest for fame and fortune of some cocky treasure hunter, and I don't think the final Shifa survivor will either."

Porter nodded. "I hope you're right."

"You'll find out soon enough," Nate called back from the driver's seat as Casablanca's skyline rose into view beyond the windshield. "We're here."

Chapter Thirty-Nine
Trust Issues

Casablanca, Morocco
Ten Days Before The Sky Opened

It only took twenty more minutes for the team to locate the home of Adila Benkirane, the last of the Shifa survivors. She lived in the penthouse of an upscale twenty-story apartment complex just off the North Atlantic Ocean. Gabriel could see why Samantha called it luxurious. The penthouse consumed the upper three floors of the complex, with seamless glass windows on all sides and a concrete balcony that jutted outward toward the ocean. Gabriel identified what appeared to be sun umbrellas poking up from the balcony, indicating there was likely a swimming pool up there. He could also see exercise equipment lining its adjacent glass window and a spiral staircase behind the equipment than spanned the penthouse's three floors. The glare of the late afternoon sun made seeing anything else impossible, but Gabriel could fill in the blanks. Adila Benkirane had obviously done well for herself in life.

The apartment complex itself was well kept. Its walls were bright white, something likely only achievable will frequent cleanings given its proximity to the ocean. The complex was surrounded by meticulously trimmed landscaping that wasn't overbearing and instead blended well with Casablanca's city aesthetic. Gabriel spotted two doormen monitoring the building's front entrance, and wouldn't have been surprised if more awaited on the inside. The only parking near the apartment complex was blocked off for valet service, so Gabriel instructed Samantha to find the closest street meter that would give them a visual angle on the entrance.

"Porter, Nadine," Gabriel said as Samantha pulled into a spot that met his demands, "I think you should try getting access to Mrs. Benkirane first. Things didn't go smoothly when we tried to see Tareq Sabir as a group. Mrs. Benkirane might be more receptive to just the two of you."

"Agreed," Porter said.

"Samantha, has your contact confirmed she's still home?"

Samantha nodded. "I received a text about five minutes ago. I also told him to grab an expensive dinner on our dime for his efforts."

"Great." Gabriel turned his attention back to Porter. "Make your case. If she's willing to speak with all of us, signal and we'll be there. If she's only willing to speak with you, be sure to take good notes."

Porter smiled. "That's one of Nadine's specialties."

After a brief eye roll from Nadine, the two stepped out of the cargo van, straightened their clothes, and set off for Adila Benkirane's apartment complex. The rest of the team watched with anticipation, none of them certain whether the final Shifa survivor would even entertain their visit. Porter had tried reaching out to her in advance of their trip, but he could never get past her servants to speak with Adila directly. Unfortunately, still clueless as to what The Veiled Bird was supposed to tell them, Adila Benkirane was the team's last shot at avoiding a needle in a haystack hunt through Spain.

"Nate?" Gabriel asked once he was certain Porter and Nadine weren't doubling back. "Can we have an unbiased conversation?"

"Sure, boss."

Gabriel wasn't looking to mince words, so he asked what he wanted to know directly. "Do you trust Porter?"

Nate laughed instinctively before realizing Gabriel was being serious. "Objectively?"

"Objectively."

Nate thought for a moment before answering. "No."

"Why not?"

"There's too much smoke," the tech engineer replied. "First, it was the white lie about the pendant drawing. Then it was his admission of underhanded business practices. Now we've got the unexplainable presence of Byron in the region. And let's not forget-"

"Oh God, please don't say it," Samantha muttered.

"-he did cheat me out of that engineering competition when we were kids, regardless of what he claims now." Samantha shook her head in disbelief, but Nate ignored her. "Where there's that much smoke, there's bound to be fire."

"Do you think he's lying about his illness?" Gabriel asked.

Nate puckered his lips in contemplation. "No. I think that part of the story is real. I've seen the bloody handkerchiefs and how he looked like he was about to keel over on us in the desert last night. He's not faking that."

"What's on your mind?" Lisa asked Gabriel.

"I don't know," he replied as he watched Porter and Nadine converse with one of Adila's doormen. "I have this feeling we're overlooking something. Maybe it's Porter. Maybe it's something else altogether."

"My money's on Porter," Nate said. "He may be dying, and he may truly be searching for the pendant to prevent that from happening, but he's also hiding something from us. Like I said, too much smoke."

The team sat quietly for a moment as Porter and Nadine's conversation with the doorman continued. They seemed to have convinced the doorman to contact Adila, for he motioned for them to wait while he exposed a cell phone and dialed.

"We could find out," Lisa said, breaking the silence. "Nate's still got a transmitter in Cannes Tower. We could activate it and see if there's anything concerning on his network."

"Two problems with that," Gabriel responded. "One, we don't actually know that Porter's keeping any secrets from us. Well... any secrets related to this mission, anyway. Two, once we burn that transmitter, we won't be able to turn to it again should the need arise."

"Three problems, actually," Nate chimed in. "Once we burn that transmitter, Porter will find out. You can kiss our contract goodbye at that point, even if he turns out to be innocent."

Gabriel chewed at the inside of his cheek as his mind did laps around his skull. "We need another way..."

"I've got an idea," Samantha said. "If Porter is hiding something, he's got to know Nate is the one most likely to expose it. Let's give him an opportunity to *reduce his risk*, so to speak."

Nate looked at her curiously. "Are you suggesting we give Porter an opportunity to kill me?"

Samantha shrugged. "Well… he doesn't have to *kill* you. We just need to set up a situation in which he could… I don't know… let you die?"

Nate blinked slowly, as if waiting for her to retract the suggestion. When she didn't, he simply stated, "I'm not on board with this idea."

"What?" Samantha asked innocently. "We run into life and death situations all the time on these missions. Let's just make sure you run into one and leave Porter to decide what to do about it."

Nate blinked slowly again. "I reiterate my position-"

"Samantha has a good point," Lisa cut in. "If Porter's the monster you think he is, he should take advantage of an opportunity to take you out of play. Then we'd know and we could pull out of this mission with our consciences clear."

"*You* could pull out," Nate said. "I'd be dead."

Gabriel sighed. "We wouldn't really let you die, Nate. We just need to find the right situation-"

Samantha shushed him. Porter and Nadine were on their way back to the van. Unfortunately, by the looks on their faces, the conversation with the doorman hadn't ended well.

Chapter Forty
Stonewalled

Casablanca, Morocco
Ten Days Before The Sky Opened

"She won't see us," Porter said as soon as he opened the van's side door. "The doorman relayed my request, but she denied it. I asked to speak with Mrs. Benkirane directly, but it was no use. We're being stonewalled."

"So now what?" Lisa asked.

Determined not to let morale fall, Gabriel answered before anyone else had the chance. "Now we go to Spain." He knew he needed to give them more than that, so he thought on his feet. "We'll hit the cities closest to Morocco first. We'll split up, check out the local bars and hotspots, and keep our ears peeled for any stories consistent with visits to the pendant. Maybe someone shares a tall tale of an injury healing extraordinarily fast or of randomly stumbling into a small fortune... things others would normally shrug off as bullshit or luck, but which we know could have a more pertinent explanation." Seeing the doubt on everyone else's faces, Gabriel added desperately, "we can even ask about The Veiled Bird. Maybe it has local meaning we aren't privy to. Someone could see the drawing and steer us straight to the pendant. We'll make copies so everyone has one to show around."

Again, the return stares were doubtful, but it wasn't as if the team had another choice. They couldn't force Adila Benkirane to see them, nor could they force her to tell them what she knew about the pendant, even if they managed to arrange an unauthorized meeting outside of her home. And without Adila, Morocco had no more useful information to yield about the Pendant of God. It was time to move on, as hard as that might be to accept.

Without acknowledging Gabriel's suggestions, Porter helped Nadine into the van. Then, as he stepped up, he broke into a bloody coughing fit, directing his expulsions to the surface of the nearby street. The tarry red substance that splatted across the ground stood vibrantly apart from the otherwise clean surface. Nadine hopped out of the van to help as Gabriel did the same, but before either of them could assist Porter, an unlikely set of hands fell on his shoulders. It was the doorman Porter and Nadine had spoken with. In an unexpected gesture of kindness, the doorman removed a cloth from his pocket and helped wipe the blood from Porter's mouth.

"*Mr. Cannes,*" Gabriel heard the doorman's voice translated in his earpiece. "*Please be patient. I have monitored Mrs. Benkirane's door for many years. She sees no one seeking the pendant until she vets their motives. She is probably vetting you as we speak. Do not aggravate your condition with worry.*"

Porter looked toward the penthouse, peering as though attempting to see Adila Benkirane watching him. Gabriel followed Porter's gaze, but the sun's reflection off the penthouse's windows blinded him.

"I pay a lot of money to keep my personal business private," Porter said. He waited for Nadine to translate before adding, "she won't find what she's looking for."

The doorman smiled at Porter's naivety. "*Mr. Cannes, you are far from being the only one in this world with money and power. If Mrs. Benkirane wants to learn the truth behind your visit to our corner of the world, she will find it.*"

Porter looked at the doorman, then back to the penthouse, then at the doorman again. "How long do these things usually take?"

"*At least a few hours,*" the doorman answered. "*Go to your hotel and take your mind off of things. Let your lungs, and your heart, rest. If your desire to find the pendant is genuine, which I believe it is, Mrs. Benkirane will send for you.*"

The doorman's actions and words were a far cry from the stonewalling posture he had assumed mere minutes earlier. "I assume you don't normally intervene when Mrs. Benkirane sends people away," Gabriel said. "Why help us?"

After Nadine translated, the doorman turned his gaze to the

splattering of blood on the street next to the van. *"I watched my father die of lung cancer when I was a boy. It's a terrible way to die... and a terrible way to live in the months leading to death. I don't wish anyone to go through that."*

The doorman looked behind him, toward the apartment complex, and shuffled nervously.

Afraid he was running out of time for inquiry, Gabriel asked, "did another man come here today asking about the pendant?"

"If you're referring to Mr. Coltrain," the doorman said, *"yes. But Mrs. Benkirane turned him away as well. His intentions do not appear to be pure, so I don't believe she will send for him as she will you."*

That was reassuring to hear. Gabriel nodded in acceptance of the doorman's answer.

"I've been away from my post too long," the doorman then said with another nervous glance towards the apartment complex. *"Please excuse me, and remember what I said about having patience."*

Porter thanked the doorman for his kindness. As he jogged back to the building. Gabriel, Porter, and Nadine piled back into the van. Lisa shot Gabriel a *what was that about?* glance, to which he responded with an uncertain shrug. The doorman's intervention seemed heartfelt. And under any other circumstances, his suggestion would have been simple to follow. An evening of relaxation in Casablanca was certainly appealing after the way the team had spent their previous night. But enjoying the evening required ignoring Porter's rapidly ticking biological clock, and spending hours waiting on a call that might never come was a gamble that carried high risk. It was questionable whether taking a similar gamble the night before had been worth it, at least regarding the mission. Gabriel wouldn't make the call this time.

"What do you want to do?" He asked Porter.

Porter stared out his window, looking toward Adila Benkirane's penthouse. Gabriel wondered if he could see the Shifa survivor up there, staring back at him, assessing Porter's motives and deciding whether she would share whatever knowledge she held with him. After a few moments of hesitation, Porter turned his sullen eyes to the team.

"Let's go to the hotel. First round of drinks is on me."

Chapter Forty-One
Patience

Casablanca, Morocco
Ten Days Before The Sky Opened

Gabriel sat back in a poolside recliner and sipped a soda. Lisa was already stretched out beside him, a long-island iced tea on the table next to her as she bathed in the warmth of the early evening Moroccan sun. A few chairs down, Porter was ignoring his drink while busying his brain with what Gabriel assumed was work. Nadine was nearby, taking a dip with the other tourists in their hotel's luxurious pool. Nate was in the pool too, playing hide and seek with a group of kids among its arched stone walkways and manmade waterfalls. Samantha had found an isolated spot near the pool's far end, where she sat with her feet dangling in the water while she toiled away on her phone, no doubt making preparations for their eventual transition to Spain.

"Mind if we talk business for a bit?" Lisa asked as Gabriel set his soda down.

"Business before pleasure," he replied.

"The Blessed Burial Ground... did you notice anything odd while we were there?"

"You mean other than the flourishing biome and pre-labeled burial vaults?" Gabriel thought hard for a moment. "Nope, can't say anything's standing out."

"Not even the arrangement of the vaults?"

Gabriel recalled the imagery of The Blessed Burial Ground in his mind. There had been three sets of vaults, one in the main chamber and one in each side chamber. The set in the main chamber had three rows, spanning from the entry stairway to the bold blue waterfall at the other end. Jalal Ismaili had been decorating Faras El Mehdi's vault at the end of the first row. Tareq Sabir's family had been mourning at the end of the second. At the end of the third-

Gabriel turned to Lisa as her implication dawned on him. "They mirror the order of death."

"It sure looks that way," Lisa said. "We'd have to match the names and order of the other vaults to official death certificates to know for certain, but it would be one hell of a coincidence if not."

Gabriel put on his devil's advocate hat. "Assuming Jalal arrived at The Blessed Burial Ground before Tareq Sabir's family, could he have moved Faras El Mehdi's burial vault into the first position? Then the Sabir family could have done the same with their vault, by default leaving the only empty vault for the last position?"

"Sure," Lisa said, "if they had all received a healthy dose of gamma radiation beforehand."

Gabriel smirked at her. "I don't recall any tools or mechanisms that could have shifted the vaults around."

Lisa shook her head.

"So what are we saying? The Shifa survivors' order of death is predetermined?"

"Barring any other rational explanation." Lisa took a sip of her drink. "But the evidence aligns. Jalal told us Faras El Mehdi acted as though he could tell he would die soon. Tareq Sabir started making preparations for his own death days ago, then set off on a trek to his grave on the very day death came for him. Again, that's a lot of coincidence to swallow."

Gabriel couldn't refute her analysis, and if coincidence had somehow defied probability, then so be it. The world was full of random events that just happened to align in coincidental ways from time to time. But predetermination was different. It wasn't a scientific concept, and Gabriel's own experience had shown that science generally explained most things, no matter how odd they may initially appear. Then again, if the Book of Damien was to be believed, the Pendant of God wasn't purely of scientific origin, and therefore predetermination fit right in to its story.

"Let's say their deaths are predetermined," Gabriel suggested. "How does it affect our mission? Beyond evidence of the pendant's religious connections?"

Lisa shrugged. "I'm still working that out." She sat up and removed her lightweight pool robe, revealing a dark swimsuit that was flattering to her body while being respectful of the local culture. "And I'm going to keep working it out from in there."

Gabriel watched her walked to the edge of the pool and dive in, her body piercing its surface as gracefully as a dolphin. He smiled. About twenty yards out, Gabriel saw Nate on the run- if that's what you can call it when ungracefully treading through chest-high water- from the group of kids he'd been playing with. Nate spotted Nadine and used her, much to her protest, as his next hiding spot. The kids were on top of him moments later, swarming Nate and taking Nadine down with him, soaking what had been a dry head of hair until that point. Nate took off 'running' again, not from the kids, but from a furious Nadine, who hollered a variety of obscenities in his wake.

Gabriel shook his head and noticed Nadine's yelling had broken Porter's attention from his work. Gabriel took the opportunity to meander over to his old friend. He sat nearby and motioned to the blueprints in Porter's lap. "Those are the same ones you were looking at on the plane, right?"

"Yep," Porter replied. "It's a prototype for a new line of construction equipment I'm thinking of launching. I brought it along in case I had time to kill, but now that I'll need to pivot my business more into the commercial and retail sectors..."

"You think Cannes International can become a big player in the construction space?" Gabriel asked.

"We already are," Porter told him. "It was never part of my master plan, but do you remember that disaster in Eden about four years ago?"

Gabriel nodded. "How could I forget? It was all over the national news for weeks."

"Well, the government put out a call to all contractors with excess capacity to help rebuild the city as quickly as possible. We were already toying with the idea of modernizing construction equipment when we got wind of the request, so we finalized a fleet of prototypes in our R&D lab and sent them to assist." Porter smiled proudly. "Our equipment did twice the work of the other contractors in half the time."

"Hmph," Gabriel said. "I didn't hear about that."

"You wouldn't have," Porter explained. "Remember, we were dealing with a fleet of rushed prototypes. We didn't have nearly the presence in Eden that more established companies in the field did. But the results were solid. Over the next two years, we shifted resources into our construction division and carved out a moderate slice of the commercial market. Today, we've got more requests for our equipment than we can push off the production line."

Gabriel glanced at the blueprints again, making note of the mechanical claw that seemed to be their focal point. "So this thing is..."

Porter pushed the blueprints aside. "Honestly, not very interesting." He grabbed a brown satchel from the ground next to him. The satchel sagged with weight as Porter swung it onto his lap. "What you'll find more interesting is what's in here."

Before Porter could share the contents of the satchel with Gabriel, a hotel concierge approached him with a silver tray containing a tented note. Porter took the note, thanked the concierge, then read its contents.

"Please tell me it's good news," Gabriel said.

Porter smiled and passed him the note. It didn't say much, but the few words it contained meant volumes:

Mrs. Benkirane requests your company.

10:00am. Don't be late.

Chapter Forty-Two
Adila Benkirane

Casablanca, Morocco
Nine Days Before The Sky Opened

The team was loaded in the van and ready to go by nine-thirty. Upon learning of Adila Benkirane's request the evening before, Gabriel called an early end to the team's recreation time. Porter arranged for an expedited dinner in one of the hotel's conference rooms so they could strategize while they ate. Gabriel opened the discussion by suggesting Samantha get eyes on Adila's residence again to ensure she didn't slip away during the night. But Samantha pointed out that she couldn't rely on the contacts she had used that day. They didn't warn her that Byron had visited Adila before the team's arrival, which meant Byron or one of his associates had bought their loyalty. Samantha offered to monitor the residence herself, but Gabriel shot the idea down. He didn't know what their day would bring once they spoke with Adila, so he wanted the entire team rested and on their A-game.

With Byron fresh on his mind, Gabriel next suggested that everyone pack their gear before going to bed. If Adila gave them the location of the pendant, there wouldn't be time to return to the hotel. Any second wasted was another second they risked Byron finding the pendant before them. Since Gabriel didn't know what Byron's intentions toward the pendant were, the conservative assumption was that those intentions would interfere with saving Porter's life.

Gabriel asked whether anyone had updated thoughts on The Veiled Bird, which no one did, and shared Lisa's theory about the Shifa survivors having a predetermined order of death. That struck

Porter's interest, but Gabriel suspected not because he had derived some impact to their mission. Porter was seeking the pendant's blessing, just as the Shifa survivors had done before him. Would he receive a predetermined date of death along with that blessing? If so, for what purpose?

The rest of the meal was spent running through a checklist of supplies and Samantha laying out travel routes in each major cardinal and ordinal direction so they wouldn't ˆwaste time once they knew their destination. When the meal was over, everyone returned to their rooms to pack and get sleep. Now Samantha watched the clock as she started the van's engine and drove toward Adila Benkirane's apartment complex. They arrived with time to spare, found street parking near the spot they had used the prior day, and unloaded, leaving most of their gear behind as not to come across as too intimidating to their civilian host.

The doorman from the day before greeted Porter as the team approached and confirmed Adila was willing to have everyone present for their conversation. He then escorted them to the first floor of Adila's penthouse, where Adila waited in a large sitting room with ample space for the team to spread out comfortably. The glass windows of the penthouse negated the need for indoor lighting during the day, and Gabriel noticed how the bright light combined with mostly white and stainless steel decor to give Adila's penthouse an almost sterile-like quality.

"Mrs. Benkirane," Porter opened the conversation, "thank you for having us. I'd like to introduce some good friends of mine. This is-"

"Gabriel Dunne," Adila cut him off in perfect English before Nadine started translating. "And his wife, Lisa, their team, and your assistant, Nadine Walsh. You can save the pleasantries, Mr. Cannes. I've done my homework."

"Of course you have," Porter replied. "I assume you know why I'm here, then?"

"You seek the Pendant of God," Adila said. "And since you've found your way to my door, you've no doubt deduced that I sought the pendant myself so many years ago."

"And received its blessing," Porter added.

Adila nodded in confirmation.

"I'm dying," Porter told her. Gabriel noticed he had a difficult time getting the words out, as if he still didn't fully accept it himself. "I never expected to have so little time, and there's so much left that I want to accomplish."

Adila eyed him as an experienced judge might eye a defendant pleading their case before the court.

"If you know anything about the pendant's current location," Porter continued, "we could really use some guidance. I'd offer you money or some other compensation..." Porter looked around the penthouse. "Obviously, you have no need. But you would have my sincerest appreciation."

"My sources tell me you don't have many days left," Adila stated bluntly.

"That's correct."

"What makes you think you can even get to the pendant in time?"

Porter shrugged. "It's the only option I have left. I'll either get there... or die trying."

Adila turned her judgmental gaze to Gabriel and the team. She didn't speak, but Gabriel could see she was incorporating their presence into her mental calculus. After a few moments, she looked back at Porter.

"A duty accepted by all who receive the pendant's blessing is to protect its whereabouts," Adila said with an air of elderly wisdom. "We guide those deserving of it to its next location, and divert those undeserving to where they belong. It's why I vet all of my guests so carefully." Adila licked her wrinkled lips as if formulating what she would say next in real time. "Mr. Cannes, if you had come to me with only your plight, I might have been willing to be your guide. But I know your secrets. You hired treasure hunters to find the pendant for you. These are not the sorts that belong anywhere near its glory."

"Please," Porter pleaded as he shot a worried glance at Gabriel, "I hired them because they're my friends, and I knew I couldn't do this alone. We go back years. They aren't here to steal the pendant. They're here to save my life."

Gabriel tried to add an objective voice to the effort. "Mrs. Benkirane, you say you've done your homework. If that's true, then you know what type of people my team and I are, and you know we respect and protect historical relics. Porter's not lying. We're here for him, not the pendant."

Adila pursed her lips in contemplation. She looked back and forth between Porter and Gabriel, updating her calculus with these new claims. After a few moments, her eyes settled on Gabriel and his team. "If you really are here for Mr. Cannes, then am I to assume you're willing to accept his fate, regardless of what that fate might be?"

Gabriel wasn't sure how literally he should take the question. Was Adila asking Gabriel if he would accept Porter's death, should his death be the mission's outcome? Or was she asking if he and the team were willing to die along with Porter, should the mission fail? The two interpretations carried quite different implications. However, Gabriel's quick assessment of Adila suggested she wasn't the type to take kindly to requests for clarification, nor was she the type to ignore hesitation in response, so he spoke without additional thought. "Yes."

As if taking a cue, Lisa added, "yes."

Then Samantha and Nadine spoke in unison. "Yes."

"Hell no," said Nate, who promptly received an elbow to the gut from Samantha. "I mean... I trust my team. So I suppose, yes."

Adila's gaze shifted to Porter. She seemed to be somewhere between pleased and disturbed by the team's near-unanimous response. Her eyes grew dark as her lips formed a mischievous smile. "So be it."

Chapter Forty-Three
Breakthrough

Casablanca, Morocco
Nine Days Before The Sky Opened

Adila asked a servant to bring her a tablet. She ushered the team to the next room over, where a ninety-inch television was mounted to the wall. Adila wirelessly linked her tablet to the television, mirroring its screen, and opened her map app in satellite view. The app automatically honed in on their current location, but Adila zoomed out enough to view Casablanca as a whole, then scrolled northeast along the coast of Morocco, over the Alboran Sea, and finally, the Balearic Sea. There, Adila zoomed in on the Balearic Islands, and continued zooming until only the relatively small Isla de Cabrera filled the screen. Its surface was covered in greenery, and Gabriel could see a small tree icon on the map with a label that read *Cabrera Archipelago Maritime-Terrestrial National Park*.

"A national park?" He asked. "Isn't that a bit public?"

"You must not know your national parks," Adila replied. "The Cabrera National Park consumes the entire Cabrera island. There is no permanent settlement in the area and visitation is limited. The natural terrain provides the perfect cover for an underground village."

"Underground?" Lisa asked.

"Oh yes. The pendant doesn't always reside in a surface level village, especially not in modern times when satellite imagery could easily expose that village."

Lisa stepped closer to the television. "According to the map's scale, the island is about six square miles. The entrance to the village could be anywhere. I don't suppose you can get us closer?"

Adila zoomed in on the mid-northern section of the island, where manmade structures were barely visible against the natural terrain. "This is Cabrera Castle. It dates back to the fourteenth century, when it was used as a watchtower to protect Cabrera from pirates. Today, it's the primary tourist attraction for those who visit the island."

"I'm guessing you aren't going to tell us the entrance to the underground village is there," Gabriel said.

"No," Adila confirmed. "But I'll share what I do know: illuminate the castle, and the path to the pendant will be revealed."

Gabriel waited for more, but it became clear after a full minute of silence that Adila had no more to give.

"That's it?" Nate eventually asked. "Some cryptic message about illuminating the castle? You want us to throw a flashlight in there or something?"

Adila blinked at him as if he were an insolent child. Gabriel stepped between them, cutting off Adila's line of sight and giving Nate a signal to shut his mouth.

"We're grateful for the help," Gabriel said.

"Yes," Porter agreed, "very grateful."

Adila frowned. "You shouldn't be. You're playing a very dangerous game, Mr. Cannes. The Pendant of God can be a blessing or a curse. Consider that before you continue your journey."

Gabriel watched the exchange between Porter and Adila curiously. Was she still concerned by his use of treasure hunters to find the pendant? Was there something more she found on Porter that she wasn't saying out loud? Could it be the secret fire that fueled Nate's observed smoke? It was clear Gabriel wouldn't get an answer right now, for Adila had already chosen to communicate her true message with a silent stare.

"I'll mull over your advice," Porter said, summoning his inner businessman. "Regardless of what happens next, I am appreciative of your assistance."

Adila smiled weakly and gave him a nod of her head, her indication that their business was complete. The team followed one of Adila's servants to her door and then to the building elevator, which they rode down to ground level. Gabriel, Porter, and Lisa each thanked Adila's doorman once more for his intervention the evening before. The team then returned to their van, where Samantha gave them a quick rundown of what she found on her phone during the brief change in location.

"Cabrera is officially part of Spain, so that tracks with our assumption about the pendant's next destination. It's remote, similar to prior pendant villages like Shifa. And as Adila Benkirane said, the entire island, as well as several hundred square miles of nearby sea, falls under the protection of the Cabrera National Park."

"How do we get there?" Gabriel asked.

"Officially, we can take a tourist boat from the Colonia de Sant Jordi on Mallorca," Samantha told him. "It's a well-developed island just north of Cabrera."

"But?" Lisa asked.

"But tourist boats make day trips, and by the sounds of it, we need to be on Cabrera at night. There's also no guarantee we can get open seats on such short notice." Samantha swiped to a new browser tab on her phone. "We can take our own boat, but legally speaking, we would need to acquire appropriate permits to visit Cabrera and drop anchor offshore."

"And if we don't bother with the permits?" Porter asked.

"Then we try not to get caught."

Porter looked at Gabriel, who in turn looked at Lisa, who gave a nod of approval. They didn't have time for legal formalities. Nate fired up the van's engine.

"Give me a direction," he told Samantha.

"Northeast. It'll take four hours to get to Tangier. From there, we'll take a ninety-minute ferry across the Straight of Gibraltar, then we'll have another six hours' drive to Alicante. There's a port there that can give us a straight-shot to the Balearic islands. I should be able to have a Leviathan watercraft delivered by the time we arrive."

"Wait," Nadine spoke up. "Couldn't we just fly to Mallorca and take a boat from there?"

"It'll put us back on the military's radar," Gabriel informed her. "We could get intercepted before we ever hit the Balearic Sea."

"What's the time differential?" Porter asked.

"Not as much as you'd think," Samantha said, checking her phone. "There're no direct flights from Casablanca to Mallorca. The best we could do is pass through Madrid, putting our flight time at about five hours. Add on two more hours to catch the next flight out of Casablanca and we're only looking at about a four to five hour total difference."

Porter looked at Gabriel, this time with a sense of urgency and determination in his eyes. "It's your turn to make the call."

Gabriel gnawed at his lower lip as he considered the alternatives. "We take a five hour hit now... or we risk a far longer hit when we reach Madrid or Mallorca, one that could end the mission altogether."

"There's something else to consider," Samantha added. "If we fly, we'll also have to abandon our van and gear. We'd be limited to whatever we could take on the plane. I won't be able to restock us on such short notice."

Gabriel took the additional cost into consideration and stared back at Porter. "You think you've got an extra five hours in you?"

Porter nodded, but with much more uncertainty than Gabriel was used to getting from him.

"Okay," Gabriel said with a heavy sigh. "Nate, let's get moving."

Nate put the van into gear, but a loud pounding on the driver's side window halted him from pulling into the street. It was Adila's doorman, and he had that same nervous shuffle about him as he had had the day before. Nate rolled down the window.

"Mr. Cannes, Mr. Dunne," the doorman's voice repeated through Gabriel's earpiece translator, *"I thought you should know. That man you asked about yesterday... Mr. Coltrain? He visited Mrs. Benkirane again this morning. She showed him the same map she showed you."*

Gabriel and Lisa shared a concerned glance. They knew what this meant, and the doorman's next words confirmed it.

"He has a two-hour head start on you."

Chapter Forty-Four
Lingering Questions

Badriouene, Morocco
Nine Days Before The Sky Opened

Nate slowed the van as the team passed through Badriouene, a small village about ten miles southwest of Tangier. It was a nice change of pace from careening along the Moroccan coast like a bat out of hell for the past three hours. The next ferry between Tangier and Algeciras, the port city on Spain's side of the Straight of Gibraltar, was scheduled to leave at four o'clock. Samantha had already booked reservations online to avoid ticket queues, but Nate didn't want to take any chances they would run into traffic or some other unforeseen delay that would cause them to miss their ride.

Conversations along way to Tangier ranged from making preparations to reach Cabrera, to whether the team would get any sleep that night, to how Cabrera linked to The Veiled Bird, and, most curiously, to why Adila would give Byron an advantage in reaching the pendant first. As far as preparations went, Samantha confirmed Porter would spend the one and a half million dollars plus fuel and delivery it would take for her to procure a Leviathan watercraft in Alicante. Porter didn't blink an eye at the request. It wasn't like a million and a half was detrimental to his wealth, but Gabriel sensed there was something more behind his agreeability. Porter seemed *emptier* than when they had first started this mission, and Gabriel wondered whether the sacrifice of his company's future had taken a greater emotional toll than Porter let on. It would explain why all other expenses seemed trivial at this point.

Regarding sleep for the night, Gabriel had already done the mental math, and it didn't look promising. The team would arrive in Alicante just before midnight. It would take between one and two hours to reach Cabrera and find a safe spot to anchor. Sunrise was around seven o'clock, so the team would then have five hours to figure out how to illuminate Cabrera Castle before they lost their opportunity and got stuck in a holding pattern until sunset rolled back around. Realistically, there was no time for sleep, which Nadine didn't take well when Gabriel shared his calculations. She insisted Porter couldn't go that long without rest, and it took Porter reminding her he may not have twelve hours to spare waiting out the next day to get her to back down from her crusade.

Lisa, meanwhile, stewed over the connection between Cabrera and The Veiled Bird. Though she already knew the definition of the word *veil*, she looked it up in an online dictionary to ensure there was no alternate meaning of which she should be aware. As expected, the dictionary defined a veil as a cover, or something meant to conceal. Given their clue from Adila Benkirane, Lisa knew it was probable the underground village housing the pendant was concealed in some fashion, so she checked that off of her connection list.

Lisa then focused on the 'bird' aspect of Faras El Mehdi's message. Some brief web searching showed that the European Union had officially declared the Cabrera Archipelago Maritime-Terrestrial National Park as a Special Protection Area, or SPA, for seabirds. Maybe The Veiled Bird was Faras' way of telling Porter to look for a hidden village among birds? It didn't align perfectly, but Lisa's experience with treasure hunting clues was that they rarely did. She shared her findings with the team, and everyone agreed it was the best explanation they had heard yet.

Last, there was Byron. Gabriel couldn't stop asking himself why Adila had given him a leg up on the team. She clearly had it out for treasure hunters. Did she distrust Porter so much that she was willing to give a rival treasure hunter an advantage over him? If so, why? If not... Gabriel couldn't make much sense of her decision. As Nate drove through Badriouene, he confronted Porter directly about it.

"What's the deal with Mrs. Benkirane wanting you to drop your pursuit of the pendant?"

Porter shook his head. "I've got no idea."

Gabriel studied his face, but it was hard to get a read beyond anything but his deteriorating condition, which was visibly accelerating despite two good nights' sleep. "Is there something you need to tell me? We're getting closer to our goal, but I don't know what obstacles lie between us and it. If there's anything you haven't been straightforward about-"

"I've told you everything of relevance," Porter said. "Mrs. Benkirane probably discovered unrelated things about me- maybe the way I do business or spend my money- that she didn't care for. Whatever it was, it didn't stop her from guiding us onward."

"Yeah," Gabriel agreed, "but she sent Byron ahead of us. At best, he's going the same route we are, in which case we'll likely wind up on the same ferry to Algeciras. At worst, he's not worried about flying, and his two-hour head start is going to turn into a seven hour one. If he gets to the pendant before we do-"

"I'm as good as dead," Porter said bluntly. "I know. But there's nothing we can do about that now. I just need to hope I made the right choice in hiring you instead of him, that seven hours won't be enough lead time for him to solve Mrs. Benkirane's clue before we have a shot at it."

Gabriel frowned. "Byron's good..."

"But you're better," Porter reminded him. "Don't worry about Byron Coltrain or why Mrs. Benkirane felt the need to saddle our mission with an additional challenge. Just do your job, and I trust you'll get me through this."

Gabriel sighed, the uneasy tension in his chest refusing to relent. His gut told him there was significance in Adila's decision to send Byron ahead. There was something he wasn't seeing, something that could potentially endanger the mission, and worse, the lives of his team. But Porter was right; there was nothing Gabriel or anyone else could do about it right now. And every thought spent on Byron Coltrain was another thought not spent preparing for the mystery that awaited on Cabrera. Gabriel needed to get his head in the game.

Chapter Forty-Five
Reunion

Tangier, Morocco
Nine Days Before The Sky Opened

About thirty minutes later, Nate pulled the van into the port of Tangier. Samantha guided him to their ferry, which had already begun boarding. Nate joined the line of vehicles pulling into the ferry's main hold, and after about fifteen minutes of creeping down the dock at a snail's pace, he parked in a growing grid of passenger cars and trucks interspersed with the occasional commercial vehicle. Once their van was surrounded and they were clear to exit safely, Gabriel opened a side door.

"I'm going to take a short walk," he told the rest of the team. "I need to clear my head. We have another long ride on the other side of the strait, so you guys might want to stretch your legs, too."

Lisa shot Gabriel an *are you all right?* glance, to which Gabriel responded with a muted smile. He was all right, but he was also finding it difficult to concentrate on solving the Cabrera Castle puzzle. His brain was pulling him in too many directions, and Gabriel thought some fresh ocean air would do him good. He stepped out of the van and followed signage to a pedestrian deck, where a crowd of other passengers had already congregated. Gabriel weaved his way to the edge of the deck and stood with his arms outstretched before him and palms wrapped firmly around the perimeter railing. He inhaled deeply, the saltiness of the humid air noticeable to his senses as it filled his lungs. Gabriel allowed the air to permeate his body before exhaling slowly and repeating the process.

He stared out at the Strait of Gibraltar. Shortly after the ferry departed, it would pass the Rock of Gibraltar, once believed to be the edge of the known world. How far humanity had come since then... it left Gabriel wondering how his world might change should the team find the Pendant of God. He supposed it depended on whether the pendant lived up to its reputation, but if so... Gabriel shook his head. He didn't need another thing to ponder over right now. He needed to focus on Cabrera, and on whatever preparations he could make to ensure efficient and effective progress toward solving Adila's clue.

"Well, look who we have here," an all-too-familiar voice said, instantly shattering Gabriel's peaceful excursion. "You must be taking the scenic route to Bilbao."

Byron knew damn well Gabriel wasn't headed to Bilbao; this was just part of the game.

"At least I'm headed toward the right country," Gabriel replied as he faced his nemesis. "Did they move Giza out of Egypt since the last time I was there?"

Byron smiled with eyes that said *touché*. "Last minute change of plans. I got a better offer."

"Did that better offer take you by the penthouse of Adila Benkirane this morning?"

Byron joined Gabriel at the railing and rested his forearms as he leaned to see the water below. "We both know where I was this morning. No sense playing coy about it now." He turned his eyes to Gabriel. "So, how do we resolve this little conflict of ours?"

Gabriel shrugged. "There's no conflict. There's just a race and to the victor goes the spoils. Speaking of, why aren't you in the air right now? You could have beaten us to Cabrera easily."

"And get blown out of the sky or sea by the U.S. military? No thanks."

Byron's response caught Gabriel by surprise. How had he known the U.S. military was a clandestine contestant in their sprint to the finish line?

Before Gabriel could devise an answer, Byron continued. "I heard you had a little run-in yourself. Good thing you had Samantha with you. What I wouldn't give to have someone so competent on my team."

Gabriel's eyes narrowed. It was one thing for Byron to know about the military; it was another thing altogether for him to know about Gabriel's encounter with them two days earlier.

"Luckily for me, whatever you guys did to knock out the military's tracking capabilities was mutually beneficial," Byron added. "They're back up-and-running, by the way. So you might want to be cautious about standing out from the crowd going forward. Especially if knocking out their systems was a one-time-only event."

"Helping the competition now?" Gabriel asked. "That's unlike you."

Byron grinned. "I've got to keep you in the race. Otherwise, where's the fun?"

Byron had never worried about maintaining fair competition or fun in previous hunts, but Gabriel supposed he owed the team one for getting the military off his back. Maybe this was his subtle way of paying back the favor. If so, Gabriel knew not to expect shared intel going forward.

"Anyway," Byron said as he stood straight and stretched his appendages, "I just thought I'd say hi before we start the next lap around the track. I've got to get back to my crew. We've got a contest to win." He took a deep breath and grimaced. "God, I hate the air around here. Can't wait to go home with my prize."

Byron clasped Gabriel's shoulder. If it were anyone else, Gabriel would have taken it as a parting sign of respect. In this case, he wished he had Samantha's reflexes so he could break Byron's hand before Byron had a chance to remove it. A moment later, Byron strolled away casually, no doubt already contemplating ways to screw Gabriel over. Gabriel may not have enjoyed running into his nemesis on the ferry's deck, but it was the fire he needed to get his mind focused on the task at hand. He hustled back to the van, where everyone except Nadine was standing around, getting the lead out of their legs.

"Byron's on the ferry," Gabriel announced.

"That's awesome," Nate replied. "He's lost his time advantage."

"Awesome from that perspective," Gabriel agreed. "But now we're about to be trapped in an enclosed space with a ruthless competitor for the next ninety minutes." Gabriel looked at Lisa. "You think you can locate Byron's vehicle without getting spotted?"

Lisa nodded. "Sure."

Gabriel turned to Samantha. "Fortify the van. If anyone suspicious gets near it, take appropriate action."

"You got it, boss."

"Tech geniuses," Gabriel said, looking at Porter and Nate, "do you two think you can put your differences aside and work together for a little while?"

They turned to each other, their eyes meeting briefly before reluctantly muttering in unison. "Yes."

"Okay. All modern vehicles are heavily computerized. Figure out how we can use that to our advantage." Gabriel shifted his gaze from one member of the team to the next, imparting on them the newfound determination coursing through his veins. "I don't want Byron Coltrain leaving this ship."

Chapter Forty-Six
Two Vans

Straight of Gibraltar
Nine Days Before The Sky Opened

It only took Lisa twenty minutes to find Byron's crew and report back to Gabriel. She spotted six men and one woman with him. The woman had short hair, wore thin-framed glasses, and appeared to be the intellect of the group. One of the men had his nose buried in his laptop and appeared to be Byron's equivalent of Nate. The rest were mercenary types- big muscles, gruff attitudes, and at least one or two concealed weapons each. They exchanged jokes crude enough to be off-putting to nearby passengers and remained oblivious as those passengers rolled up their car windows or discretely moved to the observation decks.

"I saw two vans," Lisa told Gabriel. "They're parked one behind the other in the hold above us. Byron and his primary team are in the front van with the windows down. The hired help are on their feet and crowded around the rear van. We're going to need a distraction to stand a chance at getting close."

"Let's worry about our distraction once we know our plan of attack," Gabriel replied before looking at Porter and Nate. "You two come up with anything yet?"

"Lisa, did you see any antenna wires on the vans' front windshields?" Nate asked.

"I don't think so."

"Damn," Nate said, snapping his finger. "We'll have to hardwire."

Gabriel cocked his head. "Hardwire what?"

Porter showed him a small black box with a flexible wire antenna sticking out of one end.

"Is that-"

"One of Nate's transmitters," Porter confirmed. "He brought it along in case he needed it for... *something*." Nate looked away guiltily as Porter glared at him. "Anyway, we were hoping to use it to hack the vans' remote start functions, but it looks like we'll have to go hard through a diagnostics port instead."

"One of you brought a vehicle diagnostics cable with you?" Gabriel asked.

"Nope," Nate said. "But it's a ferry. Vehicles must break down on board all the time, which means there's got to be a diagnostics cable stashed around here somewhere."

Gabriel looked at Lisa.

"I'm on it," she said before taking off at a jog.

Gabriel turned his attention back to the tech duo. "Okay, so what's the plan?"

"I didn't build my transmitter for hard-wiring," Nate said. "Once we've got the diagnostics cable, we'll need about ten minutes to surgically connect the two. After that, you'll have to pick which van you want to disable and plug the transmitter into the diagnostics port beneath its steering column. Samantha!" Nate shouted toward the back of their own van, where she was standing guard. "Did you bring any duct tape?"

"Do you really need to ask?" She yelled back.

"Cool." Nate looked at Gabriel. "Once plugged in, you'll need to tape the transmitter and cable to the underside of the steering column, where no one will see it. We're going to use Porter's tablet to hack the van's computer and run its commands through an online action randomizer. For every input the computer receives- gear shifting, braking, headlights, you name it- the randomizer will trigger a different output."

"Why not just disable the engine?"

Nate and Porter chuckled in unison.

"Because this way is much more fun," Nate then said. "Besides, a disabled engine is easy to diagnose. This solution will cause so much confusion and chaos, Byron's team won't know what's going on or how to fix it. Of course, that's assuming the transmitter stays plugged in the entire time. If it loses connection, the party's over, so make sure you tape it good."

"I love how you keep assuming I'm the one who's going to hook it up," Gabriel said.

"Samantha's busy guarding our van, and I'm sure as hell not going to risk getting caught by whatever nut-jobs Byron's subcontracted for this gig. It's not like you can send Mr. Bloody Lung over here, either." Nate pointed a thumb at Porter. "No offense."

"None taken... jackass," Porter replied.

Lisa returned with a thick black cable in tow. "Is this what you need?"

Nate examined the connector on one end of the cable. "It's perfect." He passed the cable to Porter. "We'll need to strip the sheathing on the other end. Now, be careful opening my transmitter-"

Porter slammed the transmitter against the deck so hard its outer casing shattered, revealing the intricate wiring within. "Oops," he said with zero remorse.

"Now who's being mature?" Nate asked him.

Porter picked up the core pieces of the transmitter. "Consider it a compliment. What did they teach us in school? If your invention can't take a beating, you didn't engineer it good enough."

"A *reasonable* beating," Nate clarified. "Not aggravated assault."

"Okay, you two," Gabriel said sternly.

As if Nate and Samantha weren't enough, now there was a third feisty sibling in the mix. Luckily, Porter didn't escalate the mini-feud from there. He opened a side door of their van, laid out the pieces of Nate's transmitter and diagnostics cable, and entered his focus mode as he began the intricate job of splicing them together.

"That'll take care of one van," Gabriel said. "What about the other?"

Nate shrugged. "That's on you, boss. One transmitter, one van. The nerds are tapped out."

Gabriel turned to Lisa. "Any ideas?"

Lisa thought for a few moments, her lips pursed as Gabriel could almost envision her mind scanning through a sea of possibilities. It looked as though she would come up empty, when suddenly her face lit with inspiration. "I saw a utility truck parked about five spots back from the vans!"

Gabriel was less than impressed. "And that helps us how?"

Lisa smiled. "It had a winch on the front. Let the nerds disable one van with their fancy tech. We can disable the other using good old-fashioned physics."

Gabriel returned her smile and added a smack on the lips. "Now that sounds like a plan."

"We're still going to need a distraction," Lisa reminded him.

As if on cue, Nadine rejoined the group from what Gabriel had been told was a stroll for fresh air and sunlight. She glanced at Porter and Nate huddled over their science project, then at Samantha standing at the rear of the van with the posture of a secret agent ready to assassinate someone. Finally, she looked at Gabriel and Lisa, who were still giddy with excitement. "I feel like I've missed something..."

Gabriel laughed. "You have. But we're glad you're back. We've got a job for you."

Chapter Forty-Seven
Vehicular Warfare

Straight of Gibraltar
Nine Days Before The Sky Opened

The ferry was halfway through its journey across open water by the time Gabriel and his team were ready to launch their clandestine attack on Byron. Samantha supplied everyone with walkie-talkies and agreed to monitor their chatter and advise as needed, but that was the extent of her role in the attack. She needed to stay near the team's van in the event Byron had his own counterattack in the works. Since Porter wasn't in a healthy enough condition to help execute the attack, he offered to plant himself in a discrete location and provide Samantha with an extra set of eyes. Against his wishes, Nate got roped into planting his transmitter in the rear van while Gabriel worked on disabling the front van. Lisa and Nadine were on distraction duty, which may have sounded like the easiest of the tasks required, but was actually the hardest and most critical.

"Is everyone in place?" Gabriel asked into his walkie-talkie.

He counted as each member of the attack squad responded with their affirmation. Then he told them the mission was a go and made his first move. Gabriel had already performed recon in the hold where Byron's vans were parked while Nate and Porter prepared the transmitter. He had spotted a group of eight American college students about fifty yards ahead of the vans, well within Byron's view, and he knew immediately that they would make the perfect targets for what Gabriel had labeled in his mind as Project Paranoia.

"Wow!" Gabriel said with exaggerated excitement as he approached the students. "It's so good to see some Americans for a

change! I was feeling like a stranger in a strange land around here!"
Gabriel noticed the students were looking at him as if he were a loon.
"Stranger in a strange land? King James bible? Robert Heinlein? No?"
Gabriel waved a dismissive hand. "Eh, who am I kidding? You guys
don't read that stuff. You probably read fluff fiction like the stuff
Gabriel Dunne writes."

As he had hoped, Gabriel saw sudden recognition wash over one
student's face.

"Hey," he told his friends. "Hey, this is Gabriel Dunne! I recognize
his picture from the back of that novel we had to read for class last
month!"

"You actually read it?" Another student asked. "I just watched the
movie."

"Book, movie... doesn't make any difference to me as long as you
enjoyed it," Gabriel told her.

"It was all right."

Gabriel ignored the critique. "Look, um, I'm doing some research
for my next book. I could use about fifteen minutes of your time if
you'd be willing to help. I'd even give each of you a shout-out in the
book's dedication."

The students looked at each other reluctantly before one athletic
type stepped forward. "It's not like we've got anything else to do right
now. But I want a selfie, too. My momma's a fan; it'll tickle her pink to
know I ran into one of her favorite authors."

"You've got a deal."

Gabriel's ask of the students was quite simple. First, he needed
them to pretend to be extremely interested in what he had to say,
while occasionally glancing in the general direction of Byron's vans.
Then he needed them to take some cash from him, which he told them
they could keep. Gabriel purposely dropped some of the cash to
ensure he caused a scene as the students tried to snatch it from the
wind. That way, if he hadn't had Byron's attention already, he would
have it now. Gabriel finally asked the students to disperse in pairs,
each pair headed in a separate direction. They were to stay on the
move for fifteen minutes, doing nothing but strolling aimlessly around
the ferry and avoiding Byron's vans. Gabriel would meet them back
where they started to collect their info for the dedication and pose for

whatever pictures they might want.

The students' execution of Project Paranoia was perfect. As soon as they scrambled, Byron signaled for his mercenaries to follow. Four pairs of students, four mercenaries down. Now there was only one to go. Gabriel probably could have drawn all five mercenaries from the van if he had asked the students to disperse individually, but he felt they were safer in pairs should Byron's men try anything. Gabriel could have also drawn the last mercenary away himself, but he ducked into hiding as soon as the students dispersed to remove that temptation. He couldn't be on the run because he needed the freedom to execute the next stage of the plan. Luckily, that's where Nadine came into play.

"Nadine," Gabriel said into his walkie-talkie, "you're up."

Gabriel squatted low as he traversed the perimeter of the vehicle hold. He saw Nadine strut down a stairwell far behind Byron's vans. She had changed into her tightest pants, stripped off her bra, and loosened the top three buttons of her shirt. She carried a purse to conceal her walkie-talkie in one hand and fiddled with her phone in the other. Gabriel watched as men's eyes wandered from their families, phones, and other focal points to follow Nadine's trail. *Good*, he thought to himself, *now let's hope our last mercenary is just as interested.*

Nadine strolled up the aisle to Byron's vans and nearly ran into the remaining mercenary. Gabriel saw her excuse herself with a flirtatious tone and turn to the nearest stairwell, putting her body into a full runway swing to ensure she showed off the goods. Like a dog chasing a bone, the mercenary adjusted his position to watch Nadine climb the stairs. Her instructions were to entice the mercenary to follow her once she reached the next deck. Gabriel wasn't sure how Nadine was planning to do that, but whatever she had in mind must have worked. The mercenary took a quick scan of the vicinity, then looked back at Byron's vans to confirm they were secure, then followed in Nadine's footsteps.

"Nate, go," Gabriel ordered into his walkie-talkie.

Trepidation filled the voice that responded. *"Yeah, this isn't really my thing. I'm more of a 'stay in the van' kind of guy."*

Gabriel knew they didn't have time for this. "You're going to get your ass in *Byron's van* right now or you're going to be out of a job."

"Okay, okay."

Gabriel kept his eyes on the front van, where Byron and his two primary team members were deep in conversation, for any signs of suspicious activity. Nate emerged from a nearby hallway, snuck between the rows of vehicles, quietly opened the rear van's side door, and climbed inside. He closed the van's door behind him, the only evidence of his trespassing the slight rock of the van on its hydraulics as Nate no doubt crawled his way into the front seat.

"Lisa," Gabriel said into his walkie-talkie, "our turn."

Gabriel followed Nate's path through the rows of vehicles parked in the hold. As he neared Byron's vans, he veered off toward Lisa's voice.

"I'm so sorry," she said with a woozy tone. "Everything is spinning. Do you know where the bathroom is?"

Gabriel heard his earpiece translate the response: *"Are you okay? Do you need help?"*

Great, the utility truck driver didn't speak English. Lisa was quick on her toes, though. She began making vomiting sounds and must have been putting on a good physical show as well, for Gabriel heard the truck door open, followed by the translation: *"Come, this way, this way."*

They were in the home stretch now. Gabriel hurried to the front of the utility truck and unwound its winch. He knew he needed to move quickly, because at any moment the distractions underway could fail to retain the attention of Byron's mercenaries or the utility truck driver. Gabriel estimated five vehicles' and a van's worth of winch cable, then unwound a little more for good measure, grabbed the hook at the end of the cable, and squat-jogged back toward Byron's vans. He went up the passenger side of the row because it offered more concealment than the driver's side, feeding the winch cable underneath each vehicle he passed. When he reached the rear van, Gabriel gave its side door two light pats, his signal to Nate to wrap things up. Then Gabriel crawled between the vans, lied on his back, and stretched the winch hook toward the front van's rear axle. It didn't make it.

Gabriel tugged hard at the cable, trying to gather any excess slack that might be in the line, but he was still about four inches short of his target. *Shit*, Gabriel thought. He checked his watch. It had been nine minutes since the students first dispersed. He probably didn't have time to return to the utility truck, unwind more cable, and get back to Byron's van before his attack window closed for good. Gabriel yanked on the cable again, but again it yielded no additional length. He thought for sure he had unwound plenty. Unless he didn't consider the extra distance from the end of the rear van to the front van's first axle. Or unless the cable was caught somewhere...

Gabriel followed it with his eyes, and sure enough, the cable had gotten pinched under the edge of the rear van's front tire. It had probably happened while Gabriel was signaling Nate. Gabriel rolled on his side, reached the pinch point, and loosened the cable. He collected whatever excess was in the line and determined it should be plenty. Gabriel returned to his back, ready to latch the rear axle, when his hand slipped and the metal winch hook crashed into the underbelly of the van with an audible clang.

Chapter Forty-Eight
Tension

Straight of Gibraltar
Nine Days Before The Sky Opened

Gabriel froze. He remembered the front van's windows had been down. Even if Byron and his team hadn't felt the impact of the winch hook, there was no way they hadn't heard the metal on metal clang it produced. Sure enough, the body of the van rocked as its passengers shifted inside. Then the side door slid open, and Gabriel saw Byron's shoes land on the concrete just five feet from his head. Maybe he'd get lucky and Byron wouldn't walk to the rear of the van. Maybe his rival would take a brief glance around and determine the sound had come from some other vehicle, or maybe even the ferry itself.

No such luck. Byron's shoes turned toward the rear of the van. He took a step, then another, and was only seconds from discovering Gabriel when another clang rang out. Byron's feet pivoted in place, directing his body toward the far end of the vehicle hold. Gabriel wriggled his body so he could peer between the neighboring vehicles and see whatever had grabbed Byron's attention. It was Samantha. She was sitting on the roof of an empty car, swinging what appeared to be a pellet gun on her index finger. After a few revolutions, she steadied the gun's grip in her hand, took aim, and fired a pellet at Byron's van. The pellet hit with another clang before ricochetting away.

"Real cute!" Byron called out.

Samantha took aim again, but a livid mom, crying child, and ferry security guard showed up before she could pull the trigger. The guard scolded Samantha, took the pellet gun and returned it to the child, then insisted Samantha follow him.

"Serves you right!" Byron yelled after her. Then, under his breath, "bitch."

Gabriel watched as Byron's feet stepped one-after-another into the van. He then heard the van door slam shut and breathed a sigh of relief. Gabriel made a mental note to thank Samantha for her quick thinking. He also made a note to thank Nate for calling in the calvary, for only Nate could have known about Gabriel's unforced error. Gabriel returned to his original position on the underside of the van and secured the winch hook around its rear axle. He then heard loud boots echoing from the nearby stairwell and saw a descending shadow growing larger. Gabriel checked his watch. It had been fourteen minutes since the students dispersed. When the other four mercenaries returned, they'd be coming from all angles. He and Nate needed to get out of there now.

Gabriel scooted from under the front van and crawled to the rear van's passenger side door. He patted it rapidly, his way of telling Nate *time's up*. Luckily, Nate was ready. He opened the door just enough to slip out, then followed as Gabriel led them in a squat-jog through the maze of surrounding vehicles and to a shaded hallway where Lisa and Nadine waited. They made it just in time, for the student pairs began arriving back at their car only half a minute later, and the mercenaries that followed them abandoned pursuit to corral back at their van. The team watched for signs that the mercenaries noticed anything out of the ordinary, but all appeared normal. Gabriel released a tense breath.

"Well, that was fun," he said sarcastically. Then, into his walkie-talkie, "does anyone have eyes on our van?"

"I do," Porter responded. *"The dog that was trailing Nadine scouted it out after losing interest in her, but Samantha scared him off. It's been quiet since."*

"Great," Gabriel said. "We're on our way back. Samantha's been taken into custody. You think your wallet can get her free?"

"I'm sure I can work something out with ferry security."

Porter was right. In fact, it didn't even take as large of a bribe as he thought it would to get the security guard and his colleagues to release Samantha. After a pit stop to collect the college students' names, sign a few autographs, and take selfies, the entire team reconvened at their van, which Samantha insisted on sweeping for booby traps and tracking devices despite Porter's claims that no one had messed with it. The van was clean. With only twenty minutes left on their ferry ride, Gabriel found it odd that Byron hadn't tried to sabotage them. It almost made Gabriel feel like he was the bad guy, since he was the one playing dirty in this contest. Then he reminded himself of the many reasons he had based his novels' antagonists on Byron, and Gabriel decided it was better to brush his guilt aside and take this as an unexpected win for the good guys.

When the ferry pulled into port at Algeciras, Gabriel's deck was the first to unload. Nate resumed driving duty so Samantha could return to lookout duty, which was especially important now that the U.S. military had their surveillance systems back online and could show at any moment. Gabriel instructed Nate to disembark and then find a place to idle so they could observe whether their operation had been successful. Ten minutes later, it was time for Byron's deck to unload. Vehicles streamed out without issue, and Gabriel held his breath as he counted down the rows until Byron's turn. A moment later, he saw the car ahead of Byron's front van roll forward. Byron's front van tried to follow, lurching forward maybe a half foot before hitting resistance. The mercenary behind the wheel gunned the engine, but he only succeeded in yanking the utility truck into the car ahead of it, which in turn piled into the next car, and the one after that, the bumpers of each vehicle crunching together.

The mercenary driving Byron's rear van must have realized something was wrong, for he jerked it to the right in what appeared to be an effort to escape the constricting line of vehicles. That van only went a foot or two before stopping. Gabriel saw its headlights flash, then its windshield wipers kick on. Gabriel wasn't sure what the mercenary driving was doing, but he guessed it wasn't kicking the vehicle into reverse, smashing into the hood of the car behind it, and then blaring the radio so loud Gabriel and his team could hear it from land. Nate and Porter shared a rare congratulatory smile. The engine of Byron's front van revved as it made another attempt to escape the ferry. Before it could move, the rear van thrusted forward unexpectedly, catching the front van on an angle and blowing its right rear tire. Gabriel's team cheered.

On the ferry, Byron must have given the order for both of his drivers to stand down, for the vans were now still. Byron climbed out of his van and ignored the shouting owners of vehicles that had been collateral damage in Gabriel's trap. He marched past complaining ferry workers and to the edge of the ferry deck, his eyes scanning the horizon until he spotted Gabriel. Byron stared angrily, but behind the stare was also an acknowledgement of professional respect. Gabriel had won this round, but he knew the match was far from over.

Chapter Forty-Nine
Three Bags

Alicante, Spain
Nine Days Before The Sky Opened

It was nearing midnight when the team pulled into the Port of Alicante. Activity at the port was minimal, with only one commercial barge unloading its cargo and an assortment of private yachts and sailboats anchored in the adjacent harbor dark and unmoving. Nate dropped Samantha off at the pier so she could locate their Leviathan watercraft while he scouted for a secluded parking spot in which they could safely leave the van. Gabriel woke Porter, who had dozed off a couple of hours into the drive from Algeciras, and Porter woke Nadine, who had subsequently leaned her head against his shoulder and done the same.

"Had a good nap?" Gabriel asked Porter with a smile.

The tech billionaire rubbed a hand over his groggy face. "Sorry. I didn't mean to crash on you like that. My stamina isn't what it used to be."

"Don't worry about it," Gabriel said, diverting attention away from Porter's condition. "Once the sun went down, we couldn't see the scenery anyway."

Nadine caught his eye and gave him a grateful nod.

Nate stopped the van. Lisa, who had been waiting in the cargo area, popped open the rear doors and tossed out three duffel bags she and Gabriel had spent most of the drive packing with gear. Based on Samantha's road research, they needed to be prepared for hiking, climbing, hacking, and God knew what else once they entered the underground village. Thus, their gear included ropes, hooks, bandages and other first aid supplies, flashlights, walkie-talkies, spare food and water, a collection of basic tools, as well as common electrical engineering hardware. Gabriel retrieved the bags and displayed the contents of one of them to Porter as he and Nadine stretched their legs.

"Remember how Nate was curious about lighting Cabrera Castle? There's a lighthouse at the southwest tip of the island. Its lamp runs on an automated system. We're going to drop you and Nate off nearby. Between this and your tablet, do you think you two can hack the system and gain control of the lamp?"

Porter quickly assessed the gear. "Yeah, that should do."

Gabriel zipped the duffel bag and passed it to him.

"It looks like Team Nerd is back in action," Nate said as he joined his rival. "If this is going to be a recurring thing, I'm thinking we need to establish an org chart so there's no confusion over who's in charge. Now, obviously, with my leadership skills-"

Porter shoved the duffel bag against Nate's chest, cutting him off. "You carry this. I need to get my satchel."

Nate looked at the bag, then shouted at Porter's departing backside. "The peons typically carry the gear!"

"And true leaders lead by example!" Porter shouted back.

Gabriel and Nadine exchanged a look, as if silently asking each other how they put up with their respective geniuses. Then Nadine asked, "what do you need me to do?"

"We're assuming we need to use the lighthouse to illuminate Cabrera Castle, but there could be some other lighting mechanism at the castle that we're not aware of. You and Samantha will head there. Search the castle for anything out of the ordinary, anything that could be a source of electricity or fire or anything else that could create light. The castle's a tourist destination, so there shouldn't be anything dangerous to worry about, but Samantha will keep you safe in the event something unexpected happens."

"Got it." Nadine took one of the duffel bags from Gabriel. "Three bags, three teams. What are you and Lisa going to be doing?"

Gabriel tensed. If he was being honest, they were going on a wild goose chase. But it was a necessary chase, nonetheless. "The lighthouse is on the southwest tip of Cabrera Island. Cabrera Castle is on the middle northern edge. And according to satellite imagery, there's no direct line of sight between the two. There's a hill that'll prevent us from using the lighthouse to illuminate the castle."

Nadine eyed Gabriel's bag. "You must have some mighty strong shovels in there."

Gabriel smiled in appreciation of her sarcasm. "If the lighthouse is the source of our illumination, there must be a mechanism in place to bend its lamplight around the hill. There's a rise in the southeastern quadrant of the island with an altitude similar to both the lighthouse and the castle. It's off the established tourist trails, which makes it a prime candidate to hide... something. Lisa and I are going to check it out."

Nadine nodded, but a look of worry defied her movements.

"You're wondering what the backup plan is if none of this pans out," Gabriel said.

Nadine stared hard into his eyes, confirming his presumption.

"Don't worry about that right now," Gabriel said in as comforting a tone as he could. "I know our approach feels wishy-washy, but if there's one thing my team and I excel at, it's thinking on our feet. Let's just take this one step at a time."

Nadine nodded again, this time in agreement with Gabriel's suggestion. Gabriel heard the van's cargo doors slam shut and turned to find Lisa, Nate, and Porter standing at attention. Porter had the brown satchel he had tried to show Gabriel back in Casablanca slung around his shoulder. He also had a fresh determination in his eyes, as if he could sense victory was finally within grasp.

"Ready?" Gabriel asked.

Porter nodded resolutely. "As I'll ever be."

Chapter Fifty
Isla de Cabrera

Balearic Sea
Eight Days Before The Sky Opened

Gabriel was amazed by the smoothness with which the Leviathan watercraft cut through the choppy surface of the Balearic Sea. There were traveling at just over one hundred miles per hour, forcing Gabriel to huddle with Samantha behind the watercraft's aerodynamic reinforced plexiglass windshield. Everyone else was in the cabin below, no one wanting to risk falling overboard from the minimalist deck. Samantha had informed Gabriel the watercraft was capable of reaching nearly two hundred miles per hour. But these were civilian waters, and at that speed, it would be difficult to avoid a collision with innocent sailors setting off for a night cruise from neighboring Ibiza, Formentera, or Mallorca. The Leviathan had a number of high-tech sensors and instruments to help avoid such collisions, so perhaps Samantha's concerns were overblown, but there was an additional risk of higher speeds drawing unwanted attention. Keeping the boat around one hundred would keep prying eyes from distinguishing one of the most advanced watercrafts ever assembled from some rich asshole's pleasure boat.

"How's our timing?" Gabriel yelled over the roar of ocean wind.

"We'll arrive at Cabrera Island in about thirty minutes," Samantha yelled back. "We're approaching from the southwest, so we'll drop the boys off first. I'll then take us around the southern edge of the island and find a safe spot for you and Lisa to disembark. You're going to have a hell of a hike to reach the rise you want to investigate, but it's that or drop you off on the eastern beach, where you'd have to scale a ninety-degree cliff of sharp rock in order to get inland."

"We'll take the hike," Gabriel said. "What time does that put you and Nadine at the castle?"

"Between one-thirty and two o'clock, just as planned. We'll have five hours to find the entrance to the underground village. You and Lisa are going to be the bottleneck, so hike as fast as you can."

"Will do."

Twenty minutes later, Gabriel could see the glow of civilization approaching from the distance. Samantha informed him it was coming from Mallorca. She then pointed out the blip of isolated light to the south of Mallorca that repeatedly faded in and out of view. It was the N'Ensiola Lighthouse, marking the southwestern tip of Cabrera Island. The rest of the island was invisible in the black of night from their current distance, but its silhouette slowly emerged under moonlight as they neared. Samantha used the lighthouse as her guide to get close, then turned on the Leviathan's headlamp as she skirted the rocky shore. It took about five minutes to find a low enough point for Nate and Porter to unload. They would have a quarter-mile or so trek uphill to reach the lighthouse, but Samantha assured them it would be an easy walk, for the hill was cut with a winding tourist trail. Gabriel confirmed that Nate and Porter had all the gear they would need. Then Samantha had them perform a battery and signal check on their walkie-talkies.

"Now just remember," Nate told Gabriel as he turned on his flashlight, "if I don't make it out of this lighthouse alive... Porter did it."

Gabriel and Samantha choked back laughter. Porter didn't seem amused.

"In all seriousness," Gabriel said without laughter, "if anything goes wrong, or if either of you sense danger, send a distress message over the walkie-talkies and head straight back here. Samantha will hop in the Leviathan and pick you up. Got it?"

Porter and Nate both nodded. They then waved goodbye and set off toward the lighthouse on foot. Samantha pulled their boat away from shore and proceed along the southern edge of the island. She sailed slowly, monitoring the ever-changing shoreline of Cabrera Island while also weaving between a handful of islets that hung close to the larger landmass. Soon, they reached the southeastern tip of the island, which they had barely rounded before Samantha pulled the Leviathan to shore once more.

"This is as close as I can get you without dealing with the cliff," she told Gabriel.

Lisa joined him as he grabbed their duffel bag and climbed onto the adjacent rocky beach. Nadine came up from the cabin to see them off and take Gabriel's place beside Samantha.

"How will we know when we've reached the rise?" Lisa asked. "It's kind of hard to tell one hill from the next in the dark."

Samantha tossed her a small black box with a digital screen. It was no bigger than a deck of playing cards, and on the screen was an aerial map of their current location. Lisa saw a green dot blinking along one edge.

"I've programmed the rise's global positioning coordinates into that," Samantha said. "Just follow the green dot. Unfortunately, anyone scanning for GPS receivers is going to know there's an active one on this island, but that's a risk we're going to have to take. You're going to be twisting and turning too much to follow a simple compass bearing."

Lisa gave Samantha a thumbs up and pocketed the receiver. Samantha made them go through the same checks as Porter and Nate, reminded them that they would be the laggards in reaching their destination, and reiterated Gabriel's protocol in case of an emergency. Then she turned her attention to the Leviathan's control board and guided her and Nadine back out to sea. The two were quickly gone from view, though Gabriel could still hear the Leviathan's engines echoing across the island's eastern edge.

"Care for a romantic night hike, m'lady?" He asked Lisa with debonair charm.

She stifled laughter. "You are such a dork." She then checked the GPS receiver and pointed. "It looks like we need to head that way first."

Gabriel nodded in agreement. "That's good, considering any other direction would put us right back in the ocean."

Lisa punched him playfully. Then Gabriel held a hooked elbow out and stood his ground until Lisa accepted his courting gesture. Arm-in-arm, the two set off briskly into the dark hills of Cabrera Island, braced for whatever secrets might await them there.

Chapter Fifty-One
Light

Isla de Cabrera, Spain
Eight Days Before The Sky Opened

Gabriel and Lisa didn't reach their destination until nearly three o'clock. By the time they got there, Porter and Nate had already hacked into the lighthouse's automated system and shut it down. They claimed to be minutes away from having full manual control of the lighthouse lamp, at which point they would boot the system back up, but then twenty minutes of bickering went by and they were no closer to their goal. Meanwhile, Samantha and Nadine arrived at Cabrera Castle and performed a first pass of the area. They reported no sign of electricity, no source of fire, nor any other obvious means by which to illuminate the castle. The first pass had been rushed, however, so while Porter and Nate resolved whatever differences they were currently working through, Samantha and Nadine would conduct a more thorough inspection.

After checking in on the team's status, Gabriel and Lisa tackled their own end of the mission. They began at one end of the rise and marched in as straight of a line as they could under the glow of moonlight. They swept the beams of their flashlights from side to side, their eyes following methodically, in search of anything out of the ordinary. They also ensured they took it slowly, crossing over the peak of the rise after about ten minutes and then continuing another ten down the opposing slope, until they were equidistant from where they had started. Nothing. The two had spotted nothing but green grass and waist-high shrubbery. This rise was just that: a hilly rise on a remote island with nothing to hide.

"Now what?" Lisa asked.

Gabriel looked at her with determination. "Now we go again."

Lisa didn't argue. The two had been through enough together to know even the most obvious of oddities could escape the human eye at first glance, especially in the dark. They faced their starting point and marched again, even slower this time, their eyes now familiar with the terrain and alert for anything that deviated in appearance from it. This time, Gabriel made note of an uncharacteristic dip on the southwestern face of the rise. It was as if the ground was sunken in over a circular area about nine feet in diameter. The dip was subtle, and could easily be explained by weathering on this side of the rise, but Gabriel wouldn't take even the slightest aberration for granted. He and Lisa examined the dip, especially its edges, looking for any indication that it was manmade. But they came up empty, and so they continued on, soon reaching their original starting position.

Gabriel checked his watch and could feel the pressure of time slipping away. "It's almost four-thirty." He grabbed his walkie-talkie. "Samantha, anything new on your end?"

"Sorry, boss," Samantha replied. "This place looks like your standard tourist attraction. Even if we do light it up, I don't see any evidence of a mechanism that would be triggered by light. I'm starting to feel like we've been played."

Gabriel shared a glance with Lisa. She was feeling the same.

"Nate?" Gabriel then said into the walkie-talkie. "Did you guys ever solve... whatever the hell your problem was?"

"Hang on," Nate said brusquely.

Gabriel heard a resistant whine echo across the island, as if gears were being forced to turn unnaturally. Then there was a loud click, and suddenly the lighthouse lamp returned to life, frozen on a southeastern trajectory, illuminating the hills Gabriel and Lisa had traversed to reach their current position.

"Let there be light!" Nate shouted with excitement over the walkie-talkie. "Put another notch in Team Nerd's victory column!"

"I'm thinking we need a different name..." Porter's more distant voice said.

"Great job, you guys," Gabriel told them. "For the hell of it, can you try to light the castle directly?"

"Give us a second," Nate said.

Gabriel heard more echoed squeals as Nate and Porter instructed the lighthouse to turn northern. It briefly passed over him and Lisa, then continued on, until Gabriel saw it stop on a north-northeastern trajectory. His eyes followed the light from its source, across the island terrain, and, as anticipated, directly into a hillside.

"Shit." He lifted his walkie-talkie. "Samantha, I'm guessing you're still in the dark over there?"

"That's affirmative."

Lisa frowned at Gabriel. "Maybe Nadine was on to something when she thought we were bringing shovels."

Gabriel knew she was only half joking. "No. Finding the village wouldn't require that much effort." He looked at the dark rise outstretched before them. Gabriel's instincts were rarely wrong, and his instincts told him this rise was the key to connecting the lighthouse's lamplight with Cabrera Castle. Topographically and geographically, it was the only spot on the island that was isolated from tourists and had the right height and line of sight to link the historical attractions. Gabriel opened the line on his walkie-talkie once more. "Nate, light us up."

A few loud creaks, ten second later, and the lighthouse lamp rotated to shine on the western face of the rise. Silhouetted against the incoming illumination, Gabriel turned off his flashlight and examined the freshly lit ground.

"The lamp points here," he told Lisa. "So any reflecting mechanism must be here as well."

They fanned out across the western face, pressing firmly into the ground with each step to check for inconsistencies in its composition. They felt each shrub and periodically examined exposed roots to confirm their authenticity. Gabriel even drug his fingers through random patches of dirt and soil to examine its age and compactness. As with their previous passes, nothing was out of the ordinary, until-

Gabriel paused. He took a few steps back and pushed his toe into the grassy patchwork he had just crossed. It had a slight spring to it, as if it had soaked in a recent rain. Then Gabriel stepped forward into a four-foot clearing of dirt. The ground was harder here- not unexpected, given its lack of plant life. But then, as Gabriel proceeded into the clearing, he felt his right foot land on an even harder surface, almost as if there was a layer of rock just beneath the dirt. He kneeled down and dug in with his fingers. Yes, there was definitely something under this dirt.

"Lisa," he called out like a giddy schoolboy. "Come see!"

Chapter Fifty-Two
The Disc

Isla de Cabrera, Spain
Eight Days Before The Sky Opened

In the brief time it took Lisa to join him, Gabriel had already identified a solid curved edge beneath the top layer of dirt. He clawed at the ground as he exposed more and more of the edge, which was now forming a large arc. Gabriel followed the arc in one direction while Lisa followed in the other, each of them digging a few inches deep, exposing the sides of what turned out to be a stone disc about two feet in diameter. Gabriel tried gripping the sides of the disc and turning it, but he felt no give.

"Maybe we need to dig deeper to release it," Lisa suggested.

Gabriel agreed with her suggestion and two worked to expose another two inches of stone before reaching a subsurface that was too hard to dig through with their hands. Gabriel stood and tried turning the disc again, but couldn't get it to budge. Lisa offered to help, but even with their combined leverage, the stone remained in its original position.

"There's got to be more to it," Gabriel said.

Lisa dropped to her knees and patted the dirt that still covered the surface of the underground disc. Gabriel watched her hands move to the center of the disc, then back toward the edges, then to the center again. She had felt something.

"It's not solid," Lisa said a moment later. "The center is soft."

Gabriel dropped beside her and the two dug in unison, starting at the disc's center and moving outward. They made a cavity three inches deep before hitting the same stone that composed the disc. Then they grew the cavity, using the inner edges of stone to guide their digging, until finally there was no dirt left to remove. Gabriel and Lisa stood and analyzed their discovery. There, carved symmetrically into the stone disc, was a large plus sign. Gabriel's inner child wished he were standing about forty-five degrees off the current axis so he could make a joke about x marking the spot, but unfortunately life wasn't a movie, and changing position just to get a laugh would feel forced.

"I hope you brought a really big Phillips-head screwdriver with you," Lisa quipped.

Damn, Gabriel had missed his chance. "The stone isn't reflective. There must be another piece to it... something that stands in the center depression."

"Whatever it is would have to be curved or prism shaped in order to bend light," Lisa said. "We would have spotted a large prism by now. Let's ignore flat ground and concentrate on portions of the rise with the largest arcs."

They fanned out again, this time not limiting themselves to the area of the rise illuminated by the lighthouse. It was after five o'clock now. A voice in the back of Gabriel's mind reminded him they had less than two hours left until sunrise. They had no choice but to find the other component of this mechanism and figure out how it worked before then. Gabriel reached a prominent curve in the terrain and turned on his flashlight. He examined the curve, first visually, then by touch, and concluded there was nothing odd about it. Gabriel scanned for the next curve and did the same with it. Then a third.

Meanwhile, Lisa and her flashlight had disappeared over the crest of the rise. Samantha radioed for a status update, and Lisa responded, so Gabriel knew she was okay. He heard his wife relay their discovery to the other team members and explain the search they were conducting. Then he heard Lisa stop abruptly in mid-sentence, her last sound over the walkie-talkie an unexpected yelp, before the next sound of her voice came as a shout emanating from just over the rise.

"Gabriel!"

Instantly alarmed, Gabriel abandoned his search and raced toward Lisa's voice. He huffed his way over the tip of the rise, spotted Lisa's flashlight lying idle in a distant patch of grass, then swung his own flashlight frantically in search of his wife as he stumbled down the eastern slope.

"Lisa!"

Her reply came from just ahead. "Down here!" It was followed by, "I'm okay. Watch your step."

Gabriel reached Lisa's flashlight and immediately saw what she was warning him about. Just over a foot away, the eastern slope of the rise made a sharp downward turn. Just before that, a square stone jutted from the ground at an angle that made it nearly invisible against the night sky. The only reason Gabriel spotted it was because Lisa's left shoe was laying haphazardly against the stone. Gabriel approached the drop-off slowly, retrieved the shoe, and glanced over the edge. Lisa was seated five feet below him, a group of shrubbery having broken her tumble.

"Do you mind tossing me that?" She asked, pointing to the shoe. "I'd rather not get my sock dirty."

Gabriel did as asked. "Are you sure you're okay?"

"Yeah, though I'll probably have a pretty solid bruise on my right ass cheek in the morning."

"Gabriel, Lisa, are you all right?" Samantha asked through the walkie-talkie.

"Lisa took a spill," Gabriel informed her, "but she's fine. I've got to put the walkie-talkie down to help her. We'll be dark for a minute or two."

After receiving Samantha's acknowledgment, Gabriel put the walkie-talkie away and crouched to make a controlled descent toward his wife.

"Wait," Lisa said from her perch against the brush below. "Stay there. Toss me my flashlight."

Gabriel eyed her curiously as he fulfilled the request. Lisa turned on her light, apologizing for inadvertently blinding Gabriel, then swung its beam toward the stone she had tripped over. Lisa squinted as if trying to read the smallest lines of an eye chart, moved her flashlight downward, then shifted it back toward the stone once more.

"Well, I'll be damned..." she muttered under her breath.

Gabriel climbed down to join his wife, then followed the beam of her flashlight to the square stone. It was then that he saw the stone was part of a larger object, an object partially embedded in the steep slope, overgrown with stray grasses and weeds, but nonetheless distinct from its surroundings. The object was about five feet long and three feet wide. It was curved, its concave surface facing the ground, and made of a material that blended with the terrain's natural colors. The object was also upside down from Gabriel and Lisa's current perspective, for at its top were two more square stones sitting adjacent to the one Lisa had tripped over. Three sides of a plus sign, and Gabriel had no doubt the fourth side was shoved into the ground at the top of the slope, anchoring the object in place. Gabriel checked his watch. They had found the rest of the reflecting mechanism with an hour and a half to spare. Now they had to assemble it... and pray that it still worked.

Chapter Fifty-Three
Orientation

Isla de Cabrera, Spain
Eight Days Before The Sky Opened

Gabriel and Lisa informed the team of their discovery, then carefully dislodged the reflecting mechanism from its anchor point on the slope. Lisa unburied the rest of the plus-shaped pedestal while Gabriel stood below to catch the weight of the mechanism and lower it to the ground. Once down, they examined the concave surface that was previously hidden from view. It had a metallic coating that was surprisingly free of rust and other impairments. Gabriel removed a few small vines and brushed a layer of dirt from the coated surface. Then he shined his flashlight at it to confirm it was as reflective as it appeared to be. Satisfied, he and Lisa each took an end and carried the mechanism back over the rise and to the disc they had unburied earlier. They stood the reflector upright, turned it so the metallic surface faced the incoming lighthouse beam, and set its base into the matching indentation of the stone disc.

"*Guys,*" Samantha said over their walkie-talkies. "*We've got some light over here. It's a little off-angle, but it's definitely reaching.*"

"Roger that," Gabriel responded.

He shared a smile with Lisa. The reflector was successfully redirecting the lighthouse beam toward Cabrera Castle, but they needed to make some adjustments. Gabriel asked Lisa to support the reflector while he stepped back and analyzed the angle of the incoming lighthouse beam.

"Nate?" He said into his walkie-talkie. "I need you to rotate the lamp about four degrees clockwise."

Gabriel heard the now-familiar echoed squeals of Nate and Porter forcing the lighthouse lamp gears to betray their natural rotations. The incoming light shifted to the right, nailing the reflecting mechanism head-on.

"That's perfect," Gabriel said. "Team Nerd, you're on standby. Samantha?"

"Things are brighter over here," she said. *"But I still think the angle is off."*

Gabriel rejoined Lisa at the reflecting mechanism. He noticed it leaned slightly, and when he tried to correct the lean, the mechanism wobbled unsteadily. Gabriel confirmed its pedestal was properly aligned with the indentation in the stone disc. Maybe it was damaged, perhaps from natural erosion or uneven exposure to the elements.

"Maybe we should try turning it?" Lisa asked.

"Maybe..."

Gabriel asked Samantha which direction she needed the light to shift. Then he and Lisa each took a side of the reflector and pushed counter-clockwise. It immediately tried to topple over, but Gabriel caught its weight before any damage could be done by an impact with the hard ground and stone disc beneath. Gabriel and Lisa repositioned the reflector and adjusted their grips. They pushed again, but the stone disc still wouldn't budge. They pushed harder, and the reflector tried to topple over once more.

"It's like trying to turn a stripped screw," Gabriel said. "What are we doing wrong?"

Lisa pushed gently against one edge of the reflector and examined its wobble. She repeated the act, this time watching its pedestal rock within the confines of the disc indentation. "Help me lift it out."

Gabriel did, and Lisa dropped to her knees and peered at the plus-shaped base that was giving them so much trouble.

"Of course," she said. "The shape is symmetrical on the x and y axes, but not on the z axis. One peg of the plus sign is shallower than the others." Lisa turned her attention to the stone disc, running her fingers slowly through its indentation. "It's not symmetric on the z axis either. The asymmetry prevents the reflector from being inserted in the wrong orientation." She looked back and forth from the stone indentation to the matching reflector pedestal. "We need to face the concave surface away from the lighthouse."

Gabriel waited for Lisa to stand and help him so he wouldn't risk dropping the reflector. Once they had it oriented properly, they set it back into the stone disc, where it sunk in snuggly. Something triggered beneath the disc. Gabriel heard a dull thud and saw an ankle-high puff of dirt shoot out from its edges. His pulse raced with excitement. He pushed on the reflector, but it was sturdy now. It was also facing the wrong direction, but Gabriel suspected that wouldn't be an issue for long. He instructed Lisa to resume her previous position and, after a three count, they pushed counter-clockwise in unison.

Gabriel felt the vibration of stone scraping stone as the disc finally turned. It gave resistance, but not so much that turning it was a struggle. It also seemed to have predetermined mechanical positions it fell into after each push, for Gabriel heard a subtle repetitive click that reminded him of turning a combination lock. Soon, the reflector caught the beam from the lighthouse. Gabriel and Lisa continued rotating, catching more and more of the beam, until they returned the reflector to its previous angle.

"Samantha?" Gabriel asked.

"Just a little farther," she replied.

Gabriel and Lisa pushed slowly, listening to the grind of stone and each passing click emanating from beneath the earth. They were about ten degrees past their original angle when Samantha gave them the order to stop.

"You did it!" She exclaimed over the walkie-talkie. *"We're as bright as day over here!"*

Gabriel and Lisa shared a celebratory cheer and hug.

Then Porter got on the walkie-talkie. *"So, what now?"* His voice was also filled with excitement, but underlying it was a nervous eagerness. *"Did the light trigger something? Do you see a door or a path or-"*

"There's nothing," Samantha said abruptly. She then continued in a more somber, apologetic tone. *"The light... it didn't do anything."*

Silence followed. Any semblance of joy or celebration had been instantly sucked out of the team. Gabriel knew what they were feeling, especially Porter, but he needed them to stay focused on the task at hand. Setbacks were common in their line of work. This was just the next one, and they would need to work through it.

"I know time is short," Gabriel said into his walkie-talkie, "but give Lisa and I a few minutes to assess the situation. We've come this far. There's no reason to lose hope yet."

Chapter Fifty-Four
Mind Of The Mechanic

Isla de Cabrera, Spain
Eight Days Before The Sky Opened

Gabriel put away his walkie-talkie and stared at the reflecting mechanism. Adila Benkirane had said to illuminate the castle to reveal the path to the pendant. She hadn't said that path was at the castle, only that lighting it was the key. "Put yourself in the mind of the whomever created this mechanism," Gabriel said to Lisa. "You want it to reveal a path, but only for those who know how to use it. We found the mechanism because we knew we needed to illuminate Cabrera Castle, and that doing so required reflecting the lighthouse's lamplight from this rise. But given enough time and manpower, anyone could have found this mechanism, regardless of whether they knew about lighting the castle. They would just need to scour the island from one end to the other."

Lisa continued his thought. "So if anyone can find the mechanism, you would want to lock it, so that it couldn't be turned without the proper key."

"But that leaves us in the same place," Gabriel countered. "Anyone could find the key if they searched hard enough. Likewise, anyone could determine the key's proper orientation with a close enough examination of its pedestal."

"So anyone could find the mechanism, unlock it, and rotate it," Lisa said. "But without knowing about lighting the castle, they wouldn't know where on the rotation to stop."

"Trial and error," Gabriel said. "Again, with enough time, you could test every point in the rotation. It still doesn't require knowledge of lighting the castle."

"Unless it's not enough to simply rotate into the proper position," Lisa suggested. "Maybe you need to lock in that position."

Gabriel considered the idea, then looked at Lisa with a fresh twinkle of inspiration in his eyes. "We need to remove the reflector. We need to re-lock the disc."

They each took position beside the reflector and gripped it tightly.

Gabriel counted down. "Three, two-"

"Wait," Lisa said. "You're forgetting trial and error."

He shook his head, confused.

"We can re-lock the disc, but if nothing happens, we could just put the reflector back in, rotate to the next position, and try again. There's nothing forcing us to get the position right on the first try. There's nothing forcing us to have knowledge about lighting the castle."

Gabriel's eyes scanned the reflector from top to bottom. "Unless there is. If I was designing this mechanism, I wouldn't give people a second try. Lock in the wrong position, and you're done. You weren't meant to find the pendant."

Lisa pursed her lips. "And by done, you mean..."

Gabriel shrugged. "Maybe the mechanism triggers a more secure lock, one that can only be released from inside the underground village." He recalled Adila Benkirane's words about protecting the pendant from those undeserving of its glory. "Or maybe it triggers a trap... something to remove the immediate threat to the pendant's safety."

Gabriel saw the worry on Lisa's face. He decided it was worth spending a few minutes ensuring they had the right position before re-locking the disc. First, he got Nate on the walkie-talkie and asked him to rotate the lighthouse lamp one degree clockwise. Its beam moved off-center from the reflector. Then Gabriel asked Nate to rotate two degrees counter-clockwise. The first degree properly aligned the beam, and the second pushed it off-center again. Comfortable they already had it correct, Gabriel asked Nate to return the lamp to its previous position. He then performed the same exercise with Samantha, only this time Gabriel and Lisa were the ones shifting the beam of light by rotating the reflecting mechanism one click to either side of its current position. Samantha confirmed both options yielded less light than the original.

"Okay," Gabriel sighed as he and Lisa returned the reflecting mechanism to its previous position. "That's as good of a confirmation as we're going to get."

Lisa nodded. It was clear she was still worried, but there was nothing more they could do. The time had come to re-lock the disc and accept whatever consequences came with doing so. She and Gabriel resumed their positions on each side of the reflector. Gabriel counted down again, and on zero, he and Lisa lifted the reflector. Another thud similar to the first sounded from beneath the disc. This time, no dirt billowed into the air. Instead, Gabriel heard a methodical clinking, almost as if someone were steadily reeling in a metal chain underneath his feet. The sound was dull, muffled by the ground, and it was soon followed by another stone on stone scraping in the distance. The scraping ended in another thud, one Gabriel felt vibrate through his shoes.

"What was that?" Lisa asked.

"Guys, are you okay?" Samantha said over their walkie-talkies. *"We're dark again over here."*

"Yeah, Samantha," Gabriel acknowledged. "Hang tight."

He shined his flashlight toward the moonlit silence that hung in the wake of the scraping noise. After a moment of hesitation, Gabriel and Lisa marched toward that silence together, their eyes and ears alert for any new dangers that might have been triggered by the disc mechanism. Soon, they reached the spot where Gabriel had earlier noted an uncharacteristic dip in the terrain. That dip was gone now, and in its place was a nine-foot hole in the side of the rise. It was a cavern entrance, and beyond its threshold was nothing but blackness.

Gabriel felt the hairs on his arms stick up straight as he and Lisa approached the entrance. He shined his flashlight around the edges and saw that a nearly half-foot thick stone slab had slid aside to reveal the hole. The dirt that had previously camouflaged the slab lay piled before the cavern threshold. Lisa shined her flashlight into the darkness. A tunnel as wide as the cavern opening stretched before her and Gabriel, descending at a moderate angle into an unseen world beneath Cabrera Island.

Gabriel grabbed his walkie-talkie. "Samantha? Go pick up Team

Nerd and converge on our position." He paused a moment to let the anticipation linger, then came clean with what everyone wanted to hear. "We found it."

Chapter Fifty-Five
Worthy

Isla de Cabrera, Spain
Eight Days Before The Sky Opened

It took Samantha and Nadine twenty minutes to pick up Porter and Nate, then another ten to anchor the Leviathan on the southeastern edge of Cabrera Island. Sunlight had just begun to brighten the horizon when Gabriel received confirmation that the team was on foot and headed toward him and Lisa. Gabriel didn't fret, though, for sunrise was no longer a threat to their progress. They had found the entrance to Cabrera Island's underground village, and the approaching daylight couldn't take that from them.

Gabriel recalled the lengthy hike from Cabrera's shoreline to the rise where the cavern was hidden and knew he and Lisa had time to spare. He pulled her away from her expedition preparations and walked her to the peak of the rise. They both sat, arms wrapped tightly around one another, and watched the deep oranges, pinks, and blues seep across the vast expanse that hovered above the Balearic Sea. Darkness turned to light, stars faded from view, and wispy clouds escorted the great ball of yellow and orange fire that burned millions of miles away into view. What had once been a looming deadline was now a wondrous and calming sight to behold.

Thirty minutes later, it was time to get back to work. Gabriel and Lisa returned to the cavern entrance, which was still black as night after the first couple of feet beyond the threshold, the western path receiving no benefit from the early morning sun. They dumped the contents of their gear bag on the ground outside the cavern, then made two piles: one for the equipment they anticipated needing inside; one for the gear they could leave behind until returning from their expedition. Items such as flashlights, spare batteries, ropes and carabiners, and at least one shared canteen of water were deemed necessities. Items such as compasses, flare guns, MREs, and excess water were less important and would only impede mobility.

After sorting their gear, Gabriel and Lisa examined the cavern entrance for any signs of instability or other danger, such as a sealing mechanism that might trap them inside. They found nothing of concern, so they proceeded into the first few feet of the entrance tunnel and performed a similar examination there. Again, they found nothing of concern. Of course, this was expected. Shifa and the pendant villages that had preceded it were welcoming of travelers seeking the pendant's blessing. It wouldn't make sense to booby trap the paths to them and potentially harm the very people the Pendant of God was fabled to help. Satisfied that the road ahead was benign, Gabriel and Lisa returned outside, where they were met by the rest of the team only minutes later.

"My God," Porter said, his mouth agape as he stared at the cavern entrance. "It really is here."

If by "it" he meant a hidden cave that led into the recesses of Cabrera Island, he was correct. If by "it" he meant the Pendant of God... well, that remained to be seen.

"Let's not get our hopes up yet," Gabriel said in a tone that rode the line between sage advisor and party pooper. "We've still got more journey ahead."

He and Lisa helped the other team members match their gear selection. Then they stacked their duffel bags to the side of the cavern entrance, turned on their flashlights, and marched two-by-two into the darkness. The tunnel was cool and damp. Its sides were uneven and jagged, as if bored by hand rather than machine. The tunnel's slope was gradual, but the initial stretch was so long that eventually the team lost sight of the cavern entrance. From there, silence and claustrophobia took hold, for any sound of nature outside was now too far to reach Gabriel's ears, and the back-light that had given Gabriel comfort of an escape hatch should something go wrong was replaced by swampy blackness.

"How deep do you think this goes?" Nadine asked, her voice

echoing off the surrounding rock, its reverberations emphasizing a nervousness shared by the rest of the team.

Gabriel shook his head. "The rise had a pretty high altitude. I suppose we can go until we hit sea level... which could be a while."

A while came sooner than expected, however, for soon the team spotted an opening where the edges of the entrance tunnel gave way to a more open space. They emerged into a stone antechamber large enough to hold the entire group, but just barely. The antechamber had a flat floor with rounded walls and ceilings. There were only two visible entrances to it: the tunnel the team had taken to get there, and a smaller passageway that branched off ninety degrees to the left of that. On each side of the passageway, affixed to the adjacent wall, was a stone tablet. The one to the right contained several rows of words that appeared to be written in Spanish. Lisa approached it.

"Those who seek the pendant's blessing," she translated slowly as her mind struggled to reignite foreign language skills she hadn't used in years, "must prove they are worthy. Four trials of God's gifts to man lie ahead. At the end, salvation awaits."

That was where the words ended, but Lisa shifted her flashlight beam downward, where, near the bottom of the tablet, four symbols had been centered beneath the text. The first consisted of two horizontal lines whose right ends were connected by what appeared to be a cloud. The second was a collection of jagged cracks, much like the jagged surface of the rocky tunnel the team had traversed to get here. The third was a series of wavy lines that reminded Gabriel of ocean chop. Finally, the fourth was undoubtedly a flame.

"The elements of life," Gabriel said to no one in particular. He turned his own flashlight to the stone tablet to the left of the antechamber's next passageway. Engraved on that tablet was a larger replica of the symbol with horizontal lines connected by a cloud. "And it looks like *Wind* is first."

Normally, Gabriel would have been excited by the thrill of discovery and anticipation of potentially dangerous exploration that lied ahead. But he wasn't excited, and he could see that neither was Lisa, for in her mind was probably the same thought that was currently racing through his: something about this cave wasn't right.

Chapter Fifty-Six
Red Flags

Isla de Cabrera, Spain
Eight Days Before The Sky Opened

Porter must have noticed Gabriel's and Lisa's hesitation. "What's wrong? I thought you guys lived for this Indiana Jones shit."

"When it's authentic, yeah," Gabriel replied. "But, do you have any idea how many missions we've been on where the relic we're after is neatly wrapped in a bow at the end of a telegraphed set of challenges straight out of a Hollywood blockbuster?"

Porter shrugged. "I assume most of them fit that description."

"None," Nate said bluntly. "We've never been on a mission like that."

Porter peered at Nate, confusion settling over him.

"Remember what you used to tell us about Indiana Jones?" Lisa asked rhetorically. "It's not real archeology. The thing is, it's not exactly real treasure hunting, either. No one ever leaves their treasured artifacts on weighted plates that trigger giant boulders. No one sets up elaborate challenges that serve no purpose other than to make obtaining those artifacts difficult."

"Not to mention," Samantha chimed in, "we're not just talking about an artifact here. We're talking about an entire village. How do its inhabitants get in and out? Do they have to pass the trials each time? Do the trials work the same way from both directions? Who resets the challenges after they've been triggered?"

Gabriel picked up the argument from there. "In reality, artifacts are typically passed down through generational bloodlines. Maybe they get stolen. Maybe they change hands in battle. But eventually, they wind up in the hands of someone whose entire civilization is suddenly wiped out, or someone who dies alone, or they get buried as a memento, or any number of other outcomes. The point is, an external force removes them from the chain of inheritance, and they become lost in time, until people like us find them... in tombs, in the rubble of former cities, on the ocean floor-"

"Where we don't find them," Lisa continued, "is in places that resemble Hollywood sets." She then emphasized, "places like this."

Porter's astonished gaze shifted to her, then to Gabriel. "What are you saying?" His words carried a nervous aggression. "That we shouldn't go through that passage? That we should just turn around and wait for time to run out?"

Gabriel motioned for Porter to relax. "No one's saying that. All we're saying is that this feels more like a movie than anything we've previously experienced in real life. It feels... staged. It also doesn't align with what we know about previous pendant villages. If those truly are trials that lie ahead, then by definition, there must be a meaningful level of difficulty in completing them. How are people in need of the pendant's healing supposed to get through that?"

"Not everyone requiring healing needs the pendant for the same reason," Porter said, desperately clinging to hope.

"That's exactly my point," Gabriel countered. "*Wind, Earth, Water, Fire...* there's a challenge there no matter your ailment. How can someone with bad legs get through an *Earth* challenge? How can someone with weak muscles or an unsteady balance get through a *Wind* challenge?" He stared hard into Porter's eyes. "And what about you? What happens if we get to *Water*, and it requires holding your breath for any length of time? Can you honestly tell me your lungs up for that?"

Porter, normally one to exude confidence, spoke more timidly than Gabriel had ever heard him do so before. "That's why it's called a trial, isn't it?"

Gabriel acquiesced. His gut was waving a red flag, shouting that they shouldn't proceed, that this couldn't possibly be the path to the new pendant village. But Porter was right about one thing. Aside from a vague drawing about a bird, the team had nothing else to pursue. If they turned back now, Porter's clock would certainly run out before they came close to discovering the new village's location. Gabriel looked at Lisa, his sound mind in troubling situations. She frowned, an acknowledgment that forging ahead carried an uncomfortable level of risk, then nodded reluctantly, her signal to proceed anyway.

"We'll face the trials," Gabriel announced to the group. "But take nothing you see, hear, smell- anything at all- at face value. Assume we're walking into a trap and maintain a high awareness of your surroundings at all times. Use the buddy system, same teams as before. If anything triggers a warning sign, don't keep it to yourself. Got it?"

Each team member expressed agreement. Gabriel shined his light on the stone *Wind* tablet once more, took a deep breath, and stepped toward its adjacent passageway. A hand quickly pressed against his chest, blocking his advance.

"I'm the reason you're all risking your lives," Porter said. "I'll go first. That way, if it is a trap, maybe I'll be the only one to suffer the consequences." He turned to Nate. "Team Nerd can regroup once I give the all-clear."

Gabriel nodded and allowed Porter to take the lead. He watched his friend approach the passageway and peer as far through the awaiting darkness as he could using his flashlight. The next thing Gabriel knew, Porter stepped into that darkness, and a few seconds later, he was gone. The other team members waited anxiously for a report from beyond. A minute passed. Then two. Worry grew visible on Nadine's face as she shined her own light into the passageway, as if hoping to catch a glimpse of Porter somewhere within. Another long, silent minute went by. Concerned that Porter might need his help, but already be outside of earshot, Gabriel took a step forward. Lisa grabbed his arm and shook her head: *no.*

Before Gabriel could argue, Porter's voice echoed from the passageway. "I reached the trial!" His words had a hollow tinge to them, as if he were yelling them from a far-off, open-air location. "The passage is safe! You're going to want to see this!"

Chapter Fifty-Seven
Crosswinds

Isla de Cabrera, Spain
Eight Days Before The Sky Opened

Though Porter had already vetted the passageway to the *Wind* trial, Gabriel forced the team to advance slowly and carefully. He inspected one side of the passageway as Lisa inspected the other. As Porter had indicated, it appeared safe for traversal. It took the team about five minutes to reach the end of the dark tunnel, where it opened into an underground cavern so huge that Gabriel was certain it hadn't been excavated by the pendant villagers. The cavern was partially illuminated by sunlight that pierced distant gaps in walls that were at least three or four hundred feet away. It was just bright enough that the team could temporarily put away their flashlights and allow their eyes to adjust to the dim glow that surrounded them.

They were standing on a rocky platform attached to the passageway exit. Above them, too high to see, was the cavern roof. Below was a massive ravine that flooded with darkness well before reaching bottom. A stone bridge about five feet wide and just as deep spanned the distance of the ravine. Gabriel immediately noted that it had no walls, railings, or other obvious protections from falling. At the other end of the bridge was another passageway flanked by a stone tablet... their next destination.

"Do you hear that?" Lisa asked.

Gabriel had picked up on the constant roar emanating from the darkness below shortly after entering the cavern. Now he listened closer and realized it wasn't as constant as he originally perceived. It was a series of roars, similar in sound but broken into individual segments, some overlapping and others not.

"Waves?" Gabriel asked.

"It sounds like the sea," Lisa said.

Porter turned to them. "That's not all."

As soon as he finished speaking, a second noise, this one a muted hum, filled the cavern. The hum was soon overtaken by the screech of wind as a hurricane-strength current blasted across the ravine for nearly ten seconds. Then the wind died down, the screech stifled, and the hum dissipated, leaving only the roar of unseen waves below.

Nate clicked his tongue. "I guess that's the *Wind* challenge."

Porter swung deliberate eyes to his fellow engineer. "What clued you in?"

Samantha removed her water canteen and checked its level. As the muted hum filled the cavern once more, she slid her canteen as far down the stone bridge as she safely could while keeping it centered. It stopped about eight feet away. Then the blast of wind came, and the canteen was snatched off the bridge and flung into the far darkness. No one heard whether it crashed into the unseen walls or fell into the invisible sea below.

"The wind is blowing perpendicular to the bridge," Samantha said. "I thought a full canteen might give at least some resistance..."

"A canteen is a lot smaller than a person," Gabriel pointed out. "Maybe something with a larger mass-"

Samantha cut him off. "Larger mass, but more surface area to catch the blast." She shook her head. "If any of us gets caught in that crosswind, he or she is as good as dead."

As if supporting her theory with an ominous warning, another hum and wind blast triggered. That made three in less than two minutes. Gabriel assessed the path across the ravine. At a full sprint, it would take at least twenty seconds to get to the other end. With the dim lighting of the cavern and no guardrails to provide a sense of security, the team could, at best, jog across. And with Porter's lungs working below capacity...

"We can't cover that distance between blasts," Gabriel said, pointing at the ravine. "There's got to be another way."

"What if we aren't meant to cross the bridge?" Nadine asked. "We can all hear the water down there. What if the *Wind* trial is really just a diversion from a *Water* trial we should complete instead?"

Samantha chewed at the inside of her cheek as she considered Nadine's suggestion. Then she shook her head again. "We don't know how far down that water is, but I can tell you it's too far to safely jump. We could lower ourselves as far as possible with ropes, then jump from there-"

"Even if we did," Lisa said, "those are rough waves we're hearing. They'd toss us around until beating us to death against the cavern walls."

While they were talking, another blast of wind screeched through the cavern. As soon as it calmed, Gabriel took a step onto the stone bridge.

"What are you doing?" Porter asked.

Gabriel held up a hand that signaled *give me a minute*. He counted the seconds in his head, giving himself no more than ten before he would turn back to avoid the next wind blast. He knew if there was no way to outrun the wind, and no way to get around the bridge, then there must be a way across that the team couldn't see. They needed to perform recon, and Gabriel didn't want to risk anyone else doing it. His leg muscles tried to liquify as he moved farther and farther from the safety of the rocky platform on which everyone else stood. He made the mistake of glancing into the ravine, the darkness beyond the cavern glow disorienting him, throwing off his balance. Gabriel wobbled, and in a panic dropped to one knee to avoid falling. He took several quick, successive breaths and closed his eyes to steady himself. Then he heard the muted hum and realized in his moment of panic he had lost count of his time to return.

Gabriel opened his eyes and looked to the rocky platform, where Lisa and the others were shouting in fear. Gabriel knew instantly that it was too far away. In moments, the cavern hum would be replaced by screeching wind, and Gabriel would learn the fate of Samantha's canteen. His destiny already sealed, Gabriel didn't attempt to reach safety. Instead, he insanely embraced what minuscule hope he had, turned the other way, and ran. Maybe the wind didn't cover the entire bridge. Maybe there were dead zones and Gabriel would reach one before the blast reached him. Maybe-

Gabriel's right toe caught on a small piece of stone jutting vertically from the bridge. He slammed face-first into the hard surface and felt a sudden breeze as death's screech began. With no other option, Gabriel rotated on his stomach and grasped for the stone that had tripped him. He found it with his left hand just as the wind blast arrived. His body was pulled upwards as if caught in an aerial vortex. But Gabriel held on to the stone, his fingers white with strain as he fought back against the hurricane. Then one finger began to slip. Then another. Suspended in air, nearly upside down, deafened by the storm that engulfed him, Gabriel flung his right hand around for support. He missed the stone and felt his fingertips instead drag along the smooth surface of the bridge. Despite every effort to hang on, Gabriel was no match for the powerful crosswind. His left hand lost its grip, and he felt his body rip away from the only anchor it had.

Chapter Fifty-Eight
Airborne

Isla de Cabrera, Spain
Eight Days Before The Sky Opened

Gabriel was floating free, and in that moment, he wondered if this is what it felt like to be an astronaut, or maybe more appropriately, a skydiver. He also wondered if this is what it felt like to be a spirit leaving behind a dead body. Unfortunately, he knew he would get the answer to that second question soon enough. He stared blankly at the surface of the stone bridge as it zipped by beneath him. Then Gabriel was jolted by a searing pain in his right hand, and his free float hit an abrupt stop. Looking for the source of the pain, he saw that his scraped right fingertips had instinctually latched around a second vertical stone. Reinvigorated by the prospect of survival, Gabriel pulled with all his might and secured his left hand over his right. The blast of wind began to settle, and Gabriel felt his body lowering. He oriented so he would land back on the bridge, and a few seconds later, he was no longer airborne. The screeching stopped, and the hum diminished.

"Holy shit," Gabriel muttered through stuttered breaths.

He couldn't believe he was still alive, much less safe right back where he had started his one-man standoff against Mother Nature. All Gabriel wanted to do was lie there and enjoy the cool, hard surface of solid ground against his body. But subconsciously aware that time was short, he instead sat upright and examined the vertical stones that had saved his life. Surprisingly, they appeared to be contoured to fit the natural shape of a human hand when assuming a claw-like grip. Gabriel had a vague sense he had seen their shape before. Then it hit him: rock walls. The stones resembled the handholds one might find on a gymnasium rock wall. Not only that, but they weren't alone. Now that Gabriel was closer to the ground and knew what to look for, he could see that more vertical stones were positioned periodically along the bridge in both directions. The muted hum filled the cavern again.

"Gabriel!" Lisa yelled. "Get back here!"

Gabriel held up a confident hand, hopeful she would understand his message: *he had this under control.* He dropped into a prone position and reached for the stone grips nearest to each hand. Gabriel clenched them tightly and pressed his body against the ground as the next blast of wind swept out of the darkness and smashed into the side of the bridge. This time, he didn't go airborne. The wind tried to slip beneath him, and even lifted his feet, but Gabriel's two anchor points and flat brace provided enough support to keep him secure. Though the wind lasted just as long as before, it felt as though it were over sooner, for it had been reduced from a lethal threat to moderate annoyance. This time, once the blast subsided, Gabriel rose and jogged back to his waiting team.

"What the hell were you thinking?!" Lisa hollered.

"I don't know," Gabriel told her. "I just figured there had to be a way across."

Porter smiled and gave him a congratulatory slap on the back. "That's why you're the best."

"So we just repeat what you did?" Nadine asked. "Walk when we can, keep an eye on the handholds, and drop whenever the hum starts?"

Gabriel nodded. "That's it. The wind still hits pretty hard, so you need to hold on tight..." As his voice trailed, his eyes shifted to Porter. "How's your strength?"

Porter smiled weakly. "It could be better." He then swung his satchel from around his arm and sat it on the ground. "Luckily, it won't be a problem. Do you remember back in our hotel in Casablanca when I said I had something interesting to show you?"

Porter opened the satchel and removed an oversized mechanical glove from within. He slipped it over his right hand and showed off the device, which appeared to be made primarily of a flexible cloth lined with circuitry, which was then surrounded by a metallic exoskeleton. In the palm of the high-tech glove was a glowing disc embedded in what Gabriel could only guess was some sort of launching device.

"Well?" Porter asked.

Nate cocked his head at the wearable machine. "What the hell is that?"

Porter chuckled. "You know those extension claws that elderly people use to grab things from out-of-reach shelves? Think of this as the next evolution of that product."

Taking a cue from Samantha, he removed his canteen and tossed it to the far end of the rocky platform. Then he held his gloved hand up, fingers clenched and facing away from him. Porter spread his fingers wide with visible force, the gesture triggering the launch of the glowing disc. It shot forward from Porter's palm, beamed across the platform, and smacked into the fallen canteen with a clang. The disc secured itself to the canteen's surface using a mechanism too small for Gabriel to see. Then Porter closed and re-opened his fist in one fluid motion, triggering the disc's return. It shot back across the platform, carrying the canteen with it, and slammed into place in the launching device in Porter's palm.

"Damn," Nate said with astonishment. He followed it with, "overcompensating much?"

Porter ignored him. "I'm still working out some bugs, which is why I brought it on the trip. I figured I could tinker with it in our downtime. But then it hit me that it might come in handy here on Cabrera Island. Now I'm wondering what I would have done without it."

Samantha frowned. "I'm sorry... how is that going to help you cross?"

Porter walked to the closest rock wall and grabbed a jagged protrusion with his gloved hand. He used his other hand to double tap the top of the glove, at which point Gabriel could see it tighten around the protrusion. Porter tried pulling away from the rocky surface for demonstrative purposes, but the glove wouldn't budge. He double tapped the top a second time, and then it released freely.

"You don't need your own strength when you've got the strength of technology-infused steel on your side," Porter said.

Gabriel gawked at the invention. "How does it maintain its hold?"

Porter bobbed his head. "It's a bit technical, but the glove and disc are connected by a focused array of electromagnets. The outer side of the disc is covered in microscopic diamond hooks that extend upon impact with an object and retract upon return to the glove. The hooks can penetrate most surfaces without leaving visible marks."

"Electromagnets, huh?" Nate said with a hint of sarcasm. "Not exactly ideal for the pacemaker-wearing customer base. It'd be like equipping them with loaded guns and no safety switches. I can already see the headlines the first time an innocent elderly person aims their hand the wrong way and winds up in the grave."

"For what it's worth," Porter told him, "the FDA agrees with you. They won't sign off on the device until I replace the magnets with some other technology. The problem is, I'm having trouble identifying an alternative that achieves feature parity."

Gabriel placed a comforting hand on his shoulder. "Luckily for you, none of us have pacemakers. So let's line up and get across that bridge using whatever sources of strength we've got."

Porter smiled at him, appreciative of the miniature pep talk. "Thank you, my friend."

The most recent blast of wind- the fourth since Gabriel had returned to the team- wavered in strength. Gabriel and the others fell into single-file at the start of the bridge, Gabriel in front to dictate brace timing, Samantha in the back to keep an eye on everyone until they made it across safely. A moment later, the wind died down and the accompanying hum went silent.

Gabriel glanced back at his team and shouted, "let's go!" Then he set out across the bridge to tempt death once more.

Chapter Fifty-Nine
Descent

Isla de Cabrera, Spain
Eight Days Before The Sky Opened

Traversing the *Wind* challenge went surprisingly smooth from there. Gabriel would drop and grip the nearest stone handholds at the first sound of the muted hum. Each team member behind him would follow suit, with Samantha dropping just before the hurricane winds blasted through the cavern. When the winds petered out, Gabriel would stand and resume the procession across the bridge. Rinse and repeat. The team reached the other side without incident, where a rock platform similar to that they entered on awaited. Gabriel wasted no time approaching the passageway to their next challenge and examining the stone tablet that accompanied it.

"It looks like *Earth* is next," he told the team as he stared at the jagged cracks that spider-webbed between each side of the tablet. He then turned his gaze to the passageway, which was illuminated just enough by the cavern glow for Gabriel to see what lied ahead. It was another antechamber, this one significantly smaller than the previous, and in its center was a dark hole, maybe seven or eight feet in diameter by Gabriel's best estimation, bored straight down into the earth. "Samantha, flare."

Samantha passed him the skinny red cylinder, and Gabriel sparked its chemical reaction. He held the flare ahead of him, casting a bright red glow through the short passageway and into the antechamber beyond. Gabriel inspected the walls of the passageway, once again finding no booby traps or other causes for concern. He then stepped forward slowly, the rest of the team falling into the same line they had taken across the bridge, and led the way to the dark hole that awaited.

The team had to spread out, flanking the hole's circumference, to fit everyone inside the antechamber. Gabriel kneeled down and extended the flare beyond the mouth of darkness. Much like the bridge they had just crossed, the walls of the shaft that awaited were smooth, except for occasional handholds that jutted just far enough to provide a stable grip. Gabriel couldn't see where the shaft ended, so he tossed the flare down its center, then counted the seconds as it fell, piercing the darkness and revealing more smooth surface and more stone handholds, until it clattered to a hard landing below.

"That's about two hundred feet," Samantha said. "Maybe more."

"At least there's no wind," Nate added.

Gabriel still hadn't risen from his kneel. That long of a climb was a challenge in itself, but then again, so was crossing a nausea-inducing ravine on a bridge with no guardrails. Yet the previous trial had presented an additional challenge, that in the form of vicious wind. What was the additional challenge here? There was no way the climb was as straightforward as it appeared.

"We've got a lighting issue," Lisa said.

"What?" Gabriel asked.

"We've got a lighting issue," she repeated. "The flare will provide light once we near the bottom, but there's nothing covering the first three-fourths of the climb. The light from the *Wind* cavern doesn't reach into the shaft."

"We've got flashlights," Nadine reminded her.

"True, but we need our hands for the climb." Lisa looked at Samantha. "I don't suppose you packed head lamps?"

Samantha shook her head in the negative.

Gabriel sighed. There was his additional challenge. Climbing two hundred feet when you could see where you were going was one thing. Doing it in pitch black was something completely different.

"Look," Porter said to the entire team, "I know I volunteered to go first on these trials to keep the rest of you safe, but in this case, maybe I should go last."

Gabriel cocked his head curiously.

"There's no need for everyone to climb in the dark," Porter

clarified. "Nate and I can hang back and shine flashlights into the shaft while the rest of you descend. Then I'll hold a light for Nate, and finally I'll come down in the dark."

"I don't think you realize what you're signing up for," Gabriel told him.

"Yes, I do. Besides, I'm the one with technology on his side." He held up his electromagnetic glove. "Between that and whatever light you can provide me from the bottom, I should be fine."

Gabriel looked at Lisa, who shrugged complacently.

"Fine," he then said. "But we're deploying a safety rope as far as it'll take us. We can use the bridge as an anchor. We'll lose a lot of length tying off and running the rope through the passageway, but it's still better than free climbing the entire distance. We'll secure ourselves up here and be prepared to unlink once the rope runs out. Hopefully, we'll be close to the bottom of the shaft by then. Samantha, give Porter a crash course since he's going to have to manage on his own."

"Sure thing, boss."

As Samantha walked Porter through the critical steps of securing and releasing himself from an anchor line, Gabriel and Lisa returned to the rocky platform at the end of the *Wind* challenge. Gabriel lowered one end of a safety rope on the side nearest the wind source, then stepped back and waited for the impending blast. It came within a minute, grabbing the end of the rope, yanking it beneath the stone bridge, and taking it airborne on the other side. Secure in the passageway, Gabriel allowed sufficient slack to release, then held the rope tight to prevent the wind from taking any more. As soon as the blast lost energy, Lisa ran forward and grabbed the flapping airborne end before gravity could intervene. Then she and Gabriel tied the rope to itself, creating an anchoring loop around the bridge. They triple-checked their knots, returned to the antechamber, and dropped whatever length of rope they had left into the *Earth* shaft.

Lisa hitched herself to the rope, taking lead position since she was a more experienced climber than Gabriel. Sticking to the buddy system, Gabriel went second, followed by Nadine, and, once she was done with Porter, Samantha, who again wanted to be in the rear to keep an eye on the safety of the others. The climbing group used a second rope to daisy-chain themselves to each other. When finished, they lined up along one edge of the shaft while Nate and Porter assumed their flashlight positions on the other.

"You didn't think of soliciting my input before volunteering us to stay behind?" Nate asked his thrill-seeking buddy.

"You still get the benefit of light when you go down."

"Yeah," Nate agreed, "but not the safety of being linked to the group if I slip."

Porter smiled reassuringly. "You can link to me. I'll keep a hand on your rope until it runs out."

"A hand or a knife?" Nate shot back.

Porter's smile didn't crack. "A hand," he confirmed. "We're not rivals anymore, Nate. We're Team Nerd... and we don't let each other fall."

Samantha inspected the climbing team's riggings and tested the strength of their anchor knots by having everyone lean their full body weight in unison. All safety mechanisms held. Lisa sat on the edge of the shaft, her legs dangling into Nate and Porter's flashlight beams. She took a firming breath and turned, propping herself onto her arms, before lowering to the first handhold. Lisa gripped it just as she had gripped those on the bridge. She then used the leverage of the first handhold to reach for a second. Her fingers wrapped around the jutting stone and conformed to its contours. Lisa shifted her weight, preparing to find her next target, but as she did so, the second handhold released from the shaft wall. Unprepared for the sudden loss of support, Lisa's body tore free, and with a yelp, she plunged into the open darkness below.

Chapter Sixty
Falling

Isla de Cabrera, Spain
Eight Days Before The Sky Opened

"Brace!" Gabriel screamed as soon as he saw Lisa detach.

He planted his feet and tightened both hands around the daisy-chained rope. Nadine mimicked his actions while Samantha launched herself at the nearest rock wall and clung to its rough protrusions. The rope went taut, violently yanking each of them toward the mouth of the *Earth* shaft. Gabriel teetered at the edge, his body in an unsteady tug-of-war between the combined force of gravity and Lisa's weight, and the resistance being provided by Samantha and Nadine.

He tried to lean away from the shaft, but his muscles could barely keep him from toppling over, much less provide him the leverage needed to get to safety. Gabriel saw flashes of bright light and worried that the strain was causing him to lose consciousness. Then he heard a clattering, followed by brisk shuffling, and seconds later, two sets of arms had interlocked with his own. Nate and Porter pulled Gabriel away from the shaft. Then they each clasped the daisy-chain rope and provided whatever additional support they could.

"Lisa!" Gabriel yelled, unable to see into the shaft. "Lisa, can you hear me?!"

Her reply was sluggish, and when it came, her voice was faint and dazed. "Y-yeah... I'm trying to see... there's so little light."

Gabriel looked at Nate and nudged his head. The tech engineer released the rope and returned to his flashlight, which he had haphazardly tossed aside when scrambling to help. Nate shined the light back into the shaft, eventually finding Lisa, who was now deeper than before, dangling like a fish on a line. Guided by his bright beam, Lisa spotted the nearest stone handholds and swung her body gently toward them. She tested the handholds before trusting them with her weight, then pulled herself back into a climbing position. Tension in the daisy-chain rope instantly eased, giving the rest of the climbing team freedom to move about the antechamber.

"What happened?" Gabriel called down to his wife. "Freak accident?"

"I don't think so," Lisa said. She scanned for another handhold, realizing now that they appeared to be grouped into sets of three. With her weight securely anchored to one of her current handholds, Lisa cautiously reached for the third of this set. Her initial assessment upon making contact was that it was no different from the others, but when Lisa tugged at it with force, it broke away freely from the smooth shaft wall. "They're decoys," Lisa informed the rest of the team. "Fake handholds are interspersed with the real ones. One in every set of three, I'm guessing."

Gabriel silently scolded himself. He'd suspected there would be a twist in this trial, and he had readily accepted that the twist must be the darkness in which to scale the shaft. But darkness had nothing to do with *Earth*. Gabriel should have been more diligent in identifying the trial-specific threat, and his lack of diligence had almost cost Lisa her life.

"Do you think you can identify the decoys without endangering yourself?"

Lisa eyed the next grouping of handholds. "Yeah. We'll just need to take our time. And you're going to need to watch for the ones I fell past."

Gabriel confirmed he would, then verified Nadine and Samantha were ready to proceed. Once he began his descent, Lisa continued hers. She tested all three handholds in each new group and discarded the decoys to mitigate the risk of anyone else grabbing them. Gabriel did the same for the first few sets, which Lisa had bypassed, then continued along her path. Lisa reached the bottom of the safety rope and unhooked herself. She informed the other climbers that there was a ten-foot gap of darkness between then end of the rope and the reach of the flare's glow from below, but that if they just continued straight down, they would easily find the handholds she had cleared.

Soon, Lisa reached the bottom of the shaft. Then Gabriel, Nadine, and Samantha arrived unharmed as well. Gabriel shouted to Team Nerd that it was their turn, so Porter helped Nate latch to the anchor rope, then secured a secondary safety rope between them for peace of mind. Porter resumed flashlight duty, and Nate began his descent. With the decoy handholds along one full side of the shaft now cleared, it was a much safer climb than before. But Nate's stuttered breathing echoed downward, revealing that he was uneasy. It took twice as long as it had taken the others, but he eventually reached the end of the anchor rope, detached himself, and continued into the stretch of darkness that followed. When he emerged from the other side, Gabriel saw Nate must have been disoriented by his temporary blindness, for he was no longer on the cleared side of the shaft.

"Nate, stop!" Gabriel yelled into the hole overhead. "Let your eyes adjust before you move."

Nate did as he was told, then looked around, the reason for Gabriel's intervention immediately clear. "Oh, shit."

"It's okay," Lisa said, a deliberate smoothness to her voice. "You just need to keep your weight anchored to a secure hand while you test the next set of grips with the other."

"Easy for you to say!"

Gabriel looked for a way to climb back into the shaft to help Nate, but the hole was nearly ten feet high, and there was no obvious way to reach it from the flat surface on which he and the others now stood.

"Nate, trust me," Lisa continued. "Just keep your testing hand free of any weight. Tell yourself you can't rely on it for support."

"Maybe I should go back up," Nate suggested. "I think I remember which handholds I used. I can get back on the path you already cleared."

"It's probably safer to get down here as efficiently as possible," Gabriel told him. "You don't know for sure which handholds are safe."

"Yeah," Nate said with an anxious nod. "Yeah, I do. I'm going to get back on track."

"Nate, don't-"

But it was no use. Nate had made up his mind and was already reaching for a handhold from the set bordering the darkness above.

234

He gingerly touched it with his left hand, then slapped its sides as if patting a child's cheeks. Apparently that was comforting enough, for Nate gripped the handhold and pulled his weight upward. The handhold instantly snapped from its perch in the shaft wall, and Nate plunged toward the ground below.

Nadine screamed. Nate fell so fast that Gabriel, Lisa, and Samantha had only enough time to react on instinct, and that instinct was to run beneath the shaft to try to catch him. But then Nate stopped just beyond the shaft threshold. His body was levitating in mid-air, with nothing visibly supporting its weight. Gabriel and the others were stunned with confusion, and so was Nate, until his face twisted with the onset of pain.

"Ow!" He yelled as he turned his gaze upward.

Perched on a cleared set of handholds fifteen feet above Nate was Porter. His gloved hand was extended outward, palm facing Nate's back, its electromagnetic stream pulling at the disc Gabriel assumed had lodged itself somewhere along Nate's spine.

"I can't hold this position much longer," Porter said, strain tearing at his voice. "You ready?"

"Yeah," Gabriel yelled.

Porter shut down the magnet, and Nate's fall resumed. This time, however, he only fell nine feet into the waiting arms of his teammates.

"I could use that back!" Porter yelled, his breathing heavy.

The team set Nate down and Gabriel examined his back. Sure enough, Porter's disc was embedded just above Nate's buttocks. Gabriel wiggled it loose, which took far more force than anticipated and elicited a scream from Nate as it drew blood. He held the disc out, and it glinted in the red flare light as it zipped through the shaft and returned to Porter's palm launcher.

"I'll be down in a minute," Porter said, using his glove to latch on to a handhold and provide his other muscles with relief.

With Porter still in the shaft, and Nadine standing out of earshot, Gabriel bent down under the guise of inspecting Nate's wound and subtly whispered in his tech engineer's ear. "I know we discussed testing Porter's willingness to let you die, but that was reckless. You should have waited on us to come up with a plan where you wouldn't actually get killed if Porter didn't come through."

Nate didn't speak, but he looked at Gabriel with eyes that had just been shaken by the prospect of death.

"That wasn't a test?" Gabriel asked.

Nate shook his head slowly. "It looks like I was wrong about Porter, after all." He looked away, his gaze distant and unfocused as he stared into space. "That's never happened to me before."

Gabriel rolled his eyes. "Once you get over the fact that you're human like the rest of us, you owe Porter an apology... or at least a heavy dose of gratitude."

Nate smiled half-heartedly. "I'll start with the latter."

Chapter Sixty-One
The Lock

Isla de Cabrera, Spain
Eight Days Before The Sky Opened

The room at the bottom of the *Earth* shaft mirrored that at its top. Red flare light bounced off the walls of a small antechamber bored from pure stone. Overhead was the exit from the *Earth* shaft, from which Porter had just finished his descent and now stood bent over, hands on knees, heaving for breath. Gabriel could see only one other path out of the room: a passageway embedded in the rocky wall. Beside it was a stone tablet displaying the same series of wavy lines they had seen earlier. *Water*, perhaps the deadliest challenge given Porter's physical state, awaited them.

As he had done with each previous passageway, Gabriel inspected this one for booby traps. He took his time, allotting this inspection more than double the attention he had given each of the others. When Lisa took notice and gave him a questioning look, Gabriel made a subtle nod toward Porter, his way of silently explaining that nothing was wrong, and he was just giving his friend extra time to recover.

"It's clear," Gabriel said once Porter had his breathing under control.

Porter smiled weakly and proceeded to the head of the pack. "No time like the present."

"Porter, you don't have to-"

Porter gave him a dismissive wave and shined his light into the dark passageway. Then he took a hesitant step forward, followed by another. Gabriel watched intently as Porter forged ahead, and was pleasantly surprised when his friend didn't disappear into blackness as he had done when approaching the *Wind* trial. Instead, Porter's silhouette grew smaller and smaller, the beam of his flashlight shrinking into the distance of what appeared to be an adjacent cylindric chamber. Porter stopped a little over a minute later, swung his flashlight beam across a solid surface that blocked his path, then called back to the group.

"I think you're good to enter!" His voiced echoed loudly off the curved walls.

Nate huffed. "I guess that's my cue."

He approached the awaiting passageway, confirmed that Porter still seemed to be okay in the chamber beyond, then marched forward to reunite Team Nerd. Gabriel and Lisa followed, then Samantha and Nadine did the same. They each had their flashlights out again and were scanning the walls that surrounded them. Gabriel could make out the core surface of cragged rock in every direction. He also occasionally spotted rods of stone jutting out of that rock, almost as if they had been nailed in, and each rod had a different, precision-carved symbol for a head.

"What the hell?" Lisa asked aloud.

Gabriel couldn't wrap his head around what they were seeing. "Samantha, do you have more flares?"

Samantha responded in the affirmative, then sparked two flares and tossed them to the floor in opposite directions. Their burning glows cast a dim light throughout the entire chamber, bringing the pieces of everything Gabriel had seen so far together. As he initially assessed, the room was indeed cylindrical, like an overturned soup can with a twenty-foot diameter and length of a football field. A smooth walking path spanned the middle of the curved floor, but otherwise the rest of the floor, walls, and ceiling were rough and uneven. The rods Gabriel had spotted were each about six inches long, with a diameter triple that of a standard broom handle. They were regularly spaced throughout the chamber, and Gabriel now estimated there must be at least a couple hundred of them.

"What are they?" Nadine asked.

"I think," Gabriel said with a hint of trepidation in his voice, "they're the only things keeping us from drowning right now. Listen."

Everyone grew quiet, and through their own silence, they could hear a familiar muffled roar emanating from the rocky surface overhead. Gabriel replayed their progress through the underground cavern in his mind, mapping out their initial descent, then their crossing of the *Wind* bridge, and their climb down the *Earth* shaft and subsequent procession into this chamber. If his navigation was accurate-

"We're directly beneath the *Wind* trial," Samantha said.

"But I thought there was water..." Nadine's words trailed as she realized exactly what Samantha meant by being *beneath* the other challenge. "Oh, God."

"It's okay," Lisa assured her. "There's no sign of moisture in here right now. Potential threats aside, the chamber appears watertight. Besides, if water gets in, we can float up the *Earth* shaft until we're even with sea level and then climb to safety."

That seemed to ease Nadine's nerves a little.

"You're going to want to see the exit," Porter told Gabriel, shining his light toward the solid surface that had blocked his path earlier. At the far end of the chamber was another passageway, this one with a tablet displaying a flame next to it. But the passageway was blocked by a stone door similar to the one at the initial entrance to the underground cave. On the opposite side of the passageway from the flame tablet was a second tablet with a hole in its center. Gabriel shined his flashlight into the hole and could see a recessed curvy symbol about half a foot within.

"It's a lock," he told the rest of the group. He then shined his flashlight over the hundreds of symbol-headed rods sticking out of the chamber walls, its beam creating ominous, elongated shadows on the rocky surfaces. "A lock in need of a key..."

"And each key is a potential breach in our underwater sanctuary," Nate added unnecessarily. He looked at Porter. "I suspect we're about to get wet. Are you ready for this?"

Porter swallowed hard and spoke bravely, though his face was pale with unspoken fear. "Better now than later." His words were truthful, even if less than comforting. Porter swung his gaze to Gabriel. "Tell us what to do, boss."

Chapter Sixty-Two
The Leak

Isla de Cabrera, Spain
Eight Days Before The Sky Opened

"Let's do this smartly," Gabriel said as he stepped aside. "Everyone, come get a good look at the lock. Then fan out and find the matching symbol. Don't remove it from the wall if you find it; just call everyone over for a consensus before we proceed. One missing rod shouldn't let much water in, but we have no idea what other surprises we might be in for."

The other team members acknowledged his instructions, and soon they dispersed throughout the chamber, methodically checking each stone rod for the unique curvy pattern within the tablet hole. After five minutes, there was a false alarm, with Nate finding a symbol that looked similar, but upon closer inspection, not identical to the one for which they were searching. After another twenty minutes, they hit paydirt, with Nadine finding the matching symbol at the head of a rod about two-thirds away from the locked door. The team regrouped around her and confirmed her discovery.

"Okay," Gabriel then directed, "I want you to pull the rod out and get to the keyhole as fast as you can. Samantha will go with you to ensure there are no problems. The rest of us will stay here and try to plug whatever water leak you create. Are you comfortable with that?"

Nadine nodded confidently. Gabriel counted to three, then helped her yank on the stone rod, which scraped loudly against surrounding rock as it slid free of its home. There was a loud clunk from within the hole left behind, then sea water shot through it like a wide-open fire hose, nearly taking Nadine's arm off. A series of unseen mechanisms clicked and clacked behind the chamber wall. The sounds made their way to the entry passageway, triggering the collapse of a camouflaged stone awning that slammed down in front of it, eliminating any possibility of retreat. Seeing this, Gabriel attempted to cup his hands over the stream of sea water, but the pressure was unbearable. It stung his skin and, even though they had only been exposed for a second, left his palms bright red and numb. Lisa looked around frantically for some other way to impede the flow as Nadine and Samantha neared the *Fire* trial door.

"It's okay," Porter said over the gushing stream. "Based on the flow rate and size of this chamber, I estimate it'll take at least a day for the room to reach capacity. We should be fine."

"I'd feel much more comfortable if we could slow it down," Lisa told him.

At the far end of the chamber, Nadine and Samantha appeared to be struggling with the exit lock. They had inserted the rod, then pulled it back out, re-aligned the symbol, and inserted it again. But they hadn't made progress beyond that.

"What's going on?" Gabriel called.

"It doesn't fit," Samantha called back. "It's the right shape, but it's too big!"

"What about the other end?"

"No good! It's smaller but has a different symbol!"

Gabriel looked at Lisa. Just like the previous two trials, this one appeared too easy on its surface. The heads of the stone rods were decoys, with the real keys embedded in the rocky wall, where they couldn't be observed without removing them and allowing water to breach the chamber. Now the team was trapped inside with an active leak and no exit strategy.

"Come plug the rod hole!" Gabriel yelled. "We need to rethink our approach!"

Samantha and Nadine returned with the stone rod. Lisa and Porter assisted as they brought the rod down at an angle into the water stream. The force of the incoming flow batted it off track instantly. The team lifted the rod and tried once more, but again, the incoming flow was too strong to overcome. Samantha analyzed the stream and saw it appeared weaker on the bottom edge than the top, so she guided the team into a new position and they tried again. A few seconds later, the flow ripped the stone rod from their hands and shot it halfway across the chamber.

"It's no use!" Samantha shouted over the roaring water. "We don't have the strength to reinsert the rod against a current like that!"

Gabriel glanced at the rod hole's immediate surroundings, but saw nothing that would indicate a mechanism for shutting off the water flow. "You think it's safe to assume this thing is locked in the open position?" He asked Lisa.

She had been perusing their surroundings as well. "Probably."

"Then let's not waste more time on it." Gabriel turned to Porter. "You said it would take at least a day to fill up the chamber. How certain are you?"

Porter spoke aloud as he performed mental math. "My best guess is that the water's flowing in at around five hundred gallons per minute. We're in a cylinder with a ten foot radius and maybe three hundred foot length, which works out to a volume of just over ninety-four thousand cubic feet, or approximately seven hundred thousand gallons. Divide by five hundred, then sixty... we've got twenty-three and a half hours, give or take estimation errors."

"But we still need to find the key," Gabriel said, looking at the insurmountable number of rods jutting from the chamber's walls. "And our time decreases with each new leak we create. How many rods can we reasonably inspect?"

Nate had already done the calculation. "A hundred-thirty or so. At an average of one to two rods per minute for each of us, we might get fifteen minutes before the chamber fills. If we haven't found the right key by then, we drown."

Gabriel nodded, but in the back of his mind, he knew that meant they would only get through forty to fifty percent of the rods at best. He also knew that meant they only had a forty to fifty percent chance of surviving this trial, and that was assuming everyone could operate at full speed in rising water conditions for the entire fifteen minutes. Gabriel's eyes involuntarily shifted to Porter.

"I can make it," his friend said. "I didn't come this far to let fifteen minutes and a little sea water stop me." Porter turned and gripped his hands around the nearest stone rod. "Ready when you are!"

Gabriel signaled for the others to spread and find rods of their own while he did the same. Once everyone was in position, he yelled, "pull!"

Chapter Sixty-Three
Submerged

Isla de Cabrera, Spain
Eight Days Before The Sky Opened

Prepared for the intensity of the water streams that would breach the chamber walls, each team member removed their first rod and quickly stood clear of the open holes left behind. One leak in the watertight chamber turned into seven, and no one had been lucky enough to locate the exit key on their first attempt. They each scrambled to their second, and then third rods. By the time one minute had passed, Gabriel was already starting on his fourth, and he noticed that Lisa and Samantha were as well, with the others not far behind.

They were ahead of Nate's projections, or at least, that's what Gabriel originally thought. Then he dropped his fourth rod into the pool of ankle-deep water that had already permeated the chamber and realized how much longer it took him to slosh through that water to reach his fifth rod. It would only get worse as the water continued to rise. Eventually, the team would have to swim between rods, and then remove those rods in an underwater environment. They'd be lucky to remove even one per minute each at that point, which meant they needed to move as fast as possible now to maintain the average Nate had estimated.

Compounding the slowdown were the active water streams jetting throughout the chamber. There were over forty of them now, and each had the force to sweep the team members off their feet at best, and to knock them unconscious or otherwise put them out of commission at worst. It was critical that everyone dodged the streams as they increased in number, but that required taking less direct paths between rods. On top of that, the flares Samantha had ignited were now submerged in the initial pool of water that had accumulated. That meant resorting to flashlights, which were luckily waterproof, but also consumed hands that would otherwise be used for stability while traversing the now knee-deep water and for removing stone rods from their housing.

"Anything yet?" Gabriel shouted across the growing roar of inflowing water.

Most of the team members responded negatively, but Nate responded in typical Nate fashion. "Yeah, I found the key a few minutes ago, but decided not to tell anyone to keep the suspense going!"

For once, Gabriel hoped Nate's sarcasm was serious, but a quick glance at his tech engineer revealed it wasn't. He estimated they were past sixty rods now, but the water pooling in the chamber was rising at an exponential pace. It was up to Gabriel's chest, deep enough that he found it more efficient to dive and swim to his next rod than to drag his body upright through the resistant surface. Underwater, however, was like a scene from a mesmerizing dream. The submerged flares had turned the sea water red, while criss-crossing flashlight beams pierced it to reveal discarded stone rods and their alien symbols littered across the chamber floor. Gabriel watched as two more rods splashed through the water's surface and sunk past bubbles and debris to the graveyard below. If he didn't hurry, he and his team would wind up in that graveyard as well.

A few more minutes passed, and with nearly one hundred rods removed, the exit key was still nowhere to be found. The team was treading water, and there was less breathable space left in the chamber than had already been filled. Gabriel was down to removing two rods per minute, but his arms were tiring and he knew that pace would decrease soon. Only Samantha was keeping a similar pace, with the others already down to one per minute, and in Porter's case, even less. The tech billionaire had to keep pausing for air and finding wall ridges to hold to rest his arms. He wasn't using his magnetic glove for assistance, leading Gabriel to suspect the water had shorted it out.

Gabriel pulled another rod and checked its end. No dice. He swam to the next rod and spotted Lisa streaking through the water by his side. Her facial expression was determined, though her body language showed weakness. Nonetheless, she pressed onward, breaching the surface just as Gabriel did and positioning her feet against the wall near another rod. Gabriel removed his, checked the end, and tossed it into the water. He glanced at Lisa, who was still inspecting hers, then did a double-take as he realized it wasn't her new rod she was inspecting, but his recently discarded one.

"We don't have time to second guess each other!" Gabriel yelled over the near-deafening roar of water.

"What are you talking about?!"

"I just threw that one out!"

Lisa shook her head, confused. "I just pulled this one from the wall!"

Gabriel felt time slipping away as the roof of the chamber closed in less than two feet from his head. He almost dropped the dispute to continue his key search, but his gut told him he had just stumbled on to an important detail. He instructed Lisa to hang on to her rod, then dove straight down to retrieve the one he had discarded. When he returned to the surface, his head was only one foot from the ceiling.

"Let me see!" Gabriel yelled.

Lisa held her rod out of the water, and Gabriel held his beside it. The two rods were nearly identical, except that their ends were swapped, with the larger head of Gabriel's rod matching the smaller end of Lisa's, and vice versa.

"They're a matching set!" Lisa yelled.

"No!" Gabriel corrected. "They're mirror images... distorted reflections, just like you get from water!"

Lisa shrugged as she resumed treading with both arms. "What does it mean?!"

Gabriel had figured it out, but he knew he didn't have time to explain. He dropped his latest rod and dove, swimming as fast as he could to Samantha. He surfaced beside her, his head bumping the roof of the chamber as she turned to find another rod.

"Samantha, wait!" Gabriel choked as a wave of sea water flooded his mouth. "The first key you and Nadine tried... what was the symbol on the other end?!"

"What?!"

Gabriel wasn't sure if she couldn't hear him or if she simply didn't understand what he was asking. He repeated himself. "What was the symbol on the other end of the first key?! The one that didn't match the lock?!"

Samantha spit water from her mouth as she thought. Then she said, "It was a rectangle with a ball at the end, kind of like a compressed exclamation mark!"

"Are you sure?!"

Samantha nodded, the water level rising above her mouth, leaving only her nose for air. Gabriel inhaled as deeply as his lungs would allow, then dove again. The rods were reflections of each other, and if he and Lisa's recent positions were any indication, so was the chamber itself: a cylinder, composed of one halfpipe butted up against its own reflection. Gabriel oriented underwater and identified the general location where Nadine had found the first rod. He then swam to the opposing wall and scanned the remaining symbols projecting from it. There was a triangle with a horizontal line on top, a circle with two dots on opposing outer edges, a rectangle... with a circle at one end!

That was it! Gabriel propped his feet against the wall for leverage and yanked the rod free. At the other end was a curvy symbol, a symbol that matched the one in the exit lock. Gabriel wanted to surface for a fresh lungful of air, but upon looking up, he saw his teammates were now fully submerged, and the grim realization that no air remained set over him. His chest burning, Gabriel focused his eyes on the *Fire* trial door at the opposite end of the room. He swam forward, his muscles screaming with every stroke, his reflexes trying to force a breath even though doing so would guarantee drowning. Gabriel felt his head growing light and saw his vision blur, but he was almost there. He shut his eyes and told himself not to give up, then kept pushing his arms forward and back, forward and back, propelling his body through the red water, until he reached a solid surface.

Gabriel opened his eyes, but they were of little use. He felt for the stone tablet next to the exit door, slid his hands over it until they found the keyhole, then inserted his final rod, shimmying it until its symbol aligned with the recessed carving that awaited within. The rod shifted another five inches into the lock, then Gabriel heard a series of muted clacks coming from all around. An intense rumble followed, filling not only Gabriel's ears but reverberating throughout his body. Through his blurry vision, he could see what appeared to be thick curtains of air bubbles rising from each side of the chamber. That could only mean one thing: the water was draining! Gabriel knew if he could get to the surface, fresh air awaited him there. But he had nothing left, and instead drifted into darkness, the knowledge that he had given his team a chance to survive providing him peace as his mind finally lost consciousness.

Chapter Sixty-Four
Heat Shield

Isla de Cabrera, Spain
Eight Days Before The Sky Opened

Gabriel's eyes fluttered open, revealing Lisa's face hovering overhead. "What happened?"

Lisa smiled. "You did it."

She pulled away, allowing Gabriel a full view of his surroundings. He was lying on the floor of the *Water* trial chamber, just before the *Fire* trial passageway, which was now wide open, its stone door having receded into the wall. The chamber glistened with sea water residue, and its floor was still covered by the hundred-or-so stone rods the team had removed during the trial. Gabriel's team members were huddled nearby, each dripping wet, but alive, though Porter looked as though he was in rough shape.

"I couldn't make it to the surface," Gabriel said.

"No," Lisa agreed. "But once the water started draining, I was able to get a breath of air so I could swim down and retrieve you."

Gabriel gripped her hand and gave it a gentle kiss. "I appreciate that."

Lisa shrugged. "We still have one challenge left. If we're going to die down here, we're going to die together. You don't get off the hook early."

Gabriel tried to chuckle, but his lungs still hurt. Once he had enough energy to sit up, he requested a debrief of what he missed. Samantha explained that the unlocking mechanism seemed to trigger a three-stage event. First, containment hatches sealed off the open rod holes, cutting off additional water inflow. It was Lisa's conjecture that these hatches were in their closed positions originally, and that removing the keys had opened them, resulting in the clunking noises that had preceded each water stream. Second, a motorized pumping system activated, draining the chamber of standing sea water and replacing it with outside air. Third, once the chamber was free of standing water, the passage to the *Fire* trial opened to permit their advance.

Gabriel was amazed by the intricacies that had gone into designing each trial so far, with the *Water* trial being the most intricate of them all. But he was also disturbed by something, something that had been bothering him since first learning of the elemental trials that awaited. They were dangerous- hell, deadly- and there was little chance people in need of the pendant's blessing could survive them without significant help. Whether physically impaired, or impoverished, or mentally unfocused, those in need of the pendant wouldn't have the ability or fortitude to make it this far, and there was no telling what still awaited beyond the *Fire* passageway. It reinforced Gabriel's initial belief: something wasn't right about this place.

"Assuming we make it out of here," Porter said from a seated position a few feet away, "this will make great content for your next book."

Gabriel smiled. Porter was certainly right about that, but it all hinged on his first contingency: *assuming* they made it out. Though they were three-fourths of the way through, Gabriel was growing less and less confident in their ability to succeed. This latest brush with death had simply been too close for comfort.

"You want me to do the initial scan?" Lisa asked, motioning to the *Fire* passageway.

"I'm ready," Gabriel replied. "Just help me up."

Lisa did so, then she and Gabriel approached the *Fire* passageway together. They each took a side, scanning the outer edges, then inner walls, for traps. They found nothing unusual in the first section of the passage, but they did notice a soft orange glow illuminating the path around a curve just ahead. Gabriel and Lisa took the curve together, and though the passage still had another five feet, beyond it, they could see the *Fire* chamber. It was much smaller than the *Water* chamber, a rectangular room only ten feet tall and wide, and at most twenty-five feet long. The *Fire* chamber was the most refined of the trial rooms, with a smooth floor, polished walls, and a marbled path that led from the mouth of the passageway to the far end of the room, where a modest fire burned in a recessed oven. Lining the marbled path were mermaid statues, each with a gentle stream of water arcing from their mouths. The streams of water landed beyond the marble path, on a sloped portion of the floor that must have had some type of drainage, for no water pooled in the room.

Despite a guarantee that danger lurked within, Gabriel found the room to be beautiful. His eyes shifted from statue to statue and then finally to the fire in the oven as he proceeded through the passageway. He had all but forgotten that he was still supposed to be scanning for traps, but luckily, Lisa had stayed on it for the both of them, for she quickly grabbed his arm and pulled him to a halt.

"Wait," she said, pointing at the floor just ahead of Gabriel's feet.

The first two marble tiles at the head of the floor path had more distinct edges than the rest. Upon closer inspection, Gabriel saw they were free-standing, and he suspected it was to allow them movement when stepped on.

"Pressure plates?" Lisa asked.

Gabriel nodded. His eyes then shifted to the mouth of the passageway exit, where he saw the edge of a stone door embedded in the wall to one side. "It's a trapping mechanism, just like in the *Water* chamber."

This was the point where Gabriel and Lisa were supposed to fall back and let Porter forge ahead into the next trial. They would warn him of the pressure plates, of course, but anything that happened after that was his risk to take. But Gabriel knew this was the end of their journey. There was no clear exit from the *Fire* chamber other than the passage they had taken to get in. The prize they were after was here, and the adventurer within him wanted to discover it with his own eyes. He stood straight and stepped carefully over the pressure plates.

"What are you doing?" Lisa asked.

"I just need to see."

Gabriel shifted his weight to his front foot. Feeling solid marble under it, he then pulled his other foot forward, over the pressure plates, and onto the solid path with his first foot.

"Gabriel..." Lisa said in a cautionary voice.

He kneeled down and scanned the rest of the path. It appeared safe. Gabriel then looked at the mermaid statue on his right, and its mirror image on his left, and determined that neither of them was threatening either. He took another step forward. Now he was far enough into the room to see the oven more clearly. It was carved into the stone wall, with a flat base and arching top, similar to an old-fashioned pizza oven. Gabriel couldn't feel the heat of its flames, nor smell anything burning within, but he definitely saw something beyond the wall of fire. It was something sparkling in the flickering orange glow, something hanging from a metal hook in the oven ceiling. Gabriel took another step forward, and the middle flames parted slightly, giving him the briefest view of the object. It was all Gabriel needed to make his heart leap. He had seen the golden charm in its full glory. He had seen it dangling from an equally golden chain. He had seen the intricate etchings that gave it a unique character, and he had recognized those etchings as ancient Hebrew writing. In that moment, there was no longer any doubt in Gabriel's mind: he was standing before the Pendant of God.

Chapter Sixty-Five
Fireball

Isla de Cabrera, Spain
Eight Days Before The Sky Opened

"It's beautiful," Porter said, his eyes transfixed on the hanging pendant.

He and the rest of the team had joined Gabriel and Lisa in the *Fire* chamber. They now stood in pairs of two down the marble pathway, mermaid statues to their sides and a pergola of arcing water overhead. Gabriel and Porter were at the head of the pack, sharing the joy of discovery and, in Porter's case, success. Gabriel could see on his face that he was already reveling in the thought of being healed. But even though the pendant was within their grasps, whether it contained the otherworldly power it was fabled to remained to be seen.

"Porter," Gabriel said softly, "we don't know for sure if it will-"

"It will," Porter said, anticipating his thought. He then stepped forward eagerly, but with caution, until he reached the open oven and peered within. "Is there anything specific I should look for?"

"There's no smoke buildup or burning smell in here," Gabriel said. "That suggests the flames are running on natural gas. Look for a knob or keyhole or something along those lines that we could turn to shut off the flow."

"You can't just grab the pendant with your fancy pantry glove?" Nate asked from the rear of the room with a snarky chuckle.

Porter flipped him off. "It needs to dry." He then examined the edges of the oven before moving on to the wall in which it was embedded. Porter ran his palms over the smooth surface, finding nothing on the left side. Then he performed the same procedure on the right, and about five inches from the oven's midpoint, he stopped. "There's a circular lip here. It's about three inches in diameter and maybe two millimeters deep; not enough to grab."

"Try pushing the middle," Gabriel suggested. "Like a button."

Porter did, and the circle depressed into the wall before springing outward to form a knob on a short stem. Porter turned the knob counterclockwise, and the flames in the oven shrank, then eventually disappeared. At the same time, the water streams arcing overhead lost pressure, reduced to a trickle, and then also disappeared, leaving the room pitch black and silent. Gabriel reached for his flashlight, but the orange glow of fire reappeared before he turned it on. It wasn't coming from the oven, which was still fire-free. Instead, a tiny orange flame had flickered to life in each of the mermaid statues' eyes.

"So... that's creepy," Nate commented.

Lisa examined the statue nearest to her. "It must be a rerouting system. It's a way to keep the fire alive while also providing access to the pendant."

"Yeah," Samantha agreed. Then, "but why keep it alive?"

Gabriel turned his attention back to Porter, who had turned on his flashlight and aimed the beam into the oven. "Tell me what you see."

"Not much," Porter said. "The inner walls are smooth. There's nothing in there except for the pendant and the hook it's hanging from."

"Is there an air gap around the base of the hook?"

Porter shifted his light. "Yes. Why?"

Gabriel's head slumped. He had been afraid of that.

"Remember the opening scene of Raiders of the Lost Ark?" Lisa asked. "When Indiana Jones tried to swap a weighted sandbag for the golden idol?" She motioned toward the hook.

"You think the gap allows the hook to retract once the pendant's weight is removed," Porter said. He turned his light back to the threatening mechanism. "What if I hang something else in its place? Maybe a canteen, or a wet satchel..."

Gabriel shook his head. "If the hook is a trap, it's probably one end of a precisely weighted scale. Unless you can match the pendant's weight exactly, there's nothing you can do about it. Any movement, up or down, will tip the balance and trigger whatever chain reaction it's set to trigger."

Porter stared at him. "*If* the hook is a trap."

Gabriel nodded.

"Well, there's only one way to find out."

And with that, Porter lifted the pendant from its hook and lunged away from the oven. He dropped into a fetal position, burying his head between his knees. The other team members followed suit, huddling together in the middle of the chamber, cowering from whatever harmful trap Porter had potentially sprung. But nothing happened. Gabriel was the first to uncover his face and rise back to his feet. He looked and listened for any change in the chamber, but the most he noticed was that the orange glow from the mermaids' eyes seemed a little brighter. Gabriel chalked that up to his own eyes having briefly been in darkness a moment earlier.

"Are we good?" Porter asked.

The other team members were already rising when Gabriel answered. "I think so."

Nate had used one of the mermaid statues to pull himself up. His left hand landed on its mouth as he straightened his legs. "Um, guys? There's air coming out of here."

Gabriel looked at him curiously, then darted to his own statue and held his hand in front of the mouth. Sure enough, there was a stream of air coming from the opening where an arc of water had previously originated. Gabriel looked at Lisa and Samantha, who had dispersed to two other statues. They nodded to confirm the observation.

"Have they been doing this the entire time?" Nate asked.

"Probably since the water shut off," Gabriel said. The room seemed even brighter now, and Gabriel noticed that the flames in the eyes of his mermaid statue appeared larger than before. *No*, he then told himself, *they are larger than before*. In fact, all the fiery eyes had grown and were now casting a stronger glow throughout the room. If they grew any further, they would pop right of the mermaids and...

"Oh shit," Gabriel said under his breath. Then he shouted to the others. "Run!"

His own team members didn't hesitate nor ask why. Nadine, on the other hand, stood her ground, looking confused, as Gabriel neared her.

"What is it?"

"Gas!" Gabriel yelled.

"But I don't smell anything!"

Gabriel grabbed one of her arms as Porter grabbed the other. "Natural gas is odorless!"

They drug Nadine forward, lifting her over the pressure plates that lined the entrance to the chamber before jumping past them themselves. The rest of the team was already in the passageway between the *Water* and *Fire* trials when the first mermaid flames broke free of containment. The flames contacted the gas that had filled the chamber and instantaneously exploded into an enormous fireball. It spread like a viral contagion, consuming all twenty-five feet of the *Fire* chamber in less than two seconds. Luckily, Gabriel had the sense to reach back and trigger one of the chamber's pressure plates the moment he heard the explosion begin. He yanked his arm out of the way as the stone trap door slammed into place, cutting off the fireball just as it reached the passageway threshold.

Chapter Sixty-Six
Revelations

Isla de Cabrera, Spain
Eight Days Before The Sky Opened

Gabriel didn't move. He had seen the fireball materialize, had watched its flickering tentacles swarm across the *Fire* chamber, and had felt its searing heat as the stone door triggered, providing an earthen barrier of protection just in time to prevent him and his team from being incinerated. He jumped as a gentle hand touched his shoulder. It was Lisa, checking that he was okay.

"I'm fine," Gabriel told her as he shifted into a sitting position, his pulse still racing from yet another brush with death. He suspected next time he wouldn't be so lucky. "What about the rest of you?" Gabriel called out to the team. "Is anyone hurt?"

"Only my ego," Porter replied. "I'm sorry I put us all in danger like that."

Gabriel shot him a sympathetic smile. "You were caught in the moment. Please tell me you didn't drop the pendant during our hasty exit."

Porter held it up for everyone to see.

"Good," Samantha said. "Now let's hope it lives up to its reputation. We may need it to get out of here."

"Why is that?" Nadine asked.

"Because we're trapped," Gabriel told her. "The *Fire* chamber was a dead end and removing the first key rod triggered a stone blockade at the entrance to the *Water* chamber. We might be able to clear it, given enough time, but I suspect we'll run out of energy and starve to death well before then."

"You couldn't... oh, I don't know, find a more positive way to frame that?" Nate asked.

"Don't worry," Porter said. "The power of the pendant can move those stones."

He must have known his words would draw everyone else's attention to him, for he stood and marched into the *Water* chamber with a fresh determination in his step and the others hot on his heels. The chamber was dark again, so Samantha ignited her last flare and tossed it into the middle of the room. Porter stood near it, faced the blockade of stone that stood between them and their path to freedom, and raised the pendant high above his head. Gabriel's eyes darted to the blockade, then back to Porter and the pendant. He wasn't sure if he really expected something to happen, but he hoped it would, for the alternative was too dire to think about. A full minute passed before anyone spoke.

"Maybe I'm doing something wrong," Porter said as he lowered the pendant.

"Maybe its batteries are loose," Nate suggested. "Try banging on it."

Gabriel gave Nate a look that said *now isn't the time.*

"Damien controlled the pendant through will alone," Porter said. "I'm willing it to move the stones, but it isn't responding. I'm not sure what I'm doing wrong."

Gabriel frowned. "Porter..."

"Don't say it. Don't say the pendant's power isn't real. I know it's real. I just need to figure out how to harness it." He held the pendant out toward the stone blockade and squeezed his eyes tight. Another thirty seconds passed, and the situation hadn't changed.

"Porter, please-"

The tech billionaire groaned in frustration. With his eyes still shut, he bent over and used his empty hand to stabilize himself against a knee. Then he opened his eyes and stared at the pendant, and that's when Gabriel saw a disturbing shift in Porter's expression. His mouth fell open slightly, his lips and cheeks turned pale, and a noticeable tremble took hold of his lower jaw. Porter's eyes widened in either anger or fear- Gabriel couldn't be sure which- and his grip on the pendant tightened, the muscles in his arm tensing beneath his wet sleeve. Gabriel joined his friend to make sure he was all right, and in doing so, he saw the same jarring detail that had triggered Porter's reaction. On the bottom edge of the pendant's backing, standing out clearly from the Hebrew text that adorned the rest of the artifact, was the engraved phrase: *Made in India.*

"It's a fake," Porter mumbled through staggered breathing. "We went through all of that, wasted so much time, put all of our lives in danger... for a fake."

Gabriel wished it wasn't true, but there was no denying it. Now he understood why their journey into the cave beneath Cabrera Island hadn't felt right. The entire series of events, from illuminating Cabrera Castle to surviving the elemental trials, had been staged. This place hadn't been built to house the next Shifa village. It existed for one purpose alone: to kill those who sought the pendant but weren't worthy of its blessing. Adila Benkirane had tried to warn them of this possibility. She had expressed her reservations about Porter's worthiness, and had told them that, as a Shifa survivor, her duty was to vet those worthy and unworthy unlike, and to guide them appropriately based on that vetting. Porter screamed as he hurled the fake pendant across the open chamber.

"What do we do now?" Nate asked. "I mean, it's great that we survived the trials, but we're still trapped down here. Sure, it sucks that the pendant's a fake, but it'll suck even more if we never make it out of this subterranean tomb."

As if answering his question, the sound of scraping rock filled the room as a hidden doorway nestled to the right of the stone blockade slid open. A man- Moroccan, by the looks of it- stood in a secret passageway on the other side of that door. He was carrying an oil lantern and whistled a peppy tune as he took several casual steps forward into the water chamber. Then he noticed Gabriel and the rest of the team, and that's when he froze in surprise.

Equally surprised, Gabriel said the first thing that came to mind. "Hello?"

The man yelped, turned on his heels, and retreated through the hidden doorway, failing to close it behind him. Gabriel looked at the others, who shrugged with bewilderment. Then he did the only sensible thing he could do: he took off in pursuit.

Chapter Sixty-Seven
The Observer

Isla de Cabrera, Spain
Eight Days Before The Sky Opened

Gabriel ducked and weaved his way through the cavern tunnel. Its walls were less refined than those along the main trial path, scraping at Gabriel's arms as he ran. Its ceiling was uneven, with large chunks of rock threatening to remove Gabriel's head every few feet. He couldn't see the Moroccan man, but he could hear the echo of the man's footsteps growing louder and see the light from his oil lantern brightening. Gabriel could also hear footsteps behind him and assumed his team had followed him into the tunnel. They had no idea what danger the Moroccan man might pose, but then again, it wasn't like they had anywhere else to go.

After passing what appeared to be a sealed stone door embedded in the tunnel wall, Gabriel faced a hairpin turn, followed by a steep incline as far as he could see. The Moroccan man was a silhouette in the distance, still fleeing into the darkness. Gabriel huffed his way up the incline, which lasted at least two hundred feet. At the top was a small antechamber adjacent to the next hairpin turn. Another sealed door was embedded in the antechamber wall. If his inner compass was accurate, Gabriel should be above sea level by now and probably somewhere near the middle of the *Earth* shaft. He realized these doors, which were likely invisible from the other side given the poor lighting conditions there, provided secret access points to the four elemental challenges. The Moroccan man must have paused to consider taking this access point, for he was now much closer to Gabriel as he scaled the next incline.

Gabriel continued his pursuit, straining leg muscles he rarely put under such stress. His chest burned as his lungs inflated and deflated in rapid succession and his heart pumped oxygenated blood to the rest of his body as fast as it could. Another antechamber awaited at the end of this incline. Instead of a hairpin turn, this one contained a vertical shaft down which a telescoping ladder had been deployed. The Moroccan man was already nearing the top of the ladder. Gabriel grabbed the bottom rung to prevent him from collapsing it, then asked his legs to hang in there while shifting most of his weight to his arms.

The Moroccan man disappeared from view. Gabriel passed the halfway point of the shaft and heard the familiar scraping of stone on stone as another secret door was opened. Gabriel pushed his body into overdrive and scaled the remaining rungs in less than half the time it had taken him on the previous ones. He pulled himself into the next antechamber and spotted the Moroccan man on the other side of an open passageway. The man was scrambling to find something in the rock wall beyond Gabriel's view. Assuming whatever it was would likely trigger the stone door between them to snap back into place, Gabriel charged forward, using what little energy he had left to tackle the man.

They hit the ground hard and skidded to a halt just before an abrupt drop-off. Exhausted from the pursuit and dazed by the impact with his quarry, Gabriel couldn't make heads or tails of where they were. Then he heard a muted hum, followed by screeching wind, and within seconds, a hurricane-strength current blasted by just five feet from his head. Gabriel could have gone his whole life without hearing that noise again. But here he was, back in the *Wind* chamber, and once his senses settled down and his eyes adjusted to the cavern's glow, he could see that he was on the rocky platform at its entrance.

Gabriel assessed the Moroccan man lying flat beneath him. The man was middle-aged, with well-kept hair and clean skin. From a fitness perspective, he was about average, and Gabriel suspected he could best the man in a physical altercation. The man must have suspected it too, for he no longer tried to flee nor fight, and instead spoke something in Arabic that had a touch of fear to it. Gabriel waited for his earpiece to translate, but it never did. He pulled it out and saw water glisten along its bottom edge.

"Can you speak English?" He asked his captive.

"Yes," the man said. "Please take me away from this ledge. I'm afraid of heights."

Gabriel climbed off the man, whose words removed any concern that he might be threatening, and extended a hand. The man took it and stood, then backed away from the ledge that overlooked the *Wind* ravine.

"Who are you?" Gabriel asked.

"My name is Ilias Choukri. I am The Observer."

"The observer of what?"

"Of those who come here seeking the pendant," Ilias said. "My job is to monitor their progress and report on their fates."

Gabriel asked the question he already knew the answer to. "You report to Mrs. Benkirane?"

Ilias nodded.

"And just how many people have you observed die down here?"

Ilias shrugged. "All of them. You're only the third to make it to the *Fire* trial, and the first to survive it."

Gabriel struggled to wrap his head around that knowledge. Ilias hadn't given him a number, but the way he said 'all of them' spoke volumes. "And after you observe their deaths, you report to Mrs. Benkirane... and then what?"

"Then she sends in a repair crew to reset the trials for the next treasure hunters she sends their way." Ilias must have sensed Gabriel's disapproval. "I know it sounds cruel, but you must understand, the pendant is too powerful to leave it unprotected. If it fell into the wrong hands..."

Samantha and Lisa stepped through the passageway between the *Wind* chamber and the secret tunnels.

"Where are the others?" Gabriel asked.

"Porter had to stop," Lisa said. "Nate and Nadine stayed back to help him. He's fading fast, Gabriel. We need to find the pendant soon."

Gabriel turned his attention back to Ilias. "Do you know the pendant's true location?"

"I'm afraid not," he said sincerely.

Gabriel looked to the *Wind* chamber entrance. "Is the door to the underground cavern still open? Can we leave that way safely?"

"Yes," Ilias said. "Once someone survives the trials, we are not permitted to interfere further."

Gabriel thought about asking who *we* included, but again, he already knew. "When we leave here, you're going to contact Mrs. Benkirane to tell her we survived?"

"Of course. It's my duty."

Gabriel nodded, a swirling mix of anger, frustration, and desperation behind his next words. "Tell her she'll see us soon."

Chapter Sixty-Eight
Down The Barrel

Isla de Cabrera, Spain
Eight Days Before The Sky Opened

The midday sun blinded Gabriel as he emerged from the underground cavern. It took his eyes several minutes to adjust after having spent hours in the dark, and when they did, he found himself staring down the barrel of a very large gun.

"You've got to be kidding me," he said with incredulity.

Gabriel's eyes scanned from right to left as he sized up his situation. The gun barrel aimed at his head belonged to an assault rifle, and the mercenary gripping it tightly was someone he hadn't seen since leaving the Tangier-Algeciras ferry. The same could be said for the other mercenaries standing their ground around them, each taking aim at the next of Gabriel's team members to emerge from the cavern. Behind the mercenaries waited Byron and his two core companions. The former wore a shit-eating grin, as if he had just won the lottery and planned to rub it in the faces of everyone he knew.

"Bravo," he said with a sarcastically slow clap. "You solved the mystery of Cabrera Island and returned victoriously from the village hidden beneath it. To think of all the trouble you saved me..."

"Byron-"

The rival treasure hunter held a silencing finger to his lips. "There's nothing for you to say. You bested me on the ferry. I've bested you here. Just hand over the pendant and we'll call it even." He approached Gabriel with an open hand.

"Byron, that's what I'm trying to tell you," Gabriel said. "We don't have the pendant."

Byron scoffed in disbelief. "Gabriel Dunne, the most talented treasure hunter no one has ever heard of, didn't return from the depths of Cabrera with his prize? What kind of fool do you take me for?"

"You're no fool, Byron," Gabriel said with a straight face. Then, "you finally admitted that I'm more talented than you."

Even Byron's own mercenaries had a chuckle at his expense. Byron glared at Gabriel, and his body language suggested that he might even take a swing at his counterpart, but he held his composure and pushed his open palm toward Gabriel once more.

"The pendant. Now."

After everything they had endured in the elemental trials, Gabriel didn't have the patience for this. "Search us if you don't believe me. There was a pendant down there, but it was fake. We didn't even bother bringing it back with us. The whole cave is just one giant death trap."

Byron's eyes passed over each of Gabriel's team members. After stopping on Nate, he whistled to the mercenary targeting the tech engineer. The mercenary lowered his rifle and started forward, looking a little too eager to perform the pat down.

"He's telling the truth," Porter said, his voice weak. "Coming here was a setup to steer us away from pendant's true location."

Byron motioned for his mercenary to stop. Gabriel watched the silent looks exchanged between his ongoing rival and old friend. He couldn't tell if the two were daring each other to challenge their potential bluffs or engaging in foreplay for some weird captor-captive sexual fantasy. When they broke eye contact moments later, Byron shouted orders for his men to stand down and return to their boat. Gabriel breathed a sigh of relief.

"Well," Byron said, "I suppose you still saved me the effort of wasting my time."

"Then I guess we're even for the ferry after all," Gabriel told him.

Byron smirked. "Sure, we're even. Though the same can't be said for all those ferry passengers you inconvenienced. A little birdie might have passed your names along to ferry security, so don't be surprised if they come after you with legal repercussions."

"That won't be a problem," Nate called out. "I memorized the license plates of the cars that would sustain collateral damage and already transferred a half million dollars of Porter's money to each owner."

A renewed fire erupted in Porter. "You did what?!"

Nate shrugged. "We had some time to kill at the lighthouse. You know, you really shouldn't leave your tablet logged in to your financial accounts when sharing it with someone else."

Porter took a step toward Nate, but Nadine intervened, calming him with a gentle hand on his chest. Gabriel turned his focus back to Byron.

"I guess we don't need to worry about those legal repercussions. You and me, on the other hand..."

"My team and I are going to take our boat north to Palma," Byron said. "You claim there's an underground death trap beyond that cavern door? Adila Benkirane didn't build it herself. She must have sourced workers, supplies... left some sort of money trail. Maybe that same money trail can lead us to the real pendant's location."

Honesty. It was rare between competing treasure hunters, but sometimes, in the interest of mutual progress, both parties needed to show their hands, if only to prevent further stepping on each other's toes.

"We're returning to Casablanca to confront Mrs. Benkirane directly," Gabriel said.

"What makes you think she'll be any more honest with you now than before?"

Gabriel recalled what Ilias had told him: *once someone survives the trials, we are not permitted to interfere further.* He hoped misdirection and lying fell under the purview of *interference*, and that Adila Benkirane would hold herself to the same level of integrity as her servant. "It's just a hunch," he told Byron.

His rival didn't press him further. "Good luck with your hunch." Then, as he and his core team members walked away, he shouted back, "here's hoping we don't see each other again until the next treasure drops on our respective radars!"

Yeah, Gabriel thought, *here's hoping.* Unfortunately, he had little confidence that would be the case.

Chapter Sixty-Nine
Judgment

Casablanca, Morocco
Seven Days Before The Sky Opened

After their brief encounter with Byron, Gabriel and his team took their Leviathan watercraft back to Alicante, where they retrieved their van and took turns changing into fresh clothes. Samantha then swept the van for tracking devices, finding two, and disposed of them accordingly, placing one on a boat docked at the Alicante port and placing the other on another vehicle parked nearby. Byron had to have suspected she would check for trackers, and he would know for certain when their signals diverged later that day, but until then, maybe he would believe the team took a break in Alicante before heading back to Morocco.

Porter slept for most of the drive to Algeciras, though it was uneasy sleep. When Nadine asked him about it, Porter blamed the bright afternoon sun and discomfort of the van's seats. Gabriel knew the truth, however. Porter, like him, couldn't help mentally rehearsing for their confrontation with Adila Benkirane. The woman had tried to kill them, not something either took lightly. And yet, she was the only person with information that could steer them back on the pendant's path. Both Gabriel and Porter would have to be cautious with their words and tempers if they had any chance at exploiting her knowledge.

The sun had already set by the time the team arrived in Algeciras. They rode the ferry to Tangier without incident, then drove the final stretch to Casablanca, reaching their hotel a little after eleven o'clock. They had debated whether they should drive straight to Adila

Benkirane's apartment complex, but shot down the idea on two points. First, it wouldn't be a great look for a team of armed treasure hunters to show up at a wealthy woman's home in the middle of the night, especially since she knew they were coming and might have private security or the police on standby. Second, Porter needed at least a few hours of rest in a proper bed or he wasn't going to make it to the pendant's true location, even if Adila helped them find it. Nadine also wanted to run a few tests on him, and the others would all appreciate hot showers. So they pulled into the hotel parking lot, grabbed minimal gear, and dispersed to their separate rooms, agreeing to meet in the lobby at seven the next morning.

Gabriel and Lisa were the first ones down, so they grabbed a few items from the hotel's continental breakfast to settle their stomachs while waiting on the others. Samantha and Nate were next. Nate also helped himself to the breakfast offerings while Samantha excused herself to prep the van. It was another half hour before Porter and Nadine came down, and Gabriel could tell by the somber look on Nadine's face what the holdup had been.

"Why don't you grab something for the road?" He suggested to Porter. "We all need to keep our energy up."

"I'll get something after our meeting with Mrs. Benkirane. I don't have much of an appetite right now."

Nadine bit her lip and looked away, as if stifling a protest.

"You really should-"

"I'm good, Gabriel," Porter said, abruptly cutting him off. "Let's just get moving."

Samantha had tidied up the van from the day before by the time the rest of the team joined her. Twenty minutes later, they pulled into open street parking near Adila Benkirane's apartment complex. Samantha scanned the area for signs of extra security, but saw none. Not bothering to solicit a formal invitation, the rest of the team exited the van and approached Adila's doorman. Surprisingly, he informed them that Adila was expecting them and escorted them upstairs without protest. There, Adila waited in her glass-enclosed sitting room. Her face was staunch and demeanor icy as the team took seats around her.

"So," she opened the conversation, "you made it back."

"You sound disappointed," Porter quipped.

"Disappointed," Adila agreed with a slight bobble of her head. "And surprised." She eyed Gabriel and the others. "You have talented friends. They didn't let the Cabrera trials or your condition kill you. Few people are so lucky to be so cared for."

Porter's right hand trembled involuntarily. He casually tucked it under his left arm as he leaned forward. "They're trying to save me, as I told you when we first met."

"You're not worthy of being saved," Adila hissed. "You're not worthy of the pendant's blessing. You're deceptive and manipulative in all your ways, and you should have died on Cabrera island!"

His eyes narrow with anger, Porter opened his mouth to counter her verbal attack. But Gabriel caught his attention and motioned for him to tread carefully. Adila Benkirane obviously had a deep-rooted disdain for the tech billionaire. Perhaps if he didn't respond in a way that confirmed her expectations...

"Mrs. Benkirane," Porter said calmly, "I'm not a perfect man. God knows I've done plenty of stupid and harmful things in my life. I won't pretend otherwise. But through my inventions and my company's philanthropic activities, I've also brought a lot of good to the world. I know I've still got capacity for more good in me... if only I had the time. By helping me find the pendant, you'd be granting that time."

Adila stared at him as if torn between her preconceived perceptions and his plea. A tense minute passed, then she said quietly, "you survived the Cabrera trials. No one has ever done that before. Perhaps my judgment..." She trailed off, lost in her own thoughts, as another minute slowly ticked by.

Porter lowered his head in defeat. "I'm sorry we've wasted each other's time."

He stood and helped Nadine to her feet, then motioned for Gabriel and the team to follow as he headed for the door.

"Please wait," Adila requested.

Porter stopped, but didn't give her the satisfaction of facing her.

"Mr. Cannes, you've either become a changed man or mastered your art of deception. I can't say for sure which, but even if I believed you, I couldn't help."

Gabriel glanced at her with curiosity.

"The truth is," Adila said sheepishly, "I don't know the pendant's current location. I never have."

Chapter Seventy
The Truth

Casablanca, Morocco
Seven Days Before The Sky Opened

Gabriel felt Adila's words slam into his gut, instantly knocking out of him whatever hope he had left. Their impact on Porter was even worse. His lips turned white as he stumbled backwards and nearly doubled over, if not for Nadine's support. Gabriel struggled to find words- any words at all- to make sense of the situation. All he found were questions.

"But... you're a Shifa survivor."

Adila nodded. "Yes, and if you were looking for Shifa, I could point you to the Atlas Mountains. But you already knew that."

"You told us those who receive the pendant's blessing have a duty to protect its whereabouts," Lisa reminded her. "How can you protect them if you don't know where those whereabouts are?"

"I would pose the question back to you," Adila said. "What better way to protect the whereabouts than to *not* know where they are?"

"But you also told us that you guide those deserving to the pendant's next location," Gabriel countered. "The implication was that you know where that location is."

"And I also said that we guide those undeserving to where they belong," Adila reminded him. "I was using the collective *we.*"

Lisa exhaled in defeat as she processed Adila's meaning. "You segregated the information."

"That's right. Half the survivors received the pendant's next location and were tasked with guiding the new generation of blessed to it. The other half were tasked with misdirection."

"And you were in the latter group," Gabriel surmised.

"Given my wealth and resources, it made the most sense," Adila said. "The cavern of challenges you found on Cabrera island isn't the only one of its kind. There are at least five other active decoy pendant locations spread across the Mediterranean region. There would be more, but every once in a while, knowledge of a decoy location dies along with the bearers of that knowledge, necessitating the need to create a new avenue of misdirect."

"Which your resources enabled you to do," Gabriel said, completing the thought.

He looked at Porter, who was slack-jawed with devastation. Gabriel wanted to comfort him, to point out that there were still other ways they could find the pendant, but the cold, hard truth was any of those other ways would take too long to pursue. Gabriel and his team might eventually find the pendant, but Porter would dead long before then.

"Mrs. Benkirane?" Nate addressed, nervously biting his lip. "For what it's worth, I've been on your side since the start of this operation. I've never fully trusted Mr. Cannes. He and I have a long, competitive history with one another, and I know he's not as clean as the image he tries to portray." Nate took a deep breath, as if summoning the inner courage required for his next words. "But he saved my life on Cabrera island. He didn't need to, and believe me, the temptation to let me die was probably there. Yet, he put his own life at risk to ensure I survived. No matter what he might have done in the past, that's the action of someone with at least some good in them, and hopefully someone who intends to expand upon that good in the future." Nate glanced back at Porter, a glistening of tears in his eyes. "Please help us save him. Even if you don't know where the pendant is, there's got to be some knowledge you could share to get us back on the right path."

Adila's features softened, Nate's emotional plea piercing her otherwise stoic veneer. "Faras El Mehdi."

Gabriel felt a spark ignite within him. "What did you say?"

"Faras El Mehdi," Adila repeated. "He knew the pendant's current location. My sources informed me you visited him upon first arriving in Morocco."

"That's right. But we were too late. He passed away before we could meet with him." Gabriel reached into his pocket and removed the scrap of paper containing Faras' final drawing. It had gotten soaked during the *Water* trial, and its ink had bled, partially obscuring its hieroglyphic creature. "His servant gave us this. He said Mr. El Mehdi called it The Veiled Bird. Does it mean anything to you?"

Adila took the drawing and analyzed it for nearly a minute. Then she passed it back to Gabriel. "I'm afraid not. But I will tell you this: that drawing will lead you to the pendant's location. Faras must have seen something in Mr. Cannes that I did not. He was a good man... better than most. If he left this drawing for you, it was to help you reach your goal."

Gabriel noted the personal way Adila spoke of Faras El Mehdi. He suspected they had been more than mere acquaintances once upon a time, but he would never know for certain. "Is there anything else you can tell us?"

"Just one thing," Adila said. "When the Shifa villagers were preparing to move, they contacted me to arrange their transportation. I commissioned a fleet of boats large enough to move the entire settlement in one voyage. And before you ask, I wasn't told their destination." She swallowed hard, then reluctantly spilled her final offering. "But I do know their port of origin."

"A city along the Mediterranean Sea?" Lisa asked.

Adila shook her head slowly. "No, Essaouira. Though, at the time, it was known as Mogador."

"Essaouira?" Lisa's voice quivered. "They set out on the Atlantic Ocean?"

Adila nodded, fully aware of the implication, an implication that Nate, in his usual manner, felt compelled to vocalize.

"But... that means they could be anywhere."

Chapter Seventy-One
Research

Casablanca, Morocco
Seven Days Before The Sky Opened

Following Adila Benkirane's revelations, Gabriel and the rest of the team returned to their hotel to brainstorm their next steps. Along the way, they stopped at a school supply shop to pick up a collection of physical maps meant for geography teachers to display on their walls. One was a flattened overview of the entire Earth, another focused on the African continent, another on the Mediterranean region, and another on the Atlantic Ocean itself. The team rented a business center conference room at the hotel so they could comfortably spread out while both working together and maintaining privacy.

Gabriel spread the maps out on the conference room table, arranging the focused ones in proper geographic alignment, then instructed everyone to identify the most logical destinations for a fleet of ships leaving Essaouira in the early 1900s seeking solitude from the rest of the world. The most obvious destinations were the Medeira and Canary Islands, followed by Cape Verde, which was significantly further south. Since they had already ruled out the Canary Islands as having no relation to The Veiled Bird, Gabriel assigned Samantha and Nadine to investigating any possible connections between their sole clue and the other two destination candidates.

Next up on the potential destination list was anywhere along the African coast, though Gabriel felt this was unlikely, as a land trip across the African continent would have made more sense than setting out to sea. That led to Western Europe, and by extension, Iceland or maybe even Greenland as the next most likely candidates. Gabriel assigned Team Nerd to rule out as many of those destinations as possible and to come back with a short list for consideration. Finally, there was the eastern coast of the Americas, as well as a handful of smaller islands in between continents. Gabriel suspected those represented too far of an ocean voyage to risk moving an entire village, but he volunteered himself and Lisa to explore the possibility just to be certain.

The goal of the hunt was to identify only those places that could support hiding a small village, that had some direct connection to birds, and that could reasonably be associated with the word *veil*. Given the sheer number of destinations and related factoids the team would have to process, Gabriel estimated it would take all day to narrow their candidates... and he was right. By mid-afternoon, the team had ruled out several coastal destinations for the relocated Shifa village, but had identified no actual candidates that fit their three criteria. By early evening, Gabriel could see everyone was dragging, so he requested catering from the hotel restaurant.

After being re-energized, the team kept at it another four hours, at which time Porter had a violent coughing fit that left a wad of bloody flesh on the map he'd been analyzing. Gabriel wondered just how much lung tissue a person could lose before being fully incapacitated, suspecting the answer was probably somewhere in the realm of *not much*. Nadine insisted Porter call it a night and escorted him back to his room. She didn't return, not that Gabriel had expected her to, leaving the core team to press on into the night.

By one o'clock in the morning, exhaustion had fully set in, and the team was no closer to identifying valid candidates for the pendant's current location. Gabriel spoke with hotel management about reserving their conference room through the next day so they could leave their research out and return after some rest. He then insisted his own team get some sleep and locked the conference room door before heading to bed with Lisa. Sinking into a pillow so soft it enveloped the sides of his head, Gabriel's mind swirled with ongoing mental analyses, worry that they might be too late to save Porter's life, and inner reflections on whether he could have done anything differently to achieve a better outcome. His thoughts drifted to nonsense after only a few minutes, then the comforting world of slumber embraced him...

Boom boom boom!

The noise awoke Gabriel from deep sleep. His mind was in a fog, but he thought he heard muffled yelling somewhere beyond the darkness of his and Lisa's bedroom. He turned to the bedside clock, which was blurry and painful to read with his dilated pupils. Gabriel rubbed his eyes and waited for them to adjust, then looked at the clock again. It was a little after five o'clock.

Boom boom boom!

Someone was pounding on Gabriel's hotel room door. This time, the noise woke Lisa, who stirred and then quickly rose, asking Gabriel what was wrong. A moment later, the muffled yelling repeated itself. It was Samantha.

"Gabriel, Lisa, wake up! You need to see this!"

Adrenaline kicked in, not because Samantha sounded afraid or in danger, but because she sounded excited. It was an excitement Gabriel and Lisa both recognized, the excitement of discovery. They raced to their door and flung it open, finding Samantha bursting at the seams with energy while Nate, still in his pajamas, yawned loudly behind her.

"What is it?" Gabriel asked. "Why are you up so early?"

"I never went to sleep," Samantha said with a jitteriness reflective of the claim. "There was this thought I couldn't let go of, like my brain was telling me we were overlooking something. So I started with the basics and ran through everything we knew, making sure to separate conjecture from fact and to conclude nothing without considering all possibilities."

Gabriel thought his half-awake brain caught all that. "And?"

"And I did it," Samantha said with a huge grin. "I solved The Veiled Bird." She allowed a moment for her words to register, then followed excitedly with, "I know where the pendant is!"

Chapter Seventy-Two
Unveiled

Casablanca, Morocco
Six Days Before The Sky Opened

The hotel was quiet in its early morning hours. After quickly throwing on clothes, Gabriel led his core team down to their rented conference room and unlocked the door. He inspected the large flatscreen television mounted at the head of the conference table and passed Samantha an HDMI cable with a multi-port adapter hanging from it. She plugged in her phone, then loaded a satellite image as Gabriel took a seat next to Lisa and Nate. The image showed a string of seven large land masses accompanied by a spattering of smaller ones against an ocean blue backdrop.

"That looks familiar," Gabriel said. He leaned forward and examined the physical maps spread across the conference room table. "The Canary Islands?"

"Bingo," Samantha replied.

"We discussed this when we first learned about The Veiled Bird," Lisa said. "You said the islands weren't named after the canary bird. They were named after dogs or something."

"*Canariae Insulae*," Samantha confirmed. "Island of the Dogs."

"You got me out of bed for this?" Nate asked dryly. "What's the deal?"

"The islands aren't named after the bird," Samantha reiterated, "but that got me thinking: it's awfully coincidental that they share the same name. So I did a little digging, and sure enough, the islands aren't named after the bird-"

Lisa's face lit with sudden revelation. "But the bird is named after the islands."

Samantha grinned. "You got it."

Intrigued, Gabriel stood to get a closer look at the television screen. He stared at the geographic contours of the Canary Islands' various peaks and valleys, all formed from volcanic activity years before he walked the Earth. "So you made the bird connection; what about the veil?"

"For that, I took a closer view at each of the individual islands." Samantha zoomed her satellite image in on the Isla de La Palma, filling the television screen. "As you can see, while the topography of the islands is interesting, there's nothing about them to indicate a veil or covering of any sort." She scrolled the image to El Hierro, then the Isla de La Gomera, then Tenerife. "Being volcanic islands, there's certainly room for the new Shifa village to exist somewhere underground, making the ground itself a veil, but if the village was going to move underground, it seems reasonable that Mrs. Benkirane, who has experience contracting out such operations, would have been tasked for assistance."

Samantha scrolled the image over the Isla de Gran Canaria, then Fuerteventura, and finally stopped on Lanzarote. Gabriel saw nothing out of the ordinary.

"What about the smaller islands?" He asked. "I assume when you told us you knew the pendant's location, you didn't mean we would have to island hop on a wild goose chase to find it."

Samantha grinned again. She scrolled the image northward, exposing the smaller Graciosa Island and Isla de Montana Clara. Again, Gabriel saw nothing that triggered a red flag in his mind. He looked at Samantha, but she hung on the current image, as if waiting for him to notice something he was overlooking. Gabriel scanned the television screen again, and this time, his own brain told him something wasn't right. He returned to the physical maps spread across the table.

"You're missing an island," He said after only a few seconds of analysis. "That cloud is blocking our view of the Isla de Alegranza." Gabriel pointed to the wispy white smear north of the Isla de Montana Clara. "Did you try pulling a different view?"

"Sure did." Samantha flipped to a new image and zoomed to that same section of ocean. "The first image I showed you was taken about a week ago. This one was taken about a month ago."

For a moment, Gabriel thought Samantha was pulling a fast one on him. Other than the tone of the image being slightly warmer and the angle of shadows having shifted to accommodate a slightly different position of the sun, it looked nearly identical to the first image. Samantha flipped again.

"This one was taken about a year ago." Once more, the tone and shadows shifted, but the image was nearly identical, cloud coverage and all. "Three years ago," Samantha said as she changed images again. "Ten years ago." She flipped once more, and though she had already made her point, she seized the opportunity to hammer it home. "Thirty years ago," she said with one last flip. Then she changed the screen to display a crop of all six images aligned in a two by three grid, with each containing the same obscuring cloud over the Isla de Alegranza.

"Holy shit," Nate uttered under his breath. "You really found it."

"The Veiled Bird," Lisa added. "Alegranza... that's happiness or-"

"Joy," Samantha clarified. "A fitting name, don't you think?"

Gabriel stared at the collage of images in awe. "Aerial imagery doesn't go far enough back for us to compare these against one from Shifa's days in the Atlas Mountains, does it?"

Samantha shook her head. "But if I were a betting woman, I'd put my entire life savings on that cloud not being there back then."

Gabriel nodded in silent agreement.

"How do we get there?" Lisa asked.

"We take the same route the Shifa villagers did," Samantha said. "We drive down to Essaouira and sail a Leviathan to Alegranza from there. Even though the Canaries are Spanish territory, the island itself is privately owned and- with the possible exception of the Shifa villagers- uninhabited. We shouldn't have any problem getting ashore."

Gabriel beamed with newfound conviction. "Get whatever arrangements you need to moving. We'll grab Porter. He'll want to get on the road right away." Gabriel glanced at Nate in his rumpled pajamas. "You might want to get some clothes on. Nap time's over."

He and Lisa left their other team members to prep and took an elevator to the floor where Porter was staying. They found Porter's room, then knocked loud enough to wake, but not alarm, its occupants. A moment later, they heard footsteps, then a groggy Nadine answered the door.

"What's going on?"

Gabriel spotted Porter slowly climbing out of bed behind her. "Good news. We've identified the pendant's location. Samantha's making travel arrang-"

He stopped, his ears registering a faint, but growing, sound that was both familiar and unsettling. It was coming from outside the hotel, a repetitive thumping that descended from somewhere above, grew louder as it passed the wall beyond Porter's balcony window, then slightly faded as it continued below. The nature of the noise revealed its source, a source Gabriel didn't need to see and didn't want to believe. Lisa barged past Nadine and peered around the curtain hanging over Porter's window. When she looked back, the fear in her eyes confirmed what Gabriel already knew.

"It's a Phoenix chopper. The military's found us."

Chapter Seventy-Three
Hunted

Casablanca, Morocco
Six Days Before The Sky Opened

Gabriel rushed to Lisa's side to assess the situation. Outside, the Phoenix chopper hovered a few feet off the ground just outside the hotel's front entrance. Four soldiers dressed in dark army gear and carrying assault rifles unloaded from the chopper. They made hand signals to each other, splitting into two groups as the chopper lifted away. One group then entered the hotel through its front doors while the other jogged along its perimeter until it was no longer in visual range.

"We have to assume they know which rooms we're staying in," Gabriel said. "Grab only necessities and a change of clothes. We've got less than two minutes to get out of here."

Porter and Nadine did as he instructed. Lisa returned to the hallway and monitored each direction for activity. When Porter and Nadine were ready, she gave the all-clear and led the group toward the nearest stairwell.

"Where are Nate and Samantha?" Porter asked as they hustled along.

"We split up downstairs," Gabriel told him. "Don't worry; Samantha can take care of the both of them."

They arrived at the stairwell. Lisa opened the door quietly and listened. At first there was silence, but then radio static echoed from somewhere below. Lisa began backing away from the approaching noise, but then the elevator at the other end of the hallway dinged. Gabriel waved wildly to draw everyone's attention, then pointed upward as he mouthed *the roof*. Lisa held the stairwell door open as Gabriel ushered Porter and Nadine inside. Taking over for his wife, Gabriel then guided the stairwell door shut just as the elevator doors at the other end of the hallway slid open, revealing the unmistakable pattern of army camo within.

Porter was in the lead now, with Nadine holding his arm to help him maintain balance, as they crept step by step toward the next floor. They weren't silent, but they were quiet enough that their noise was masked by the rapid footsteps of the soldiers approaching from below. They put one floor of distance between them and their entry point, then another, before the soldiers stopped in the stairwell, apparently having reached their destination. Gabriel motioned for everyone to remain still. He heard a stairwell door open, then more rapid footsteps, then the same stairwell door shutting once more. Porter heaved a sigh of relief.

"We're not out of the woods yet," Gabriel told him. "Those soldiers are going to see the state of your room and know we fled. They'll assume we're still somewhere in the hotel."

"Change your clothes," Lisa instructed. "We'll need to blend in as much as possible once we get outside." She pointed to a trash chute embedded in the nearby wall. "You can dispose of your pajamas there."

Porter and Nadine stripped, favoring survival over modesty, while Gabriel weighed their options.

"Continue to the roof or hightail it to the lobby and hope those soldiers don't retreat before we get there?" He asked Lisa.

"The roof," she said adamantly. "There's a fire escape on the rear side of the hotel. We can take it down while the soldiers are occupied searching in here."

Gabriel gave her a nervous thumbs-up. Porter and Nadine finished donning their street clothes and disposed of their pajamas as ordered. Then the group resumed its upward climb, this time more concerned with speed than quietness. They reached the roof hatch two minutes later, which Gabriel was thankful for, as Porter's movements were growing feebler by the second. Unfortunately, they still had a long trek down, though at least gravity would be on their side for it.

Gabriel climbed out onto the gravel surface that covered the top of the hotel. It took him a moment to reorient in the dim pre-dawn light, but he quickly identified the rear of the hotel and scouted for the fire escape Lisa had noted. The others were out of the stairwell by the time he found it, so he waved them over and they began their exterior descent. The hotel's backside faced a dark alleyway sandwiched between two buildings, so if they could just get far enough down the escape ladder to break free of nature's glow, shadows would protect them the rest of the way.

A loud squeal bounced off the alleyway walls as bright artificial light temporarily illuminated trash bins and exposed utility infrastructure below. Samantha and Nate, the latter still in his pajamas, had flung open a rear door at ground level and were now racing down the alleyway at full speed. The door slammed shut behind them, returning the alleyway to darkness. Gabriel paused his descent and almost called out, but then another light entered his vision, this one originating from above and directly focused on his fleeing team members. A Phoenix chopper with a mounted spotlight glided into the intersection where Samantha and Nate now stood. They pivoted away from the chopper, but a stream of bullets kicked up dirt and rock at their feet, forcing them to halt. Two soldiers slid down rappelling ropes, and in less than a minute, they had both Samantha and Nate in handcuffs.

"Shit," Gabriel whispered.

Things had just gotten significantly more complicated.

Chapter Seventy-Four
Caught

Casablanca, Morocco
Six Days Before The Sky Opened

Gabriel and the others waited in stillness as the Phoenix chopper landed and the soldiers loaded Samantha and Nate on board. Then they held their breath, hoping they wouldn't be spotted, as the chopper lifted off, returning the alleyway and adjoining intersection to uneasy silence.

"Now what?" Nadine asked, her nerves making her lip quiver.

"We keep going," Gabriel said. "We can't change what's already happened."

He continued his descent down the fire escape, aware of the coldness that his words conveyed, but reminding himself that Samantha and Nate would be all right. They were in trouble, for sure, but it wasn't anything a good lawyer couldn't handle. Porter, on the other hand, was already living on borrowed time... and *living* was putting it nicely. Gabriel had to secure his escape above all else.

They reached the bottom of the fire escape and headed toward the intersection at the opposite end of the alleyway from where Samantha and Nate had been caught. Once they reached the corner of the hotel, Porter buckled over, wheezing and clenching his chest in pain.

"I know this is hard on you," Gabriel said, "but we've come so far. Just push a little farther."

Porter flashed him a difficult smile and tried to stand, only to buckle over once more. This time, the buckling was accompanied by a yelp of agony, followed by Porter spitting blood onto the ground.

"I'm slowing you down," he gasped. "You need to go ahead. I'll catch up when I can."

"We aren't leaving you," Lisa told him.

Porter shook his head. "We all know that a chain is only as strong as its weakest link." He dropped to his hands and knees, then shifted onto his buttocks. "This chain's going to snap if you keep me in it right now. We can't afford that. Get out of here and find a way to draw the military's attention away from the hotel. I'll stay hidden until then. We can regroup in front of Mrs. Benkirane's apartment complex... let's say, in two hours?"

Gabriel looked at Lisa with uncertainty. She frowned, but nodded in agreement.

"Fine," Gabriel said. "Two hours. Not a moment later."

"I'll make sure he gets there," Nadine said.

"No," Porter objected. "You go with them. I need you to stay safe."

"And I need to make sure you stay alive long enough to make it to the rendezvous point." Despite her nerves, Nadine's posture was rigid. "I'm staying with you."

Gabriel heard the thumping of Phoenix chopper blades in the distance. "One way or another, we need to move now."

It was obvious Porter wanted to argue further, but he either didn't have the energy or knew it would be a waste of breath. He motioned for Gabriel and Lisa to be on their way as Nadine helped him up and escorted him to a dark nook where industrial pipes and utility meters were bolted to the hotel's rear wall. Gabriel looked around the hotel's rear corner for hostiles, then, not seeing any, signaled for Lisa to proceed into the intersection. They were halfway across, briefly illuminated by street lights, when a commanding voice called for them to stop.

Neither Gabriel nor Lisa bothered searching for the source of the voice, but it and the gunfire that followed originated from somewhere high, likely from one of their hotel balconies. The two reached the other side of the intersection and dashed down a second alleyway as the thumping of chopper blades grew louder behind them. They heard more voices and felt the ricochet of warning fire bouncing off their legs as the next intersection approached. They dashed out of the alleyway and turned left to put a building between themselves and their rear pursuers. But no sooner had they broken into the open that they crashed head-on into another pair of soldiers. Gabriel and Lisa struggled, but they were no match for their military-trained opposition. The soldiers spun them both around, pressed them into the ground, and slapped handcuffs around their wrists.

"Get up," one soldier barked as he yanked on Gabriel's arms.

Gabriel obeyed, and the soldier turned him so they were eye-to-eye.

"Where's Porter Cannes?" The soldier asked.

Gabriel played dumb. "Who?"

The soldier swung the butt of his assault rifle into Gabriel's abdomen, eliciting a pained groan. "Where is he?!"

While Gabriel took the brunt of physical and verbal abuse, Lisa was putting her brain to work. "We sent him ahead!" She yelled from her prone position. "We thought you had him already!"

Smart, Gabriel thought. She was giving them reason to abandon the hotel.

"Is that right?" The soldier interrogating Gabriel asked.

"Yeah," Gabriel lied. "He was the first one out of the building. But obviously you don't have him, which means you're never going to catch up to him now." He tried to sound as authentic as possible, hoping his goading would create a sense of urgency for the soldiers to expand their search grid. For good measure, he added, "Porter's too resourceful. He'll be out of the country within the hour."

The soldier eyed Gabriel suspiciously, and for a moment, Gabriel thought his ruse had failed. But then the man lifted his radio and pressed the talk button.

"Command, come in."

"This is Command," an electronic voice responded.

"We've got the Dunnes in custody. It looks like the primary target has already evaded our net. Please advise."

There was a long pause, then the electronic voice replied, *"bring the Dunnes back to base. The locals will hit the streets soon. We're going to start an international incident if you don't get your choppers out of there by then. We'll have to locate the primary target another way."*

"Roger that," the soldier said. He clipped his radio to his belt and turned his attention back to Gabriel. "This way."

The soldiers led Gabriel and Lisa back down their most recent alleyway and ushered them into the intersection where they had first been fired upon. A Phoenix chopper was standing by in its center, two additional soldiers flanking it with their weapons at the ready. Gabriel paused at the chopper door, knowing that once he and Lisa were on board, there would be no further opportunity for a last ditch escape effort. The soldier escorting him must have sensed his trepidation, for he nudged Gabriel's spine with the barrel of his assault rifle. Gabriel got the message and climbed aboard, taking a window seat to which he was fastened with an additional set of handcuffs.

Once he and Lisa were secure, the chopper lifted slowly, its pilot careful to stay clear of the surrounding buildings. Gabriel glimpsed a slight motion out his window and looked to see Porter and Nadine watching him from their dark nook behind the hotel. His initial feeling was one of relief, for his friend hadn't been caught, and the military was abandoning its search, which would give him an opportunity to flee the area. But then Gabriel realized he had overlooked a crucial detail in their haste to escape their military pursuers: he hadn't shared the pendant's location with Porter or Nadine.

How could I have been so stupid? Gabriel asked himself. He had been with Porter when the military arrived at the hotel. It had never even occurred to him they might get separated, or even worse, that everyone with knowledge of Samantha's discovery might get caught. Yes, Porter and Nadine were free to continue the search for the pendant, but as far as they knew, it could be anywhere along the Atlantic Ocean's great expanse. They didn't know the solution to The Veiled Bird. They didn't know about Alegranza. And worst of all, there was absolutely no chance Porter would survive long enough for Gabriel to tell him.

The treasure hunter turned sorrowful eyes to Lisa. "We failed."

Chapter Seventy-Five
Caged

U.S. Black Site, Morocco
Six Days Before The Sky Opened

As best Gabriel could tell, the Phoenix chopper followed a southeastern trajectory out of Casablanca. Open terrain marked with agricultural plots, stretches of rocky hills, and lesser traveled roads passed underneath as the chopper glided farther and farther from civilization. Soon, Gabriel spotted an approaching settlement. It spanned a three to four acre plot of arid land surrounded by enough undeveloped territory that it would be unlikely Moroccan civilians would stumble upon its location. Within the settlement were a variety of tents and other temporary shelters of thick green canvas. Each was capped with a camouflage tarp that blended with the Moroccan landscape. Gabriel could see military personnel moving about the settlement, and a second Phoenix chopper currently landing on one of two crudely marked helipads on the eastern edge.

"You could have left us at our hotel, you know," Gabriel yelled to the soldier nearest him. "The accommodations here seem a little... lacking."

The soldier adjusted his grip around his assault rifle. "You'll have plenty of time to air your grievances with General Sikes once we're on the ground."

General Sikes... well, at least now Gabriel knew who was in charge of this clandestine circus, not that it did him any good. He watched the blades on the second Phoenix chopper slow and eventually stop. Then a platoon of soldiers disembarked with Samantha and Nate in tow. They were escorted to what Gabriel presumed was a holding tent on the northern border of the encampment.

Next, it was his and Lisa's turn. Their chopper descended next to the other, its engines shut down, and the armed soldiers climbed out before turning and ordering Gabriel and Lisa to follow. They both knew there was no point in being defiant, and that compliance and diplomacy were probably the best tactic for securing freedom, assuming freedom was even an option. After being released from their handcuffs, they followed their escorts to the same tent as Samantha and Nate. Inside was a row of portable metal cages, each large enough to hold a single human adult, but not much else. Samantha and Nate had already been dispersed into the first two cages, leaving three others free for use.

"Do we get to pick our rooms?" Gabriel asked.

One of his soldier escorts shoved him toward the third cage. Gabriel stepped inside and watched closely as the soldier closed and locked the door. It used a standard bolt and padlock mechanism, where a metal bolt passed through custom fitted shafts on both the cage door and body, then a heavy padlock threaded through aligned holes in each to prevent the bolt from retracting. It was a pretty simple mechanism. The problem was that it was also highly effective. Without bolt cutters, a blowtorch, or the padlock key, Gabriel was stuck.

Lisa was guided into the fourth cage and secured the same way. This time, Gabriel watched the key to Lisa's padlock, which the locking soldier passed to another, who then dropped it in a velcro pouch on his vest before leaving the tent.

So much for that, Gabriel thought as his eyes haphazardly scanned the interior of the tent for a blowtorch. There wasn't one. In fact, there wasn't much at all in the tent except for a folding table covered in paperwork, an uncomfortable looking folding chair beside it, and an electric fan that didn't exactly cool the place down, but at least kept the air circulating enough to prevent it from getting stale.

"General Sikes will be with you shortly," one soldier told the team.

Then they all left. Gabriel was surprised not even one stayed behind to guard them. Then again, he had already accepted there was no breaking out of these cells. Even if there was, it was unlikely they'd make it out of the encampment without being caught. And if, by some miracle, they pulled that off, they'd probably die of thirst, starvation, or exposure before finding their way back to civilization. So in hindsight, it wasn't all that surprising after all.

"This is fun," Nate said dryly as he plopped down on the hard ground. "You think they'll bring me a change of clothes? They tore my pajamas getting me out of the chopper."

Samantha rolled her eyes and turned to Gabriel and Lisa. "Sorry guys. I should have been monitoring the military's movements once we returned to Morocco."

"It's not your fault," Lisa said. "None of us stopped long enough to consider the military might be closing in. Besides, you were busy doing something even more important: solving The Veiled Bird."

"Speaking of which, did anyone see what happened to Porter and Nadine?"

"I don't think they got caught," Gabriel told her. "They were still free when the military pulled out of Casablanca."

"Thank God," Samantha said. "Porter will have to arrange his own boat to Alegranza, and we'll have to hope the village welcomes him instead of challenging him, but at least he has a chance." She must have seen the dire look that washed over Gabriel's face. "What?" She asked. "You told Porter where the pendant was, right?"

"Everything happened so fast..."

Samantha's shoulders slumped. "So he has no idea." She dropped to the ground and cradled her knees. "We should have gotten moving sooner."

"We couldn't have known this was going to happen," Gabriel reminded her. "And we can't change what's happened already. We need to focus on getting out of here instead."

"You can't brute force these locks," Nate said.

"And the soldiers stripped me of my emergency gear," Samantha added. "The only way we're getting out of here is if they let us out."

Unfortunately, that was the same conclusion Gabriel had already reached. "Let's hope this General Sikes is a reasonable man."

"And that he gets here soon," Lisa added.

Gabriel nodded, then stared at the bottom edge of the surrounding tent, where a strip of light from the rising sun snuck through the gap between canvas and earth. As the morning progressed, that light grew brighter and whiter. And as the afternoon slipped away, it grew dimmer again and took on hues of yellow and orange. As evening set it, the light faded, until it was replaced by the darkness of night. Through all that time, soldiers had occasionally checked in on the team, brought them sufficient food and water, and arranged periodic excursions to portable restrooms. They never brought Nate new clothes, never engaged in conversation beyond the immediate reason for dropping by, and never acknowledged General Sikes' ongoing absence, which continued into the next day...

Chapter Seventy-Six
Twenty Questions

U.S. Black Site, Morocco
Five Days Before The Sky Opened

"Am I organic?" Nate asked as he lied on his back, staring at the taut inner lining of the tent roof.

"Yes," Samantha said.

"Do I typically have a warm color?"

"No."

Nate rubbed his chin. "Am I a reptile?"

"No." Samantha stretched her neck, releasing several audible cracks. "Seventeen questions to go."

This was their third game of Twenty Questions since waking up that morning. It was also the seventh game the team had played to keep their wits about them as they sat in their cages with little other access to stimulation. Nate was the first to float the idea, challenging Lisa to a game of I Spy. Lisa won, earning her the right to challenge Gabriel, who then challenged Samantha after achieving his own victory. Unfortunately, they quickly ran out of objects to spy, so Nate suggested a new game: Charades. He volunteered to be the first to make an ass of himself, then passed the privilege to Gabriel, who was in the middle of acting out *Planet of the Apes* when soldiers arrived to check if they needed bathroom breaks. The embarrassment was enough to get Charades placed on the team's figurative blacklist.

"Am I a plant?" Nate asked.

"Yes."

The team played multiple best-of-five Rock, Paper, Scissors bracket tournaments, challenged each other to Name the Movie based on obscure quotes- that one was quite popular- and took turns being Simon during increasingly challenging rounds of Simon Says. Nate really put their brains to the test when he insisted they attempt playing Chess, with each person mentally keeping track of board positions and move histories. That worked for five moves for Gabriel and Nate- seven for Lisa and Samantha- before discrepancies arose between the players and Nate admitted what everyone else had already known: the idea had been futile from the start.

"Am I poisonous?"

"No," Samantha said. Then she clarified, "not with typical use, anyway."

Nate pondered over her emphasis. "Are parts of me commonly consumed by mouth?"

"Yes."

"Raw?"

"Yes..."

Nate noticed the way she hung on that response. "And dried?"

"Yes."

"Are my leaves used as an herb for cooking?"

"Yes. Eleven to go."

Even with the vast variety of cooking herbs in the world, Gabriel suspected Nate would nail this down with over half his allotted questions remaining. The team leader tuned out their makeshift game show and shifted his eyes to the crack of light slipping between the tent and the ground. That light had been what first woke him up that morning, as dawn replaced the long darkness that came before it. But it had changed little since then, casting a constant, bright white glare into the tent that occasionally dimmed before quickly returning to its former state.

Gabriel deduced it was overcast today, which was great for keeping the temperature in the tent comfortable, but terrible for monitoring the time of day. Maybe it was still morning, maybe it was late afternoon- he honestly had no idea. The soldiers had only brought them one meal so far, but was that breakfast or brunch? It wasn't like this was a five-star hotel with a guarantee of three solid meals per day.

"Italian cooking?" Gabriel heard Nate ask in the background.

"Yes."

It had been at least twenty-six hours since they had been captured. More importantly, it had been at least twenty-six hours since they, and their knowledge of the pendant's location, had been separated from Porter. Was their old friend still alive? Was he still on the run? Maybe he had returned to the hotel's conference room and pieced together the same clues that had led Samantha to her discovery. Maybe he was too weak to do anything, and was lying in hiding, awaiting death's embrace. In fact, Gabriel wondered, maybe that was the reason General Sikes had been ghosting the team. The military didn't need them to turn over Porter or to abandon their search for the pendant. They just need to incapacitate the team long enough to ride out Porter's reaming lifespan... and they were doing a hell of a job at that so far.

"Are my leaves long and thin, like tree needles?" Nate asked.

"Nope."

"Are they-"

Nate stopped as the tent's door flap pulled back, filling the open space with the same overcast glare that had been peaking along its lower edge. Two soldiers Gabriel recognized from previous visits filed in, and behind them came a hard-edged man that effortlessly carried the weight of authority on his shoulders. He marched slowly past the cages, one foot in front of the other, eying his captives as if deciding which he would shoot for his next meal. Once he reached the end of the group, he flipped on his heels and doubled back over his previous steps, stopping at the folding chair and swinging his legs around it to face Gabriel. Had he spread his open crouch toward the team in some show of machoism? Probably not, but Gabriel couldn't help the thought from entering his mind.

"I'm General Morris Sikes," the man said, stating the obvious. "I hear you've been waiting to speak with me?"

Gabriel stared at the man, earned hostility welling within him. He would try to keep his cool, try to be diplomatic and reasonable, if for no other reason than to garner his team's release. But it was already clear from the way in which they'd been taken, the mind games General Sikes had played in keeping them waiting, and the manner by which the man had stepped into this tent like his shit didn't stink, that this wouldn't be a friendly conversation.

Chapter Seventy-Seven
Face To Face

U.S. Black Site, Morocco
Five Days Before The Sky Opened

Gabriel leered at the military official seated across from him. "We're U.S. citizens visiting Morocco for business reasons. We've broken no laws. Under what authority are you detaining us?"

The edge of General Sikes' lip curled upward. "Team Dunne... clandestine treasure hunters, and quite skillful ones, from what I've been told. I'm afraid your business has become a matter of national security. That's the authority I'm holding you under." He chuckled under his breath. "And don't get me started about breaking laws."

Gabriel noticed General Sikes flicked his gaze to Samantha with those last words. "We've been hired to find an ancient relic for an old friend," he said, trying to steer the conversation back on course.

"The Pendant of God," General Sikes acknowledged. "I've been briefed. And while I have my own doubts about the pendant's mythos, there are some in the government that believe its legend. They also believe the pendant poses a threat unlike any we've faced before, should it fall into the wrong hands, of course."

"We have no intention of letting that happen," Lisa said. "We need the pendant to heal someone; nothing more."

"Porter Cannes. Yes, I've been briefed on him, too. I've got to say, if there was ever an example of *wrong hands...*" The general shook his head. "I guess you're just too close to see it."

"Porter's not the enemy here," Samantha said, her dagger eyes clearly indicating who she felt was. "You detained us because you want him to die."

"I can't control his medical condition," General Sikes replied, the ice in his voice chilling even from a distance. "And if you must know, we would have detained him too, given the chance. We can't have something with as much potential for destruction as the Pendant of God winding up under the control of such an egotistical and ruthless man."

"Are you suggesting you're any better?" Gabriel was pushing his limits, but hey, he asked the question nicely.

General Sikes shook his head. "No. Something like that has no business in the military's hands, either. The fact that I can recognize that is why I was chosen for this mission."

"What exactly is your mission?"

"To prevent Porter Cannes from obtaining the Pendant of God until such a time that he's no longer a threat. You're his greatest asset in that pursuit. By stopping you, we've effectively stopped him."

"So the U.S. government has no interest in obtaining the pendant for itself?" Lisa asked.

General Sikes' lip curled again. "It's not our primary purpose for being here. But if the opportunity arises, yes, I'm under orders to secure the pendant and return it to the states."

"For what purpose?" Nate asked.

"That's above my pay grade."

"That's comforting."

General Sikes' eyes shifted back to Gabriel. "We could work together, you know. Perhaps a deal to earn your release?"

"Let me guess. Retrieve the pendant for the U.S. government?"

"And cut Porter Cannes out of the loop," General Sikes added. "Let his cancer have its way with him... if it hasn't already."

Gabriel tilted his head so General Sikes wouldn't see he'd hit a sore spot. Porter didn't have much time left when the team got captured. And though Gabriel couldn't tell exactly how much time had passed since then, he knew with every breath he took, Porter was one second closer to meeting his maker. The one bright spot was that even General Sikes didn't seem to know Porter's current condition, which meant there was a chance, however small, that he was still alive. "Your briefing about me and my team must have been lacking. Otherwise, you'd already know we'd never take that kind of deal."

"Yeah, I know. But it was worth a shot anyway." General Sikes leaned back casually, as if he'd reached the end of his formal script and was prepared to improvise. "Porter Cannes is going to die one way or another. Whether it happens while you whither in boredom in these cages or while you're out there chasing down the religious relic to best all others is up to you. If it was me, I'd prefer the latter."

Nate mimicked the general by leaning casually against the bars of his cage. "I guess that's what makes us *us* and you *an asshole.*"

General Sikes shrugged. "You're entitled to your opinion." He stood and pushed the folding chair under the adjacent desk. "Now, if you'll excuse me, I've got... well, anything other than this to do. But don't worry. We'll continue to take good care of you, and I'm sure we'll release you soon enough. You'll even get a formal apology from the U.S. government for mistaking you for terrorists. Can't have anyone back home thinking we purposefully detained American citizens on foreign soil."

"Some cover story," Samantha said. "It'll be interesting to see how it plays out in the media once we tell our side of things. Or in court, for that matter. Ever heard of depraved indifference? Let Porter die and you'll become quite familiar with the phrase."

General Sikes stood tall and puffed out his chest, reflecting her words the way Superman might reflect bullets. "Wasn't it you who aimed a loaded rocket launcher at my men the other day? I wouldn't even need to perjure myself to swear on a bible that they were on a routine reconnaissance mission and not even carrying live ammunition at the time. Hardly a threat to justify such a lethal response." Samantha flinched. It was barely noticeable, but enough to confirm General Sikes had her dead-to-rights. "Yeah, I think the mistaken terrorist story will play out just fine. And Porter Cannes will be an unfortunate casualty that could have been avoided... if only you hadn't given us reason to classify you as hostiles."

Shit, Gabriel thought. *They'd been played.* The scare tactics in New York to put them on edge, the helicopter standoff on the way to Safi... they were part of a larger strategy to get the team to take aggressive action against the military- which they had done- and in turn, justify their detainment. Worried they might dig themselves into a deeper grave if they kept talking, Gabriel motioned for Samantha to back off. General Sikes caught the gesture, but didn't comment on it.

"My offer stands until Porter Cannes' cancer nullifies it," he said on his way out of the tent. "Let me know if you change your minds."

And then General Sikes and his escort were gone. The team stood in silence for over a minute. Gabriel and Lisa shared an unspoken look that said *we've got to figure a way out of here*. Samantha stewed on her own actions and the precarious position in which she had now put the team. Nate did what Nate does best.

"So," he said, breaking the silent tension. "Are my leaves flat and floppy and typically rolled before cutting?"

The others turned, staring incredulously, before Samantha replied in a dry, humorless drawl, "yes, Nate. Yes, they are."

Chapter Seventy-Eight
Fireworks

U.S. Black Site, Morocco
Five Days Before The Sky Opened

The overcast glow lining the bottom edge of the tent eventually faded, yielding to the darkness of the next night. Gabriel felt the heavy weight of defeat press upon him. Now he knew it had been at least thirty-eight hours since they'd gotten caught. He recalled Porter's last coughing fit in Casablanca, the one that had given him insight into the bloody mess Porter's sickness was making of his lungs. He remembered how feeble Porter had looked getting out of bed and then attempting to flee the military's assault. Then he tried to project what that would look like thirty-eight hours later. It wasn't a pleasant thought.

Gabriel and the team had discussed taking General Sikes' deal, not that their acceptance would be authentic. They looked at it as their only plausible means of release, and told themselves that, once free of the black site, they could disappear from the military's radar and resume helping Porter. There were two problems that prevented the idea from moving forward. First, they would eventually get caught again. And once that happened, the government would likely prosecute them for treason... and win. Second, Gabriel had already concluded that General Sikes was an intelligent man. He would likely see through the ruse and put safeguards in place to prevent the team from deserting. Then they'd be stuck giving the U.S. government exactly what they wanted- which they probably wouldn't do- or getting charged with treason, hence ending up in the same place as the first scenario. Needless to say, accepting the general's deal, authentic or otherwise, wasn't an option.

That left a greater problem, just not for Gabriel and the team. Porter would indeed die. Gabriel tried to take solace in knowing that healing Porter had been a long-shot from the outset, that it was contingent on both the success of a mission with little to go on and the mystical powers of an ancient relic turning out to be real. But that brought little comfort. Over the course of the mission, Gabriel had come to believe that the Pendant of God was real and that it could heal Porter. Nate had told him where there's smoke, there's fire, and despite all the setbacks they'd endured, Gabriel could smell a thick plume of smoke. He could even visualize that smoke, its gray wisps wafting through the gap between tent and ground.

"What the hell is that?" Nate asked.

Wait... Nate could see it too?

"Smoke," Samantha said. "Something's on fire out there."

Then they heard the first boom. It was close, yet high, and it rattled the tent's support bars as its shockwave spread outward from its source. Lisa shot Gabriel a confused glance. Then another boom sounded, followed by a third. Though Gabriel couldn't see what was happening outside the tent, he could hear the sounds of soldiers scrambling, of weapons being deployed and then discharged into the darkness, of heavy coughing as the smoke cloud outside grew thicker.

"Is the base under attack?" Nate asked. "By whom?"

More booms, this time much closer. Soldiers hollered at one another to take cover, then fired more bullets, the short, random bursts signaling they had no idea what or where their target was. General Sikes stormed into the tent, the same two soldiers that had joined him earlier at his side.

"Is this you?" He demanded.

Gabriel shook his head. "We don't know what's going on."

Before the general could interrogate him further, Gabriel heard a whistling noise as a small dart with a feathered tail shot into the tent and embedded itself in General Sikes' neck. Two more darts followed, and within seconds, all three military men dropped to the ground, their bodies rag dolls. The tent door flapped open, and a familiar, albeit wholly unexpected, face emerged from the outside darkness.

"Byron? What-"

Two of Byron's mercenaries followed him into the tent. They both carried bolt cutters and proceeded to snap the locks on each cage. Outside, the explosions and aimless return fire continued.

"Please tell me you didn't actually use live rounds against a U.S. military base," Gabriel said.

"What kind of chump do you take me for?" Byron released Gabriel's bolt and swung his cage door open. "Those are a bunch of rampant teenagers launching fireworks and smoke grenades from cover on the other side of a hill. We paid them to provide a distraction."

"A distraction from what?"

Byron squeezed Gabriel's cheeks like a grandmother might squeeze those of her grandchild. "From rescuing you, of course! Let's go. We can explain everything once we're away from here."

"We?" Gabriel asked.

But Byron didn't answer. The rest of the team was free, so Byron's mercenaries poked their heads out of the tent, then signaled for everyone to follow as they jogged into the darkness. The black site was barely visible and scarcely recognizable between the natural darkness and clouds of suffocating smoke that Byron's hired help had launched. The mercenaries followed what appeared to be a predetermined path, avoiding the edge of camp where most of the action was underway. They passed some soldiers who were too busy heading toward the fray to notice them, and those that did they subdued with the same tranquilizer darts they had used on General Sikes. The noise of the fireworks intensified, as if building toward a New Year's Eve climax.

"That's our warning sound," Byron yelled to Gabriel as they ran. "We've only got a minute or two left before they run out of stock."

"Where are we going?"

Byron pointed straight ahead. Between billows of smoke, Gabriel could see the edge of the base camp. Just beyond that were two cargo vans with flashing hazard lights. The fleeing group stepped up their speed as the last of the firework booms faded and unsettling quietness returned. Byron removed a palm-sized, square device from his pocket.

"I was hoping I wouldn't have to do this."

He lifted a trigger guard and pressed a glowing green switch. A series of explosions broke out across the camp. Illuminated by rising fireballs all around, Gabriel saw truck hoods and engine parts blasted into the air and broken hubcaps and shredded rubber skidding across the ground. The series of detonations culminated at the makeshift helipads, where the cockpit of each Phoenix chopper was suddenly engulfed by red and orange flames.

"I thought you weren't a chump!" Gabriel yelled at Byron.

"Well," the rival treasure hunter replied, "you know me!"

They reached the vans as a new level of chaos swamped the military base. Now Gabriel could see that one van was the lesser damaged one from his and Nate's sabotage on the Tangier-Algeciras ferry. The other was their own, magically transported from where they had left it in Casablanca.

"How did you-"

"Hot-wire," Byron said. "Though it was a bitch to do. You must have installed a custom safeguard on the ignition shaft."

Gabriel glanced at Samantha, who returned a sly smile.

"There's someone who wants to speak with you," Byron continued.

He pulled open their van's side door, revealing Porter and Nadine inside. Porter was slumped to one side, his eyes sunken into dark pits, a sag to his face that Gabriel didn't remember, and a constant tremor running through his right arm and leg. He frowned. Gabriel suspected it was partially an apology for the current situation and partially out of shame.

"Sorry," Porter said in a low, raspy voice. "It was the only way."

Under any other circumstances, Gabriel would have chastised his friend for getting into bed with Byron Coltrain. But tonight, he was just happy to see Porter was still alive.

Chapter Seventy-Nine
Partners

U.S. Black Site, Morocco
Five Days Before The Sky Opened

Samantha reached inside each van and killed their hazard lights. She also disabled their interior courtesy lights to create as much cover of darkness as she could. The chaos inside the base camp would settle now that Byron's distractions had been exhausted. Soldiers would soon discover General Sikes' unconscious body and initiate a search for their escapees. Gabriel and the rest of the team knew it was imperative they flee the area as soon as possible, but they also knew that couldn't happen until business was concluded.

"What were the terms of the deal?" Gabriel asked Porter.

"Byron rescues you," he said in an increasingly hoarse voice. "We let him tag along to find the pendant."

"How do you like that?" Byron said, gleefully slapping Gabriel's shoulder. "We're partners now."

Gabriel couldn't stand the idea, but the deal had been struck without his say, and Byron had already fulfilled his end of the arrangement. "What happens after we find the pendant?"

Porter shrugged weakly. "We work out a new deal. Byron's already assured me he won't interfere with me receiving the pendant's blessing. He's also assured me he'll behave and do things our way, which I take to mean he'll negotiate in good faith regarding the pendant's ultimate fate."

Byron gave a firm nod of agreement. Gabriel caught a look of concern on Lisa's face. She, like him, knew Byron's assurances were fickle at best. He'd look for every opportunity to renege if it suited his own interests.

"Fine," Gabriel said. "We're partners until we find the pendant, and then we have a good-faith discussion about where to go from there. But Byron, the moment you or your team members step out of line, our partnership and any subsequent trust is over. Got it?"

"Whoa, whoa, whoa," Byron said, holding his hands up as if to say *don't shoot*, "I'm not the one who's been playing dirty lately. But I agree. Our trust is contingent on my team following the Dunne code. I promise we'll play nice."

"Good. Now let's get out of here."

Samantha was already behind the wheel of their van. Nate climbed into the front passenger seat as Gabriel climbed into the back. But as Lisa followed, Byron, who hadn't bothered returning to his own van, raised his hand in objection.

"Hold it right there," he said, loud enough for everyone to hear. "Lisa needs to go in my van. I'll be going in yours."

Gabriel poked his head out. "No one mentioned that in the terms of the deal."

"That's because it wasn't in the terms of the deal," Byron acknowledged. "But it's a demand I'm making now, and it's non-negotiable. Despite any arrangement we might have, we're both going to look for ways to screw over the other. It's in our nature. The only way to ensure we all reach our destination together is by intermingling our teams. Lisa can go with mine. I'll go with yours. That way, no one gets left behind."

Gabriel looked at Lisa, his way of leaving the decision to her. She nodded reluctantly, then climbed down and transferred to Byron's van, where his short-haired intellect greeted her and showed her to an open seat. Byron climbed into Team Dunne's van and helped himself to a spot behind Gabriel.

"Isn't this fun?" He asked with the most jolly, punchable face Gabriel could imagine. "Who knows? This could be the start of a beautiful friendship."

"I doubt it," Gabriel said.

He leaned over and slammed the van's door. Seconds later, they pulled away from the black site. Soldiers heard their engines rev and ran to investigate, but by then, the vans were speeding into uninhabited Moroccan territory. Gabriel heard the soldiers shouting as they fired a few rounds at them. A couple of bullets ricocheted off their van's metal body, but that was the only resistance they endured. They were quickly out of accurate firing range, and thanks to Byron, the military currently had no viable means of pursuit.

"So," Byron asked once they were clear of the base, "where are we headed?"

"Essaouira," Gabriel answered truthfully, so Byron could communicate it to his van's driver. "I'll tell you the next destination once we get there."

Byron shook his head. "Such distrust..."

"With good reason." Gabriel looked at Porter, who had barely moved since the rescue operation. "Are you going to hang on another eight hours or so?"

His response was barely visible, but Gabriel was pretty sure Porter had nodded his head.

"We tried to get you out sooner," Nadine said. "But it took time to find Mr. Coltrain, then to locate the black site, then to gather the gear we needed,..." She stroked Porter's cheek affectionately. "I never imagined we'd be cutting it so close."

Gabriel nodded. He hadn't expected it to come down to the wire either, but there was nothing they could do about that now. The key was to keep moving forward, no matter what. "Samantha? How are we as far as preparations go?"

"I got one of my contacts moving on sourcing a Leviathan before we were captured. I just need to let him know to double the order and where to leave them." She glanced in the rearview mirror at Porter. "We're probably going to need a portable gurney, too. I have spare phones and earpieces in the back. Fish a set out for me and I'll get the ball rolling."

"Is there anything else we need?" Gabriel asked as he unbuckled his seatbelt and climbed into the cargo area.

"Shouldn't be. The van's still fully stocked, minus whatever Byron might have lifted for himself." The rival treasure hunter gave her reflection an innocent shrug. "We'll make do with what we've got and hope we don't run into anything too unexpected once we reach our destination."

Gabriel found the stash of phones and earpieces. He brought a pair to Samantha, then reclaimed his seat in front of Byron.

"Essaouira's a port city," Byron said with the tone of someone fishing for details. "And you're requisitioning high tech speed boats. Is there an island retreat in our near future?"

Gabriel didn't give him the respect of turning around. "I told you we'd share that information once we get to Essaouira."

He heard the soft squish of Byron leaning back against his leather seat. "I guess I'll just have to be patient until then... partner."

Gabriel shuddered as the word oozed into his ears. Part of him wished he was still in his cage in the military black site. But that part of him also knew it meant condemning Porter to certain death. He would suck up his disdain for Byron in order to help his friend, but he wouldn't honor this partnership for even a moment beyond that. Worse, he knew Byron wouldn't either.

Chapter Eighty
More Time

North Atlantic Ocean
Four Days Before The Sky Opened

It took four and a half hours for the team to reach Essaouira. Half the city had already gone to sleep while the other half energized the local nightclubs, bars, and public spaces. Samantha guided their caravan to the western port, where a modestly sized nondescript wooden crate awaited their arrival. That was the gurney Samantha had requested, which she unpacked and set up while they waited for delivery of their Leviathan watercrafts. Once complete, Gabriel and Byron helped Porter onto the gurney. It was then that Gabriel noticed how frail his friend had become. Even though there was no way Porter's muscles could have atrophied over such a short period, they may as well have, for it was clear he couldn't use them. Likewise, Porter's lungs weren't permitting much air intake, and so the tech billionaire refrained from attempting any physical movement if he could help it.

The Leviathans arrived an hour later. Samantha finished prepping 'go bags' with whatever gear they might reasonably need on Alegranza and shared her mental packing list with Byron's team so they could do the same. She also shared earpiece translators from Byron's stash to assist with communication once they found the pendant's new village. They loaded the Leviathans, wheeled Porter aboard, and distributed their intermingled teams among the vessels, maintaining the same arrangement they had for the vans. Gabriel shared their destination just before it was time to set sail, but insisted Byron's team let Samantha lead the way to retain control over their approach to the island and any unexpected encounters they might have along the way.

By two o'clock, they were skimming across the Atlantic Ocean. Again, they had to limit their speed to one hundred miles per hour, not for fear of hitting pedestrians in the dark of night like in the Balearic Sea, but for the risk of crashing into an uncharted islet between Essaouira and Alegranza. Though the chances were minimal given the Leviathans' object-collision technology, any collision at higher speeds would bring their journey to an abrupt end, and spell death not only for Porter, but for everyone aboard. That cost was too high to take even small chances with.

"How are you doing?" Gabriel asked Porter when he woke from a nearly two-hour nap.

"I'm still breathing," his friend replied, barely audible over the noise of the Leviathan cutting through waves above deck. "How long do we have left?"

"We should reach Alegranza any minute now."

Porter nodded and looked away despondently. "We're so close to victory, and to think, I may not live long enough to embrace it."

"Don't talk like that," Gabriel said. "Those are the words of a quitter. The Porter Cannes I know isn't a quitter."

"Those are the words of a realist," Porter corrected him. "And I'm very much one of those. Let's face it, time's not on our side, and you and I both know there's an uncertain amount of it that still stands between us and the pendant."

"Uncertain doesn't mean too much. It just means we don't know."

Porter smiled in appreciation of his optimism. Then he sighed and closed his eyes. "If only I had a little longer..."

Gabriel opened his mouth with a response that had been lingering on the tip of tongue, then held back from saying it. He didn't want to upset Porter in his dying state, but there was something troubling, something that, given the current situation, could have made all the difference in the world. If Gabriel didn't ask now, he might never get another chance.

"Porter... you had more time."

Porter opened his eyes and stared at Gabriel, as if he knew where the conversation was headed. "You saw the dating of the scroll, didn't you?"

Gabriel nodded. "Why'd you lie about it? You could have contacted me weeks sooner. We could have found the pendant long before your condition deteriorated to this point."

Porter averted his eyes, which glistened with tears. "Chalk it up to arrogance. I thought I could find the pendant on my own. I was determined to save myself without the need for anyone else's help. After a couple of weeks passed with no significant progress, I realized I was being a fool."

"But why lie about it?" Gabriel pressed.

"Imagine you're trapped in a burning building with two options: pick up the phone and call the fire department to save you, or try to battle the flames yourself, given no training and insufficient resources. Which would you do?"

"Call the fire department, of course."

"Now imagine you did the other, and even though you made it out alive, half your body is covered in burn scars for the rest of your life. Would you be forthright about your idiocy if someone asked you how it happened, or would you simply say you got trapped in a burning building?"

Gabriel lowered his head in contemplation. "I see your point."

"My stupidity may very well have killed me," Porter continued. "I suppose we'll find out shortly. Unfortunately, if that turns out to be the case, a man like me has little chance of getting into Heaven. I've indulged in the pleasures of humanity too much for that."

"You believe in Heaven now?"

Porter frowned. "Seeing what we've seen this past week, knowing what I know now... I believe in something. Maybe it's not a traditional Heaven or similar plane of existence, but I know something more extraordinary than this mortal world awaits. It must; otherwise, how could the pendant do the things it does?"

"We still don't have proof-"

Porter chuckled. "I think we have sufficient circumstantial evidence at this point." He closed his eyes again, musing over the idea. "If whatever exists beyond mortality is a traditional Heaven, I sure wish its ruler would be a bit more lenient about admission standards... at least for the next twelve hours or so."

Gabriel wasn't sure why, but that gave him a good laugh. "The standards have pretty much been set in stone for thousands of years now."

"Well," Porter said with a lighthearted shrug, "when you find the pendant, ask whomever has it to see if it can bend the rules for my wayward soul. I figure if anything has the power to breach the gates of Heaven, it's that."

Gabriel put a consoling hand on his friend's arm. "We won't let it come to that."

He heard a knocking overhead, Samantha's way of getting his attention without leaving the wheel. Gabriel excused himself from the conversation with Porter and joined her up top, salty mist pelting him as he made his way to the boat's shielded control panel.

"What's up?" Gabriel asked.

"We're here!" Samantha yelled over the roar of the ocean.

She pointed straight ahead. At first, Gabriel saw nothing but the black horizon. But then his eyes adjusted to the stars and moonlight, and an approaching silhouette took shape. It was an island rising from the depths, dark among the waves, and partially shrouded by a thin, white haze. That haze stretched over the island from end to end, and grew thicker as it rose in altitude, where it would completely block the land mass from an overhead view. Gabriel took a moment to let the visual sink in, and in his peripheral vision, he saw Lisa was doing the same from the second boat, which had pulled alongside for a better view.

Gabriel wanted to remember this moment forever. It was the moment all their hard work on this mission had finally paid off, the moment they had reached the destination that had so far eluded their greatest efforts. Only one phrase could capture such a moment, one phrase that left Gabriel's lips with a tenor of reverence and awe that rivaled Alan Grant's when life found a way in *Jurassic Park*: "The Veiled Bird."

Chapter Eighty-One
Into The Veil

Alegranza, Canary Islands
Four Days Before The Sky Opened

The Leviathans approached Alegranza from the northeast. Samantha insisted they slow to a crawl as they neared, for between the pre-dawn darkness and white mist that now surrounded them, visual acuity was severely impaired. Once she had a firm sense of the island's perimeter, Samantha guided their fleet eastward along the coast. She was looking for the Punta Delgada Lighthouse, built in the 1860s to help prevent ships from grounding themselves in the Alegranza shallows. It wasn't the lighthouse Samantha was interested in, per se, but the ocean dock it sat adjacent to. It would provide them a safe place to disembark and secure the Leviathans until their return.

Around four-thirty, Samantha spotted what she'd been looking for. The lighthouse wasn't operational- no doubt intentionally shut down by the Shifa villagers to conceal their location- but its whitewashed walls stood out noticeably from its dark and hazy surroundings. Samantha guided the team on an arcing path around the lighthouse's headland, which jutted out eastward from the main island until sloping into the ocean, creating a minefield of rocky obstructions separated by dangerously shallow water and obscured by foamy ocean chop. Even more cautious now that their destination was so close, Samantha swung wide to avoid all collision threats, then cut back toward the island, this time approaching the lighthouse from its headland's southern shore.

There, she spotted the ocean dock, a long rectangular slab of stone that extended southward from a manmade path that ran to the base of the lighthouse. Samantha pulled around to the less choppy western side of the dock, where rope posts and a low boarding zone awaited visiting vessels. She left room for Byron's crew to pull in behind her, then began disembarking procedures.

It took another thirty minutes for everyone to unload, gear up, secure the Leviathans, and run through their game plan. According to maritime records Samantha had gathered, they had docked on the eastern tip of Alegranza. To their north was low-lying coast and a beach, both ideal terrain for establishing a temporary settlement, but also a little too exposed to ships that happened to pass by. Gabriel reasoned that if the pendant villagers wanted to retain their secrecy, they weren't likely to have settled there. To the south was a series of small mountain ranges. These were less ideal for settlement, and would also leave the pendant villagers exposed to passing ships, unless they settled high enough to hide in the misty veil, but that would make daily life quite difficult. As with the north, Gabriel assessed the likelihood of finding the pendant there as low.

That left two locations which were more promising. The first, but slightly less promising, was at the opposite end of the island from where they were now. There stood the Caldera de Alegranza, a half-mile wide crater that served as a reminder of the island's volcanic origins. Though part of Alegranza's southwestern coastline, the Caldera de Alegranza's high walls and concave center were perfect for concealing a mobile village from outsiders. In fact, Gabriel would have ranked it his most promising target for the pendant's location, if it weren't for one small, but highly significant detail: that was the mouth of a volcano. Sure, the likelihood of a dormant caldera suddenly spewing fresh magma was exceptionally low, but there was still something disturbing about living atop one of the most violent and explosive weapons at Mother Nature's disposal.

That focused Gabriel's attention on the center of the island. It was higher and drier than the northern shore, but not as high and unlivable as the mountainous southeastern shore, and it was just as concealed as the Caldera de Alegranza. He decided that was the team's first destination. They would travel as a unified group into the heart of Alegranza, and if they came up empty, they still had the option of continuing on toward the caldera. It was both the most promising and most efficient trajectory, and efficiency was crucial at this point.

"Are you ready?" Gabriel asked Porter, whose gurney was angled slightly upwards so he could be part of the action.

"Life's not waiting on me to be ready," Porter replied with as much of a smile as he could manage. "Let's go."

Gabriel and Byron each took a side of the gurney as Samantha and the mercenaries formed a side-by-side armed escort along the dock. They wheeled Porter toward the shore, Nadine, Lisa, Nate, and Byron's right hands bringing up the rear. This wasn't how Gabriel had imagined this mission playing out when he first accepted it, but then again, life had a habit of throwing people curve balls. As they set out into the looming mist, he told himself that none of it mattered, as long as they succeeded in saving his friend.

Chapter Eighty-Two
Unseen Resistance

Alegranza, Canary Islands
Four Days Before The Sky Opened

Samantha's estimates put the center of Alegranza between a half mile and full mile from the lighthouse. On flat, open terrain, that would have taken the team only fifteen minutes or so to cross. On the uneven, mist covered land of Alegranza, she suggested doubling that expectation. It was just after five-thirty when the team departed the dock, still too early for the sun to light their way. As they soon discovered, flashlights were useless too, for as soon as the team marched inland, the mist grew so thick that it diffused their beams, diffracting them in every direction and creating a persistent wall of blinding glare. Luckily, the water molecules that comprised the thick veil overhead were also diffractive. They collected and dispersed moonlight throughout its puffy mass, providing the team with just enough of a natural glow to see a few feet ahead at all times.

"It's like walking through a dream," Lisa said.

Gabriel agreed. If someone had told him he'd been kidnapped and dropped off on another planet, he wouldn't have been able to argue otherwise. Here, there was no sign of humanity. There were no buildings, no artificial lights, no sounds of people gathering en masse. If Alegranza was home to any plant life, Gabriel had yet to see it. He didn't hear any animals, not even insects or birds, and the rolling mist that surrounded him both consumed and revealed an endless supply of volcanic rock underfoot, as if the team were walking in place on nature's treadmill.

"Everyone stop," Samantha barked from somewhere ahead.

Gabriel couldn't see her. Hell, he couldn't see half of their expanded team members. He only knew they were still there because he could hear them shuffling or see the mist flowing around what he presumed were their bodies. "What's going on?"

Samantha broke through the fog ahead. She was smacking the side of her compass the way a child might smack a malfunctioning toy. "Something's interfering with my reading."

"Maybe it's the volcanic activity in the area," Lisa suggested.

"I don't think so. It was working fine until just a moment ago."

Gabriel glanced at Nate for ideas, but he just shrugged.

"How confident are you we were on the right path before your compass went on the fritz?" Byron asked.

"Confident," Samantha said.

"Then let's just keep marching straight."

"That's easier said than done when you can't see where you're going. We could veer off trajectory and never know it. We could even wind up going in circles."

Gabriel considered the risk. "The island's not that big. We know approximately how long it should take to hit shore, which means we'll know if we veer off that bad. We also know the terrain at each shoreline, which we could use to adjust course if needed. The worst that'll happen is we lose time." He looked at Porter, who nodded nervously. "We've got to try to keep moving."

"You got it, boss." Samantha disappeared into the mist to resume her position at the front of the parade. But only seconds later, she returned, her pistol raised in a two-hand grip. "Byron, what the hell are you up to?"

The rival treasure hunter released Porter's gurney and raised his hands innocently. "I don't know what you're talking about."

"Your men," Samantha said. "Where'd they go?"

Byron shook his head.

As far as Gabriel could tell, his responses seemed genuine, but he couldn't take any chances that Byron was executing a secret plan to retrieve the pendant himself now that he knew its location. "Lisa, keep your eyes peeled for anything funny back there." Silence. "Lisa?"

Gabriel turned and found a fleeting wisp of mist where Lisa had previously stood. She wasn't the only one gone, either. Byron's techie was missing, and his intellect looked scared for her life as she stared at the empty space where he had been moments sooner.

"Everyone, huddle up around the gurney!" Samantha shouted.

Gabriel unholstered his gun, and Byron must have felt comfortable enough Samantha wouldn't shoot him that he did the same. They turned their backs to one another, Porter lying on the gurney between, and aimed their weapons toward the walls of mist that rose on every side. Samantha, Nate, Nadine, and Byron's intellect joined them.

"No one fire unless you have a visual on the threat," Gabriel said. "We don't want to hit our own people out there."

For nearly a minute, all was still. Gabriel scanned the mist for any signs of movement beyond the constant flowing and twirling of white. He wanted to call out for Lisa, but he knew she wouldn't respond. Besides, sound was the enemy right now. Gabriel couldn't see whomever was picking off his team from beyond the mist, but that meant they couldn't see him either. Noise would give away his position.

"We can't just stand here," Byron whispered. "We're sitting ducks."

Gabriel and Samantha exchanged looks to confirm they were both in agreement. They needed to get to the new Shifa village. If this invisible threat was from there, then perhaps they could explain the innocent nature of their voyage to Alegranza and resolve any misunderstanding. If the invisible threat wasn't from there, then maybe the villagers at least knew what to do about it. Either way, the village was still their destination, and Gabriel had to hope Lisa would be all right until they got there.

"Samantha, which way?" Gabriel asked quietly.

She pointed.

"Okay," he then said to the group, "on three, we run. Byron and I will still stay on the sides of the gurney. Nate, you take the back. Rolling will be too slow. We need to lift and carry."

Nate and Byron nodded. Gabriel scanned the mist once more, and seeing no changes, he lifted a fist for all to see. Then he raised a finger. *One*. The other team members tensed. *Two*. They shifted their bodies to face the trajectory Samantha had indicated. Gabriel inhaled deeply to fill his lungs with oxygen, then raised his final finger. *Three*.

Gabriel, Byron, and Nate lifted Porter's gurney as the others dashed ahead of them. The sound of padded footsteps filled the air. Gabriel heard a thud from somewhere, then rustling. He tried to tune it out as they carried Porter onward, the mist blowing past them faster than it had before. Gabriel didn't know if Samantha and the others were still out in front or if they too had been taken one by one, swallowed by the mist as though some supernatural creature lurked within it. Then a shadow filled Gabriel's peripheral vision. He looked to the side just in time to see a large boulder break through the wall of white. It swept Byron's legs from under him the way a bowling ball knocks away pins. The rival treasure hunter fell, and with no support on that side of the gurney, Porter crashed down with him. At the same time, a billow of mist shot forth behind Nate.

"Look out!" Gabriel yelled.

But it was too late. Two pairs of arms reached out of the mist, one to wrap around Nate's body, the other to cover his mouth. The arms yanked him into the fog quicker than he could scream. Gabriel pushed the overturned gurney aside and kneeled to help Porter. His friend stared at him with fearful eyes, and Gabriel realized a moment too late that Porter wasn't looking at him, but looking *behind* him. He felt a muscular arm encircle his waist. Gabriel grabbed his gun and swung its barrel toward the source of the arms, but the weapon was ripped from his hands before he could pull the trigger. Then a muscular hand covered Gabriel's mouth, and he felt himself ripped backwards, away from Porter and into the mist, which filled his vision with white.

Chapter Eighty-Three
Speechless

Alegranza, Canary Islands
Four Days Before The Sky Opened

"Well," Nate said in an exceptionally sarcastic tone, "this feels familiar."

Gabriel opened his eyes to find himself lying on a hard rock floor. He sat up slowly, then rubbed his aching neck, his fingers pausing over the raised bump where his mist attackers had injected him with what he now knew had been a fast-acting sedative. Gabriel tried to look around, but the room went crooked and spun off-axis.

"Don't move too fast," Lisa said, kneeling to help keep him balanced. "It takes a couple of minutes to fully wear off."

"Lisa? You're okay?"

"I'm fine," she said. "We're all fine. We're just-"

She motioned behind her back with a hand gesture that was weak with helplessness. Gabriel followed with his eyes, more slowly this time, and saw the vertical bars of the wooden cage that surrounded them.

"Well, shit," he said.

"Exactly," Nate chimed in. "We could have hung around the U.S. black site if we'd known this is where we'd wind up. At least they fed us pretty well."

Gabriel ignored him. "Porter?"

Lisa pointed to his left. About ten feet away, Porter was stretched out on the ground, having not yet woken from his sedative. Nadine was sitting next to him, her eyes puffy and red as she stroked his back. A few more feet behind Porter was Byron, who looked like he was still in a daze, as though he had woken around the same time as Gabriel. His two right hands were by his side to welcome him back to consciousness. His mercenaries were dispersed throughout the large cell, none looking amused by their predicament.

"I assume they stripped us of our gear?" Gabriel asked.

"Just our weapons," Samantha told him. She was leaning back in one corner of the cell, her body still and eyes closed, as if preserving energy. "They left everything else."

"Anything useful to get us out of here?"

"Of course," she said, opening her eyes to look at him. "But they've got two guards watching the door, and we already know they've got the upper hand in the mist, so what's the point of trying to escape?"

Gabriel hated when her logic was so sound, or at least, he hated it when that logic wasn't something he wanted to hear. He scanned the room that surrounded the makeshift cage. It was also made of wood and contained no decoration or accessories. The wood was old, its grain stressed by years of dryness, its color a ghostly representation of the vibrancy Gabriel assumed it once flaunted. Periodic holes allowed in light from outside...

Light, Gabriel thought. The sun had risen while he was asleep. How much time had gone by? Was Porter really still out because of the sedative, or was there a chance he wouldn't wake at all? Gabriel prayed it wasn't the latter, not when they were so close to achieving victory. *Okay,* he confessed inwardly, *maybe not that close...*

A shirtless, muscular man entered the tent. His skin was pale from a lack of sun, but he clearly hadn't been hurting for protein. He wore decorative jewelry around his neck and one wrist, and his shorts appeared to have been made from animal hide, but without the processing of modern clothing manufacturing. The man approached the cage and observed its inhabitants.

"Hi," Gabriel said, unsure what else he should do. "I'm Gabriel Dunne. I'm afraid we've had a misunderstanding."

The man ignored him and strolled down the length of the cage. Gabriel glanced at Lisa, who shrugged with a *don't look at me* kind of attitude, then followed the man.

"I was wondering if we could speak to your leader." Gabriel heard how ridiculous he sounded the moment the words left his mouth.

Alegranza may have been indistinguishable from an alien world, but this was still Earth and this man was still a human being. Gabriel shouldn't be speaking to him as if he had green tentacles and googly eyes. "I'm sorry. What I meant to say-"

The man stopped and slammed his palm against the wooden bars. Gabriel perceived the move as an act of aggression, so he shut up. But then the man hit the bars again anyway. This time, he got Nadine's attention, which was apparently what he wanted. The man pointed at Porter and twirled his finger as if to say *rise and shine*. Nadine stopped rubbing and instead shook Porter's shoulder. His eyes fluttered open, but they were glazed over and distant, his mind still somewhere else. The shirtless man hit the bars a third time.

"Hey," Nadine whispered to Porter. "You need to wake up."

Porter's eyes swung from one end of their sockets to the other. Then they focused on Nadine, and Gabriel saw signs of sentient life as Porter reached up to touch her face and give her a reassuring smile. Satisfied that Porter was finally awake, the muscular man turned back the way he had come.

"Wait," Gabriel said. "Won't you at least talk to us?"

His subsequent exit told Gabriel the answer was *no*. Feeling as though he had lost all control over the situation, Gabriel sighed and leaned his head against the cage bars. He had barely gotten a moment of sulking out, however, when the muscular man returned, this time with ten other similarly dressed, similarly decorated, and, oddly enough, similarly muscled men with him. The ten men spread out with equal number lined up on each side of the cage door, essentially forming a corridor of flesh between the cage and the building's exit. The original muscle man unlocked the cage door and opened it wide. Gabriel looked questionably at the door, then at the man, then back at the door again. The man grunted and waved his hand in a gesture meant to usher his prisoners out.

Nate jumped at the opportunity. "You don't have to tell me twice."

"I'll watch over him," Samantha said before following.

Byron went next, taking his entire team with him, while Gabriel and Lisa assisted Nadine in getting Porter to his feet. Another person entered the tent. This one was a young man, perhaps in his teens, with scruffy hair and the body of someone who ate only when he needed to.

He pushed Porter's scuffed-up gurney down the corridor of men and rolled it to a stop next to its awaiting patient. Then, without a word, the young man left. The others helped Porter onto the gurney, then Gabriel and Lisa each took a side while Nadine held Porter's hand for comfort. They wheeled their feeble friend down Muscle Alley, toward the daylight streaming in from outside, and toward the unknowns that awaited them there.

Chapter Eighty-Four
The Thousand Year Man

Alegranza, Canary Islands
Four Days Before The Sky Opened

As Gabriel's eyes adjusted to the bright glow of sunlight, two things quickly became apparent. First, even though the primary mist cloud still hovered overhead, the sun's rays diffracting throughout its mass, no mist extended down to ground level, enabling Gabriel to see clearly in every direction. Second, near-vertical rock walls stood tall in the distance, surrounding them on all sides. This latter observation could only mean one thing: they were inside the Caldera de Alegranza.

The lead muscular man guided the team over the expanse of gently sloped volcanic rock that formed the center of the caldera. Erected across the expanse were more wooden buildings. Most were small houses, but there were also clusters of outhouses here and there, a few larger buildings with open sides that appeared to be common areas of some sort, a handful of barns occupied by common livestock, and a centralized structure that Gabriel assumed was either a town hall or house of worship. That's where the team was being taken.

As they headed toward it, Gabriel also noticed potted gardens accompanying most houses. Hardy fruits and vegetables dominated the gardens, which were tended to by young children in simple clothing. Adults, on the other hand, seemed occupied with more traditional chores. Groups of them surrounded communal washing basins, which numbered one for every eight to ten houses, by Gabriel's estimate. A handful of them stoked fires in stone pits and made cooking preparations in makeshift kitchens dominated by cast iron and rock. Others carried supplies from one end of the village to the other, laid out utensils in the common areas to prepare for a meal, or wrangled in stray children who had run off to play.

"We're actually here," Gabriel said to Porter in disbelief.

His friend was watching the Shifa villagers with both wonder and curiosity. They were gears in a well-oiled, if old, machine. Each seemed to do his or her part, and each seemed happy to serve, as if this was all they could ever want from life. Some villagers eyed Gabriel and the team with... well, Gabriel wasn't quite sure. It could have been simple interest, or maybe even a bit of contempt. Perhaps it was mistrust, or possibly fear. The looks were inconsistent and difficult to read, and Gabriel couldn't separate his interpretation of them from the knowledge that he and his team were intruding on these people's otherwise peaceful lives.

They reached the centralized structure. The lead muscle man pushed open the oversized wooden doors, which creaked on their hinges in protest. He then lead the team inside, where a spacious sanctuary awaited. Old-fashioned lanterns hung from rope overhead. Stone benches flanked a center aisle that stretched toward a raised pulpit, and on that pulpit stood a ceremonial stone table and matching throne. As Gabriel filed down the aisle with his team, he made eye contact with a robed man seated on the throne. The man's age was difficult to nail down, for he had the staunchness of someone who had long ago experienced life and persevered through its difficulties to earn his current place, yet his skin was smooth like a child's and his posture pristine.

The man held up a hand when the team had gotten close enough, so they stopped. Behind them, the other ten muscular men entered the sanctuary and spread along its perimeter, each one taking up post in a predetermined, equidistant position that ensured Gabriel and his team remained surrounded. Their leader shut the sanctuary doors and posted himself in front of it, blocking the only visible exit from the building. All eyes turned to the robed man on the throne, who then spoke in a firm voice that echoed off the sanctuary's walls. His words were foreign, a language that sounded familiar, but that Gabriel couldn't identify, so he waited for his earpiece to translate.

Only it didn't. Gabriel wondered if his earpiece's battery had run dry, but when he looked to Lisa, it was clear hers hadn't made the translation either. The robed man repeated himself, and once again, the earpieces failed to translate. Gabriel glanced at Porter, who shrugged, unsure what had gone wrong. On the pulpit, the robed man displayed a sly smile.

"You didn't think to program your technology for ancient Hebrew dialects?" The man asked in perfect English. His eyes locked onto Porter. "A silly oversight, considering the quest you were undertaking."

Now everyone looked at Porter, awaiting his response. Diplomacy training told Gabriel that this was a make or break moment. First impressions could foster deep, cordial relationships or create insurmountable rifts between parties that would otherwise get along. The robed man was testing Porter, opening their conversation by insulting the very things he had built his life around: his intelligence and technology. Porter had every right to respond with hostility, and perhaps that's what the man wanted. Or maybe he wanted to see if Porter would keep his cool... just like with his age, it was hard to get a read on him.

Gabriel hoped Porter would take a non-aggressive approach, perhaps by showing humility and admitting the oversight. But what Porter did was even better. He said nothing at all. He looked as though he wanted to, but he kept his jaw relaxed and his mouth devoid of words. The robed man frowned.

"Mr. Cannes, you are a media-savvy man. I find it hard to believe the cat's got your tongue." He paused a moment, giving Porter an opening to lash out, but Porter remained quiet. The robed man's frown turned to a subtle smile. "Very well."

He stood from his throne, and as he did so, something fell from the folds of his robe. It was circular and golden, and gleaming in the lantern light. It hung from the robed man's neck just the way the Moroccan scroll depicted it would.

"My God..." Gabriel uttered.

"No, Mr. Dunne," the robed man said, "I am not your God."

"But you wear his pendant," Porter said, finally letting words loose. "Who are you?"

The robed man turned toward him, the pendant around his neck glowing with celestial glory. "You haven't figured it out yet?" He shifted his gaze to Lisa, then Gabriel. "Surely you have by now, Mr. and Mrs. Dunne."

Lisa shook her head. "But that's impossible."

The man glanced down at the pendant hanging from his neck. "That's what I thought, too, when I was first granted this."

Porter tugged at Gabriel's arm. "Tell me. Who is he?"

Gabriel could hardly believe it himself. But the evidence added up. The ancient Hebrew dialect, the air of experience, the body of youth, the honor to wield God's power on Earth. "Porter…" Gabriel looked once more at the robed man as chills ran through his body. "That's Damien."

Chapter Eighty-Five
A Question Of Worth

Alegranza, Canary Islands
Four Days Before The Sky Opened

Porter stared in disbelief. "Damien? As in *the Damien*?"

"Whom else did you think you would find at the end of your journey?" Damien asked.

"But that would make you-"

"Very, very old," Damien finished, as if he didn't want to hear the number. "Unfortunately for you, Mr. Cannes, that also makes me quite knowledgeable."

"Unfortunately?" Gabriel asked. "Why is that?"

"Because you've bet on the wrong horse, Mr. Dunne," Damien said matter-of-factly. "Your heart was in the right place; I'll give you that. But Mr. Cannes' heart is, quite frankly, not. You should have never helped him find the pendant. You should have left him to his disease; let nature run its course."

"Harsh words for someone who's dedicated lifetimes to helping people," Lisa pointed out.

"You speak as though I've claimed to be a saint," Damien said. "I'm no saint, Mrs. Dunne. I'm a man, flawed like the rest of you."

"But you wield God's pendant. You're a vessel for his forgiveness and love."

"And I was a vessel for his might first," Damien reminded her. "I have the blood of hundreds of thousands on my hands. Some of those, like Lyrus, needed to be removed from this world to make it a better place. But others? They were ordinary men: sons, husbands, fathers... pressured into joining a tyrant's army to protect their own bloodlines.

They were better men than Mr. Cannes, more honest, more loyal, and yet I slaughtered them along with the rest."

"So all of this was for nothing?" Nadine asked, tears welling in her eyes. "After everything we've been through, after pushing the limits of human endurance, you won't help him?"

Damien's face softened. "I can see your heart is in the right place, too, Ms. Walsh. I'm sorry you fell in love with such a terrible man."

Nadine turned and buried her face in her palms as sobs escaped her. Gabriel took a step toward Damien, fire in his veins.

"How can you be so heartless? You say you're a man, but you stand up on that pulpit exercising the judgment of a god. So, which are you really? Because a man would understand that people make mistakes. A man would recognize that people can change, that they can atone for those mistakes. And a man would be able to show compassion for a fellow man in his greatest time of need."

Gabriel half expected Damien's guards to advance on him as a protective measure, but surprisingly, both they and Damien remained at bay. The sanctuary grew thick with tension, and only Nadine's sobs were heard as Gabriel waited for a response. Damien placed a hand over the pendant and closed his eyes, breathing rhythmically, as if in search of inner peace. When he opened his eyes, he had a newfound awareness in his expression.

"I'm sorry," he said. "You're right, Mr. Dunne. Having carried this dual blessing and burden for so many years, having witnessed so much... sometimes I lose sight of my place. Sometimes..." He paused as if his words were difficult to push out. "Sometimes I lose faith in the ability of man to change for the better." His eyes honed in on Porter once more. "Mr. Cannes, stand up."

Porter looked at him like he was crazy.

"He can't!" Nadine screamed through her sobs. "Don't you see that?!"

"He can," Damien argued. "The human body is capable of amazing feats when the alternative is death. How do you think he made it this far?"

Porter rolled to the edge of the gurney and winced as he swung his legs over the edge. Gabriel helped him down, then supported a portion of Porter's weight to help his friend maintain balance.

"Step forward," Damien ordered. Then he added, "alone."

Gabriel glanced at Porter with uncertainty, but his friend nodded, letting him know that certainty no longer mattered. He had to do this. Byron and his mercenaries stepped aside to make a path for Porter, who shuffled down the central aisle one inch at a time, his body perpetually on the verge of collapsing onto itself as he creeped toward Damien. Damien made no effort to help, and instead watched intently, as if Porter's gait would reveal his inner nature. Porter's forehead broke into a sweat. His breathing was more labored that Gabriel had ever heard it before, and he swayed like a fragile tree in a storm. It was painful to watch, and Gabriel suspected it would've been even more painful if he could see the agony on Porter's face, something Damien appeared immune to.

"That's far enough," the village leader said when Porter was two feet shy of the pulpit. He kneeled as Porter lifted his chin to meet Damien's judging gaze. The two stared each other down for over a minute, one a man of earthly power, the other a wielder of God's power, each assessing, each planning his response to the other's next move. "You've been through a lot to get here, Mr. Cannes," Damien eventually said. "But are you worthy? That's the real question. Could someone as vile and backhanded as you have truly become a changed man?" Porter remained silent. Damien peered past his eyes, as if looking into Porter's very soul. A moment later, he broke their connection and stood. "You can stop crying, Ms. Walsh. Mr. Cannes has twenty-two hours left before he faces a judgment much greater than my own."

He said it so casually, the words almost floated in one of Gabriel's ears and out the other. But then Gabriel realized the significance of what he had just heard. Was Damien simply estimating how much time Porter had left? Surely he couldn't make such an assessment from a visual exam alone. But that would mean he was tapping into the pendant's power, and if true, that would mean twenty-two hours was no guess. It was a fact. Gabriel thought back to their time in The Blessed Burial Ground, to how the burial vaults had seemingly been arranged in order of death. That had been no accident. The Shifa survivors knew when they would die, because Damien knew when they would die.

Holy shit... Gabriel thought.

"Twenty-two hours," Damien repeated. "You are all welcome to stay here during that time. And sometime before then, I will make my final decision whether to cure Mr. Cannes."

Nadine stifled her sobs and looked up from her glistening palms. "You mean-"

"Yes, Ms. Walsh. I'll give him a chance. But that's all it is. I make no guarantees. And when time runs out, if I stand by my original decision not to help him, I expect all of you, Mr. Cannes included, to accept that decision with grace."

Gabriel seized the offer before anyone gave Damien a reason to rescind it. "You have a deal. Thank you."

Damien sought confirmation from Porter. "Well, Mr. Cannes?"

Gabriel could see that Porter was contemplating something. He hoped his friend wouldn't say anything to screw this up. Twenty-two hours was plenty of time to change Damien's mind. They just needed to go with the flow.

"One request, please," Porter said, stealing Gabriel's breath.

Damien raised an eyebrow. "Yes?"

"May I see it? Up close, I mean."

He had asked with a sense of humble reverence, and though Damien appeared apprehensive at first, the village leader walked to the side edge of the pulpit, came down its steps, and approached Porter. He stopped a foot away and silently challenged Porter to close the remaining gap. If he wanted to see the pendant close up, he would have to earn it. Porter shuffled, one foot and then the other, one inch, then a second, until he had crossed all twelve between himself and Damien. Though tottering, he was still standing. His eyes traveled from Damien's face, down across his neck, and to his chest, where the Pendant of God hung among the leader's robes. Porter stared, a combination of sad longing and pervasive hunger emanating from within him.

Don't do anything stupid, Gabriel thought to himself. *Just thank him and walk away.*

Porter was entranced by the pendant. He cocked his head as he examined its contours, followed its molded fasteners to the equally golden chain from which it hung, looked up at the tender neck of the person who wore it...

Come on, Porter.

...then Porter's eyes lowered to the pendant again. This time, his head bobbed slightly, his acknowledgment that it wasn't time yet. He had to be patient and await Damien's decision. Porter closed his eyes and turned his head away, revealing a tear streaming down his cheek. Damien waved his hand toward his lead guard, who in turn opened the sanctuary doors.

"You're free to do as you please. I'm sure the villagers will take good care of you. I'll send a messenger when I'm ready."

"Thank you," Lisa said on behalf of the entire team.

She, Gabriel, and Nadine helped Porter back onto the gurney as the others filed out. Then they followed, back onto the caldera, with some comfort knowing that time was finally on their side.

Chapter Eighty-Six
Village De Alegranza

Alegranza, Canary Islands
Four Days Before The Sky Opened

Gabriel made sure to ask the actual time of day from the first villager he saw once outside the sanctuary. The villager, who introduced herself as Esmerelda, informed Gabriel that it was just past eleven o'clock. Porter overheard the time, and he didn't need to ask why Gabriel had wanted it. Esmerelda then let Gabriel know that lunch was nearly ready. She said the villagers rarely woke early enough to prepare breakfast for the entire community, so any pre-dawn risers would snack on fruits or breads while everyone else waited for their first big meal to come at an early lunch. There were enough open seats for half the team at the common area building closest to the sanctuary, and enough for the other half at one closer to the center of the caldera.

Byron offered to take his crew on the farther walk, but Gabriel didn't like the thought of letting his rival treasure hunter off the leash when impressions made over the next twenty-two hours were so crucial. At the risk of prodding Byron's suspicions, he suggested they remain commingled, with members from each of their teams dividing among the common areas. In the end, Samantha, Nate, Byron's equivalent of Nate, and the mercenaries trekked to the far building, while everyone else moseyed to the closer one.

For such simple people, Gabriel was shocked at how well they could cook. He didn't know if it was the freshness of the meats and vegetables, the seasoning from cast iron cooking, years of experience, or something else altogether that made the meal so delicious, but it ranked with some of the best he'd ever had. It was presented on clay and ceramic dishware that appeared to have been collected from a variety of civilizations over a multitude of generations. The hodgepodge of materials, colors, textures, and designs would have looked sloppy when combined on the same table, if it weren't for how historically fascinating they all were.

"Don't even think about stealing that," Gabriel joked after noticing Lisa eyeing a particularly beautiful set of hand-blown glassware. "We have to be on our best behavior."

She rolled her eyes at him as Porter cracked a weak smile from his gurney.

"So," Gabriel then said to the villagers at the table, "what's it been like living in the Caldera de Alegranza for... what's it been? Ninety years or so?"

The villagers shared a laugh.

"What did I say?"

They looked to a middle-aged man who had earlier introduced himself as Santiago. He, like the rest of the villagers so far, had treated Gabriel and the team with kindness, though in Santiago's case, there had been noticeable reservations to that kindness. Gabriel suspected he was somewhat of an alpha male, at least for one sect of villagers, and he still wasn't sure whether their new arrivals were as benign as they claimed to be. Considering the team showed up armed to the teeth with lethal weapons, Gabriel couldn't fault him for that.

"We just didn't realize we looked so old," Santiago said, drawing another laugh from the villagers.

In fact, only two people at the table looked older than Santiago, and not by more than five to ten years. The others were still quite youthful. "I'm sorry, I just assumed..."

Santiago held up an explanatory hand. "This village has been around for ninety-seven years. But we are only its present inhabitants. We are born, we live our lives in service to God, have kids that can someday take our place, and then return to the earth as scheduled. Sometimes new villagers join us from the outside. Sometimes existing villagers leave of their own accord to pursue personal passions. But none of us have nor desire Damien's immortality."

"Interesting," Gabriel said.

"Why not?" Porter then asked.

The question seemed to catch Santiago off-guard. In fact, it seemed to catch all the villagers off-guard, for they stopped eating and stared at him as him he had just said something blasphemous.

"It must be hard for someone like you to understand, Mr. Cannes. But we villagers... we see the plight of those who come seeking the pendant's blessing. Most of us have no interest in experiencing that plight for ourselves. Most of us have no interest in the material aspects this world has to offer, even the ones who leave. No, we live only to serve God, and we embrace the day he calls us to be by his side once more."

Porter seemed conflicted by the response. "But you seem so happy here. Wouldn't you want to hold on to that happiness as long as humanly possible?"

"We do hold on to it," Santiago said. Then he emphasized, "as long as *humanly* possible."

Porter frowned. "You know what I mean."

Santiago took a heavy breath. "Mr. Cannes, I trust you've looked into Damien's eyes. I trust you've seen the torment that rages within them, the constant push and pull between having one foot in humanity and the other in godliness. We weren't meant to carry that type of burden, and certainly not for as long as Damien has. Honestly, I don't know how he does it. But I have no desire to carry that burden myself. None of us do."

Porter's eyes passed over the villagers at the table: men, women, children, all having reached some sense of mortal peace that still evaded him. His sunken eyes drifted downward in contemplation. "I guess I see your point."

Santiago gave him an affirming nod, and the eating at the table continued. Nadine offered Porter some food, but he refused it, his eyes still lowered and his face stoic in thought. Gabriel hated seeing his friend so troubled, but there was nothing he could do about it. Porter's life would either be extended or extinguished in less than a day. Either way, he had to find his own peace before then.

Chapter Eighty-Seven
Moving On

Alegranza, Canary Islands
Four Days Before The Sky Opened

After lunch, Nadine asked whether there was somewhere private Porter could rest. It turned out that Damien had already instructed the villagers to dismantle the wooden holding cage from that morning, and to replace the cage with enough cots to accommodate the entire team. As Porter and Nadine excused themselves, Byron pulled Gabriel aside to have what he referred to as a "professional chat."

"We need to find our guns," Byron said to open the conversation.

"Okay, that's a hard stop right there," Gabriel told him. "We're not going to do anything to piss these people off or put Porter in a bad light. Damien told us we were welcome. Clearly, our weapons are not."

"Damien?" Byron asked. "You mean the guy with eleven guards big enough to snap our necks with their pinky fingers? Oh, and let's not forget the vessel of God's vengeance he wears around his neck."

"I think you just made my point. Even if you had your guns, what good would they do?"

"Maybe provide some protection," Byron exclaimed. "We're at this man's mercy. The second he decides we aren't welcome anymore-" He drew his finger across his neck as if slitting his throat.

Gabriel sighed, exhausted by this argument already. "If Damien decides we aren't welcome anymore, he'll order us to leave. Peacefully. He has no reason to kill us."

"Oh, yeah?" Byron asked.

Gabriel could sense the know-it-all attitude behind the rhetorical question. "What?"

"Why did it take us so long to find this place? We've both been hunting it for over a week. Your friend has been on the verge of death the entire time, so I assume you haven't been wasting that time with a Moroccan vacation. What gives?"

Gabriel played along to humor him. "The location was a closely guarded secret. As you know."

"Exactly!" Byron leaned in closer and spoke barely above a whisper. "You say Damien has no reason to kill us. I say he has every reason. We threaten his secret."

Unfortunately, Gabriel couldn't argue against that, especially considering it wouldn't be the first time someone had tried to kill him to protect the pendant's location.

"As agreed, we've been doing everything your way until now," Byron reminded him. "But I need you to meet me in the middle on this. We've got to be prepared to defend ourselves should the time come. Let my men and I find the guns. I promise we'll be discrete and we won't touch them. Reconnaissance mission only. That way, *when* we need them, we'll know where to get them."

Gabriel's gut told him to deny Byron's request, but his brain knew if he didn't give Byron something, the rival treasure hunter would go to even further extremes. "Fine. Reconnaissance only."

Byron smiled and gave Gabriel's shoulder a friendly slap. As he jogged away, Lisa took his place.

"What was that about?"

Noticing Santiago watching him from a distance, Gabriel replied, "I'll tell you later."

For the next few hours, they and the rest of the core team roamed the Village De Alegranza, speaking with villagers and observing the daily activities taking place. One thing Gabriel immediately noticed was that not all the villagers were as well versed in English as Damien and Santiago. Most of them spoke Spanish, which, unlike ancient Hebrew, his earpiece translator handled perfectly. At first, Gabriel thought it odd that the village represented the culture of the country it currently resided in, but then he considered what Santiago had told them earlier. The villagers lived out normal lifespans, and those lifespans were shorter than the time the village remained in any single location. In hindsight, it made complete sense that later generations of villagers in any one location would adopt that location's cultural norms, including names and languages. Obviously, it made no difference to Damien, for Gabriel assumed he could assimilate to any culture with ease.

The other thing that stood out, though not so immediately, was that many villagers appeared to be hauling supplies out of the village itself. They would head toward the caldera's southern wall and eventually disappear into the mist. Even weirder, those same villagers would return anywhere from thirty to sixty minutes later, empty-handed. When Gabriel intercepted one of them and asked what they were doing, the villager made a vague reference to *cleaning up*. He looked nervous when he said it and hurried off in what was clearly an attempt to avoid being pressed further. Determined to find out what was going on, Gabriel found Santiago and asked him instead.

"We packing up," Santiago told him without hesitation.

"Packing up? For what?"

"To move on, of course. I'm afraid our time on Alegranza is quickly coming to an end. Soon, we'll set sail for our new home."

"You still have your fleet from ninety-seven years ago?" Lisa asked.

Santiago chuckled. "Of course. How else could we leave an island in the middle of the ocean?"

Nate looked confused. "Ninety-seven years is a long time for ships to take the ocean's abuse and still be seaworthy."

"They haven't been exposed to the ocean's abuse," Santiago told him. "South of the caldera is a hidden lagoon protected on all sides by volcanic rock. A small cave on the island's southern shore provides ocean access. The fleet is parked there, and one of the many tasks villagers have had over the years is maintaining it."

Gabriel shared a look of astonishment with Lisa. Every new fact they had learned since arriving had left them with a sense of awe and inspiration. It was as if they were living their own adventure movie, fulfilling the dream of discovery they had shared in their youth. This time, however, Gabriel's awe was quickly replaced by guilt, for he recalled his earlier conversation with Byron and the motivation for compromising about their guns. That motivation was null and void if the village was about to relocate.

"Why do you need to move now?" He asked. "I hope it's not

because of us."

Santiago shook his head. "No. It's because Adila Benkirane will pass soon. When she does, there will no longer be Shifa survivors to direct the needy our way."

"I thought Mrs. Benkirane's role was to deter people from finding the pendant," Samantha pointed out. "Technically speaking, shouldn't you have moved already?"

Santiago smiled. "She got you here, didn't she? Regardless of one's role, they have the potential to serve as beacons on the path to the pendant. But our last beacon is about to go dark. So now it's time to set up a new village and send out new beacons to light the way to glory."

"When are you leaving?" Lisa asked.

"Once Damien makes his decision about Mr. Cannes. We can have the entire village dismantled by tomorrow afternoon and set sail by tomorrow night."

"Can?" Nate asked with trepidation. "Or will?"

Santiago smiled again. "Will. Damien has already made the call." He looked past the team, to someone waving excitedly from the village's border. Santiago waved back, then took a deep, satisfied breath as his smile expanded into a large grin. "Well, it looks like they're here."

Gabriel glanced at Lisa, but she shrugged with the same confusion as him. "Who's here?"

"I thought you would've guessed that on your own," Santiago said. Then, with continued satisfaction, he ended their suspense. "The new survivors, of course."

Chapter Eighty-Eight
The New Survivors

Alegranza, Canary Islands
Four Days Before The Sky Opened

Santiago informed Gabriel that he and the team were welcome to bear witness to the transfer of responsibility that was about to occur. He also encouraged Gabriel to wake Porter for the ceremony, for if Damien were to grant him the pendant's blessing, it would be his duty to join this first generation of beacons lighting the path to the pendant's new home. Gabriel sent Lisa and the others ahead to the sanctuary, where the ceremony would take place. He then performed a quick search for Byron to let him know he could abandon his quest for their guns. But neither Byron nor his mercenaries were anywhere to be found. His two right hands were relaxing in the shade of one of the common areas- if being frustrated with an unexplainable lack of internet connectivity could be considered relaxing- and claimed to have no idea where their boss had gone.

Unwilling to risk missing the ceremony, Gabriel gave up searching for Byron and returned to their jail-converted-to-sleeping-quarters. There, he found Porter already awake and propped in a sitting position on his gurney. He was smiling at Nadine when Gabriel entered, and for a change, it wasn't a smile forced through a wall of pain or self-sorrow. It was loving and genuine and, surprisingly, full of hope.

"You look like you're in better spirits," Gabriel said.

"I guess you could say I've reached a point of acceptance," Porter replied. "When Damien first told me how much time I had left, I wasn't sure how to feel. Sad? Angry? Relieved? I've spent so much time worrying about when the end will come that I stopped paying attention to what was most important in the here and now." He squeezed Nadine's hand. "Now I don't have to worry. Come nine o'clock tomorrow morning, I will probably be dead."

"Porter-"

"Hear me out," Porter pleaded. "There's a certain catharsis in knowing when your time will run out. It's giving me the chance to spend my final hours the way I want to spend them, to prepare my legacy for after I'm gone, to express to those I care about how I truly feel, so that there's no bad blood once I've departed this world." He looked at Gabriel. Though his eyes were still sunken, and his face still warped from the damage of the disease within, Porter had an undeniable calm about him. "I'm a realist. And as a realist, I know it's extremely unlikely Damien changes his mind about me. If he does, great, I get an unexpected new lease on life. But if he doesn't, I want to make sure I spend my final moments properly. Speaking of..."

He held out his hand for Gabriel to shake.

"What's that for?"

"It's me thanking you. You'll get paid, too, of course," Porter added with a laugh. "But I wanted you to know how grateful I was for your effort to save me. If I die tomorrow, it's not because you failed. You completed your mission. You found the pendant while I still had some life left in me. What happens next, good or bad, is solely on me."

Gabriel shook his friend's hand firmly, then leaned in for a brotherly hug.

"So," Porter said when they broke their embrace, "what'd you come here for?"

A sudden sense of urgency returned to Gabriel. "There's something we need to see."

He and Nadine wheeled Porter's gurney to the sanctuary. Inside, the ceremony was just beginning. Villagers filled the stone benches to each side of the central aisle. A collection of nearly thirty people representing a variety of ages, genders, socio-economic classes, and cultures stood in the aisle as Gabriel and his team had done earlier. Damien was on the pulpit before them, organizing rows of envelopes that lined its ceremonial table. Lisa waved Gabriel over to a rear bench, where the team had saved space for him and Nadine. They positioned Porter's gurney next to the bench, where he would have an obstructed view of whatever was about to transpire.

"Thank you all for returning," Damien said to his new arrivals. "I apologize for any inconvenience it might have caused you on such short notice. I promise to be quick." He picked up an envelope from the table. It had a name on the front, but the name was illegible from the back row. "As you know, the one price for receiving the pendant's blessing is to commit yourself to its service when the time comes. For some of you, that will mean identifying future blessing recipients and guiding them to me. For the rest, it will require bravery when the pendant is threatened, and the resolve to do what's necessary to keep it safe." He held the envelope up for all to see. "Inside these envelopes are instructions containing our village's new home, the role you will serve for it, and how long you can expect that service to last."

Lisa glanced at Gabriel with a face that asked *is he saying what I think he's saying*? Gabriel suspected he was.

"When I call your name," Damien continued, "please approach to receive your letter. Some of you share personal relationships with others in the room. To that extent, I cannot prevent you from discussing your responsibilities with those with whom you are acquainted. However, I do expect you to maintain the integrity of any confidential information you receive. Always remember what's at stake if you don't." Gabriel thought he caught Damien shooting a quick glance in Porter's direction, but it might have been an artifact of the lantern light reflecting off his pupils. "Thank you again. Once you have your envelope, you may return to your assigned ship, and a villager will escort you home." Damien looked at the envelope in his hand, then announced the first name. "Merida."

Gabriel was surprised by the simplicity of the ceremony. There was no pomp and circumstance, no religious incantation spoken, no physical ritual undertaken. There was just the reading of names and the distribution of envelopes, like a graduation ceremony without all the dressing up. When it was over, the Alegranza survivors exchanged brief, cordial conversations with the villagers in attendance, likely catching up on their lives in the time since receiving the pendant's blessing. After that, they departed as quickly as they arrived, and the village returned to its pre-ceremonial state. Waiting until everyone else had left to wheel Porter's gurney out of the sanctuary, Gabriel watched his friend slowly stroking his chin with a shaky hand. Though Porter's mental state appeared unaffected by witnessing the ceremony, it was clear his gears were turning. About what, however, Gabriel couldn't begin to imagine.

Chapter Eighty-Nine
Arsenal

Alegranza, Canary Islands
Four Days Before The Sky Opened

The team spent the rest of the afternoon helping the Alegranza villagers gather and pack their belongings. Even Porter lent a hand, folding an endless stream of children's laundry that Nadine would feed him, then stack for Esmerelda to take to the fleet. Gabriel hoped Damien would see Porter doing his part, perhaps earning him goodwill with the man who controlled his destiny. But Damien never emerged from the sanctuary following the new survivor ceremony. How could he pass judgment on Porter if he made no effort to observe Porter's actions? Maybe he had other, less obvious eyes on Porter, who would report their observations back to him in secret. Then again, maybe Porter was right about his chances of changing Damien's mind. Maybe Damien had already made his decision and was waiting for the clock to run out to reveal it.

"What's going on over here?" Byron called out as he and his two right hands neared the laundry folding station.

"The villagers are packing up to move," Nadine told him. "We're helping them out."

"They can't do it themselves?" Byron asked without compassion.

Gabriel didn't want his toxicity anywhere near Porter right now. "Can I talk with you?" He pulled Byron aside, far enough that no one would overhear their conversation. "What happened with that thing we talked about earlier?"

"The guns? Oh, we found them. The villagers had them stashed in a cluster of outhouses on the edge of the village. Funny enough, we

342

wouldn't even have searched there, but we were out that way and one of my men couldn't hold it-"

"I don't need to hear about your men's bowel movements," Gabriel interjected. "Please tell me you left everything just the way you found it."

Byron smiled, but it wasn't a comforting smile. "Didn't I promise you we would?"

Gabriel gave him an accusatory stare.

"Okay, okay," Byron said. "Yes, I was tempted to have my men relocate the guns. But you see, it wasn't just our weapons in there. There were all kinds of artillery dating back at least fifty years. There were loads of standard guns, of course. But there were also grenades, a couple of long-range sniper rifles, a bazooka... Gabriel, they have a bloody bazooka! And the ammo to go with it!"

Gabriel didn't like where this was headed. "But you didn't touch them, right?"

"We didn't touch them," Byron confirmed. "There was no way to do it discretely in the daylight. But tonight-"

"No," Gabriel said with staunch determination. "Not tonight. Not tomorrow. We leave the weapons alone. With the village moving, Damien has no incentive to harm us, which means we have no need to defend ourselves."

Byron silently hemmed and hawed over Gabriel's line in the sand. It was clear the two were at an impasse, but per their agreement, this was still Gabriel's show until Porter's business with the pendant was complete.

"Fine," Byron eventually said through gritted teeth. "But I want you to stew on something: if Damien allows his unsolicited visitors to leave this village so peacefully, why are all their weapons still here? It's almost as if... they never actually left." He gave Gabriel's should a firm squeeze. "You think about that."

Then Byron retrieved his right hands and stormed off to do whatever it was he was going to do to pass the time. As much as Gabriel didn't want to admit it, Byron had made a valid point. Maybe Damien had let prior armed visitors leave in peace, only without their weapons, to prevent those weapons from causing future bloodshed in the world. Or maybe Damien's facade of peace was just that: a facade, hiding something more sinister underneath.

"Now do you want to tell me what that was about?" Lisa asked.

She, Samantha, and Nate had walked up behind him unnoticed. They must not have heard the conversation, or Lisa wouldn't have needed to ask, but clearly they knew something wasn't kosher between Team Dunne and Team Coltrain. Gabriel told them everything, and Samantha promptly took off, vowing to monitor Byron's men closely for any unusual activity. Lisa floated the idea of coming clean with Damien to give him a chance to move the weapon cache before Byron had what they all agreed would be an inevitable lapse in judgment. But there was still the risk that Byron was right about Damien, and if he was, tattling would be a fatal mistake. In the end, the team agreed to sit on their knowledge and remain alert. With any luck, the next fifteen and a half hours would go smoothly, and then their team, as well as Porter and Nadine, would be on a plane back home, without a care in the world about the machinations of Byron Coltrain.

"Hey!" Porter hollered in a raspy, but surprisingly upbeat, voice. "Are you guys plotting how to divvy up my company once I'm dead or something? These clothes won't fold themselves."

He was grinning, something that had been noticeably absent in recent days. Gabriel motioned for him to hold on. Then the team hastily wrapped up its discussion and returned to laundry duty.

"Sorry," Gabriel told Porter. "Team business."

"Anything I need to be aware of?"

Gabriel didn't want to burden his friend unnecessarily. "Not at the moment. If it becomes an issue, I'll let you know."

Porter's look said he wasn't accustomed to being out of the loop, but either he trusted Gabriel enough to let it go, or he had accepted a reduced level of control as his life neared its end. "Okay." He pointed to the remaining pile of unfolded clothes. "Well, if it's not too much trouble, I need all hands on deck to finish this. Santiago stopped by while you were having your little powwow. Damien wants us to join him for dinner in thirty minutes."

Chapter Ninety
Last Supper

Alegranza, Canary Islands
Four Days Before The Sky Opened

While the team helped Porter wrap up folding clothes, a group of villagers assembled wooden picnic tables in a large u shape in front of the sanctuary. Apparently, everyone was going to eat together this evening. Shortly after six o'clock, children dashed around the village to round up villagers and visitors alike. A particularly jovial pair hijacked Porter's gurney and wheeled him down to the feast area, parking him at the corner of the head table. Esmerelda showed Nadine to a seat beside him and encouraged the rest of the team to disburse as they saw fit. Byron and his crew stuck together, filling an entire picnic table adjacent to Porter. Team Dunne split up to mingle with their hosts in a show of appreciation.

By six-thirty, plates and cups had been filled. Damien emerged from the sanctuary and took a seat at the center of the head table, from where he could see all the other diners. Even though his position was one of honor and authority, he didn't behave superiorly to those in attendance. He sat among them as one of them, listening to recounts of the day's events, sharing laughs at the more comedic stories being told, and repeatedly complementing and thanking the meal's chefs for their hard work on the eve before their departure. Halfway through the meal, he offered a toast to the Alegranza villagers, expressing his gratitude for their years of service to God and wishing them many years of happiness to come.

Gabriel noticed a hint of sadness to Damien's words, and it occurred to him it must be difficult to spend a lifetime in evolutionary stasis, witnessing the birth, growth, and eventual death of all those around you, only to then abandon the home you've shared with them for all those years, and then to repeat the pattern somewhere new. The mental fortitude required was beyond his grasp of understanding.

"So, Damien," Nate called out during a lull in conversation. "Where are your guards? Do they get their own feast out in the mist to keep those muscles in shape?"

The villagers grew quiet as half of their eyes fell on Nate and the other half fell on Damien. Clearly, Nate had broached some taboo subject. Gabriel silently winced.

"Did I say something wrong?" Nate asked.

Damien stared at him sternly for what felt like an eternity. But then he chuckled and stood up as if to say *challenge accepted.* Damien waved a deliberate hand through the air, and in response, the wind surrounding the dining tables kicked up. Eleven miniature whirlwinds formed and swept past the crowd, collecting every spec of dust and rock particle in their paths. The whirlwinds converged in a row behind Damien, and the particles within them took shape. Gabriel felt his jaw drop as those shapes formed the silhouettes of men and then turned into actual men. Eleven muscle-laden, flesh and bone, men. The whirlwinds dissipated.

"Holy shit..." Nate muttered.

"You mean these guards?" Damien asked with an amused grin.

Gabriel couldn't find his voice. It had been just that morning on the boat to Alegranza that he had told Porter they had no proof of the pendant's godlike power. Now Gabriel wanted to tell his friend to consider that statement revoked.

"You have the power to create life?" Lisa asked, her mouth also agape.

Damien let her believe it for just a moment, then replied, "no; at least not outside of traditional methods of procreation." That elicited a laugh from the older villagers. "The pendant's power isn't absolute, and creating life is an ability God reserves for himself."

As usual, Nate was confused. Though in this case, he wasn't alone. "But you just-"

"These men are empty bodies, nothing more," Damien explained. "Their sentience is simply an extension of my own. Didn't you wonder how I defeated Lyrus' army? Me, a single man?" He motioned to his soulless guards. "The pendant allowed me to be more than one man. In fact, I became nearly one thousand men in my battle with Lyrus. Though I don't think I have that much strength in me these days."

"So that was you that grabbed us in the mist," Samantha deduced.

Damien nodded. "The pendant provides us with all the protection we need. And when not in a state of defense..." Damien snapped a finger, and the eleven guards instantly dissolved into dust and debris that dropped into piles on the ground.

Nate's eyes went wide. "Did you just see that?" He asked the rest of the team. "He just blipped them out of existence! He's like a pendant-wielding Thanos!" No one replied. "Thanos?" Nate asked. "The Avengers?"

"I believe Thanos was a villain," Damien said, surprising Gabriel with his contemporary knowledge. "Hopefully you don't think that's an accurate representation of me."

Nate's cheeks reddened. "No. I'm sorry. I was just excited." Then he whispered under his breath, "please don't blip me."

Damien rolled his eyes and looked at Gabriel. "He must test your patience sometimes."

"All the time," Gabriel confirmed.

He might have said more, but he was still in a state of shock from what he had just witnessed. Damien nodded and sat.

"Speaking of villains," he then said with a clearing of his throat. "Mr. Cannes, tell me what you've learned since arriving at our island village."

Now all eyes turned to Porter, who straightened his body as best he could.

"Well, I've learned that the pendant is real... and that its powers are truly are godlike."

Damien stared at him as if that was a no-brainer.

"I've learned time is precious," Porter continued in a rare show of emotional fragility. "And I've learned that I've wasted most of mine on things that simply don't matter."

That seemed to intrigue Damien. "Go on."

Nadine gripped Porter's hand to lend him strength. "I've seen the joy your people have. Joy that has nothing to do with material possessions or technology or one's social status. I've seen the joy in human connection... and in a belief that extends beyond the boundaries of scientific logic."

"And what has seeing that joy taught you?"

Porter's eyes welled with tears. "That I wish I had more time." His lip quivered with emotional strain, and his already raspy voice cracked with pain. "Not for the reasons I approached Gabriel with. Not to continue building my empire, or to get my name on more buildings or more products. Not to make more money or claim more fame. I want more time to... to..." He looked at Nadine, who smiled warmly. "I want more time to live the life I've been ignorant of missing all these years. I want a do-over... a chance to try again, to be better than I was the first time around."

Damien's head lowered as he processed Porter's words. After nearly two minutes of silence, he stood and looked Porter in the eyes. "Rest easy, tonight, Mr. Cannes. I'll give you my answer first thing in the morning." Damien then turned his attention to the villagers. "Rest easy, all of you. We have a long journey ahead of us tomorrow."

And with that, Damien stepped away from the table, returned to the sanctuary, and shut the doors behind him.

Chapter Ninety-One
Early Warning

Alegranza, Canary Islands
Three Days Before The Sky Opened

Following dinner with Damien, the team and villagers alike retreated to their sleeping quarters to recover from the day's physical and emotional strain. Gabriel was concerned Porter wouldn't be able to sleep. After all, every minute he spent with his eyes closed was another minute not spent living. For someone with years ahead of them, this was no big deal. For someone with only hours... Gabriel didn't want to dwell on it. He assured his friend that he thought dinner went well, and that nothing Porter had done since arriving on Alegranza would have made a negative impression on Damien. Porter thanked him and, with the help of Nadine's soft hand stroking his head, fell quickly asleep, no energy left to ride out what might be his last night on Earth. The others followed suit, though Gabriel forced himself to stay awake until he was certain every member of Team Coltrain had passed out. Then Gabriel allowed slumber to take him too, and soon the morning came.

"Mr. Dunne," a soft voice whispered. "Mr. Dunne, wake up."

Gabriel opened his eyes, but saw only darkness. "What-"

A hand covered his mouth.

"Don't talk," the voice said. "Just get up quietly and come with me."

When Gabriel's eyes adjusted, he identified the owner of the voice as Santiago. The villager stepped back to give Gabriel room to rise from his cot. Lisa was still snoring lightly next to him. Nate and Samantha were also asleep nearby, and Porter and Nadine were in the same position they had been in the evening before. His mental fog lifting, Gabriel had a sudden sense that something was wrong. He spun to check on Team Coltrain, but to his relief, every member was still there and still sound asleep.

"This way," Santiago whispered.

Gabriel followed him as he navigated past the rows of cots and out of the sleeping quarters, then waited as Santiago softly closed the door. It was still dark outside, too, with no sign of dawn nearing, and the village was quiet.

"What time is it?" Gabriel asked.

"Around five o'clock."

Four hours. That was the first thought that popped into Gabriel's head. Porter had four hours left, and he wasn't even awake to experience them. "What's going on?"

"Damien would like to speak with you privately," Santiago said. "He's made his decision."

Gabriel wasn't sure how to interpret that news. If the decision was already made, what was the point of a private conversation? And since when did Damien care about Gabriel's opinion, anyway?

"Let's go," Santiago told him.

He led Gabriel to the sanctuary, where Damien stood atop his pulpit, staring at a collection of documents strewn across the surface of the ceremonial table. Damien thanked Santiago, who excused himself so the two could speak alone, and Gabriel couldn't help notice the ominous thud that echoed off the sanctuary walls as Santiago shut the creaky doors behind him.

"My apologies for waking you so early, Mr. Dunne," Damien said. "Please, come join me."

He motioned to a set of stairs at one end of the pulpit. Gabriel was hesitant, feeling as though climbing those stairs was the equivalent of violating hallowed ground. But Damien seemed insistent, and if the wielder of God's might thought it was okay... Gabriel joined him at the ceremonial table. Now that he was closer, his eyes scanned the documents piled there. There were too many to fully comprehend, but over and over he saw the name 'Cannes,' sometimes on a folder tab, sometimes at the top of a report, and once beneath an old photo lifted from government identification.

"What's this?" Gabriel asked.

"Research," Damien said. "It's everything I could collect on Mr. Cannes on short notice."

Gabriel recalled the struggles Byron's team had trying to get internet on this island, and he sure as hell hadn't seen any sophisticated technology, or even antiquated technology, for that matter, since arriving. "How did you get it?"

"A final favor from Adila Benkirane. I dispatched a courier to her the moment you landed on my shores." Damien shuffled through some documents. "What we have here is Mr. Cannes' life story, at least in so much as it was documented. It begins with a promising young man blessed with an engineer's brain, someone with the ability to bring great good to the world. But soon, the story takes a disappointing turn." Damien located a photograph of Porter, still back in his youth, holding up a shiny gold trophy. "I believe you're familiar with this particular part of the tale. That promising young man becomes obsessed with being the best, and can't stand the thought that anyone else might be superior to him. He cheats his way to the top of an engineering competition, besting your teammate in the process. It's not the most egregious thing a man could do, but it taught Mr. Cannes an unfortunate lesson: that he didn't need to play fair to get ahead in life."

"Nate could never prove-"

"Mr. Bellows doesn't have the resources I do," Damien said before Gabriel could continue. "Besides, the trend continues. Mr. Cannes cheated in his academic pursuits." He tossed a manilla envelope Gabriel's way. "He cheated in his business dealings." Another envelope. "He hid crimes from the governments of multiple countries." Damien added a spiral dossier to the pile. "And when he couldn't hide them, he bribed others to turn a blind eye." This time, he tossed down a stack of bank statements. "Arguably, he's even cheated in his pursuit of glory by hiring a group of lowly treasure hunters to do his dirty work for him."

Gabriel's head snapped to attention.

"I'm not talking about you, Mr. Dunne," Damien clarified. "I'm talking about the other one. You're perhaps the one honest influence on Mr. Cannes' life."

"For what it's worth," Gabriel defended, "Porter only hired Byron out of desperation."

Damien smiled, but Gabriel sensed it was a smile of pity. "You have such a blind spot for your friend, because you have such a good heart. You don't accept who he is because you don't want him to be that person. You want Mr. Cannes to be a good man, but I assure you, he isn't."

Gabriel stared at the documents. They were undeniable proof that Porter's history was filled with wrongdoing, and though he hadn't thoroughly examined them himself, deep down he knew Damien was telling him the truth. But that highlighted an important distinction. "Isn't... or wasn't?" Gabriel asked. "Porter's never claimed to have a clean history, and clearly he hasn't, but what about now? What about the person he is today? The person you spoke with last night?"

Damien took a heavy breath. "Admittedly, there is little information on Mr. Cannes' more recent activities. But a zebra's stripes don't change overnight."

"Even when that zebra is staring down the barrel of a hunter's gun?"

Damien paused, thinking. "Maybe," he then said. "And for what it's worth, his words last night almost convinced me. But I can't make such an important decision on hypotheticals. I'm afraid extending Mr. Cannes' life might do the world more harm than good."

Gabriel shook his head in protest. "No, he-"

"I asked you here early so you would know what's coming. So you could help soften the blow and comfort your friend as his final hours tick away."

"Damien, please-"

"I'll wake him by six o'clock. That way, he has a few hours to say whatever goodbyes that need to be said."

Gabriel pleaded. "You can't let it end this way. Not after all we've been through."

"I can," Damien assured him. "And I will. I won't heal Porter Cannes and risk him bringing more deceit, more lies, and more damage to this world. It's better off without him."

"Damien-"

Damien held up a firm hand to quiet Gabriel, then ended their discussion with a single, conclusive phrase. "My decision is final."

Chapter Ninety-Two
The Coup

Alegranza, Canary Islands
Three Days Before The Sky Opened

Gabriel stared at Damien in disbelief. So this was it, the end of the line for Porter. They had found the pendant, but fallen short of convincing its wielder to grant him its blessing. Given Porter's recent outlook on what little life he had left, Gabriel wondered whether the news would even come as much of a blow. Maybe it was hitting Gabriel harder than it would hit anyone else, because regardless of the fact that he had found the pendant, he viewed healing Porter as the true measure of this mission's success, and it was clear now he wouldn't attain it.

"Mr. Dunne," Damien said, "I-"

An explosion went off in the distance. Then Gabriel heard a series of pops- gunfire- followed by screams. The sanctuary doors flew open, and Lisa, Samantha, Nate, and Santiago raced inside. There was another explosion as a fireball lit the horizon outside. Samantha and Santiago slammed the doors.

"What's going on?" Gabriel asked.

"It's Byron," Lisa told him.

Santiago picked up the explanation from there. "After dropping you off, I saw him leading his team to the outskirts of the village. By the time I realized what they were doing, I couldn't stop them. I didn't know what else to do, so I woke the rest of your team and led them here."

More gunfire rang out.

"Where's Porter?" Gabriel asked.

"Unconscious," Samantha said as she looked for a way to secure the doors. "Nadine's still trying to wake him."

Gabriel turned on his heels to face Damien. "Isn't there something you can do?"

Damien was already on it. With fire in his eyes, he waved a hand in front of him and brought his muscled guards back to life. Then he sent them forth into the dark of early morning. With the doors briefly opened, Gabriel could see villagers scrambling in a panic outside. Santiago called those closest into the safety of the sanctuary.

"We need to go out there and help," Gabriel told Damien.

"No, Mr. Dunne. You need to stay right here."

"But your people-"

"My people are in God's hands now."

With just over a dozen villagers now in the sanctuary, Samantha and Santiago shut the doors once more. Gabriel heard the gunfire again, this time closer than before. One stream of it came to an abrupt halt, at which point Gabriel heard a grown man cry out for help, before a sickening crunch silenced him. Byron called for his mercenaries to regroup and focus their fire. Then there was an explosion, and a second close behind it. Damien twitched.

"What is it?" Gabriel asked.

"They've destroyed three of my guards."

Byron shouted additional orders to his men. The gunfire ceased altogether, permitting villagers' screams to reach the sanctuary walls. Then a rapid succession of explosions rattled the lanterns hanging overhead. Damien looked dejected.

"You've lost more?" Gabriel asked.

"I've lost them all."

Damien was trembling, not with fear, but with anger. He bent and slammed his palms against the pulpit floor. Loud scraping noises filled the sanctuary air as its stone benches shifted autonomously. They rammed together and twisted unnaturally before rising as a giant golem, a bulky, lifeless creature imbued with Damien's rage that towered over mere men. Samantha and Santiago began opening the sanctuary doors to allow the golem passage, but the doors exploded inward, sending their limp bodies flying and shooting shrapnel onto the others.

"Samantha!" Lisa screamed.

Gabriel saw one of Byron's mercenaries holding a smoking bazooka just across the field outside the sanctuary. Then his view was obstructed by the stone golem, which charged forward, shaking the ground with every step. The golem swept the mercenary off his feet and crushed him and his bazooka like bugs. Grenades rolled in from every direction, stopping at the golem's feet. They exploded seconds later, toppling the golem's upper half, which continued to swing its arms with rage. Damien's body shook, as if the damage to the golem were damage to him. He pressed his palms harder into the floor, and Gabriel saw the golem's leg debris gather around its base, reforming the broken appendages.

But it was too late. Another round of grenades rolled in, blowing off the golem's right hand, then part of its head. Byron's remaining mercenaries advanced, firing bullets at the debris to keep it from drawing back together. Byron himself emerged from the attack squad, a modest cube of plastic explosive in his hand. He slammed the explosive against the golem, then turned and ran as he activated its trigger, blowing the golem apart once and for all. Damien fell backwards with a cry of pain. Gabriel helped him back to his feet as the attack squad advanced on the sanctuary. Meanwhile, Lisa made her way to Samantha's scorched body.

"Gabriel! She's not breathing!"

An explosion tore through the sanctuary roof behind Gabriel and Damien. Another punched a hole in the front wall. Then a third blasted straight into Lisa, filling her torso with shrapnel.

"No!" Gabriel screamed.

He raced to his fallen wife as Byron and the mercenaries breached the sanctuary threshold. Heaving, Damien held a hand straight out before him, calling the forces of gravity to bend to his will. An invisible force lifted the intruders off the ground, then squeezed their bodies, forcing them to drop their weapons. Gabriel reached Lisa, whose clothing was soaked with blood.

"Lisa?" He asked. But she was unresponsive.

"I have killed thousands of men stronger than you," Damien growled at Byron. "Did you really think you could take my pendant by brute force? Did you really think I wouldn't respond in kind?"

Nate reached Gabriel. "Is she okay?"

Gabriel shook his head. There was so much blood, and Lisa's body was growing colder by the second. He looked hatefully at Byron and his men, dangling helplessly, like fish on a wire, and all he could hope was that Damien would kill them quickly so he could return to using his pendant for healing. Then the shot rang out...

It was a single, loud pop, and before it even reached Gabriel's ears, its accompanying sniper round had already reached its destination at the back of Damien's neck. But it didn't hit Damien. Instead, it sparked as it cut across a single link of his pendant's chain. Damien's hold over the intruders ceased, their mangled bodies dropping to the floor as the pendant fell from his neck. Gabriel felt time slow to a crawl as the mystical artifact plummeted toward the floor, as a small, glowing disc shot toward it, latched onto it, then yanked the pendant sideways in defiance of gravity.

He was already an emotional wreck, with Lisa's fate hanging in limbo, but as Gabriel's eyes followed the pendant's path across the length of the sanctuary, what he saw crushed his very soul. The pendant landed in the palm of Porter's magnetic glove. Porter himself, hunched and trembling, snapped a high-tech fastener around the broken link, then swung the chain over his own head. The transformation that followed was nearly instantaneous. Porter's trembling stopped. His muscles straightened and his body bulked out where it had previously withered. His sunken eyes rose to their natural depth. His drooped face lifted, and his lungs filled with fresh air as he took a deep breath of renewed life. Porter was no longer a feeble man succumbing to disease. He was no longer the man Gabriel remembered prior to his disease, either. He was now more than man. He was, for all intents and purposes, a god.

Chapter Ninety-Three
A Changed Man

Alegranza, Canary Islands
Three Days Before The Sky Opened

Porter stretched his open hands before him and stared in bewilderment as he flexed his fingers. Open and shut, open and shut, as if he couldn't believe the strength that flowed through them once more. He looked down at the rest of his renewed body, feeling muscle and thick padding where his flesh had previously been stretched tight across bone. Then Porter's eyes found the pendant draped over his chest. He touched it cautiously, as if afraid its power might scorch his fingertip. Then, confident it wouldn't hurt him, he held it up to eye level, where he could take in all its splendor, and smiled victoriously.

"Porter, why?" Gabriel asked.

He ignored the question while he continued to revel in his triumph. When finished, he let the pendant drop back to his chest and answered his inferior's question. "I told you, Gabriel, a man like me will never get into Heaven. My paradise is here, in the mortal world, and this was the only way to ensure I'd get the glory I deserve."

"You have no right to bear that pendant," Damien said from the pulpit. "You have no concept of the magnitude of destruction you could unwittingly unleash. Please, return it to me. Nothing you've done can't be undone, but I need the pendant to make that happen, and I need it soon. I'm the only one capable of reversing what's taken place here."

Porter was unmoved by his request. "Why would I want to reverse it? I've got my health back and I've got the pendant. It's time for immortality to serve a new master."

"Porter..." Gabriel said, his tears falling on Lisa's bloody body. "Please."

"I'm sorry, Gabriel. I never wanted you and your team to get hurt." He held up a finger, eliciting brief hope in Gabriel before his words subsequently crushed it. "But there's no point in healing Lisa. Or Samantha, for that matter." Porter retracted his finger. "You've all seen what I've done. You all know what I'm now capable of. If I let you live, you'll try to stop me. It's in your nature."

Gabriel's lip quivered with anger. "You're supposed to be better than this! We risked our lives to save you, so you could use your gifts to make the world a better place!"

"I know," Porter said with the vaguest sound of regret in his voice. "And that's what's going to make this next part even harder."

He waved a hand toward Byron and his three remaining mercenaries. The men were bent in awkward positions, their bones broken and muscles torn, yet they were still alive, twitching and drooling as they waited to be put out of their misery. Porter concentrated and did just that. Their bones shifted back into their proper positions, their muscles regrew under the skin, and their external scrapes and bruises faded, leaving pristine skin behind.

"About bloody time," Byron grumbled as he pushed himself back to his feet.

"Shut up and finish the job," Porter ordered.

Byron nodded. He removed a Bowie knife from its belt sheath and marched toward Gabriel and Nate, its smooth blade reflecting lantern light into their eyes as he approached. Gabriel took a defensive stance, but before he could act, Nate lunged toward Byron, deflecting his knife wrist while snatching his pistol from its holster. Instead of immediately firing upon Byron, Nate swung the weapon toward Porter and repeatedly pulled the trigger until no bullets were left in its clip. The first bullet missed, but the others struck Porter, first in his chest, then his gut, then in his neck and head. And each bullet left an open entry wound that sealed itself with fresh flesh and skin within seconds of impact.

Porter was left physically unharmed, but emotionally, the attempt on his life sent him into a rage. He shot his magnetic disc into Nate's chest and pulled him across the sanctuary floor. When Nate's floating body neared, Porter released the disc and caught his would-be assailant by the neck. He squeezed so hard Gabriel could hear Nate's innards squishing.

"I meant what I told you before," Porter growled. "You are the brightest tech engineer I've ever known. But that was the dumbest thing you could have done just now. I was hoping we could work together. I was hoping you would learn from all this that being honest is the path to mediocrity, not success. I was hoping to have a friend, a partner, to help me take this-" He patted the pendant. "-to the next level, to bring mysticism and science together in harmony. But I see that can't happen now. You won't ever be the person I need you to be. And given your intelligence, that makes you a threat."

Nate pulled at Porter's hand to loosen the grip on his neck, but it was a futile effort.

"Unfortunately," Porter said. "threats must be eliminated."

Gabriel heard a sickening crack and saw Nate's head flop unnaturally to the side. "No!"

Porter tossed his competitor's body away, as if discarding a wad of trash. Then he looked at Byron's mercenaries. "Well, what are you waiting for?"

The mercenaries stood there, confused, until Porter nudged his head toward Damien. Then they got the message. They cocked their assault rifles, took aim, and filled Damien's body with bullets. Gabriel saw bits of bloodied robe rip into the air as the former pendant bearer fell to his knees, then collapsed face first onto the pulpit, dead.

"I put my trust in you," Gabriel cried. "Despite what everyone said, I believed you had a good heart. How-" He stopped, knowing his words were falling on deaf ears.

Porter sighed, then gave Byron a reluctant nod.

"It's nothing personal," the rival treasure hunter said as he resumed his advance on Gabriel.

Gabriel dropped back into a sitting position. He had no more will to fight, no more conviction to save himself when he had nothing left to live for. He saw Byron's knife swoop in, felt its tip pierce his chest, press through his ribs, and cut into his heart. He stared at Lisa's face, the last image he wanted passing through his brain, before all went dark...

Chapter Ninety-Four
Crosswalk

Alegranza, Canary Islands
Three Days Before The Sky Opened

The darkness was all-consuming. There was no light to be seen, no air to be breathed, no ground on which to stand, nor physics by which to be bound. Gabriel felt no pain where his mortal wounds had been incurred. In fact, he felt nothing whatsoever, physically or emotionally, as if all nerves and any emotional processing had been chemically blocked. Yet, he continued to exist. He remembered what had just transpired, but felt disconnected from it, as though it were a dream. But it wasn't a dream... he knew that for certain. Were the nerve endings in his brain firing off whatever electrical charges they still carried while awaiting death's embrace? Or had death already taken him, and this was something else altogether?

Gabriel saw a distant, flickering light. An invisible hand pulled him toward it, and as he neared, the light grew. There was movement within it, shadowed objects darting back and forth with urgency. As the light overtook the darkness, those shadowed objects took form. One was Esmerelda. She was in the sanctuary, shouting orders to other surviving villagers in Spanish. Foolishly, Gabriel expected his earpiece translator to convert her words to English, but, of course, he had no earpiece translator in this non-corporal existence. Esmerelda pointed, and as she moved her hand, the air behind her rippled like waves on the surface of water. Gabriel noticed her voice was distant, as if she wasn't really there. Or perhaps he was the one who wasn't there...

He followed Esmerelda's outstretched finger to one of the picnic tables from the previous night's dinner. The villagers had brought it and three others into the sanctuary and lined them side-by-side in the center of the room. Two men deposited Nate's limp body on the table Esmerelda had indicated. Lisa and Samantha's bodies were already on two of the others. Gabriel moved closer to his wife, and for just a moment, sorrow broke through the chemical block that had otherwise deadened his feelings.

Esmerelda continued barking orders and pointed to the final empty table. The soft glow of dawn peeked in through the sanctuary's damaged perimeter as the villagers shuffled to one side and retrieved a fourth body. They carried it to the empty picnic table and plopped it on top, just as they had done with the previous three. Gabriel looked, expecting to see Damien's bullet-ridden corpse on display, but instead, he was staring at his own reflection. His skin was pale and his eyes were lifeless, and his clothes were soaked with the blood that had emptied from his sliced-open heart.

"What-"

"I'm sorry," Damien said behind him. "I meant to get here before you saw that."

Gabriel spun to face the deceased village leader. He wasn't part of the action in the sanctuary. His movements didn't ripple the air and his voice was loud and clear. Like Gabriel, he also seemed to no longer be bound by the laws of physics.

"What is this?" Gabriel asked. "What's happening here?"

Damien pressed his lips together in a mournful smile. "I'm afraid there's no easy way to say it. You died, Gabriel." He looked at the others on the picnic tables. "You all did. Well, we all did, I should say."

"And what's this? The afterlife?"

Damien chuckled. "No, this isn't the afterlife. Think of this as a crosswalk, somewhere that connects the here-" He motioned to the sanctuary. "-and the there." He gave a casual glance in no particular direction.

"And what are we doing here?"

"Me?" Damien asked. "I'm just here to keep you company... and perhaps share a few tidbits of knowledge. You, on the other hand, you're holding tight."

"Holding tight for what?"

Damien pointed toward the picnic tables. Esmerelda was standing over Samantha, dabbing her wounds with a wet cloth. Behind her, a child carried a large glass jug filled with a thick, golden fluid that reminded Gabriel of honey. Only this honey also contained minuscule metallic flecks suspended throughout.

"You may have noticed that I and all others blessed by the pendant are very protective of it," Damien said. "Possibly to the point of paranoia. That's because Mr. Cannes wasn't the first to try to take the pendant from me."

That grabbed Gabriel's attention.

"About eight hundred years after defeating Lyrus, I let the wrong person join my village. I knew he envied the pendant, but like you with Mr. Cannes, I wanted to believe he was better than his envy. Little did I know, he was amassing a rebellion within my own ranks. When they struck..." Damien shuddered at the memory. "I almost lost the pendant and my life that day. I vowed to never let my guard down like that again and implemented measures to ensure only the right people were funneled to the pendant. You've seen that process in action with your own eyes, and for a long time, it worked flawlessly... until you came along, that is."

Gabriel shook his head. "I never meant to harm you or your village."

"I know," Damien said with an understanding smile. "But Porter Cannes is a cunning man. We would have never allowed him to reach Alegranza on his own, but his hiring of you subverted our process. You helped him survive the Cabrera challenges. You helped him solve The Veiled Bird. You convinced all of us who wanted to turn him away that we were wrong and that he was worthy of being saved. He used you, Gabriel, because he knew you were the only one who could get him the treasure he wanted so dearly."

Again, emotion broke through Gabriel's otherwise deadened state. This time it was shame.

"Good," Damien said. "That's your connection to your mortal body showing through. That means it's not too late."

Gabriel looked at him curiously. "Too late for what?"

Chapter Ninety-Five
Wayward Souls

Alegranza, Canary Islands
Three Days Before The Sky Opened

Damien turned once more to the picnic tables. Esmerelda had finished dabbing Samantha's wounds and was now in the middle of spreading the golden viscous fluid over Lisa's impaled torso.

"Even though I had a vetting process in place, I knew I couldn't fully eliminate the risk that someone might get the upper hand on me one day. I needed a failsafe, something to protect me and my people, should I ever lose control of the pendant. So, one night, I took the pendant to the shop of a blacksmith who had received its blessing. I used his grinding stone to shave the outer coating of metal from the pendant's circumference. Then I took the shavings to an apothecary who'd also been blessed, and I asked him to prepare a tonic from them. That tonic, to be precise."

Esmerelda finished with Lisa and moved on to Nate, spreading the golden fluid around his disjointed neck. Now Gabriel understood what he was watching.

"That can bring us back?"

Damien's face told him it wasn't so simple. "The tonic can heal your bodies; I performed a test long ago to confirm it works. But a body is just that. It needs a soul to inhabit it. Yours is still tethered, but the others..." Damien hesitated as his eyes drifted over each of Gabriel's team members. "If they've moved on, not even the pendant's tonic can bring them back."

Gabriel watched Esmerelda and the child move from Nate's table to his own. It was then that a peculiar thought struck him. "Why are they saving us? We brought Porter to Alegranza. This whole thing is our fault."

"They're saving you," Damien said flatly, "because I told them to."

Gabriel didn't understand. "You can speak to them, even though you're... whatever we are?"

Damien shook his head in the negative.

It took Gabriel a moment, but he realized there was only one other possibility. "You told them before we died. You knew this was going to happen."

Damien frowned. "I knew it was a strong possibility. The pendant doesn't grant omnipotence. But it does provide insight, and when combined with as many years of experience as I've had dealing with people, well, you learn to predict things with a high degree of certainty."

"If you were so certain, why didn't you stop it? You could have had Porter exiled. You could have had your villagers move the hidden arsenal. Hell, you had the power to do just about anything you wanted to prevent this outcome!"

"Everything you've said is true," Damien admitted. "But therein lies the curse of the pendant bearer. Though I expected this outcome, there was still a chance, no matter how small, that Mr. Cannes would choose the other path. That he wouldn't take the pendant by force and instead await my decision." Damien flashed Gabriel a comforting smile. "That's where your instincts served you well. You weren't wrong about Mr. Cannes' ability to change; you were just wrong about his willingness. And despite what I told you this morning, if he had accepted my decision with humility, I probably would have healed him."

"Why?"

"Because then I would have known with complete certainty that he had indeed changed for the better. You see, that's the gift God has bestowed upon humanity: the freewill to choose one's path. Regardless of how I expected this to play out, it wasn't my place to take that choice away from Mr. Cannes, even given the high cost of choosing poorly."

"So instead of preventing him from taking the pendant," Gabriel reasoned, "you enacted a failsafe that would allow us to return and take it back."

"Not *us*, Mr. Dunne."

There was a gravity to his correction that Gabriel had been aware of, but ignoring, since their conversation first began. He looked at Esmerelda, who was carefully blotting the incision in his chest with the pendant's tonic. Then he looked at the child by her side and saw that his jug was nearly empty. That's when Gabriel realized there was no fifth picnic table, and Damien's body was right where he had last seen it, face down on the pulpit, still and lifeless.

"Why didn't they resurrect you?" He asked.

"Because there wasn't enough tonic for all of us," Damien said. "When I took the pendant to the grinding stone, I could feel its stability faltering with each shaving I removed. I shaved enough to create the one jar of tonic, but I feared taking any more would cause the pendant to break, unleashing God's power onto this world. It contains but a fraction, but even that is more than this universe could possibly withstand. It would mean the end of everything."

Gabriel considered the implications. "You could have let me go instead. You could have had Esmerelda heal you in my place."

"I gave her explicit instructions to prioritize you and your team over me," Damien informed him. "You know Porter Cannes, and you won't be blindsided by his true nature again. That makes you the world's best hope of stopping him."

Gabriel felt guilt wash over him. It wasn't brief like the other emotions, but instead lingered, tearing at his conscience.

"The connection between body and soul is strengthening," Damien said with glee. "Don't feel bad, Mr. Dunne. I've walked the Earth for more years than most men could even imagine. It's time for me to go home."

He looked toward the picnic tables once more, and following his gaze, Gabriel could see the effects of the pendant's tonic underway. Aside from her tattered clothing, Samantha appeared almost totally normal, not a speck of burnt flesh anywhere in sight. Lisa's torso was smooth again, no shrapnel protruding from it and no scars where that shrapnel had once stood. Nate's neck had straightened, and Gabriel's chest wound was nearly closed.

"It's working," he said under his breath.

"It's healing your bodies," Damien confirmed. "Now they need your souls."

Gabriel felt weight returning to him. He felt his heart beating, felt his lungs rising and falling, felt the cool morning air on his body's skin as soul and corporal form became one once more. "Wait," he said. "How do I stop Porter? How does anyone stop a god?"

Damien placed a reassuring hand on his shoulder. "He's not a god. He's a man crazed with power. There've been many before him, but if you don't find a way, there'll be none after."

"You didn't answer my question."

"It's not an answer I have," Damien admitted. "But I trust you'll figure it out. That's why I chose you over me."

Gabriel's emotions had fully returned, and he found himself tearing up at Damien's words. He had barely known the man, but through the shared experience of death and what comes after, they had become kindred spirits. Bright light began to overtake the sanctuary, signaling their time together was coming to an end. Gabriel wasn't sure why, but he had a strong feeling he'd never see Damien again.

"Best of luck," he said, "whatever comes next for you."

"You too, Mr. Dunne," Damien replied cordially. Then, as the world around them grew blindingly white, he added, "for everyone's sake."

Chapter Ninety-Six
Awake

Alegranza, Canary Islands
Two Days Before The Sky Opened

Gabriel opened his eyes. He expected to see the overhead lanterns and partially destroyed roof of the sanctuary, but instead, bright sunlight cast thin streams through a covering of deteriorated wood. Gabriel was back in his team's sleeping quarters. But how...

"Whoa, whoa, whoa," Lisa said as he jolted upright in a panic. "Take it slowly."

Gabriel's eyes found her. She looked absolutely radiant, definitely alive, and showing no signs of the physical harm she had endured during Porter's and Byron's attack. She wore villager clothing, and the streams of sunlight filtered down around her, casting an angelic aura around her frame. Gabriel wrapped his arms around her and squeezed like he had never squeezed her before.

"I thought I'd lost you," he choked.

"We thought we'd lost you too," Lisa replied.

When they broke their embrace, Gabriel saw that Samantha and Nate were also standing nearby, wearing similar villager garb. Samantha gave Gabriel a less intense, but equally compassionate, hug.

"Welcome back, boss."

When she stepped away, Gabriel looked at Nate.

"I'm good," he said, waving a hand in front of his neck. "I don't think I'm going to be in the mood for tight squeezes anytime soon."

Gabriel smiled with understanding.

"Do you remember what happened?" Lisa asked him.

"Yeah," Gabriel said before kicking into leader mode. "We need to stop Porter before anyone else gets hurt."

"Funny," Nate said. "The first thing out of each of our mouths was *how the hell are we still alive.*"

"I already know about the pendant's tonic," Gabriel told him. When the others stared at him as if he'd been holding pertinent information from them, he added, "it's a long story. I'm not even sure how much of it is real."

"Get talking," Nate said.

Before Gabriel could oblige, however, Esmerelda and two villagers Gabriel recognized as Nestor and Ramon entered the building. Gabriel smiled to show his gratitude as they approached, but his gesture was met with a slap that stung his left cheek. Esmerelda launched into a tirade Gabriel couldn't understand and didn't have an earpiece translator to assist with. Luckily, when she was done, Nestor relayed the message, albeit without the slap.

"She says it's your fault Damien is no longer with us. She says she's spent the last twenty-six hours wondering whether saving you was all for nothing."

"Wait," Gabriel interrupted. "Twenty-six hours?"

"That's how long we've been unconscious," Lisa explained. "The rest of us only woke an hour or two before you, and even then... let's just say it took a while before our brains accepted what was going on."

Esmerelda unleashed a new round of verbal assaults. It was clear from her tone that she wasn't getting any happier.

"She's says you need to get off your ass and get to work," Nestor translated. "Mr. Cannes doesn't have a head start yet, but he will if we delay much longer."

Gabriel's head hurt, trying to process the fragments of information. "How can he not have a head start? If we've been out twenty-six hours, he could be back in the United States by now."

Esmerelda turned her verbal assault on Nestor, who argued back in Spanish for several rounds before Esmeralda threw her hands up in frustration and found a seat.

"You must not know," Nestor said to Gabriel.

"Know what?"

"Mr. Cannes left the village shortly after the attack on the sanctuary," Ramon chimed in. "We think it's because he sensed he would go into stasis soon."

"Stasis?"

"It's like a state of hibernation," Nestor said. "Using the pendant drains extraordinary amounts of energy. After Damien would perform a blessing, he'd need anywhere from an hour to half a day for his body to recover. He could always sense when his body was about to give out, and would isolate himself during the recovery period to protect the pendant while he was unconscious."

"Damien had much more practice with the pendant than Mr. Cannes," Ramon added. "He used to tell us stories about being in stasis for days following even minor use. Over time, he learned to be more efficient with both his energy expenditure and replacement."

"But Mr. Cannes hasn't learned that yet," Nestor continued. "He'll need at least a day or two in stasis from using the pendant to heal himself and Mr. Coltrain's team. We've already lost one waiting for you to wake. So the next twenty-four hours will be crucial."

Esmerelda grumbled something from her seat.

"What did she say?" Lisa asked.

Nestor sighed. "She wants to know how you're going to get the pendant back."

Gabriel felt all eyes, including those of his team members, swing to him. He gulped, then answered as honestly as he could while remaining upbeat. "We still need to work out the details on that."

"*Dios Mio!*" Esmeralda exclaimed as she slapped her hands on her thighs in frustration.

Gabriel didn't need translating as she then stormed out of the building. He was glad Nestor and Ramon were more levelheaded, but he could see the disappointment on their faces when he revealed he didn't have a plan to stop Porter yet.

"We just woke up," Gabriel told them. "Please, give us time. We'll figure this out and loop you in before we execute. You have my word."

Both Nestor and Ramon eyed him as if they weren't sold on his request, but it wasn't as though they had another option.

"Just remember," Nestor said, "time is of the essence."

He followed in Esmerelda's footsteps. Ramon did the same, but stopped just short of leaving.

"If you need help figuring out where to start, you might want to speak with Mr. Cannes' lady friend."

"Nadine?" Lisa asked. "She's still here?"

Ramon nodded. "She's with the children. She is..." He seemed as though he didn't know quite how to describe Nadine's condition, but what he said next gave Gabriel a good idea of it. "I don't think she knew what Mr. Cannes was planning to do. Her heart and her mind are aching. We've offered her shelter here as long as she needs."

"You're not moving the village?" Samantha asked.

Ramon shrugged. "What would be the point? Besides, Mr. Cannes destroyed our fleet on his way out. The lagoon is awash with wreckage. We have no way to leave."

"I'm so sorry," Lisa said with noticeable sincerity.

"Save your apologies," Ramon replied, not with hostility, but with a deep yearning. "Speak with Ms. Walsh. Figure out what Mr. Cannes plans to do next. And once you know that, determine how you'll relieve him of the pendant before he succeeds. That can be your apology."

Ramon said nothing more and left.

Nate released a nervous breath. "That was intense." He sat and rubbed his forehead. "Look, I don't mean to be the negative one in the room, but hunting down madmen with weapons of godlike power isn't exactly our cup of tea."

"No," Gabriel agreed. "It's not. But today we need to."

"Why?"

"Because the fate of the world is at stake."

Again, his teammates' eyes turned to him.

"What do you know that we don't?" Lisa asked.

Gabriel recalled Damien's words about Porter being the last power-crazed man to walk the Earth, supposedly because there'd be no Earth left if they didn't stop him first. What could Porter possibly have planned? If healing himself and achieving immortality wasn't the end goal, then what was? Gabriel didn't want to tell his team about his time in the *crossroad*, as Damien had called it. He figured his team would think he was crazy. Hell, he even thought he might be a little crazy. Sure, his visions had revealed the healing process that brought the team back from the beyond, but maybe those visions hadn't been the observations of a tethered soul, but rather the residual processing of his dying mind as he lay unconscious in the sanctuary. If so, he'd never truly spoken to Damien, and anything Damien had told him was just his own mind trying to piece together an explanation for the unfolding events. Then again, it felt real, and Gabriel's gut told him it had been real. Regardless, the risk was too great to ignore.

"I'll tell you about it while we walk," he said. "Let's go find Nadine."

Chapter Ninety-Seven
Scorned

Alegranza, Canary Islands
Two Days Before The Sky Opened

When the team emerged from their sleeping quarters, they were startled to find a clear sky hovering overhead. With the pendant's loss, the mist shrouding Alegranza had vanished, allowing vibrant sunlight to wash over the island. Gabriel shared his encounter with Damien in the not-quite-beyond as the team crossed the village grounds. They took the tale in stride, not once questioning Gabriel's sanity, which made him wonder whether they were just humoring him or if they had experienced so much supernatural phenomena on this mission that a conversation between wayward souls now classified as normal.

The village was in tatters, with evidence of Byron's attack everywhere the eye could see. House walls had crumbled, common areas displayed fresh bullet holes in their already worn wood. Shrapnel and casings littered the ground, except where surviving villagers had swept them into piles to clear safe walking paths. Those that didn't survive had been lined up outside the sanctuary and respectfully covered with sheets. Based on the imprints, not all were adults...

"How could he?" Lisa asked.

Gabriel had always known Byron was scum, but this... it was a senseless massacre. It would have been more advantageous for Byron to sneak up on the sanctuary and launch his attack there, rather than blast his way through the village. All Gabriel could think was that he and his men must have been spotted, and once the first bullet was fired, others woke, giving him no choice but to continue the onslaught.

They found Nadine seated at a table outside one of the common areas. She was staring at a group of children too young to understand what had transpired as they played simple games to occupy their minds. She was staring... but she wasn't really watching. Her eyes were blank, as if all connection to humanity had been sucked from them. They had dark rings around them which hovered over a red nose, sore from so much crying and wiping. As the team neared, Lisa put a halting hand on Gabriel's chest.

"Let me take the lead," she said.

Gabriel nodded, then waited several feet back as Lisa joined Nadine and opened a soft conversation. He couldn't make out their words, but Nadine was being responsive, if brief, with those responses. Gabriel hoped she knew something, and more importantly, that she was willing to share it. Otherwise, they'd be planning their next steps based on speculation. Speaking of-

"Samantha?"

"Yes, boss?"

"No matter what we learn here, we're going to need to get off this island. Can you check on the Leviathans? I'm guessing Porter and Byron didn't leave us one, at least not intact, so you may have to get alternate transportation rolling."

"Good idea."

Ever the bravest of the team, she immediately set off on foot, heading northeast into uncharted territory, alone and unarmed. Gabriel would have been more comfortable sending someone with her, but Lisa was making headways with Nadine, and soon he would need Nate's brain to help deduce whatever Porter's goal might be. Fortunately, with Porter and Byron gone, the island should be threat-free.

"Gabriel," Lisa said. She waved him and Nate over, stepping aside so they could stand close to Nadine. "Tell them what you told me."

Nadine looked up at Gabriel, her previously blank eyes now filled with remorse. "I swear I didn't know what he was going to do. He kept me in the dark, just like you."

Gabriel glanced at Lisa, who gave a subtle nod to affirm she believed Nadine's claims.

"After your team left to warn you of Byron's attack, Porter opened

374

his eyes and told me not to worry. He was faking being unconscious. He said it was all part of his plan. I- I didn't know what that meant," she stammered, "and he said he didn't have time to explain, but that I should wait for him there. He said he would be back shortly, and then we'd be able to go home. I tried to tell him to wait, that we had four more hours, but he wouldn't listen."

"What happened when he came back for you?" Gabriel asked.

"He couldn't find me," Nadine said. "I hid in another building. I didn't want to be a part of whatever he was doing. I didn't want to hurt these people." She looked back at the children as she spoke. "I could see our sleeping quarters. Porter, Byron, his team, and at least six other men I'd never seen before came back for me. I saw Porter had changed. I saw he had the pendant around his neck, and that's when I knew what he'd done."

"These other men, were they villagers?" Lisa asked.

Nadine shook her head.

"That explains the attack from all sides," Gabriel said. "Byron must have had a second crew of mercenaries sneak onto the island to aid in the sanctuary assault. Damien was distracted by us and passing judgment on Porter. He didn't know a secondary threat had shown up." Gabriel looked back at Nadine. "Then what?"

"Porter got angry. He turned over every cot, looking for me. Then he stormed out, and I thought he was going to use the pendant to find me, but- something happened to him. He suddenly looked weak. Not sickly, like he's been, but just... drained."

"He was going into stasis," Gabriel said to Lisa, who nodded.

"He must have felt whatever was happening, because then he shouted for Byron to get moving, and they left the village. I was so afraid it might be a ruse that I didn't leave my hiding spot until a group of children found me there hours later. I just- I-"

Though Nadine had appeared all out of tears, her body found an untapped reservoir within her. She turned to the side, sobbing, and her face landed against Nate's thigh. He wasn't the most emotionally supportive person on the team, but he must have felt a connection to Nadine's plight, for he sat down and put an arm around her, allowing her to empty her tears into his chest.

"I'm sorry," she said after composing herself a couple of minutes later. "I didn't mean to-"

"It's all right," Nate assured her.

Nadine dabbed her swollen eyes, then looked up at Gabriel once more. "So, what else can I do for you?"

"We were hoping you could help us stop Porter," Lisa said, cutting to the chase. "Before things get worse."

"Do you think you can do that, Nadine?" Gabriel asked.

Her face firmed as she gave him a resolute nod. "Yes," she said, her voice strengthening with her conviction. "Yes, I'll help you. Let's stop the bastard... and put him in the ground where he belongs."

Chapter Ninety-Eight
Puzzle Pieces

Alegranza, Canary Islands
Two Days Before The Sky Opened

"Okay," Gabriel said. "What do we know?"

He, Lisa, Nate, and Nadine were back in their sleeping quarters. They had cleared one cot to use as a makeshift conference table and were spread around it, ready for their brainstorming session to begin.

"Porter's an asshole," Nate said.

"True," Gabriel agreed, "but unhelpful. What else?"

"He's a liar, a cheat, a backstabber," Nate rattled on. "He owes me an engineering trophy, and I never did get that apology."

Nadine shot him a subtle, appreciative smile.

"Also all true," Gabriel said. "Still unhelpful, though."

Nate snapped his fingers. "Okay, how about this: Porter's got the pendant."

"Obviously," Lisa said, "but at least it's relevant. I'll build from that. What's he want the pendant for? Besides healing himself, I mean."

"Immortality," Gabriel answered. "He mentioned it to Damien during the attack."

"But if it was only immortality," Nate said, "we could just let him keep the damn thing. He doesn't deserve it, but living forever doesn't put the rest of the world at risk. He must want something more."

Gabriel stewed. He had a thought, but it wasn't without contradiction. "Porter mentioned something about getting into Heaven on the way to Alegranza. He brought it up again during the attack. Given he's spent most of his life as an atheist, it's an odd desire."

They each sat on that thought for a moment, until Nate waggled a finger in Gabriel's direction.

"You've got it wrong. Porter didn't say anything about getting *into* Heaven. He said a man like him *wouldn't* get into Heaven."

"No shit," Nadine muttered.

Her commentary didn't break Nate's stride. "He also followed that with a claim that his paradise was here, on Earth."

"Hence the desire for immortality," Lisa said.

"No," Gabriel said, the pieces of information finally starting to click, "not just immortality. He wants his paradise. He can't get into Heaven, so he wants to bring Heaven to Earth."

Lisa's arm hairs stood on end. "Surely the pendant doesn't have that ability."

"I wouldn't think so," Gabriel said. "We already know the pendant's power is limited, and Damien was clear that Porter is no god. He can't make the pendant do things God didn't empower it to do."

Nate's eyes rose from deep concentration, a heightened state of fear within them. "Unless he enhances the power that's already there. Do you remember right before Porter..." He hesitated, as if disturbed by the memory. "...right before he decided my brain no longer needed to speak with my spine? He said he was hoping I would be his partner. He wanted my help *taking the pendant to the next level*. He said we would bring mysticism and science together in harmony."

"He's going to augment the power of God with the power of science," Gabriel said. "But how?"

Nadine dropped onto the cot behind her, her eyes wide with distress. "The machine..."

"What?" Gabriel asked. "What machine?"

"The one he's building on the roof of Cannes Tower," she said. "The one he's been working on for months. Day after day, slaving over those damn blueprints."

Gabriel and Nate's gazes met.

"The blueprints he's been working during our mission?" Gabriel asked. "I got the impression it was some sort of next generation construction equipment."

"Porter told me he was designing a new method for hazardous waste disposal," Nate said.

Lisa shook her head. "Clearly, Porter lied. What is it, Nadine?"

"I have no idea," she said. "I just know that, aside from his pendant quest, it's been the thing consuming most of his time." An idea seemed to strike her, for she jumped from the cot and found the backpack she'd brought to Alegranza. She dug through it and removed her tablet, which she turned on and tapped with her fingernails as it went through its boot process. "Porter made me download all of his important files in case something happened to his tablet while we were away." The tablet's home screen popped up. "I don't have much battery left, but maybe there's enough that you can make something of it." She clicked through a series of folders, then opened a replica of the blueprints Porter had lied about. "Here," she said, passing the tablet to Gabriel.

He laid it on the conference cot and hovered overhead with the others. There, on Nadine's screen, was the upright mechanical claw with pinched fingers that Gabriel had seen when eavesdropping on their flight to Morocco. Beneath it were layered platforms covered in circuitry, with exposed cables running into the ground, or as they knew now, rooftop, below.

"Talk to us, Nate," Lisa said.

"Porter told me-"

"Throw out anything Porter told you about the blueprints," Gabriel said. "Look at them with your own eyes. Tell us what *you* see."

Nate nodded and stared at the blueprints. He pinched the screen to zoom in on certain sections and to read tiny labels of technical jargon the others didn't understand. Then he zoomed out to see the bigger picture again, the wheels in his brain turning at full speed as he tried to envision what use a design like this might have. "Well, we all see the claw. I don't think it's any stretch to assume it's meant to securely hold the pendant." He pointed to curvy lines snaking out of the claw. "Those wires? They're high capacity electrical cables, and this layered platform they're connected to... I think it's some kind of parallel generator system. Well, the top two platforms, anyway. The bottom platform is essentially a giant heat sink."

"Like in a laptop?" Lisa asked.

"Exactly like a laptop. You've got a source of power feeding a centralized processor, and a mechanism to syphon heat away so it doesn't melt down."

"What are these?" Gabriel asked, pointing to standalone structures away from, but still wired to, the main unit.

"I think they're high capacity solar cells and batteries. Probably for backup power if the dual generators fail mid-operation."

"And that operation is..."

"As best I can tell," Nate said, "pump as much power as possible into the claw. There are some sort of custom plates on the claw's fingertips. I'm guessing those are the mechanisms that will then transfer that power to the pendant."

"How much power could Porter possibly draw?" Lisa asked. "It's not like Cannes Tower is constructed on top of a geothermal vent or hydroelectric dam or anything."

"No," Nadine chimed in, "but it's connected to them."

The others turned to her, slack-jawed.

"Porter insisted Cannes Tower be a hub of energy. He's wired into the city, into dams in Washington, Virginia, Michigan... you name it. He's got a direct draw from The Geysers in California. He's even tapped into an undersea grid that connects to a series of custom geothermal harvesters on the floor of the Pacific Ocean. And that's not even mentioning his nuclear sources. Believe me, whatever power he needs, he can pull it."

Silence. Then Nate turned away from the group, his face pale.

"I'm going to go throw up now."

Chapter Ninety-Nine
The Common Outcome

Alegranza, Canary Islands
Two Days Before The Sky Opened

"So, do you think he can really do it?" Lisa asked Gabriel. "Can Porter really open the doors to Heaven and merge it with Earth?"

"I honestly don't know. But that's not our biggest concern."

"The merger of Heaven and Earth?" Lisa questioned, as though he were an idiot. "With Porter as ruler? There's something more concerning than that?"

"How about the end of everything?" Gabriel asked, his voice deadly serious. "Damien made a limited quantity of his emergency tonic because he feared taking additional shavings from the pendant would break it, releasing God's power and destroying the universe. If Porter pumps too much energy into that thing-"

"-he could inadvertently kill us all," Lisa finished. "Which is exactly what could happen if he succeeds, too."

Gabriel cocked his head.

"Think about it. The pendant contains only a fraction of God's power. Where's the rest?"

"With God," Gabriel answered quickly.

"And where is God?"

Gabriel suddenly realized where she was going with this. "Oh shit. Whether Porter breaks the pendant or opens the doors to Heaven, the outcome is the same. That's why Damien said Porter would be the last power-crazed man on Earth. One way or another, he's going to bring about the end of the world, and he doesn't even know it."

Lisa looked at Nadine. "If we could get in touch with him, tell him what's going to happen, do you think he'd back down?"

Nadine's down-turned lips said it all. "He threw away his precious company. He threw away the one person who loved him. And he threw away his only friend." She set her sad gaze upon Gabriel. "There's nothing he wants more than this. And there's nothing we can say to convince him otherwise."

"We don't have to," Nate said, his voice suddenly hopeful. "Forget negotiating. We have an opportunity to stop Porter ourselves."

Gabriel scoffed. "Unless you've figured out how to overcome his new godlike powers..."

Nate grinned. "He's going to do it for us."

Either Nate had lost it, or he had a sudden stroke of genius. Gabriel hoped it was the latter. "Go on."

"Look at the blueprints," Nate said. "There's no platform, no seat, no bed or couch or anything similar to stretch out on. When the pendant is in that claw, it won't be on Porter's neck."

Gabriel grabbed the tablet and zoomed in on the main unit. "Hot damn, you're right."

"Is it really that instantaneous, though?" Lisa asked. "I mean, when he takes the pendant off-"

"He loses all godlike abilities," Nate said.

"You weren't conscious when Damien lost the pendant," Gabriel explained. "It was like flipping a light switch. The moment it left his neck, he was a normal man again. He was mortal."

"He was vulnerable," Nate emphasized.

"That's right," Gabriel said. "That's our chance. The moment Porter puts that pendant in the machine, we need to be there to take him out. We won't know if it'll take five hours or five minutes for the pendant to unleash God's might, so there's no room for error. We subdue Porter, we retrieve the pendant, and then we destroy that machine before anyone has a chance to use it again."

"One problem," Lisa said. "We have to get off this island first."

"Good point. Let's go find Samantha."

They exited the sleeping quarters just in time to see Esmerelda gathering nearly twenty villagers in the middle of the caldera. She was barking orders at them, and they were nodding in response, as if the task they'd been assigned was one of utmost importance. A minute later, Esmerelda dismissed them, and the villagers took off as one large group toward the southern caldera ridge. Samantha approached her, flanked by Nestor and Ramon, and appeared to communicate gratitude. Then she spotted the team, excused herself, and joined them.

"What was that about?" Gabriel asked.

"The Leviathan's were gone," Samantha said. "Porter must have taken one for himself in case he entered stasis before they reached dry land. Byron and his team must have taken the other."

"Can't you call your source and order another one?" Nate asked. "I know it might take a few hours..."

Samantha held up her backup phone, which was split open on one side and half melted on the other. "It was with me during the attack. I kind of wish they'd saved a little of that tonic for it."

Nadine pulled out her tablet. "I've got satellite connectivity. You can-" The screen went black. "Damn."

"Battery?" Gabriel asked.

Nadine nodded.

"What about your phone?"

"I don't know what happened to it. I had it before the attack, but I lost it sometime afterwards."

Gabriel looked at his other team members. "Does anyone still have a working phone or tablet?"

"Our tablets are either in Casablanca or with the U.S. military," Lisa reminded him. "And my backup phone looks worse than Samantha's."

"Nate?"

"I left mine on the Leviathan," he said with a frown.

Gabriel had brought his backup phone with him, but its battery was already half-drained when they arrived at Alegranza. He had little hope it had held out the past two days while constantly trying to ping satellites through the mist. He found his backpack and checked anyway. No luck.

"I don't suppose the villagers have any advanced communication technology lying around?" Gabriel asked. "Or maybe just an electrical outlet?"

"No," Samantha said, "but they're going to help us another way.

That crew you just saw is headed down to the lagoon. Esmerelda ordered them to salvage whatever it takes to reconstruct a single ship seaworthy enough to get back to Essaouira. They're going to work through the day and night if necessary."

"Day and night, huh?" Gabriel asked rhetorically. "Porter could be out of stasis by then."

"I know," Samantha said. "But it's all we've got."

Once again, time wasn't on the team's side. And once again, there was nothing Gabriel could do about it. As soon as Porter was out of stasis, he would return to New York, to Cannes Tower, to supercharge the pendant and try to achieve his ultimate glory. Gabriel feared if they weren't ahead of him, or at a minimum close behind, there wouldn't be enough time to prevent him from setting catastrophic events into motion. They had a general game plan, and they still needed to map out its details, but Gabriel suspected they'd have quite a long boat ride during which to do that. For now, they needed to focus on the bottleneck keeping them from moving forward.

"Well," he said, "what are we standing around for? Let's help build a ship."

Chapter One Hundred
Ocean Bound

North Atlantic Ocean
One Day Before The Sky Opened

Alegranza's hidden lagoon would normally have been a place of beauty, a quiet retreat to which one could go to escape the pressures of life and relax among the splendor of Mother Earth. But when Gabriel and the team arrived there, it looked like a war zone. Chunks of broken ships dotted the lagoon as though they were unnatural islands. Torn pieces of metal and wood bobbed with the gentle current coming in from the ocean. The villagers' supplies, which they had already loaded in preparation for their move, were waterlogged, broken, had sunk, or were washing out to sea.

But the team of villagers corralled by Esmerelda didn't let this bother them. They worked diligently to identify the most salvageable pieces of shipwreck they could find. They built a temporary dock from which they could work on those pieces, and by nightfall, they had already pieced together a rough skeleton of what would become the sole useable vessel on Alegranza. Gabriel and the team were tasked with less-specialized, but nonetheless critical, duties to aid in the ship's construction. Nate and Nadine were on *pump patrol*, manually scooping water from the in-progress ship to help keep it afloat. The others on drying duty. Gabriel and Lisa were responsible for hoisting soaked sails up the sheer lagoon walls, where a combination of gravity and wind would hopefully dry them enough for use. Samantha was responsible for extracting water from machinery that would help steer the ship and returning it to working order.

By two o'clock in the morning, the vessel's body was ready. By three, the machinery had been installed. By four, the sails were attached. And by five, the team was gliding down the tight rock tunnel that led out to the Atlantic Ocean. Samantha estimated it would take eight hours to reach Essaouira, nearly four times what it would have taken if they'd still had a Leviathan. They'd continue to be cut off from the rest of the world during that time, with no way to know whether Porter had awoken from stasis, whether he had already returned to New York, or whether his machine had been activated. The one bright spot, or perhaps black spot depending on how one looked at it, was that they would know if Porter unleashed the power of God... at least for a half-second or so before it wiped them from existence.

Eight hours was plenty of time to work out the team's next steps. Once they reached Essaouira, they would rent a new van and find the nearest electronics store to get Samantha back online. She would arrange for new passports and return flights from Marrakech to the United States, assuming no other city would get them home sooner. She would also get the ball rolling on a delivery of armaments back in New York, including an attack helicopter, sniper rifle, rocket launcher, and a variety of semi-legal sidearms. No longer tapped into Porter's finances, Gabriel could feel their bank account draining with each additional suggested purchase. He worried what state it might be in when they completed their mission, but he supposed even a drained bank account was better than having no bank account nor anything to spend it on should the world be destroyed.

The original plan had all five team members on the first flight out of the Marrakech Menara Airport, but Gabriel overrode that idea, unwilling to put all their eggs in one basket. He instructed Samantha and Nate to take the first flight so they could get home and finish preparations for their coming incursion with Porter. When Samantha asked if the others would be on the next flight, Gabriel beat around the bush a little too much, making her suspicious that he had something else in mind. When Gabriel came clean with his alternate idea, she wasn't thrilled.

"Are you out of your mind?" Samantha asked, turning away from their ship's wheel for only a second before it tried to veer off-course. "They'll never let you leave Morocco!"

"That's why I'm sending you and Nate ahead," Gabriel said. "If we don't make it back, then it's up to the two of you to finish the job."

"You'll be lucky if General Sikes even hears you out."

"It's a risk we have to take," Gabriel told her. "Once we get to Marrakech, it's another... what... sixteen hours until we land in New York? We could be too late. The U.S. military already has resources stateside. At best, they stop could stop Porter without us. At worst, they could slow him down."

"At worst," Nate corrected, "they stop Porter and take the pendant for themselves. I'm not sure I trust it in the military's possession any more than in his."

"Agreed," Gabriel said. "But it staves off the destruction of the universe. We can deal with the repercussions after-the-fact."

"All of this is assuming the black site is where we left it," Samantha reminded him. "And that General Sikes will both listen to you and take action on your intel."

"Once he knows Porter has the pendant, he'll act."

Samantha didn't argue further, but her posture and facial expression made her feelings clear. Gabriel had already done the math, though. After reaching Marrakech, he'd lose several more hours returning to General Sikes' black site, and an unknown number more trying to convince the general that they needed his help. But even then, it would place defensive resources in New York faster than Gabriel could get there himself. The stakes were too high to put the burden on his team alone. He had to try to get General Sikes on board, even if it meant delaying, or risked canceling, his own rendezvous with Porter. This wasn't about him, his team, or their personal vendettas; this was about saving the world.

Chapter One Hundred One
Sikes

U.S. Black Site, Morocco
One Day Before The Sky Opened

The team arrived in Essaouira just before one o'clock. As expected, both their passenger van and Byron's cargo van were gone. Luckily, there was an auto rental shop a short walk away, and an electronics store just a five-minute drive from there. Nate took driving duty to Marrakech while Samantha made all necessary arrangements in the back. The team met her document forger a few blocks away from the Marrakech Menara Airport. Samantha distributed properly stamped passports and matching government identification to everyone, along with top of the line walkie-talkies. Gabriel joked he didn't think they were strong enough to connect cross-continent, but no one laughed. It was a tough day to be a comedian.

Outside the airport terminal, Samantha made a last ditch effort to convince the others that visiting General Sikes was too risky, but Gabriel reiterated his faith in her and Nate to stop Porter if he had made the wrong call. Soon, Samantha and Nate were on their way through airport security, and Gabriel, Lisa, and Nadine were back on the road, heading northeast on a trajectory opposite to the one they had used to flee the U.S. military only days earlier. It was nearly six o'clock by the time they neared their destination.

"You might want to slow down," Lisa cautioned. "They're likely to shoot first and ask questions later If they see an unmarked van hurtling at them at high speed."

Heeding her warning, Gabriel eased up on the gas pedal. It was probably for the best, anyway. While they had a general idea of where the black site had been located, they didn't have exact coordinates. And in this uninhabited region of Morocco, the environment all had a sameness to it, making recognition of anything they had seen in the dark days ago extremely difficult. Gabriel continued on the heading he thought gave them the best shot at intercepting the black site for another ten minutes. Then he started questioning whether his inner compass was malfunctioning, until Nadine spotted a light off to their right.

"There!" She said, pointing.

Gabriel looked and saw the dim glow emanating from behind a hill maybe a quarter of a mile away. "What do you think?" He asked Lisa.

She nodded. Gabriel turned the steering wheel, guiding the van toward the left edge of the hill. As they neared, the glow grew brighter and expanded to the horizon that flanked the hill. Then camouflaged tarps and tent roofs came into view, and Gabriel smiled at their small success. His smile quickly dissipated, however, when a stream of bullets kicked up dirt just in front of the van, causing Gabriel to slam on the brakes.

"Get out of the van!" An authoritative voice shouted from somewhere in the dark.

"You're trespassing in a military outpost!" A second voice shouted. "Kill the engine and step out with your hands up!"

Wow, Gabriel thought, *they must have stepped up security since his team's prison break.* He also thought it was quite hypocritical to claim that Gabriel, Lisa, and Nadine were trespassing, when he suspected General Sikes' entire operation was an unauthorized occupation of Moroccan soil. Nonetheless, he didn't want to get shot, so he turned off the van and stepped out as instructed. Lisa and Nadine did the same. Two soldiers appeared from the darkness, flashlight-equipped assault rifles raised.

"Identify yourse..." The soldier trailed off as he saw the face at the end of his light. "Hey," he told his partner, "they came back."

The second soldier jolted, as if shocked by Gabriel's and Lisa's stupidity. "Makes our lives easier. I guess they want to go to prison for treason."

"We need to speak with General Sikes," Gabriel said. "It's urgent."

"General Sikes will speak with you when his schedule permits," the first soldier responded. "But don't worry; you're not going anywhere for a long time. I'm sure he'll see you eventually."

Lisa cut in. "Tell the general the weapon he was worried about is real. Tell him it's on its way back to the U.S." She paused as the soldiers shared dubious glances with each other, then added, "tell him Porter Cannes has it."

That seemed to make them understand the gravity of the situation. They lowered their weapons and ordered Gabriel, Lisa, and Nadine to follow them into the black site. Given the mayhem Byron had caused a few days earlier, Gabriel thought the encampment was looking pretty good. The wrecked trucks and a pile of their debris had been clustered together in an otherwise empty section of the camp. A few new trucks, though not as many as had been lost, had replaced them. At least one Phoenix chopper was operational again, for Gabriel saw a pilot inside, preparing for flight. It was impossible to tell whether the second Phoenix chopper was also operational or just taking up helipad space while waiting on repairs.

The team arrived at a large tent near the center of the encampment. The soldiers instructed them to wait while the first went inside, presumably to relay their information to General Sikes. Less than a minute later, the general stormed through the tent's front flaps, veins popping from his forehead and smoke firing from his ears.

"You stupid son of a bitch! Didn't I warn you about Porter Cannes?!"

Gabriel held up a hand to show he didn't come for a fight. "We know, General. And if we could turn back the clock, we would. But right now, we've got to focus on stopping Porter before he uses the pendant to destroy... well, everything."

General Sikes looked at Lisa. "What the hell is he talking about?"

"He has a machine," Nadine said. "He has a machine that's going to amplify the pendant's destructive power so much it might literally bring an end to all life."

Sikes eyed her suspiciously. "You're Porter Cannes' assistant, aren't you? At work and in the bedroom, from what I hear. Why should I trust you?"

"General," Gabriel interjected, "Nadine had the rug pulled out from under her, just like us. She's trying to help."

Sikes must have noted the sadness that crept over Nadine's face, for he backed down from pressing her. "Are you absolutely sure the pendant can even do the things it's fabled to do?"

"We've seen it in action," Gabriel said. "It's not a fable anymore. This is real."

Sikes squeezed his closed eyes, as if fighting off an oncoming migraine. "Well, it sounds like you've all gotten us into one hell of a mess." He opened his eyes and honed in on Gabriel. "Why'd you come back to me?"

Chapter One Hundred Two
Defensive Planning

U.S. Black Site, Morocco
One Day Before The Sky Opened

Lisa presented the team's pitch. "Porter's machine is in New York. If we can stop him from using it, we can stop him from destroying the world. Given our mutual interest in that outcome, we thought you might be willing to work together."

General Sikes didn't respond immediately. Gabriel could hear his heavy, nasal breaths as he considered the proposition and likely weighed it against the alternative of locking the three of them up and taking matters into his own hands. They had, after all, screwed the pooch thus far. Without confirming his position, Sikes continued the conversation. "Where's Porter Cannes now?"

"We don't know," Gabriel admitted. "Probably catching a flight to the U.S., if he hasn't already. We flew in through Marrakech Menara Airport. My best guess is that he'll fly out the same way."

"Why not just fly himself?" Sikes asked. "Or teleport or something?"

"I'm not sure the pendant gives him that ability," Gabriel said. "I don't know; maybe it does. The only thing we know for certain is that its powers do have limits. That, and they come with a cost."

General Sikes raised a curious eyebrow.

"Using the pendant takes a massive toll on the body," Lisa told him. "It sends the user into a hibernation-like state, called stasis, to recover. Porter's already experienced it once, so it's unlikely he'll use the pendant to get home unless absolutely necessary. It'll be quicker for him to sneak back into the U.S. like a normal person instead of waiting out stasis a second time."

Sikes shook his head, clearly having trouble wrapping his brain around all of this. "What else can you tell me?"

"He'll be traveling with forged paperwork," Gabriel said. "And he may or may not be accompanied by Byron Coltrain, though Byron will probably have forged paperwork, too."

"Byron Coltrain is in the custody of Morocco's Sûreté Nationale. He and his team were detained while trying to run illegal weapons across the Morocco-Algeria border. An acquaintance reached out to me to check if I was using them as off-book resources."

Gabriel couldn't help himself from smiling just a little at the news.

"But as far as Porter Cannes goes, a records hunt won't help," Sikes said. "We'll need visual identification. Assuming he's already left Marrakech, where's his next stop?"

"Lisbon," Lisa said. "Assuming he sticks with the quickest trip back."

"Then D.C.," Gabriel added.

General Sikes chewed his lip. "We can't do much about Lisbon. I'll send his photo to their security department, but we don't have jurisdiction and they won't prioritize a U.S. fugitive over their own security concerns. Washington, though... that's going to be our best shot at intercepting him before he gets back to New York. I've got a friend there, General Francisco Javez. He got himself into hot water recently and could use a win. He'll help us."

"I thought the U.S. military couldn't operate on domestic soil," Lisa said.

"It can if there's an active terrorist threat," Sikes told her. "As far as I'm concerned, that's exactly what Porter Cannes has become." His eyes narrowed in on Gabriel and Lisa. "The only remaining question is what to do with the two of you. You did, after all, knowingly help this terrorist obtain his weapon of mass destruction."

"You know that's not what really happened," Gabriel told him.

"Yeah, I know," General Sikes admitted. "But there's no way to survive this without things getting messy, and the media's going to need someone to blame to put the public at ease. A story about innocent treasure hunters that got in over their heads isn't nearly as sexy as one about rogue treasure hunters that were in on it from the start." He pursed his lips in thought, letting the false narrative hang out there for a few seconds longer than Gabriel would have liked. "Luckily for you, the Moroccans have a rogue treasure hunter in custody already. As long as they're willing to expedite him..."

"I'm sure you can work that out," Gabriel said. "We need to get moving."

He grabbed Lisa's hand and turned away from the general, only to find himself staring into the freshly raised assault rifle of the soldier who had stayed behind.

"You told us we were Porter's greatest asset," Gabriel reminded Sikes. "Damien implied we're now his greatest adversary. Don't make the mistake of sidelining us."

"Damien..." Sikes whispered.

"Yes," Gabriel said. "*That* Damien. I told you the pendant's power was real."

Gabriel wasn't sure whether General Sikes had been operating on strategic auto-drive or simply out of his military duty to stop Porter, but he must have been doing so despite a heavy dose of skepticism, for Gabriel could see that skepticism wash away in an instant. The general motioned for his soldier to stand down.

"I'd like Ms. Walsh to stay here to provide intel," he then said. "You have my word she'll be returned safely to the U.S. when this is over."

Gabriel and Lisa looked at Nadine. From their viewpoint, it was her decision.

"Okay," she agreed.

Gabriel and Lisa gave her nods of gratitude, then started back toward their van.

"What are you two going to do?" General Sikes called after them. "If the pendant really can do everything it's fabled to do, you don't stand a chance. You're not even armed."

"The pendant can do all those things," Gabriel reaffirmed. "But Porter can only do them while he wears it. If you guys can't stop him, we're going to separate him from it."

Sikes chuckled. "Treasure hunters..."

Gabriel nodded.

"All right, then," he said with uncharacteristic gusto. "Go get that treasure."

Chapter One Hundred Three
The Calm Before

Flight 4965: LIS to IAD
One Day Before The Sky Opened

Gabriel watched with unease as their plane rose off the runway at Humberto Delgado Airport. He and Lisa had made it back to Marrakech in time to catch the ten o'clock flight to Lisbon. They touched down around midnight local time, still seven in the evening in the United States, and quickly sought a television airing international news. They found one in a largely unoccupied bar and asked the bartender to turn up the volume. The lead story was about a climate crisis conference underway in Europe. Following that were reports about a cybersecurity incident at a large international bank, a shortage in grain production due to poor weather conditions, and rising economic tensions between Eastern and Western nations. When the U.S. was finally mentioned by name, it was in a story that covered the rollercoaster ride its stock market had been on for the past few days.

There was no mention of Porter, or the pendant, or any global catastrophes that signaled the end of the world was upon them. And it stayed that way for Gabriel and Lisa's entire four-hour layover. During the wait, the two treasure hunters found the airport's security office and name-dropped General Sikes to get face time with the current head of security. He informed Gabriel and Lisa that he had received a photograph of Porter, and that his entire team was keeping a lookout, but that they hadn't spotted him yet. Gabriel wondered whether that meant they had been too late getting off Alegranza and recruiting General Sikes' help, or too early, and Porter wasn't yet out of stasis.

The thought was still bothering him as the ground fell away

beneath his plane. In one hour, it would be midnight in the U.S. Gabriel imagined an old-fashioned clock chiming twelve consecutive dongs, slowly, deliberately, demanding the attention of those who heard it as it warned them the final day of human existence had finally arrived. He knew it was nonsense, of course, that the final day of existence would no more be tied to the Eastern time zone than to any other time zone. Hell, for all Gabriel knew, the final day was already half over, but that was a thought he had no interest in entertaining. Lisa squeezed his hand.

"It's going to be all right. We can't do anything for the next seven and a half hours. We'll get an update once we're on the ground in D.C. and go from there."

"I just can't help but wonder if we made the wrong choice going to the black site," Gabriel said. "What if we had a chance to get the jump on Porter, but we squandered it?"

"Then Samantha and Nate will get the jump on him for us," Lisa replied. "For now, get a drink and shut your eyes. We need to be rested when we get back to New York."

Gabriel knew she was right, but he also knew there was no way he was getting rest until this was over. His brain wouldn't stop processing the possibilities, coming up with contingencies, mulling over the mistakes he had made and determining how not to make them again... it was exhausting, and it would remain relentless until Porter was subdued or the world was destroyed, whichever came first.

The pilot's voice buzzed over the plane's intercom system. *"Ladies and gentlemen, welcome aboard Flight 4965, with service to Washington, D.C. We should have smooth sailing for the duration of our flight, so feel free to move about the cabin as needed. However, we do have a full flight tonight, so we ask that, when possible, you keep the aisles clear for others. Thanks and have a wonderful flight."*

Gabriel inhaled deeply to help calm himself. As the pilot had reminded him, the plane was quite full, with only one empty seat Gabriel had noticed during takeoff. He supposed he needed to be thankful that he and Lisa had even gotten on board. They had to purchase tickets in separate sections of the plane, but Gabriel's neighbor was nice enough to swap seats to reunite the couple. Seven and a half hours... that's how long he would be in the dark. That's how long until he reached home soil and learned whether he was too late to avoid the dire fate that loomed over the world. Gabriel had to find a way to shut his mind down during that time, or he would go mad as the seconds ticked, ticked, ticked ever so slowly while God knows what was happening on the ground below.

"Maybe the stewardess has a mild sedative," he said to Lisa.

She let him out of their row. Gabriel strolled down their side aisle, spotting a stewardess prepping a meal cart just ahead in the galley. He felt his eyes burning and head pounding from the combination of a lack of rest and typical airplane pressure.

"Excuse me, Miss?" Gabriel said politely.

"Yes, sir?" She replied in English, but with a noticeable Portuguese accent.

"Do you have anything for passengers struggling with nerves? Something to relax them during the flight?"

"Nothing official," she said. Then, reaching for her handbag, she added, "but I keep these with me for the few times we are stuck in a bad thunderstorm." She showed Gabriel a bottle of over-the-counter pills. "The instructions say to take one, but I usually need two to really feel the effect." She popped the top off the bottle and presented its open end. "Just don't tell anyone I gave them to you."

Gabriel smiled, grabbed two pills, and promised to keep it a secret. The stewardess prepped him a glass of water and wished him an uneventful rest of his flight. Gabriel returned to Lisa and showed her the pills.

"Can you memorize what these look like in case they turn out to be poison?" He asked.

"You think a stewardess you've never met is trying to poison you? You really do need sleep."

Gabriel chuckled and tossed the pills in his mouth. He gulped them back with the glass of water, then settled into his seat and waited for the effect to take hold. Twenty minutes later, his mind was still racing, and he wondered whether the stewardess' pills were just placebos, something she kept on hand to give passengers so they would relax even though they hadn't ingested a single gram of medicine. It wasn't a bad idea...

Gabriel looked around the cabin. A handful of passengers had gotten up to use the restroom or dig belongings out of their bags or to stretch their legs, but everyone else was settled in, either reading books, playing games, napping, or watching the highly edited in-flight movie. Gabriel's eyes found the empty chair from takeoff. He supposed whomever had booked that ticket had simply missed the flight. But if so, why hadn't the airline given the seat away to one of the three people that had been in line behind him and Lisa, and subsequently got put on a waitlist?

Gabriel stared at the empty space above the chair a little longer, and for a moment, he pictured the silhouette of someone sitting there. Had that been his imagination, or was it a memory? Had someone actually been sitting there at one point? If so, where were they now? Gabriel's brain tried to decipher reality from fantasy, but a sudden fog had overtaken it. The answers to those questions no longer mattered. Nothing mattered, except for the sweet escape of peace and relaxation that embraced him. And soon, Gabriel was asleep.

Chapter One Hundred Four
The Storm Begins

Washington, D.C.
The Day The Sky Opened

"Gabriel, wake up," Lisa's distant voice said. "Gabriel, we're here."

Gabriel felt her tapping his shoulder, gently at first, then more aggressively as she prodded him awake. He opened his eyes and saw the familiar interior of Flight 4965. Seatbelts were clicking all around, and passengers were rising, collecting their bags from overhead bins and lining the plane's aisles. A soft, blue glow filtered through the plane's windows as dawn prepared itself on the horizon. Gabriel checked his watch. It was six thirty. The plane had landed right on time, and now he and Lisa had one hour to freshen up before their connecting flight back to New York.

"Have I been out this whole time?"

Lisa laughed. "Thankfully. I checked your pulse a couple of times to make sure you were still with me. Whatever that stewardess gave you, it did the trick."

Gabriel looked behind him and spotted the stewardess in question, who gave him a friendly wave followed by a questioning thumbs-up. Gabriel returned the thumbs-up with a grateful nod. Then he swung his eyes forward, to the empty seat he recalled bothering him as he passed out. It was still empty, and no one around it seemed concerned, so Gabriel brushed off his worries as paranoia and prepared to exit the plane.

"Good morning, ladies and gentlemen," their pilot's voice said over the intercom. *"We'll be opening the doors shortly. I've been asked to inform you that there will be an enhanced police presence*

when you exit the plane. Rest assured, there is no cause for alarm. Unless you're asked otherwise, proceed past them and on to your destination. Thank you."

Lisa shot Gabriel a quizzical look. "General Javez?"

"Maybe so," he replied.

The two waited patiently as passengers ahead of them unloaded. Then they followed the line out of the plane's primary hatch, through the jetway, and into the awaiting airport terminal. It was there that they realized *enhanced police presence* was an understatement. Ten uniformed men, five on each side of the jetway door, stood with sheets of photographs in one hand and their other resting on the grips of their pistols. Beyond them, additional patrolmen, some with K-9 assistants, paced the terminal floor.

Passengers were apprehensive as they filed past the rows of armed officers. They, like Gabriel and Lisa, kept their heads down and continued on their way, unsure what to make of the unexpected arrival party. Gabriel even wondered whether this actually had anything to do with them, or whether the airport had received warning of some other threat during their flight. But then an officer at the end of the right row held up a hand to stop him. The officer checked his photograph sheet, eyeing both Gabriel and Lisa, then spoke.

"Mr. and Mrs. Dunne, please follow me."

There was no point in arguing. The officer led them past the remaining patrols and down the main terminal walkway. He stopped outside a nondescript door being guarded not by a policeman, but by someone who was clearly military. After a brief exchange with the military man, the officer opened the door and ushered Gabriel and Lisa inside. The hallway beyond was dim and lined with uniformed soldiers carrying assault rifles. At the end of the hallway was a makeshift security room, where additional soldiers stood at attention while someone of authority spoke in hushed tones with a second individual whose black slacks and white button down made him look out of his league.

"General Javez," the escorting officer addressed. "I have the Dunnes. There's still no sign of Porter Cannes. The plane is nearly empty."

"Thank you," the man of authority said. He interrupted his conversation with the other civilian in the room and turned his full attention to Gabriel and Lisa. "Mr. and Mrs. Dunne, I am General Francisco Javez. I'm under the impression you already know why I'm here?"

"Yes," Gabriel said.

"Good." General Javez paced around a conference table in the center of the room. Upon it stood a laptop connected to some sort of specialized antenna. General Javez glanced at the screen, which was facing away from Gabriel, as he passed. "We were worried you wouldn't make it. Seven and a half hours off the grid while trapped with a dangerous madman is a risky move."

Gabriel didn't understand. "What are you talking about?"

The general stopped pacing. "You don't know? We assumed that's why you picked Flight 4965."

"Why we picked..." Lisa shook her head. "I'm afraid we're in the dark here, General."

General Javez spun the laptop to face them. On the screen was a black and white still frame taken from a security camera. It showed Porter passing through a jetway door.

"When was this taken?" Gabriel asked.

"Seven and a half hours ago," the general said, his demeanor turning deadly serious. "In Lisbon."

"No..." Lisa muttered.

"That's right, Mrs. Dunne. Porter Cannes was on your flight."

"But we would have seen him."

"The empty seat," Gabriel said, now realizing why it had bothered him so much. "He was in the empty seat." Gabriel had seen Porter, not from the front where he would recognize him, but from the back, another silhouette among the many strange silhouettes before him on that plane. He pictured it again in his mind, and he knew... "I can't believe I didn't consider it."

Lisa rubbed his arm. "You were exhausted."

"You said his seat was empty?" General Javez asked.

"Yes," Gabriel replied. "For almost the entire flight."

"That suggests he spotted you. And instead of risking you seeing him, he hid." The general looked away, as if troubled by a thought. "It makes me curious, though, why he didn't just kill you up there. He must have had the opportunity."

"He already had us killed," Lisa said. When the general frowned at what he must have assumed was a fancy metaphor, she added, "literally. When he spotted us alive on the plane, he probably panicked. He wouldn't know if he was going crazy or if we were really there. And if we were really there, he probably figured there was something supernatural at play."

"Which means killing us would have required him using the pendant," Gabriel surmised.

"And that would have sent him into stasis, which now, knowing he's back on someone's radar, he would want to avoid at all costs."

General Javez's eyes swung back and forth between Gabriel and Lisa. "I feel like I haven't been fully briefed on what's happening here."

"There's no time for that now, General," Gabriel said. "We have to catch our next flight and get back to New York. If Porter landed with us, the clock is ticking."

A soldier popped his head into the room. "General, the plane's been emptied and searched. There's still no sign of Porter Cannes. But someone prematurely triggered the baggage compartment door from the inside shortly after the plane stopped. We found two unconscious baggage handlers at ground level."

A cell phone rang, and the other civilian in the room answered. He listened for nearly a minute, acknowledging whomever had called him with the occasional *uh-huh*, then hung up and looked at General Javez. "That was air traffic control for the Jet Center. A private charter plane just took off a few minutes ahead of schedule. It's headed northeast."

"Destination?"

"Its flight plan says Scranton, Pennsylvania." The civilian took a noticeable gulp. "But its trajectory puts it on track for Philadelphia."

"Or New York," Gabriel said, mentally extending that trajectory past Philly.

General Javez thought for a moment. "We don't know that for certain."

"Yes, we do," Lisa said.

Gabriel backed her. "General, you may not believe everything we've told you just now, but if you're going to believe one thing, make it this: that plane is carrying Porter Cannes. He's on his way home."

Chapter One Hundred Five
Race Against Time

Flight 4833: IAD to LGA
The Day The Sky Opened

General Javez agreed to treat the wayward jet as their primary threat until they could confirm otherwise. He informed Gabriel and Lisa that the skies would remain open for now, but he couldn't guarantee they'd stay that way, for the moment the public learned they'd blasted a plane out of the sky, the Federal Aviation Administration would put all airports on lockdown. Gabriel asked the general to ensure that any planes in mid-flight were grounded instead of left to circle aimlessly, and he promised to do what he could. Then Gabriel and Lisa ran to catch their connection to New York.

They were once again cut off from active communication with the outside world, but this flight had seatback screens receiving live cable television, so they were able to monitor the news as they watched the ninety minutes it would take to reach LaGuardia slowly tick away. For the first half of the flight, the news was business as usual, covering that day's human interest stories, any tragedies from the night before, and local weather and traffic. But then, with forty-five minutes still to go, a reporter cut in on one station with a rumored report of a private jet out of Washington, D.C., now missing from radar and last spotted near Trenton, New Jersey. The reporter didn't have any more details at this time, but promised to return once he had learned more.

Gabriel tapped nervously, waiting for the moment their pilot would inform them that the FAA had enacted precautionary measures and frozen all scheduled flights. He flipped from one channel to another, but no one was covering the missing plane. It wasn't until fifteen minutes later that the original reporter popped back in with an update. This time, the details had expanded. An anonymous source out of Dulles air traffic control had supposedly told the reporter the plane was believed to have been hijacked. Government officials wouldn't substantiate the claim, but photos and videos of the enhanced police presence in Dulles International Airport were circulating social media, adding fuel to the fire.

"We won't make it," Gabriel said.

"We just need thirty more minutes," Lisa replied hopefully.

Coverage of the missing jet spread to all other news channels. It became the story of the moment, worthy of the advertising dollars spent to fill time between reports. Another ten minutes passed, then the media caught wind of military aircraft launching from airfields in New Jersey and New York. The government continued to refrain from comment and simply assured the public that they were monitoring the situation closely and didn't want anyone to panic. A local feed from Hoboken, New Jersey, showed that's exactly what was happening as concerned residents began clogging the already backed-up roads to put distance between themselves and any potential threat.

Fifteen minutes left, Gabriel thought as he checked the time.

Lisa gripped his hand tightly, still holding out hope. Gabriel saw breaking news banners pop up on nearly every screen in the plane. Reporters from every network were now claiming the missing jet had been spotted. It had been on track for Manhattan, but Air Force fighters had used warning fire to divert it off-course. The jet was currently over Union City, New Jersey, running parallel to Manhattan island. It wasn't responding to requests for contact.

The speaker above Gabriel's head buzzed as their pilot opened the intercom. *"Ladies and gentlemen, as you're already aware, there's a safety issue in the skies near New York. The FAA has ordered the immediate grounding of all aircraft along the east coast."*

Gabriel held his breath.

"Luckily for you," the pilot continued, *"LaGuardia is our closest airport. Please buckle your seatbelts immediately. We'll be landing shortly."*

Gabriel released his breath with a relieved shudder. Lisa smiled and kissed his cheek. They were on the ground ten minutes later, having safely landed at LaGuardia. The plane pulled to an empty terminal jetway, and the pilot ordered its passengers to disembark in a hasty, but orderly, fashion. Gabriel and Lisa followed the steadily moving flow of passengers down the airplane aisle, then broke into a run as soon as they had space to spread out in the jetway. They raced into the terminal, oriented themselves, then ran toward the exit.

Every television in the airport was consumed by coverage of the wayward jet. Suddenly, all screens filled with a zoomed-in ball of fire as the jet was struck by a missile. Gabriel and Lisa froze to watch its metal carcass drop out of the sky. The reporter on their current screen was ecstatic, barely able to control his babble, but Gabriel heard him say something about Manhattan's Upper West Side. Apparently, the jet had curved back in to take another shot at the city, and that was pushing its limits too far.

"Come on!" Gabriel yelled, pulling Lisa toward the exit.

Just before hitting the streets, they saw images of Phoenix choppers hovering over the city. Then they saw one channel that had a camera at the jet's wreckage site. It looked like a scene no one could survive, yet a moment later, a sheet of metal shot out of the wreckage, and behind it, Porter stepped from the flames like a demon emerging from Hell. Gabriel heard gunfire from television speakers as he and Lisa passed through LaGuardia's exit doors. People outside the airport were following the news on their phones, from which Gabriel heard screams and explosions.

"That dude just jumped onto the side of a building like Spider-Man!" One man exclaimed.

More explosions, along with gasps from the residents and tourists watching their cell phone streams in disbelief. Gabriel fished his walkie-talkie out of his pocket and switched it on.

"Samantha, Nate, are either of you there?" He asked.

"I'm here," Nate responded. *"Welcome home! Not a moment too soon, by the way."*

"We're at LaGuardia," Gabriel said, cutting through the chitchat. "We need to get back into the city. Any advice?"

"Avoid the main roads," Nate told him. *"It's chaos out there. The subways are still running, but probably not for long. Get moving while I assess the situation. I'll report back shortly."*

"Roger that," Gabriel said as he lowered the walkie-talkie.

"The Astoria-Ditmars subway platform is a ten-minute drive from here," Lisa said. "We can take neighborhood streets to avoid traffic jams."

Gabriel nodded and looked for an available taxi. There were none, but there was one yellow cab pulling away with its *off duty* lights lit. Gabriel jumped in front of it, drawing a string of choice phrases from its driver.

"How'd you like to make a quick thousand bucks?" Gabriel hollered back at the man.

He rolled down his window. "What?"

"A thousand bucks for a ten-minute ride. What do you say?"

In true New York fashion, the driver didn't hesitate. "Get in."

Chapter One Hundred Six
Back To The Beginning

New York, New York
The Day The Sky Opened

"Snap out of it!" Lisa shouted.

Gabriel broke free of his trance. The city was growing darker by the second, the gashes in the sky blotting out the sun, the sea of blood-red clouds and stars within floating and sparkling overhead like something out of a science fiction movie. The air had already grown colder, and the tornado-like winds whipping through the streets carried an iciness that cut to Gabriel's bone. Just ahead, the two Phoenix choppers aligned themselves with Cannes Tower. They launched a barrage of missiles at the roof, where Porter's machine was already pumping energy into the pendant. The missiles exploded short of their target, and for the briefest second, Gabriel saw the otherwise invisible barrier that had blocked them illuminate with electricity.

"He's using a sonic fence to protect the machine!" Gabriel yelled over the noise of nature spinning out of control. "Just like we have around the manor!"

"We're going to need to shut it down!" Lisa replied.

The Phoenix choppers disengaged as Gabriel and Lisa raced for the front entrance of Cannes Tower. The few employees that had remained inside were now fleeing for their lives, apparently finally realizing that their employer was objectively insane. Gabriel and Lisa pushed through the front doors and entered the abandoned lobby.

"Nate?" Gabriel said into his walkie-talkie. "It's time."

"You've got it, boss." He went quiet for almost two minutes, then came back on, his voice more elated than Gabriel had heard it since

their pendant mission first began. *"We're in! The transmitter's live, and I've got control over Porter's security system! Time for Troy to fall!"* He paused, then reluctantly added, *"if you can do it in the next six to ten minutes, that is."*

"Don't worry Nate, it looks like Porter's help has abandoned him. I think we've all the time we need."

Samantha cut in. *"You might want to look out a window and reconsider that."*

Gabriel lowered his walkie-talkie and looked out the glass front of Cannes Tower. A bright streak of light fell from overhead and landed on the street, scorching its way through the top layer of concrete and into the earth below.

"What the hell?"

Another streak fell, leaving behind a smoke trail as if it were a miniature meteor. Then two more followed.

"Stardust," Lisa said, her voice breathless. "The sky is literally falling."

"Nate," Gabriel said into his walkie-talkie, his nerves beginning to frazzle, "get us up to the eighty-third floor... right now."

"You know that's nowhere close to the roof, right?" Nate questioned.

"Yes, but I also know how Porter thinks. Everything tied to the pendant will be concentrated on that one floor, including access to his machine."

There was a pause, then Nate returned with, *"the unmarked door!"*

"You got it."

Nate remotely summoned the central elevator and overrode its security card scanner. He ensured its environmental systems were still active, then commanded the elevator to take Gabriel and Lisa to the eighty-third floor. Despite the terror of their current predicament, Gabriel found the *bong* of the elevator as it released them to their destination just as ear-pleasing as the first time he had heard it. He and Lisa waited in the eighty-third floor entry corridor as Nate overrode the security on the airlock that guarded the Old World changing room.

"We'll need containment suits," Lisa told Gabriel as they proceeded past the benches and lockers that awaited them there.

"Let's just contaminate the damn place," Gabriel said as he proceeded directly to the next airlock.

"You're forgetting about the disinfecting chamber."

Gabriel paused. *Oh yeah, he might want a contamination suit for that.*

Their team members' names had been unceremoniously removed from their original lockers. Nonetheless, Gabriel flung them open, only to discover they were empty. Lisa checked the rest of the lockers on that side of the room while Gabriel rummaged through the other side. Nothing. There wasn't a single contamination suit to be found.

"Nate," Gabriel said into his walkie-talkie, "open the next airlock."

"*But you-*"

"Do it, Nate," Lisa ordered, grabbing the communication device.

She and Gabriel were on the same page. They didn't have time to hunt down contamination suits. Gabriel couldn't remember how long the poisonous gases lingered in the disinfecting chamber before its ventilation system kicked in, but they were going to have to hold their breath for however long it took. If they couldn't... well, at least they wouldn't be missing much of whatever life they would have had left otherwise.

The airlock door hissed as it slid into the ceiling. Gabriel and Lisa stepped into the sterile disinfecting chamber. As soon as the airlock closed behind them, they each took a deep breath. Gases spewed from the steel tubes overhead. Gabriel recalled them blocking his vision on his first pass through, but they were taking their sweet time getting to that point now. He felt pressure in his lungs, and a nagging urge to take a breath. He told himself breathing meant death, but that went against his bodily instincts, and his inherent reflexes wouldn't believe it. They pressured him even more, creating an ache in his chest and demanding that his respiratory system respond.

The gasses clouded Gabriel's vision, and just when he thought he couldn't hold out any longer, he heard the ventilation system kick in. Its sound was enough encouragement to withstand his body's cravings for just a few more seconds. The air cleared enough for Gabriel to see Lisa's strained red cheeks. He held up a firm finger, signaling for her to hold on, and then an affirmative buzzed echoed through the chamber. Gabriel and Lisa dropped, gasping for oxygen as Nate overrode the next airlock. When they recovered, Gabriel and Lisa stood, then, hand-in hand, proceeded into the Old World, where this entire mess had first begun.

Chapter One Hundred Seven
Whatever It Takes

New York, New York
The Day The Sky Opened

Gabriel gazed at the ancient scrolls on display in high-tech examination rooms as he and Lisa marched down the abandoned eighty-third floor hallway. He recalled Porter telling him they had been arranged in chronological order, with the oldest scrolls near the entrance and the Moroccan scroll that had served as the backbone of Porter's quest at the far end. That felt like an eternity ago, and things had changed so much since then. Now Gabriel and Lisa were literally walking through history, record after record of the good the Pendant of God had brought to the world. Porter had corrupted that good, and it was only fitting that as they bounded toward present day, they bounded toward their final confrontation with him as well.

"Nate, can you hear me?" Gabriel asked into his walkie-talkie.

"Yeah, boss," Nate replied, his voice a staticky mess.

"Have you figured out how to disable Porter's sonic fence yet?"

"No. Unfortunately, it doesn't appear on his security grid. I bet the paranoid bastard hard-wired it into his machine's power supply."

"Meaning?"

"Meaning I can't do anything about it," Nate said. *"You're going to have to deal with that yourself."*

Gabriel winced. It was just one more thing on his already overcrowded plate. Somehow, he needed to shut down the sonic fence, remove the pendant from Porter's machine- which he was certain would have failsafes to prevent him from doing so- destroy the machine, and figure out what to do about Porter *and* the pendant before the U.S. military made that decision for him. "Okay, just work on the door."

Lisa pointed to an upcoming hallway intersection. She guided Gabriel down the right-hand path, which was a short stretch to the side of the room, where a featureless steel door sat embedded in the wall. Its only obvious method of interaction was a neighboring touchscreen, on which lines of code were currently racing by.

"Almost there," Nate said. The code halted, and the door clicked. *"You're clear."*

Gabriel watched the door slide into the wall, revealing a claustrophobic shaft with a metal staircase behind it. Freezing wind and a blood-red glow filtered down from over seventeen floors above.

"It leads directly to the roof," Gabriel said. "This is it."

Lisa nodded and stepped forward, but Gabriel held her back. They couldn't just rush up there with no weapons and no plan. All Porter had to do was wait them out until his destruction was complete. Gabriel needed a wildcard, something to level the playing field. He retreated down the short hallway to where it intersected with the central aisle, then looked at the scrolls hanging nearby, and the multitude of cutting-edge technology that had been used to analyze them. He had hoped to find something he could both conceal and use as a weapon if needed, but everything in the nearby rooms was fairly benign. Of course they were. There was too much historical importance here to risk a rogue instrument wreaking havoc on any of it. Then again...

Gabriel recalled one of Nate's rants during their first trip to the Old World: *What a conceded jackass! He'd blow up all this history, destroy any evidence about the pendant's existence, just because he didn't get his way?* Nate had been referring to the fact that near the entrance to the Old World was an unassuming cylinder Samantha later identified as a thermobaric bomb. Even now, Gabriel could see the blue glow of its top ring reflecting off the far laboratory wall.

"Samantha?" He said into his walkie-talkie. "That thermobaric bomb... any chance Porter would have networked that thing?"

Samantha's voice came back with just as much interference as Nate's. *"Probably. Porter would've wanted the ability to detonate it remotely if the need arose."*

"Nate, do you think you can hack it?"

There was a pause, then Nate replied, *"if I could identify it. All that alien shit in that room is coded with generic labels. I can power each of them down, one at a time, until one of you sees the bomb go dark. Then I'll know I have it."*

Gabriel looked at Lisa. "Did you hear that?"

She nodded.

"I need you to stay here to help Nate locate the bomb on the network. Once he does, get the hell out of this building."

"You can't seriously be thinking of detonating that thing," Lisa said.

"I'm going to do whatever it takes."

He could tell she wanted to argue, but she was smart enough to know this needed to be done. Lisa grabbed her own walkie-talkie and proceeded back to the Old World entrance. "Okay, Nate. I'm heading to the bomb now. Start power cycling."

"Yes, ma'am."

"Hey, Nate," Gabriel then said, "if I give the word, you blow the bomb. No hesitation, no questions asked. Got it?"

There was a delay, then Nate responded, an uncharacteristic seriousness about him. *"I've got it, boss."*

Gabriel heard helicopter blades approaching the building. "Samantha, is that you?"

"Yeah," she said. *"We're here. I don't know what you plan to do on that roof, but you've got air support if you need it. There's a switch on the side of your walkie-talkie that says 'auto voice detection.' Flip it and we'll be able to listen to everything happening down there."*

Gabriel flipped the switch, then tested the detection feature to ensure it was working. He looked across the floor at Lisa, who was now standing next to a device Gabriel had once thought was the scariest thing he could imagine, but which now seemed so insignificant compared to what was happening outside. Lisa looked up, worry in her eyes, and mouthed the words *be careful*. Gabriel mouthed back *I will*, then blew his wife a kiss and began his climb toward the impending apocalypse.

Chapter One Hundred Eight
Man Versus God

New York, New York
The Day The Sky Opened

Gabriel could barely comprehend the hellscape that awaited him on the roof of Cannes Tower. The gashes in the sky had fully overtaken the normal shades of blue and gray that served as Earth's trademark color palette. Stardust was now falling all around, and nearby buildings were ablaze from their impact. Clouds of ash swept through the air on gusts so cold they could have blown down directly from space itself. And inside the sea of blood-red clouds and stars above, a thunderstorm of unimaginable proportions had begun, putting on a spectacle of lighting blasts that raised the hair on Gabriel's skin with each discharge. This wasn't Heaven. If anything, Porter was raining down Hell on Earth, and despite what Damien had told him, Gabriel was way out of his depths to do anything about it.

He shook his head, clearing the negative thought. He *could* do something about it. He just needed to focus on the task at hand. Gabriel drew his gaze down to the rooftop, where Porter's machine hummed and vibrated with intense energy. It looked just as the blueprints had described: a centralized claw the size of a car, facing upwards, atop layered platforms almost as big as the roof of Cannes Tower itself. In the claw's grip was the Pendant of God, glowing so brightly Gabriel could only glance at it before looking away. And at the opposite end of the roof, watching with glee, was Porter. Gabriel took a series of nervous breaths, clenched his fists, and walked toward his former friend.

"So that was you," Porter called out as Gabriel approached. "On the plane. I told myself I must have been hallucinating... some side effect from using the pendant. But I couldn't take any chances." Porter was panting heavily, the toll of invoking the pendant's power to reach Cannes Tower weighing on him. "You shouldn't have come back, Gabriel. There's nothing more you can do."

"Porter, I know what you want," Gabriel said. "But this isn't it. Look around you. Does this look like Heaven? The power you're unleashing is tearing open the very fabric of space. You're going to destroy us all!"

"So be it," Porter said, his voice stoic. "I'd rather not exist than be at the mercy of a God whose views don't align with my own."

Gabriel shook his head in disbelief. "Do you hear yourself? Those are the words of a madman!"

"Call me what you want, Gabriel. It won't change anything." He turned to his machine. "As you see, I'm already well on my way to victory. I've taken every precaution. No one can stop what's happening but me. Not you, not dead old Damien, not the military... just me."

Barely recognizable as his inner ego consumed whatever good had once been within him, Porter had just confirmed what Gabriel had already suspected. The machine had failsafes and only Porter could override them, which he wasn't willing to do. Gabriel would soon have the thermobaric bomb at his disposal, but he couldn't use it until the pendant was clear of the machine's charge. Otherwise, he'd risk breaking the pendant and his effort would be for nothing. He had to persuade Porter to separate the two...

"Fine," Gabriel said. "You're on your way to victory, but you're not there yet. And you know what else?"

Porter raised his brow curiously.

"You're still mortal."

Gabriel rushed forward, tackling Porter head-on. Without the pendant's power, and drained from previously using it, the tech entrepreneur crumpled under Gabriel's weight. He barely put up a resistance as Gabriel placed both hands around Porter's neck and squeezed as hard as he could.

"You'd rather not exist than be at God's mercy?" Gabriel asked. "I won't let that happen. I'll send you to God before your machine finishes the job. Your soul will exist in perpetual misery for the rest of time."

Veins protruded from Porter's forehead as his face turned blue. He tried to pry off Gabriel's hands, but didn't have enough strength left. Gabriel continued to squeeze, his conscience screaming at him to stop, telling him that this wasn't the way. He hadn't tackled Porter intending to kill his former friend, but he was about to do just that, his anger and fear taking hold over his actions, leading him down a dark road he would have normally avoided.

"Killing me-" Porter choked. "Killing me... won't do you any good."

Gabriel eased up. Porter was right. Killing him might seal his fate with God, but it would do nothing to save the rest of the world. The machine would continue pumping power into the pendant, the gash overhead would continue to grow, and eventually the Earth, and then the universe itself, would be torn to shreds. Gabriel released Porter's neck and stood back, giving his former friend room to recover. Meanwhile, his brain was spinning. Those words Porter had spoken... they sounded so familiar. Where had Gabriel heard them before?

Porter pushed himself to his knees, then slowly returned to his feet. He looked weak, like he might pass out at any moment, but just like when his cancer had come for him, he stood in unfathomable defiance. Gabriel stared pitifully at his former friend, and doing so triggered an odd memory: *it's not real archaeology*. Strange... that's what Porter used to tell him and Lisa when they held their Indiana Jones marathons. Gabriel pondered over the memory. Indiana Jones...

He suddenly realized why Porter's words had triggered him. They were similar to the words Indiana Jones had spoken to Walter Donovan when held at gunpoint to retrieve the Holy Grail. Shooting Indiana wouldn't help Donovan, because only Indiana could successfully complete the grail challenges. Gabriel remembered Donovan's solution, and it sparked an idea. He held his walkie-talkie high to ensure the rest of the team could hear him, confident that Samantha would understand the reference, then quoted:

"You know something, Dr. Jones? You're absolutely right."

Porter's face dropped as he processed Gabriel's words. Before he could move, a sniper shot cracked through the sky overhead, and a single round planted itself in Porter's gut. He doubled over, his mouth gaping with pain as blood poured from his wound.

"It's your choice, Porter," Gabriel said. "Bleed out and spend an eternity with a God you never believed in and want nothing to do with…" He motioned to the machine. "…or heal yourself. The pendant is right there, after all."

Porter glared at him, hatred beaming from bloodshot eyes. For a moment, Gabriel thought he might let himself die out of spite. But then Porter's desire for immortality got the better of him. He pulled out a handheld tablet no larger than an oversized cell phone and entered a long passcode on its digital keyboard. Gabriel heard something powering down and saw a brief flash as the sonic fence disengaged. Porter pulled himself across the sonic threshold and up the stairs that led to the machine's claw. His gut still oozing bodily fluids, he crawled to one of the claw's fingers and entered another passcode on a small touchscreen embedded in its side. He stopped short of tapping the final character of the passcode, scanned for Samantha's helicopter, then repositioned himself to obscure her line of sight. Then he made his move.

Porter disengaged the claw and caught the pendant in mid-air as its fingertips spread. Samantha opened fire on him with her sniper rifle, but it was too late. Porter was in possession of the pendant, and it protected him from her second attack. Not only that, but it had already healed his gut wound. Gabriel saw their opportunity slipping away.

"Samantha, the pendant!"

Another sniper shot cracked through the air as a bullet slammed into the upper edge of the pendant. The impact had enough force behind it to knock the artifact from Porter's grip. It flew across the rooftop, clearing his machine, and skidded to a halt on the gravel surface. Gabriel and Porter exchanged competitive glances, then both took off at full speed on a collision course with the pendant and each other.

"Lisa!" Gabriel shouted as he ran. "Are you clear?"

"*Yes!*"

"Nate!" He then yelled. "Get ready!"

Against all probability, Porter was closing in just as fast as him. Gabriel pushed himself to run harder than he had ever run before.

Then, with the pendant only a few feet away, he dove with an outstretched hand. He felt his fingers scraping across gravel, felt the pendant's chain catch between them, then felt its metallic surface slide into his palm.

"Now!"

Porter's weight landed on top of Gabriel. "It's not going to be that easy."

He got his own hand on the free edge of the pendant just as the thermobaric bomb detonated beneath them. Its blast incinerated the Old World, tore downward through several floors beneath, and erupted upward, engulfing the roof of Cannes Tower and obliterating everything on it. Protected from death by the pendant's power, Gabriel's and Porter's charred bodies were nonetheless blown from the roof as it exploded. With each of their lives dependent on their shared grasp of the mystical artifact, they plummeted in a free fall toward the ground below.

Chapter One Hundred Nine
Nature's Course

New York, New York
The Day The Sky Opened

The world was dark. Beneath Gabriel's cheek was the cold, rough surface of concrete. Above him was an immense pressure, something that had caved in on top of him and was actively attempting to crush his body. Opening one eye and straining his neck as far as it would turn, Gabriel saw the slab of concrete and steel that rested on his back. It had him pinned, with only one arm free, wedged through a gap in his enclosure, where it was exposed to the freezing vortex that still swirled through New York's streets. Gabriel felt the metal curve of the Pendant of God in his free hand and breathed a sigh of relief. More importantly, he didn't feel the tug of Porter's hand competing for its possession.

Gabriel blinked, shaking his mind free of the haze that had temporarily suffocated it. He remembered the explosion as Nate detonated the thermobaric bomb. He also remembered simultaneously willing a protective shield around the pendant, uncertain whether it would survive the blast without its own layer of godly armor. Then he remembered being blinded by intense light and seared by unfathomable heat. It had been an odd sensation, feeling his skin burn to a crisp, enduring the crunch of his shattering bones as the concussive force of the explosion passed through him, and yet experiencing no pain. Gabriel remembered he and Porter hurtling through the air, slamming into the ground, and the impact breaking Porter's clutch on the pendant. He had seen his former friend's body bounce several feet before debris rained down on the two of them, placing Gabriel in his current predicament.

Now, summoning the pendant's power, Gabriel flexed his upper back and heaved, lifting the concrete and steel slab until it slid off to one side, freeing him. He then stood upright and looked at the mystical artifact in his palm. It was tarnished, most likely from Porter's machine, and a small dent marked the spot where Samantha's sniper round had jolted it loose from Porter's hand. But otherwise, it appeared intact. Gabriel's will for a protective shield had thankfully done its job, preventing the pendant from breaking and keeping its power contained within.

So much destruction over something so small...

A yellow glow reflected off the pendant's surface. For a moment, Gabriel thought he'd relaxed too soon. Perhaps he had been too late protecting the pendant from the bomb. Or maybe he had somehow released more energy from the pendant than what he needed to free himself of his concrete prison. But then Gabriel realized the glow wasn't emanating from the pendant itself. It was coming from the sky, where a small gap had opened in the otherworldly field of stars, allowing a single ray of sunshine through. A second gap appeared near the first, then several others. With the pendant no longer amplified by Porter's machine, the tears in Earth's sky were shrinking... healing, just like a medicated flesh wound.

"Gabriel!" Lisa yelled.

He turned to see her only fifty feet away. Elation filled her face as she sprinted forward, jumping over scorched earth and fallen debris, until she landed in Gabriel's open arms. The two held each other tightly as stardust stopped falling, the hurricane-strength winds weakened, and the rips in the sky continued their recession, multiple streams of sunlight now dotting the ground below.

"We did it," Lisa said.

Debris rustled to the side of them, catching their attention. A hunched figure rose slowly from the ash, shaking off layers of dust and gravel that had amassed on top of him. Defensively, Gabriel shifted his grip to the pendant's chain and swung it over his head. Then he stood between the figure and Lisa, ready for its impending attack.

"You can stand down, Gabriel," Porter said, his vocal cords strained and weak. "I'm done fighting."

He pushed his way through the piles of debris that separated him from Gabriel and Lisa. His muscle control was unsteady, his balance off-kilter. When Porter reached a clearing, he dropped onto his buttocks, gasping for air. It was clear he would go no farther. That's when Gabriel saw the dark red blood on Porter's hands, and the broken rod of rebar lodged in his side.

"It didn't have to be this way," Gabriel said. "You could have played it straight. Damien might have healed you. You could have continued living."

"What can I say? I guess I... chose poorly." Porter laughed with self-pity before a jolt of pain turned his laughter into a contorted wince. When the pain passed, he saw that neither Gabriel nor Lisa had shared in his humor. "Oh, come on. Don't tell me you don't get the reference."

Of course, Gabriel got the reference. It was from Indiana Jones and the Last Crusade, when Walter Donovan got his comeuppance after forcing Indiana to lead him to the grail room. He just didn't think there was anything funny about the current situation. Porter's eyes shifted to the sky, where Samantha and Nate's helicopter hovered overhead.

"Is Nate up there?" He asked.

Gabriel nodded.

"Can I speak with him?"

Gabriel's walkie-talkie had been incinerated along with the upper portion of Cannes Tower, so he looked at Lisa, who begrudgingly offered hers to Porter. Porter took a deep breath- perhaps in need of air, or perhaps building up his nerve- then opened the line.

"Hey Nate? By now, you must know the truth about that engineering competition we were in as kids." Porter sighed. "Oh, who am I kidding? You've always known the truth. You're the one person who had me pegged from day one. For what it's worth, I'm sorry. I'm sorry I cheated. I'm sorry I lied about this mission. I'm sorry I... killed you. If I could take it all back, I would. But it's a little too late for that."

Porter closed the line and waited for a reply.

"Hey, Porter?" Nate said after only a moment's hesitation. *"Fuck you."*

Porter scoffed. "I suppose I deserved that." He passed the walkie-talkie back to Lisa, then looked at Gabriel with apologetic eyes. "You guys had better get out of here. The military will be back soon now that the sky is clearing." He pointed at the pendant around Gabriel's neck. "They'll want that."

Heeding his warning, Lisa stepped away to radio Samantha and Nate to descend and pick them up. Confident he wasn't a threat in his current condition, Gabriel kneeled down next to Porter.

"Did you mean it?" He asked. "What you told Nate?"

"About being sorry?" Porter asked.

"No. About taking it back."

Porter nodded weakly.

Gabriel lowered his gaze to Porter's rebar wound. "If you die now, your path is set. There is no happy ending for you."

Porter's eyes were growing heavy. "Yeah, I know."

Gabriel shifted his gaze to the pendant as he recalled his own experience at the starting line to eternity. "Damien told me that God's greatest gift to humanity was the free will to choose one's path. If you had more time... not in your cushy life or with your technology empire, and most like behind bars... but if you had more, would you choose a different path?"

Using what appeared to be every ounce of energy he had left, Porter said, "absolutely."

And then he fell unconscious. Behind Gabriel, Samantha and Nate's helicopter was touching down. Lisa tugged his arm.

"Let's go."

But Gabriel resisted. He stared at his fallen friend, saddened by the trajectory his life had taken, and debating whether Porter deserved one last chance to do the right thing. Damien had risked his life to give Porter that opportunity. Was it beyond Gabriel to do the same?

"Gabriel," Lisa insisted, "we need to go now."

Gabriel had to know. Had Porter's brush with godliness and subsequent implosion finally changed him for the better? Could he serve humanity for good, atoning for the terrible mistakes of his past? Could-

"Gabriel?" Lisa asked.

"He deserves a chance," Gabriel whispered.

He held his open hand toward Porter's wound, then willed the pendant to work its magic.

Lisa's eyes went wide. "What are you doing?"

Gabriel ignored her and concentrated. He felt the pendant's energy surging within him, felt its healing ability extend into his fingertips, and felt it release toward Porter. The broken rebar was expelled from Porter's body as his muscles and organs stitched themselves back together. His flesh sealed shut, his blood cells multiplied, replenishing what had been lost, and within seconds, consciousness returned. Porter looked down at his freshly repaired body, then looked at Gabriel with astonishment.

"You-"

"I'm giving you a chance," Gabriel said. "*One* chance, to pick the right path this time. Please don't waste it."

Porter smiled, then Gabriel stood and turned to Lisa, whose expression spoke volumes about her disagreement with what he'd just done. He gave her a look that said *trust me* and proceeded to their waiting helicopter. Behind him, Gabriel's pendant-enhanced senses could hear Porter rising. He detected his former friend following and picking up speed. He heard Porter whistle in a uniquely stuttered pattern that no normal person would use. And then he felt the high-tech fastener Porter had secured around the pendant's broken chain release itself. Gabriel's sense enhancements ceased immediately as the pendant fell from his neck, toward the ground, where Porter's readied hand swooped in to intercept it...

Then Porter broke into a debilitating coughing fit. He missed the pendant, which bounced against the concrete with a clank, landing near Lisa's shoe. She picked it up and secured it in her pocket. Gabriel faced his former friend, who was staring at a wad of bloody flesh on the pavement before him.

"What did you do?" Porter demanded.

"Exactly what I said," Gabriel replied. "I gave you one chance. I healed your body, but returned the cancerous mass to your lungs. It would have remained dormant as long as you walked the proper path, but the moment you deviated, it awoke to finish its job."

Porter was shivering with rage. "You've murdered me..."

"No," Gabriel corrected. "I simply did what Damien told me I should have done all along." He frowned, genuinely unhappy it had turned out this way. "I let nature run its course."

Fuming, Porter lunged at him. But another coughing fit seized the tech entrepreneur's lungs, sending him flailing to the ground once more. This fit differed from the others, however. It never let go of its stranglehold on Porter. It sent his body into violent convulsions that tore muscle and broke bones. When it ended, it only did so because Porter's life had finally been extinguished.

"I'm sorry," Gabriel whispered over his still body.

Lisa wrapped her arms around him and gave a comforting squeeze. Gabriel felt warm tears streaking down his cheeks, but he didn't have long to mourn, for soon an all-too-familiar sound kicked them back into action. It was the thump of Phoenix chopper blades, and it was quickly getting closer. Gabriel spotted the pendant's chain poking out of Lisa's pocket.

"This isn't over yet."

Chapter One Hundred Ten
Closure

New York, New York
The Day The Sky Opened

"What are we going to do?" Lisa yelled as she and Gabriel reached their team's helicopter.

By the sound of it, the Phoenix choppers were closing in fast. Gabriel knew there was no way to outrun them. He also knew they wouldn't stop their pursuit until they'd recovered the pendant. He thought about hiding it, then playing dumb when asked where it was, but that ruse would only last so long. Gabriel was also pretty certain General Javez would have troops on the ground in a heartbeat to scour the area should the pendant mysteriously disappear.

"I don't know."

Nate leaned his head out of their chopper and pointed at the pendant, now back in Gabriel's hands. "You seem to be getting pretty good at using that thing. Why don't you just make those helicopters *have an accident*, if you know what I mean?"

"Stupid idea," Gabriel said. "But I'll take it under advisement."

Nate shrugged.

"He's not wrong," Lisa said. "It would buy us some time."

"But that's all it would do," Gabriel told her. "It would confirm we have the pendant in our possession and make us the military's top target. I'm not looking to spend the rest of my life on the run. Are you?"

Lisa didn't bother shaking her head.

Samantha chimed in over her walkie-talkie. *"Whatever you're going to do, do it now. You've got two minutes, tops, before they're all over us."*

Gabriel instinctually looked to the now blue sky to spot the approaching Phoenix choppers. He didn't see them, but he did see a few remaining blood-red gashes that were slowly shrinking into nonexistence. Gabriel looked at the pendant, then scanned for the nearest gash, which was still the size of a football field and located just south of them.

"I have an idea!"

Ten seconds later, their helicopter was carrying the entire team skyward, toward the southward gash, with Lisa holding Gabriel's feet as he leaned out the side and carefully removed a rocket from the helicopter's left launcher. Once he had a good grip on it, Lisa helped pull him in. Then Gabriel sat on the helicopter floor with the rocket in his lap.

"Here you go," Nate said, passing him a roll of silver duct tape.

Gabriel held the pendant against the side of the rocket and placed a temporary piece of tape to hold it in place. Then he did the same with its broken chain. He passed the tape to Lisa, suspended the rocket by its ends, and watched as she unspooled the tape round and round, wrapping and then rewrapping, as if securing linens around a mummified limb.

"Is it just me," Nate asked, "or does this feel sacrilege?"

"It would be sacrilege to let a military body have this kind of power," Gabriel replied.

Lisa exhausted the roll of tape, which had completely smothered the pendant and its chain, securing both to the rocket's side. Gabriel gave the silver bulge they created a hardy wiggle to ensure it wouldn't break free during launch, then returned to the side of the helicopter. With Lisa's help, he replaced the rocket in its launcher. Then he saw them: two Phoenix choppers, maybe a hundred, hundred-fifty yards away, on a path to intercept.

"Gabriel Dunne," a voice said over Samantha's cockpit radio. *"This is General Javez. We need you to land immediately. My men will escort you to a holding area to await my arrival."*

Samantha glanced over her shoulder. "Well?"

"Ignore him," Gabriel instructed. He climbed into the co-pilot's seat and looked out the cockpit window. The gash was just ahead, but now half of its original size. With a smaller border, it was shrinking rapidly. The helicopter slowed its ascent. "What are you doing?"

"It's not me," Samantha said. "There's resistance. It's like we're suddenly flying into a headwind."

Gabriel felt his hairs stand on end, static electricity filling the air. Within the gash, a lightning storm continued, powerful bolts shooting across the backdrop of red stars and clouds. Familiar, freezing air whipped downward, slowing the helicopter even more.

"How much farther can you push it?" Gabriel asked.

Samantha shook her head. "Not much."

"*Gabriel Dunne,*" General Javez's voice returned, "*this is a military order. Land your helicopter now, or we'll be forced to shoot you down.*"

"Don't respond," Gabriel told Samantha. "It's the only way we can claim ignorance once this is over." The helicopter shuddered violently. "Buckle up, back there!" Gabriel yelled to Lisa and Nate.

Samantha pressed toward the gash until the helicopter could no longer overcome its resistance. Warning lights flickered to life and alarms buzzed as the vehicle threatened to stall.

"This is it!" Samantha hollered. "I'm arming the launcher now!"

She flicked up a plastic red cover and flipped the switch underneath.

"*Gabriel Dunne, I know you can hear me.*" General Javez said over their radio. "*Our sensors are showing you just activated your missile guidance system. If you fire at my men-*"

Gabriel found the radio's volume dial and spun it all the way down. A stream of bullets whizzed across the cockpit window. It was warning fire, which meant the Phoenix choppers were within attack range. Trying his best to ignore that fact, Gabriel looked straight ahead, but the view was no more comforting. The gash- now the last remaining gash- was only fifty feet away, but it was down to the size of a small swimming pool.

"Samantha?"

"The targeting system's struggling," she said. "There's nothing for it to lock onto!"

A stream of bullets traced along the roof of the helicopter. That was warning number two, and Gabriel was pretty sure there wouldn't be a third. Ahead, the final gash was down to the size of a typical sedan.

"Samantha, you're going to have to do this manually!"

"Just give it another second..."

A bright light caught Gabriel's eye. Passing through the center of the gash was one last piece of stardust. He heard a steady tone as their aiming system locked on, saw Samantha slam a button, and felt a jolt as the rocket carrying the pendant tore out of its launcher. It left a thin smoke trail as it blasted across the sky, through the otherworldly opening, and smashed into the burning speck of stardust. The resulting explosion pulsed outward in the flash of an eye, like a sun going supernova. A fraction of it slipped through the gash as it sealed. The wave of energy dispersed as it entered Earth's atmosphere, but not before crippling all three helicopters in the area.

"Hang on!" Samantha yelled.

The nose of their of aircraft tipped downward. Then, with alarms blaring, it sped toward the ground below. Samantha tried to control the crash as much as she could, but the impact was still brutal, first knocking off the helicopter's landing gear, then sending it into a skid across the concrete until it smashed headfirst into the side of a building.

Chapter One Hundred Eleven
Blue Skies

New York, New York
The Day The Sky Opened

Gabriel opened his eyes. His head was pounding, his neck ached, and he was pretty sure his right arm was broken. But he was alive, and for that, he was grateful. A shower of sparks shot out of the busted cockpit panel before him. Somewhere in the distance, police and ambulance sirens wailed in unison. Gabriel could smell smoke, though he wasn't sure if it was from their helicopter or the burning buildings in the vicinity. He could also see sunlight through the cockpit's cracked side window. Bright, warm, victorious sunlight...

"Oh good," Samantha said, "he's awake."

She was standing outside the helicopter, blood seeping from a fresh wound in her forehead and her arms covered in scrapes and cuts. Beside her, Lisa was bent over Nate. She seemed to be all right, though the same couldn't be said for Gabriel's tech engineer, who had a glistening gash running from the top of his skull down the side of his neck. Lisa was nursing it with supplies from an emergency first-aid kit.

"I bet now you wish you'd kept the damn thing, huh?" Nate asked Gabriel with a smile.

Gabriel smiled back, then unbuckled himself and used his good arm to climb out of the helicopter. Aside from the structural damage that had already been done, the fires that still burned, and the eerie emptiness of its streets, the city was back to normal, with blue skies above signaling better times to come. Gabriel and his team had staved off a universal apocalypse, and though they were banged and bruised, they were walking away with their lives intact.

"We still need to get out of here," Samantha reminded them as the distant sirens drew closer. "I saw the Phoenix choppers as we went down. They couldn't have crashed more than ten or twelve blocks away. We have to assume the soldiers on board are headed this way."

"We should probably give the military some time to cool down before interacting with them," Lisa added.

"Agreed," Gabriel said. Then he looked around, something about their crash site striking him as vaguely familiar. They were nowhere near Cannes Tower- or what was left of it- but nonetheless, Gabriel felt as though he'd been here recently. He located the street sign posted at the nearest corner. "Thirteen and Third..." he muttered to himself. Then, with his memory jogged, Gabriel turned to his team. "Samantha? Do you still know how to hot wire a car?"

Less than five minutes later, the team was cruising through the mostly empty streets of lower Manhattan. Gabriel's car, which he had ditched while in government pursuit two weeks earlier, was still parked right where he had left it. Its windshield had been plastered with parking tickets, and someone had decorated its trunk with some rather impressive spray paint art. But luckily the garage owner hadn't had the vehicle towed, nor asked the police to put a boot on it. So, one broken driver's side window and twist of ignition cables later, and it was ready to flee the government once more.

Locals who hadn't evacuated the city were just starting to come out of hiding, still unsure what to make of the destruction around them or what had caused it. Up ahead, Gabriel could see the bright red glow of taillights. They would soon run smack into the traffic jam that had formed when Porter's hijacked jet first threatened the city. Though it would slow their escape, General Javez's men didn't have a clue what method of transportation they were using to get back to Artifact Manor. Besides, chances were the traffic would conceal them better than any open road as they worked their way there. Their mission was finally over, and the team was headed home.

Chapter One Hundred Twelve
The Day The Sky Closed

New York, New York
The Day The Sky Closed

That afternoon, Gabriel and Lisa sat holding each other on the couch of their downstairs great room. Upon their return home, both had showered, and Lisa helped Gabriel get his arm in a sling to keep it stable until they could see a doctor for a proper cast. Then they went downstairs, where they sat quietly, no interest in turning on a television and seeing coverage of Porter's aftermath in Manhattan. Gabriel was getting tired now. It wasn't a normal tired, like when the body doesn't get enough rest, but something more intense and more draining. He surmised he was going into stasis, the price for using the pendant in his battle with Porter. But he didn't mind. It had been a long couple of weeks; a few days of hibernation was a welcome reprieve.

Gabriel's only regret, as he sat there, feeling the stasis slowly pull him away from conscious thought, was that he had nothing to show for this mission. His home was a miniature museum, a treasure trove of memories of the missions he'd been on or the deals he'd made to keep a cherished piece of history close to his heart. Now, he'd just completed his greatest mission yet, and despite there even being an empty display case on the great room bookshelf, Gabriel had nothing to put inside it. The Old World and any evidence it contained were gone. The Pendant of God was gone, though Gabriel imagined it hanging in there, his great room lighting reflecting off its shiny surface. It would have made the perfect addition. And yet, Gabriel knew he had made the right decision to let it go.

When Nate made his snarky pendant comment following their rougher-than-expected landing, Gabriel had a moment where he'd wished he'd kept the artifact. He would have used it to heal everyone on the spot. But that was exactly the problem. The pendant, when not in proper hands, was an ever-tempting crutch, a permanent get-out-of-jail free card for any predicament. Gabriel would have used it at the crash site, and the next time his team got in a jam, he would have used it again, and the next time…

It was a vicious cycle, and Gabriel wondered at what point he would use the pendant not to heal, but to take the offensive before his team got hurt to begin with. That was the next logical evolution of its usage. And after that, how long until Gabriel used it not to protect his team, but to help him successfully complete a mission? And then later to avoid exerting effort on missions altogether? Such a slippery slope, one that any man, no matter how noble, could fall victim to. Porter was just further along in the process from the start. Damien… well, Damien was different. Damien wore the pendant for thousands of years without succumbing to its temptations. God chose him to be its bearer, perhaps because he was the only who could bear it properly.

"What, you haven't started writing your new book yet?" Nate asked as he and Samantha trampled into the room, already in pajamas, even though the day had plenty of hours remaining.

"I think I'm going to let this story simmer a bit," Gabriel told him. "It's still a little fresh for the page."

Nate shrugged. "Suit yourself. But don't come crying to me if you never get to write it once they throw our butts in prison."

Samantha punched his arm. "I already told you, we're not going to prison."

Lisa looked at her quizzically. "How do you figure?"

"They've got nothing to throw at us in court. Despite his threats, General Sikes won't disclose anything that happened overseas given the clandestine nature of his operation. As far as what happened here…" Samantha paused, as if still reviewing her thought process for reasonableness. "Well, any admission of our role would require a simultaneous admission of the pendant's existence. Given the religious and political ramifications of that, I'd say we're good."

"They don't have to mention the pendant," Nate argued. "They could say Porter had developed some experimental weapon that went haywire."

"And then try to persecute us for stopping it and ensuring it could never be used again? No lawyer worth a damn would pursue that angle." She looked at Gabriel and Lisa. "The more I think about, the more I wonder whether our doorbell will even ring. I suspect it will, and that General Javez will drag us in for intimidation tactics and questioning. But at the end of the day, my gut tells me we'll be right back here, doing what we always do."

"Let's hope so," Gabriel said.

Samantha excused herself to make a snack. Nate told her he'd be right behind her, but hung back for a moment, darting out one side of the great room and quickly returning with his backpack in hand.

"What's up?" Gabriel asked.

"Do you remember how we were racing against the clock back in Morocco once we figured out Porter's plan? Well, we were in such a hurry that when Samantha and I hopped out at Marrakech Menara Airport, I accidentally grabbed your backpack instead of my own."

Gabriel chuckled. "It's okay. You can keep it."

Nate opened the top and held it within his reach. "I actually think you're going to want it back. It's still got your bloody clothes in it from when Porter staged his little coup on Alegranza."

Gabriel took the bag and waited for further explanation, but Nate offered none. Instead, he winked deviously and jogged off to join Samantha. Gabriel shot Lisa a *what the hell?* look, then reached into the backpack and removed his clothes. They weren't just bloody; after sitting in his bag for days, they didn't smell too great either. Finding nothing beneath the clothes, Gabriel wondered what joke was flying over his head. He shoved the dirty wad back into the bag, but stopped when the muffled sound of crinkling paper caught his attention. Curious, Gabriel moved his hand across the pile of clothing, squeezing section by section until he had honed in on the source of the crackling. It was coming from his pants' pocket.

Gabriel opened the mouth of the pocket and slipped his hand inside. His fingers extracted the rumpled paper within, which he passed to Lisa before tossing the backpack and clothes to the floor. Lisa held the paper where both of them could witness its unraveling and began to flatten its creases. A smeared black line appeared. It was connected to two others, which branched out further from there. As Lisa continued unfolding, the hieroglyphic bird and its overlapping veil took shape. Gabriel's tired face split into a wide grin.

He stood and took The Veiled Bird from Lisa. He would eventually perform some restoration work to remove its creases, clean up the smeared ink, apply a protective coat to prevent fading... that sort of thing. But for now, he just wanted to see it where it belonged. Gabriel opened the door of the empty bookshelf display case and gently set The Veiled Bird on an angled pedestal within. He then shut the door, returned to the couch and Lisa's arms, and stared. Between the warmth of her embrace and the pleasure of seeing his unexpected souvenir among the other artifacts Gabriel had collected over the years, he felt his body relax. His mind drifted somewhere else, somewhere quiet, hidden within the recesses of his psyche. Then, without further delay, stasis took hold. The last thing Gabriel saw before he succumbed to a deep, peaceful slumber was The Veiled Bird, which he took comfort in knowing would be there, waiting patiently in his collection, when he awoke again.

Author's Note

I hope you enjoyed *Pendant of God*! Gabriel Dunne and the rest of the Artifact Manor team will return in a future adventure.

If you'd like to stay informed about my works, get notified about special promotions, and receive free bonus scenes from my story universes, sign up for my "mostly monthly" newsletter at https://www.christophergcalvin.com.

I appreciate all feedback, so please consider leaving an honest rating and review with your retailer of choice. Doing so will help other readers discover the world of *Pendant of God*. Thank you for supporting my work, and I hope you'll join me for another story in the future!

- Christopher Gorham Calvin

Printed in Great Britain
by Amazon

29212079R00245